The Bearer of the Seed

RECORDS OF THE THREE REALMS

Book 2

The Bearer of the Seed

RECORDS OF THE THREE REALMS

Book 2

Joshua Killingsworth

ISBN 978-1-7341255-2-8 (Paperback)

ISBN 978-1-7341255-3-5 (eBook)

Edited by Cynthia Shepp

JoshuaKillingsworth.com @WriterJMK

Mystic Fox Publishing

To all the victims of genocide.
May we never forget.

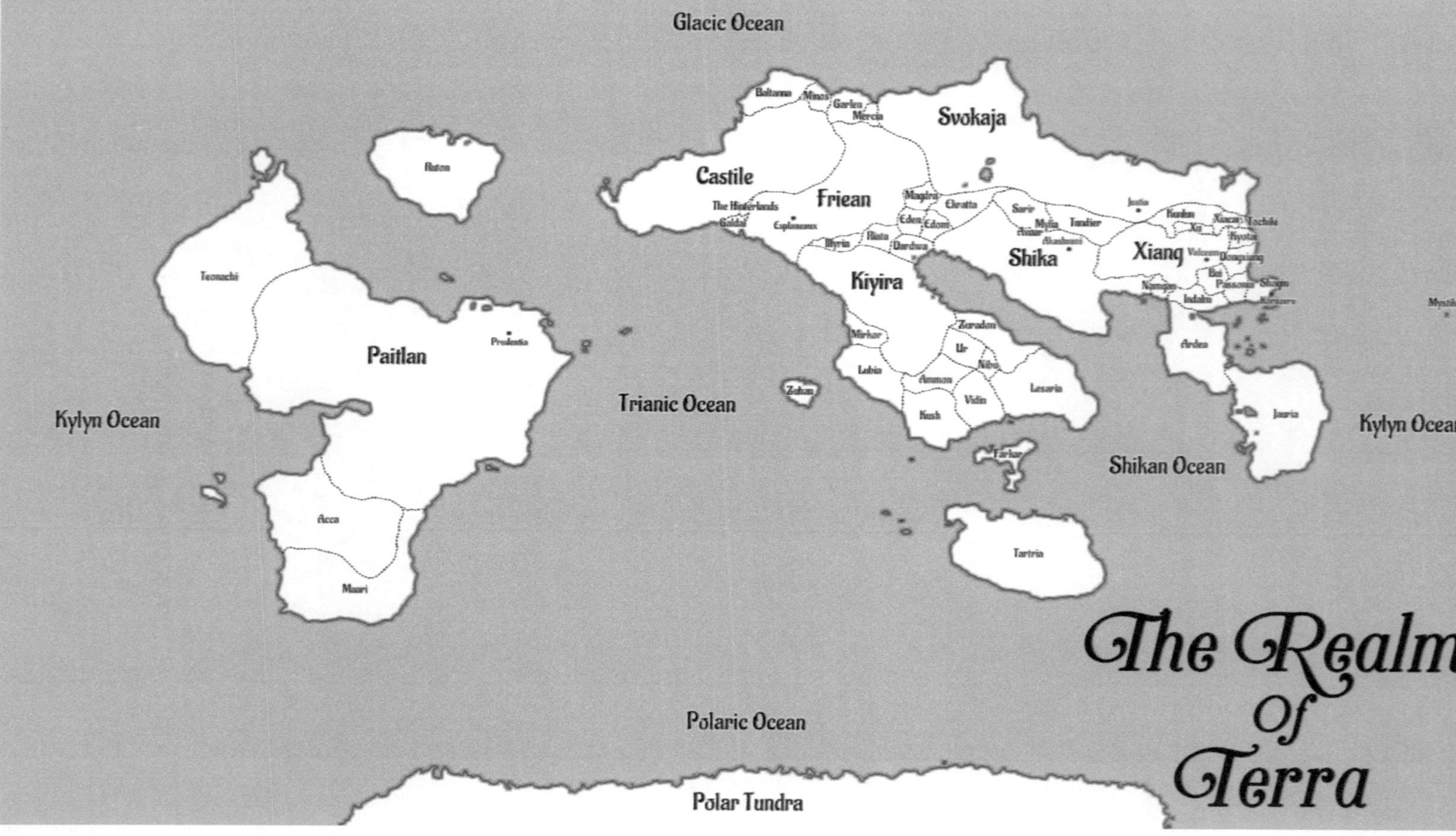

The Realm of Terra
Glacic Ocean
Kylyn Ocean
Trianic Ocean
Polaric Ocean
Polar Tundra
Shikan Ocean
Kylyn Ocean
Baton
Paitlan
Teonachi
Prudentia
Obu
Acca
Mauri
Zohar
Castile
The Hinterlands
Galdal
Esplaneaux
Friean
Illyria
Riata
Dardwa
Eden
Edom
Magdra
Chratta
Kiyira
Mirhor
Lubia
Zaradon
Ur
Amman
Nibo
Vidin
Kush
Lesaria
Svokaja
Sarir
Avian
Mylia
Akashuni
Tundier
Shika
Xiang
Justia
Kunlun
Xu
Xucar
Tochiki
Ryota
Valeggno
Dongxiang
Bai
Namigan
Pansona
Shinjin
Indalu
Koruwu
Ardea
Jauria
Mystikos
Farhac
Tartria

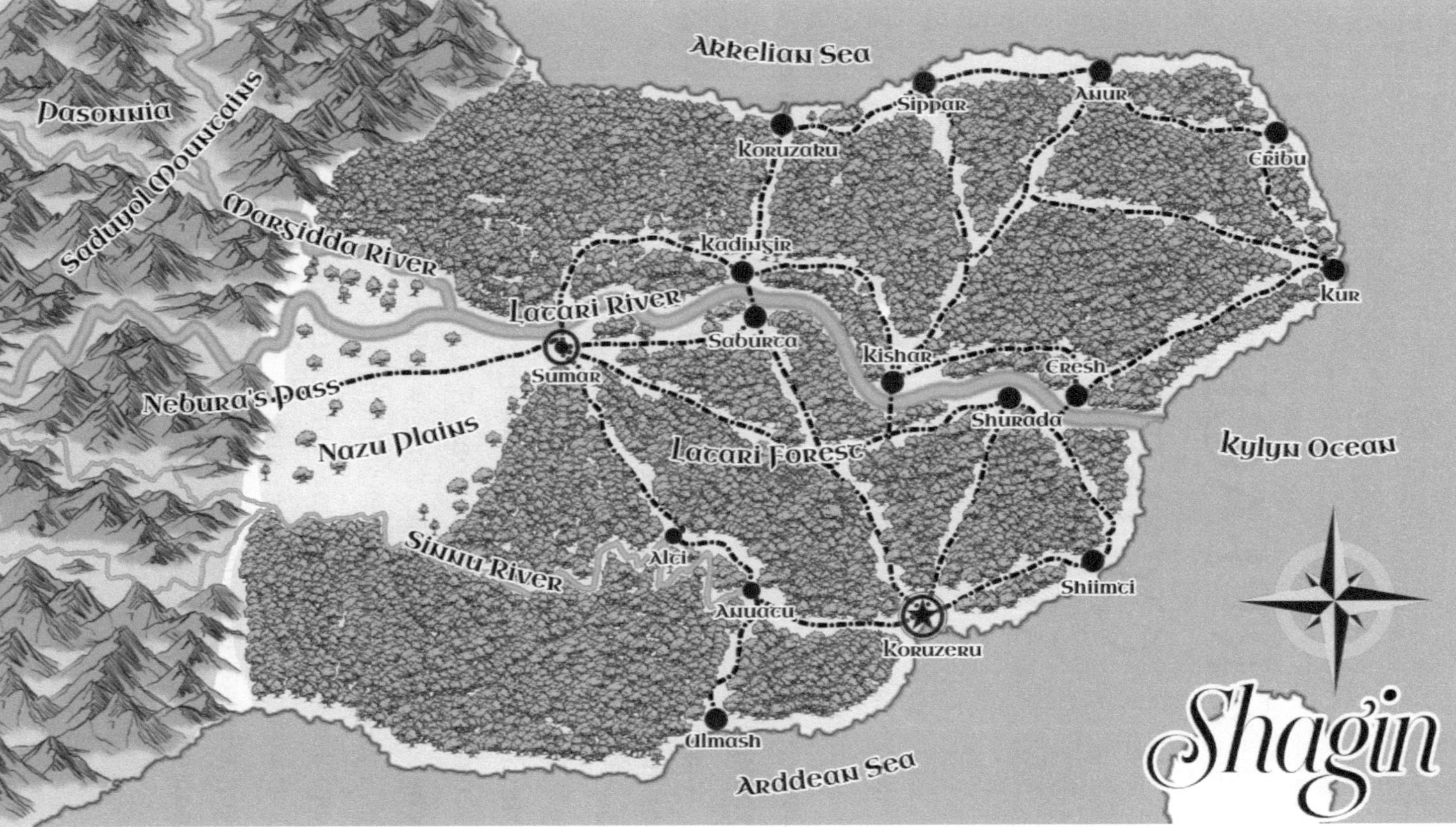
Shagin
Akkelian Sea
Kylyn Ocean
Arddean Sea
Pasonnia
Sadugol Mountains
Marsidda River
Nebura's Pass
Nazu Plains
Sinnu River
Lacari River
Lacari Forest
Sippar
Ahur
Koruzaku
Eribu
Kur
Kadinsir
Saburta
Kishar
Eresh
Shurada
Sumar
Alci
Anuatu
Koruzeru
Shiimci
Ulmash

PREFACE AND CONTENT WARNING

THIS BOOK CONTAINS SCENES of a graphic nature and may not be suitable for all audiences. Chapter 14 depicts extreme violence and hatred. Rape is discussed in this chapter, though not depicted.

Each act of cruelty shown in Chapter 14 is either lifted or inspired by a real-world parallel. As I did not shy away from the gruesome actions of humanity's worst past, I understand that Chapter 14, which illustrates these horrible acts, is not for the faint of heart. Those sensitive to extreme actions of cruelty should skip that chapter, though I believe it is worth reading. I believe it is a powerful chapter that highlights what humanity is capable of when we allow hate to flourish.

If you are interested in further reading on the topic of genocide or dehumanization, I recommend visiting geno cidewatch.com or checking out either The Lucifer Effect by Philip Zimbardo or Less Than Human: Why We Demean, Enslave, and Exterminate Others by David Livingstone Smith.

Thank you for undergoing this journey with me. I hope you enjoy the story.

Joshua Killingsworth

CHAPTER ONE

THE CHOSEN DAY HAD arrived. Kari ascended the stairs to the Hall of Heaven and Earth, flanked on by her guard. It was strange. She had fought against tyranny, oppression, and juggernauts of might and strength, but this would be her greatest challenge. Once she entered the hall, her guards would no longer be able to protect her. They would depart, leaving her to fend for herself.

Kari's footsteps echoed against the marble stairs. Her dress, a silk ruqun, flowed eloquently in the breeze, its crimson color and gold embroidery a symbol to her status as empress. A golden phoenix adorned her skirt. Her brown hair was held up with an azure fengguan—a phoenix crown—adorned with nine phoenixes made of inlaid kingfisher feathers, topped with twelve golden dragons, and inset with precious pearls and gems. Specially made, the diadem was substantial in both weight and duty.

Her guards bowed in reverence before allowing her to enter. High Chancellor Cai Ren, her chief advisor, waited for her in the antechamber to the throne room.

"My lady." He clasped his hands together, bowing. Kari motioned for him to rise. "Administrator Zhouren sends a gift a wine—*the scoundrel.* He is calling for your death."

"He's not the only one," Kari said. She stared at the door to the throne room as her body quivered with apprehension. For most of her life, she was proud of her eyes. Vibrant eye colors were a Shagin trait, and hers fairly glowed green. Only now, she wished she could hide them and what she was.

Could she do this? Could she face the Guardian's ambassador with courage and turn his heart? A lump formed in her throat. There was no changing his mind. Rational people did not call for genocide.

"You'll do fine," Cai Ren said, noticing Kari's apprehension. "Show strength and prove to the nobility you truly have the mandate of heaven, or it will be civil war."

Kari's brow furrowed as she stared at him with her mouth agape. He smiled sheepishly as he rubbed the back of his neck.

Kari took a deep breath, pushing her anxiety down. She could do this.

Once she stepped through the door, she was on her own. Cai Ren couldn't assist her.

The Guardian had exterminated her people, and now his ambassador was seeking an explanation for her existence. It was an absurd request, on which her empire hinged. Her nobles and lords questioned her ability to rule. If she didn't prove the mandate of heaven, the right to rule, was indeed hers, they would revolt.

Kari entered the massive throne room filled with hundreds of ministers and lords. They kowtowed, bowing their heads. The nine grand pillars stretched to the golden ceiling. She made her way to the high dais in the center, escorted by Cai Ren. He would be with her, but only in a silent capacity.

She climbed the marble steps to the crimson-and-gold throne at the top of the platform. Two sizeable golden dragon statues flanked either side of the dais. It felt as if they watched as she ascended the stairs to the Throne of Unity.

She wished she didn't have to sit alone. The stage allowed her to be gawked at by the courts. Her only comfort was Cai Ren, who stood behind her.

As she sat, the entire court rose in unison, then dropped to their knees. Together, they proclaimed, "May grace and peace be with you, Your Majesty."

The ambassador didn't waste time. Charging forward between the rows of ministers, he stopped just shy of the dais. He held up a silver medallion with the symbol of the Guardian etched in it—a triskelion of three interwoven spirals. His stern look sent shivers through Kari.

"You've read my request, so what is your response?" he demanded, stomping his foot like a petulant child.

A silent chill fell over the Throne Room, all eyes fixated on her. The officials waited for her reply.

It was her throne, her court, yet, she was the one on trial. What kind of response could she give? How was Kari supposed to justify her existence?

The Guardian's ambassador continued to glare from the base of her dais. It was odd. Here she sat, the Empress of Xiang, surrounded by hundreds of her court officials, yet she was alone.

"Would you like me to repeat the question?" the ambassador snarled, stepping forward and placing a foot on the bottom stair of the dais. His tight clothes and large fur cloak marked him as a foreigner in a land accustomed to loose-fitting robes and silk. Despite being a stranger to Xiang, he wielded power and authority in equal respects to her, if not more so. He spoke for the Guardian of the Three Realms, after all. It would be scandalous for any other foreigner to show such disrespect, but for him, it was tolerated, accepted even.

Kari averted her eyes, not knowing how to answer. She had been preparing for this meeting for over a month. Well, putting it off was more accurate. A disturbing silence washed over the court as they waited for her to reply. Her reign had just begun, and there were already rumors of dissent and murmurs of civil war among them.

High Chancellor Cai Ren cleared his throat, taking his place at Kari's side. His face pointed straight ahead at the ambassador, but his eyes cut toward Kari in a silent reminder for her to show strength. He had been persistent in chastising her whenever her resolve faltered. Weakness only made the court question if she genuinely possessed the mandate of heaven.

Kari shook her head, straightening her posture. What was she doing? She had to face this with courage or risk undoing so much. If the court thought she had lost the mandate of heaven, she could lose the throne, bringing back the very tyranny she fought against.

"I grow tired of waiting." The ambassador climbed the stairs, stopping one short of the top. The officials gasped and murmured at his lack of respect and decorum. If he had been anyone else, he would be reprimanded and barred from the palace. And if she had been anyone else, he would be executed. "You are a Shagin! Explain yourself!"

Kari sighed, hanging her head. What could she say? Shagin was an all-female race who believed in the "wrong" god. For that, they were outlawed and murdered. The few Purge survivors now lived in exile on their sacred island of Mystikos, hidden away from the world. As far as the rest of the world was concerned, Shagin were extinct, except her.

"I am the empress of Xiang. This is my throne. I don't have to explain my existence to you," Kari said. The only reason the Guardian had sent an ambassador and not an assassin was because she was empress of one of the most powerful nations on Terra. Hopefully, that was enough to keep him at bay.

"You do realize it's a crime to be Shagin?" the ambassador demanded.

"It's a crime to be born?" Kari leaped to her feet, then stared at the ambassador. The officials murmured even more at her outburst, and Cai Ren buried his face in his hands. Kari didn't care. There was no arguing with him or the Guardian. All pretenses of civilized debate ended at the murder of her people.

"The fourth amendment of the Triune Concordat clearly states Shagin are the enemies of humanity, and we must purge them. Xiang is in direct violation of the laws of the gods, and it now risks losing its sovereignty. There is only one remission that will restore justice."

"There is no justice in genocide!" Kari's aura flared, and spirit energy surged through her body. Light flashed at her fingertips. This man knew nothing of justice.

"My lady," Cai Ren said, placing a hand on her shoulder.

Kari closed her eyes and took a deep breath, regaining control. A part of her knew Cai Ren was right. She couldn't afford to give in to her anger and let the Guardian see the monster they feared. It wasn't fair. It was hypocrisy, a double standard the Guardian and his ilk didn't have to maintain. They could act like brutes, and the world would still revere them.

"The empress has shown compassion and restraint. She possesses none of the qualities of the old Shagin," an official shouted. Kari smiled; at least not all of her court had turned on her. Though she had shown them she was no different from them, the misconceptions of Shagin remained.

"The Shagin are monsters!" The ambassador turned away from Kari, speaking directly to the officials. "They have ransacked the world before, times beyond counting. They have stolen children, bewitched men, and now they have returned. Not just returned, mind you, the Shagin menace has already conquered this nation and enslaved you all. Yet, you defend this monster?"

"That is enough!" Kari balled her fists, then started down the stairs. Cai Ren grabbed her shoulder, pulling her back to the throne. She didn't fight him. If she descended to face the ambassador on his level, it would symbolically signal she wasn't worthy of her throne. Kari took a deep breath, relenting, and retook her seat.

The ambassador pointed at her in defiance. "Even now, she seeks to silence reason. She murdered the emperors. How many more will you let her kill? How many more nations must fall to her rule before you act? Except by then, it will be too late. Stand with the Guardian and cast out this vile creature!"

The throne room erupted in chattering officials arguing with each other.

"He speaks the truth. We are all doomed!" an official cried.

"You dare to question the will of heaven?"

"We must comply with the Guardian or lose our nation."

"Stand with the empress."

"Should a girl decide our fate?"

"Silence!" Cai Ren bellowed, and a sudden hush fell over the court.

"Chancellor, I beg of you," the ambassador said, turning toward Cai Ren. "I'm not asking you to execute her, just turn her over into my custody."

She was the empress—one without a say in her court. Kari slouched. She wanted to fade away—be anywhere but here.

"You have gone too far." Cai Ren had been an ally throughout the ordeal that put Kari on the Throne of Heaven. It was nice to see him defending her, even if it broke decorum. "You have insulted the heavens and the daughter of heaven. If you do not show respect to our empress, we will not show respect to you. Guards, show this barbarian to his quarters. Maybe tomorrow, if you have learned respect, you can be granted another audience in front of this court."

Kari sighed in relief as the guards escorted the ambassador out. She rubbed her forehead, grateful it was over. But it was just another delay. She would have to face the ambassador again. This time, she would need a better response. She feared if she kept stalling, the ambassador would lash out and try to take her life. It was what the Guardian wanted. Yet, she welcomed the deferrals.

Her court had just assembled, but she was tired. With a gesture, Kari dismissed them and retired to a rear antechamber.

She could breathe again. After she removed the phoenix crown, she untied her brown hair, letting it flow freely.

"Thank you for that," Kari said as Cai Ren entered the chamber behind her. She rested her crown on the altar before kneeling on a red cushion in front of a small table. Kari motioned for Cai Ren to join her on the opposite side.

"You shouldn't have ended court so early," Cai Ren chastised her. He refused the seat, pacing like a vulture circling its prey. "It makes you look weak. Like you are running away. Not to mention all the business you must attend to other than this fruitless inquiry from the Guardian."

"I know," Kari said, rubbing her burning eyes. She couldn't even bring herself to look at him. He had trusted in her for so long, yet it seemed she was always letting him down. "I just couldn't take anymore after hearing that barbarian talk so disparagingly about my people. I'm exhausted."

"Don't let his words get to you. Everyone in this nation knows your heart." Cai Ren stopped, stroking his black goatee. "But still, the fact remains that you *are* Shagin."

"Do you think I should just lay down my life because of what I am?" Kari shot to her feet, her voice louder than she intended.

"Not at all." Cai Ren held up his hands in a calming effort. He motioned for her to retake her seat as he knelt on the red cushion opposite her. "But you have to admit his suspicions seem warranted, at least from an outsider's perspective."

"I've done nothing to him—or anyone for that matter," Kari interjected. She dropped to her knees, defeated. It didn't matter what she did. Shagin were different. They were monsters to the rest of the world.

"The last time the Shagin were seen, they went to war against the Guardian. Now the Terran Union is in shambles, if you can even consider it still exists at all. The union is merely a name now," Cai Ren explained. He leaned over the table, clasped her hands in his. "They have a right to fear you. To fear what you can do. Your achievements cannot be understated. In a few months, you went from songstress to attendant to empress."

"If you recall, you're the one who pulled me into this to begin with," Kari said, tugging away. She stared at the decorative ceiling. Beams of gold accentuated the crimson wood. Jade figures rose from the floor to the ceiling—a tiger, a tortoise, a dragon, and a phoenix. It was a lavish room in a decadent palace centered in an impoverished city, and her subjects expected her to restore prestige to the land. Even her silk ruqun with its crimson pattern and gold phoenix embroidery only served to mask what was underneath. "I never asked for any of it."

"You saved this empire from tyranny. For that, you have mine and so many others eternal gratitude. But as you said, you didn't ask for this." Cai Ren stared, unblinking. "Abdicate the throne."

"Abdicate?" Kari asked, taken aback. "To whom?"

"Without an heir of your own, as High Chancellor, you would abdicate to me," Cai Ren said, returning to his feet. He began to pace again. "It is not an easy decision to make,

I understand. With you as empress, I feel war will come to this nation. If you abdicate, you can show the world your graciousness. They will see you not as a conqueror, but for what you truly are—a savior."

"I don't know," Kari said. On the one hand, Cai Ren knew far more about politics than she did, but something about abdicating didn't sit right. He had pushed for it when she ascended the throne, and she had refused. It wasn't like she desired power or even wanted to be the empress, but giving it up would invalidate the sacrifices made to achieve it.

"So long as you are empress, I can only do so much to protect you. But as a hero of the people, I can shield you from the Guardian," Cai Ren pleaded.

"I can protect myself." That was clear for all to see. She had defeated a peerless warrior thought to be undefeatable, and she had spent the time since then training. The strength of her spirit energy greatly surpassed what it had been months ago.

"Then do it for the people of Xiang. We are barely maintaining control of the kingdom as it is. The fall of the Tian has weakened the resolve of various warlords. Without their support, we cannot maintain order. Many doubt following a Shagin."

Kari winced at his words. Even the people she saved still thought of her as a monster. "If the Guardian comes with his army, they might not side with us. This nation will fall."

Kari placed her face in her hands. The pressures of the throne were overwhelming. Too many lives depended on her every action. Perhaps it was best to give the kingdom to Cai Ren. "It is something to consider."

"Please do." Cai Ren said, shooting her a sideways look.

"I have to go." Kari stood and clasped her hands, a sign of respect to her advisor. "I have somewhere I need to be."

Kari bid farewell to Cai Ren, summoning a sedan chair to return her to her small house. She had chosen to stay in the home she had when she was an attendant. It was the only place she felt safe. Wanting nothing to do with the Emperor's Mansion, she refused to live there. Besides, she couldn't stand any reminders of what the Tian brothers did to her.

Unfortunately, that might be hard now. Kari placed her hands on her stomach. Damn those bastards.

CHAPTER TWO

Kari grunted as the eunuchs bumped along, shaking the sedan chair. She pulled the red silk curtain closed, not wanting to see anyone. It was awkward having her subjects carry her, and she tired of the presence of people. Preparing and waiting for the court proved tumultuous. Now, her emotions fluttered with what the future may bring.

The guards set the sedan chair down at the entrance of her house, then helped her dismount. Kari squinted as sun rays reflected off the golden roof. She took a deep breath, but the crushing fear of her anxiety dwarfed her best efforts to calm herself. The doctor she had requested knelt before her as she descended.

"May grace and peace be with you, Your Majesty," the doctor said, averting his gaze.

"Thank you," Kari said. She still wasn't used to the reverence everyone showed her. "You may stand."

"My lady, are you ready?" Doctor Liujilai asked as he stood.

"I am," she lied, but it no longer mattered if she was ready. She needed to know. Kari took another deep breath, motioning for him to follow. "You may come with me."

They toed off their shoes, then the doctor followed Kari through the two entrance doors into her house. The first led into a vestibule with a decorative screen painted with a golden peacock. A second led into the inner courtyard.

Kari had taken great efforts to beautify her garden. She always carried a small pouch of seeds tied to her waist, which she'd collected from the Imperial Gardens. Using her plant magic, she'd grown the most beautiful assortment of flowers. Lavender, orchids, and roses filled the small courtyard.

In the center was a tall cherry blossom tree. She had used her power to grow it to its adult height. Unfortunately, the blossoms were out of season by the time she planted the tree. While she could use her energy to force the tree to bloom, it just didn't seem right to do so.

They crossed through the stone path to her bedchambers. Kari slid the door shut and sat on her bed, waiting for the doctor to begin.

The doctor bowed again out of respect before approaching her. "Any symptoms?" the old doctor asked, crouching in front of Kari.

She shook her head. "I don't believe so. I haven't been sleeping well, but I think that's due to stress."

"I see. So, how long has it been?" the doctor asked, placing a hand on her forehead. His hands were cold and clammy. Was he as nervous as she was?

"About three weeks," Kari replied. Her cycle was usually regular. She had thought it was merely the stress of recent events and assuming control of the throne, which caused her to be late, but after three weeks, she was beginning to worry. The Imperial Brothers had abducted her, and to save her friends and end their tyranny, Jiaorong forced her to sleep with him. It wasn't what she wanted, and now it seemed the cruelty he inflicted was yet to end.

"I see." The doctor took Kari's wrist, placing two fingers on the inside and his thumb on the out. He tilted his head, closing his eyes as if he were listening for a faint sound. After a short while, he opened his eyes and smiled. Dread filled her. She wasn't sure if him smiling was a good sign. "Congratulations, you have a happy pulse."

"A happy pulse? What does that mean?" Kari asked, but she already knew the answer. Her query was more in pursuit of a response to dispel her fears, which she did not expect to receive.

"It means that soon, you will have an heir to your throne." Damn.

Kari placed her hands on her stomach, feeling like she was going to throw up. Why? Why did she have to be pregnant? And why with his child?

Kari would do just about anything not to be. She had sacrificed so much, given up so much of herself to the

Tian brothers to end their cruelty. Why was she now being forced to give even more of herself? It didn't seem fair. The Fates must despise her.

The doctor waited for her reaction. Sensing her apprehension, he raised his eyebrows in concern.

"Thank you for your assistance. But please don't tell anyone." They would find out eventually, but she needed time to get used to it first.

"You want it to be a surprise?" the doctor asked.

"Something like that." Kari stood and walked toward the open window, staring into the courtyard.

"Of course, Your Majesty." The doctor bowed and left, leaving her alone with her thoughts.

Kari crashed onto her bed, her head slamming on her soft pillow. This was a nightmare. She would never be able to forget. Never be able to escape what they did to her. It was her worst fear come to life.

Again, she placed her hands on her stomach. It seemed so flat and tiny. It was hard to believe she was carrying a baby. She was only seventeen, too young to have a child of her own. This wasn't how she wanted it; she wasn't ready.

She draped her arms over her face.

"Not that bastard's child."

Kari shook her head. No, the little one would be hers. She sat up, staring at her belly.

"I will love you forever," she lied, trying to convince herself more than her unborn child. She didn't feel love toward it, more like dread and regret. Surely her feelings would eventually change. At least, she hoped so.

The night came. With it, the company of friends. Kari ignored her servants' request and dismissed them early, making the tea herself. She found tea to be quite therapeutic. It wasn't even the tea itself, but the preparation she enjoyed the most—finding the right balance of heat and water and the combination of leaves. But most of all, it was the sound of pouring the tea ever so slowly into brittle cups and listening to the change in decibels as it filled.

She poured Ina a cup from her jade tea set. When she offered Ronin a cup, he refused and held up a bottle of rice wine instead. She had invited them here to tell them the truth—that she was expecting—but now she wanted to do anything else. If she could run away, she would. It was a silly thought; these were her friends. They should be the first to know.

Ina was a lovely young woman, slightly older than Kari with jet-black hair, phoenix eyes, and porcelain skin. Kari's closest friend, her heart's sister, Ina's tragic life mirrored her own. Her blue-and-white ruqun accentuated her natural beauty.

Ronin was the brother Kari had never known. He was a Kitsuno Kai, a wolf among men. An expert swordsman, his ghostly presence still sent chills down her spine. He was never without his double kodachis, which he wore underneath his trademark ankle-length black coat. His entire wardrobe was black, except for the light blue sash he wore beneath his outerwear. When she met him, his very demeanor filled her with dread, but they shared the same father. Because of that, he became her most trusted ally through the horrible ordeal with the Tian.

"So, what did you want to talk about?" Ina asked, setting her tea down.

Hesitating, Kari bit her lip. She wanted to tell them about the life she carried. Desperately, she desired to lay her burdens at their feet. She needed their support more than ever. But still, she couldn't bring herself to say the words. It would make her situation real.

What would Ina think? Would she blame herself? After all, Kari first laid with Jiaorong to save Ina's life. Ina had shown her gratitude by standing by her side in Kari's final confrontation with Jiaorong, but now it didn't feel like enough.

Kari closed her eyes. It wasn't fair for her to burden them. Not yet, anyway. It wasn't Ina's fault. It was Jiaorong's and his alone.

Kari had to change the subject. "Cai Ren asked me to abdicate. Since I don't have an heir, as High Chancellor, the throne would fall to him."

"Cai Ren is a snake," Ronin said, downing his rice wine. "He only wants you to abdicate so that he can have power. That's been his plan from the start."

"But why shouldn't she abdicate?" Ina protested. She studied Kari. "I'm not saying you should, but you should do what makes you happy."

"What makes me happy?" Kari's words trailed off as she placed a hand on her stomach. She was a blossom forced to bloom out of season. In that regard, it no longer mattered what she wanted. They'd taken the choice from her, just like so many others. "I don't even know what that is anymore. I never had a choice in any of this. What do you think I should do?"

Ina had been a victim of the Tian's harem, too. They shared the same struggles. Surely, she would have the answers.

"I fear the direction the nation will take without you as its leader," Ina said. Smiling, she took another sip of her tea. Kari returned the gesture. She was glad her friend enjoyed her tea. It was a small joy, but that was all she could hope for sometimes. "Cai Ren would have no use for a harem, but he is a traditionalist. If he takes the throne, it will only undo what little change you've already accomplished. Women will still be second-class citizens. Eventually, the harem will return. But I know you don't want this life. I see the stress it places on you; you're not happy. But I also know the sacrifices you've made to get here, and I would hate for it to all be for nothing. Maybe you should nominate your successor?"

"You can't," Ronin said, lounging in his chair. "Succession is passed through blood, not proclamation. If you attempt that, there will be revolt and power struggle. You would plunge the land into a civil war."

"If it has to be a blood relative, what about you?" Kari asked. "Isn't that an option? After all, you know more..."

"I refuse," Ronin said, cutting her off. Eyes narrowing, he sat upright. He tapped the table with his index finger in cadence with his words. "The Kitsuno Kai won't stand by anyone but you. The empire is severely weakened. If the throne doesn't demonstrate strength, it will be civil war. Let me lead the Kitsuno Kai, and we will secure stability through whatever means necessary. That way, you can focus on doing what you feel is right."

"How am I supposed to know what's right and wrong?" Kari asked. It was all too much. When she was fighting a tyrant, it was so much easier to understand what she should do, what was right. She'd had to make hard choices—had sacrificed so much—to end the oppression, but she understood what was right. Here, she didn't comprehend anything. There was too much gray, too much pressure. She wanted nothing more than to go back to being a simple songstress, but she'd moved beyond that modest life. The entire world knew about her—the sole Shagin who had toppled a nation.

"I hope I'm not intruding," Cai Ren said, entering the great room.

"You are," Ronin said bluntly.

"How did you get in?" Ina asked.

"I'm sorry, my lady." Cai Ren bowed toward Kari. "Since you had forgone any personal servants to attend to your needs this evening, I didn't want to disturb you, so I let myself in."

Sighing, Kari rubbed her hand through her brown hair. "We were just discussing our plans for the future."

"Then perhaps your chief advisor should be present?" Cai Ren demanded.

"It doesn't concern you," Ronin said, jumping to his feet. He glared at Cai Ren. His right hand twitched and flexed, hovering over the hilt of his kodachi.

Ignoring the aggression, Cai Ren turned his nose up in disdain. "Your Majesty, may I speak with you in private?"

"Of course." Kari nodded. A fight breaking out between the men was the last thing she wanted. Especially since Ronin didn't know the meaning of restraint, and he very well might cut Cai Ren down.

Ronin dropped into his chair, but he did not take his eyes off the other man. Cai Ren flicked his sleeve in contempt before leaving the great room with Kari following behind.

The moon was poised high in the dark sky. The cool summer breeze rustled the flowers and leaves, sending a refreshing scent of nature to Kari's nostrils. They took a seat on a bench in the center of the courtyard underneath the tall cherry tree. Even though they weren't in season, the tree was still beautiful.

"The night's beautiful," Kari focused her gaze on the moon as it peeked through the leaves of the tree. "It took me a while to notice how lovely the palace is. But it's all a façade. I know what lies beyond these walls, a city of depression and sorrow."

"You seem melancholy. Have you already heard the news?" Cai Ren asked, his expression stern and solemn.

"No, what news?"

"Eastern Xia attacked Sui Han." Cai Ren said. "Administrator Yoon is dead. It appears it will be civil war after all."

"How? When?" Kari's heart sank. Administrator Yoon had been one of her few allies and a friend.

"Yoon took casualties in our attempted capture of the capital. His alliance with you demonstrated him as a traitor, at least to those loyal to the Tian." Cai Ren stood, then turned his back to Kari. "Perceived weakness and moral justification seem to be all that was needed."

"They must know we won't stand for this?" Kari said, louder than she intended.

"I don't think they care." Cai Ren cut his eyes toward her, pacing in circles. "There are rumblings of dissent among the other lords as well. It won't be the only rebellion. The warlords are geared up for battle."

She didn't have the resolve to fight a war. Too many people would die, and she didn't want their deaths on her hands. She already carried too much blood. How much more could she take?

"What do I do?"

"The solution hasn't changed. We have to show strength and crush these rebellions." Pausing, Cai Ren rubbed his chin. "We've talked about this before, but perhaps you should abdicate to me. I don't believe you have the heart for this."

"Maybe that would be for the best." Kari stared at the ground, chest tight and breathing shallow.

"The role you are best suited for is that of champion of the people. I can rule and accomplish that which you are unable. Together, we are stronger, but only if we play to our strengths."

"It's strategy," Kari surmised, exhaling.

"Precisely," Cai Ren replied, his expression softening. "And with me on the throne, more of the traditional lords will be willing to accept my rule."

Cai Ren's words pierced Kari's heart.

"Because I'm a woman?" She stared at the moon. Ina was right—nothing would change. Everything they went through would be meaningless.

"To put it bluntly, yes."

Kari stood and approached Cai Ren, staring up at him. "And then what? What was the point of all of this if nothing changes?"

"Listen to reason," Cai Ren said, retreating. "As you stated, this is strategy. As a eunuch, I am less then a man and never intended to inherit the mandate of heaven. Do you think I won't get resistance as well for being what I am? This might not be a perfect option, but it's the best we have available. We cannot focus on what we want, but about what the land needs. Xiang is steeped in traditions, which you can't change. They will kill you before they allow that."

"What's going on out here?" Ronin asked, entering the courtyard. Ina followed closely behind.

"We could hear you from inside," Ina said, sliding the door shut behind her.

Cai Ren paced around the cherry blossom. "We were just discussing Kari abdicating the throne."

"I'm uncertain. I would like time to think it through," Kari said. If she stepped down now, the harem would return. Not under Cai Ren, but his successor. She placed a hand on her stomach. But if she kept the throne, she could ensure the harem didn't return, at least for a few generations. Her bloodline, the Shagin bloodline, was all female.

Maybe, when the time was right, she could even use her power to bring the rest of Shagin to the mainland and save her people. She smiled at the thought.

"Think this through? You've had time enough," Cai Ren spat. "A decision must be made now! You do not have the strength to destroy these rebels. They will continue, and they will grow in number if we do not act now! You are a good woman, but I fear your sentiment will doom us all."

"I know I can't put this off forever, but I need a little more time to think through the implications," Kari said. He was right. She didn't have the willpower to wage war, but there was still so much she could accomplish. Somehow, she would find a way.

She gazed at the moon. Its light reflected on her, the same way she wanted her light to reflect on the world.

A white ball struck her cheek, sending a jolt of pain across her face. The ball erupted on impact, filling the air with powder and smoke. Kari swatted at the smoke. Her knees buckled, and she collapsed to all fours.

She coughed, her arms trembling to support her weight. What happened?

Ronin drew his kodachis, then lunged at Cai Ren.

Cai Ren hurled another white ball. It struck Ronin's chest, exploding into a puff of white smoke. Dropping his swords, Ronin fell to his knees.

"You bastard..." Ronin's eyes rolled back into his head, and he collapsed to the ground.

"Ina," Kari cried. "Run!"

Ina gasped, her eyes wide as she sprinted to the other side of the courtyard. Cai Ren took out another white ball from his robes, flinging it at her. The ball struck her in the back, and the white smoke coated her. Ina fell to the ground without resistance.

Kari struggled to her feet, focusing her spirit energy. Her hands tingled, but her power didn't manifest. She had to get out of here. Her survival was crucial. Cai Ren would pay for this.

She darted for the nearby wall. Her vision blurred and spun. As she leaped at the wall, she grabbed hold of its top ledge. Her muscles ached, her arms shaking as she pulled herself up. Her lungs were on fire, and her skin burned at the effort.

"Why won't you stay down?" Cai Ren threw another ball at her.

It struck the wall beside her. The blast of smoke sent her careening to the ground. She screamed, landing with a thud.

"Breathe deep, my friend," Cai Ren said, standing over her.

Her body ached and burned. She reached out to Cai Ren, her arm trembling. She wanted to ask him why he'd done this, but only groans escaped her lips. Body convulsing, she rolled onto her back, gripping her spasming chest.

She couldn't breathe.

Was this her death?

Her body went numb, and her arms fell to her side.

Blankly, she gazed at the moon. The shining orb doubled before her world faded to black.

CHAPTER THREE

KARI BLINKED AS HER eyes adjusted to the light, and the world came back into view. Her head smacked against the wooden floor, sending a jolt of pain through her skull. She laid in the back of a carriage, Ronin and Ina beside her, still unconscious. When she tried to place her hands on her head, she couldn't. Someone had bound her hands in front of her. Not this again.

A single soldier garbed in gray lamellar armor with a straight short sword strapped to his waist sat in the back with them, while another soldier drove the coverless carriage. They were amid a massive caravan of some forty or fifty wagons heading across a large field toward a city near the woods.

Armed soldiers filled some of the other carriages, while others were prisoners with their hands bound. By the look of the architecture, they were no longer in Xiang. The buildings lacked the decorative curved roofs. Instead, they were square and consisted of elaborate systems of decorative posts extending down the sides of the buildings. The posts were set about a foot away with beams connecting them to the building at regular intervals. They descended the corners and around the windows, forming a decorative railing that started from the roof and moved down, framing the windows, connecting to the sills, and extending to the ground.

"It's about time one of you is awake," the soldier said. "You've been out for days."

That explained Kari's empty stomach and dry mouth. Possibly even the general sense of fatigue she felt, although that could be the lingering effects of the white poison powder.

Kari glared as she crawled to sit upright on the bench. She nudged Ronin with her foot. His eyes shot wide, and he glanced around their surroundings.

He held up his bound hands. "Lovely." He sighed.

"Who are you?" Kari asked the guard. She pulled on her bindings, but it was no use. Her spirit energy was gone. Without it, her enhanced strength was gone, too. "Where are you taking us?"

The soldier smiled. "You'll find out soon enough."

Kari stared at Ronin. They shouldn't have much issue escaping, at least if they were at full strength. She wasn't sure about him, but her head was still fuzzy from whatever poison Cai Ren had used. It might be better to wait until the effects entirely wore off before fighting their way to freedom.

Ronin must have thought the same. He wasn't making any effort to flee just yet. He knelt beside Ina, trying to wake her. He seemed to have a plan already. At least, Kari hoped so. Why else would he take the time to wake Ina? He never seemed to be overly fond of her before. In fact, he didn't seem to be overly fond of anyone.

Kari didn't have much in the way of weapons. Her seed pouch and Ronin's swords were gone. That just left her light powers.

"So, you're the famous Shagin empress? You don't look so impressive to me."

"I'm not the Shagin empress," Kari glared at the soldier. "I'm Shagin who just so happens to be the empress of Xiang."

"Not anymore, you're not." The soldier laughed.

Kari balled her fists. She pulled against the bindings wrapped around her wrists, but they did not give. Resistance was useless until her spirit energy returned. She hadn't gone through everything in Xiang just to end up as another prisoner riding to an unknown fate.

Ina stirred, and Ronin helped her onto the bench.

"Quiet back there," the driver demanded. "We're approaching Sumar. We don't want a fuss when we arrive. That goes for you too, Irfan. Shut up and sit down. Once we are there, we'll get our reward."

The name Sumar sounded familiar, but Kari couldn't place from what nation. Either way, it confirmed her fears, Xiang was long behind them.

"Hear that, princess? Don't go making a fuss just yet. I hear they have big plans for you."

Kari clenched her jaw. She didn't like this. There was no telling how long her spirit energy would be gone. She was done being someone else's prisoner. As soon as she had enough strength, she was getting them out of here.

They could easily lose their captors in the woods. That was where her plant magic gave her the upper hand, not to mention her newfound light abilities. She had experimented over the past month with different light constructs. The light whip was the easiest to use, but she was sure she could make a tool for just about any need.

The forest looked ancient. Even from a distance, the trees looked more massive than any she had seen before. They had to stand nearly three hundred feet high with trunks nearly forty feet round.

The soldier cut his eyes from her to the forest.

"Look familiar, Your Majesty?" He grinned. "It should. That there is the Latari Forest."

Kari's heart nearly stopped. A wave of panic washed over her. Not here. Anywhere but here.

"The Latari Forest, but that's…" Ina stopped mid-sentence. She placed her hands on Kari's. "Why would they take us here?"

"We're leaving," Ronin flexed and pulled at his bindings, trying to break free.

This was where she was going to die—where her people had been hunted down, tortured, brutalized, and murdered. The largest genocide in history—the Shagin

Purge—occurred here. Before them were the remains of the Shagin Nation.

Damn it! Kari didn't have so much as a tingle from her spirit energy. She yanked on her bindings. Without her aura, though, there was no give.

"What are you doing? Stop that," the soldier demanded.

"Fool, release these bindings now, and I'll let you live." Ronin stood, facing the soldier.

This couldn't be happening. Why did the world hate Shagin so much? If Cai Ren wanted the throne, she would gladly give it to him. All that she wanted to do was to live, but her life was outlawed. Her existence was a crime against humanity. For that, she had to die. That was their law. That was their morality.

Humanity was corrupt. The entire human species could be so barbaric and unjust. To condemn an entire group of people to die was the highest act of cruelty. These people did not know her. She hadn't done them wrong, but because of her blood and heritage, she had to die with the rest of Shagin.

Kari's face reddened as rage flared inside her.

If they wanted her life, they were going to have to take it. Kari wasn't going to lie down and die just because they demanded it. She would meet their injustice with her own justice and vengeance for her slain sisters. Kill them all if she had to.

Kari stood. Her weak legs buckled beneath her in the bouncing carriage. She wasn't sure if that was the side effect of the poison or her trembling emotions at this point, but it didn't matter. Nothing was going to stand in her way. "Ina, are you ready?"

Ina nodded in reply, and Kari cut her eyes toward Ronin. A large smirk formed on his face.

"What the devil's going on back there?" the driver demanded.

Without hesitation, Ronin lunged at the soldier. With his hands still bound, Ronin grabbed the soldier's sword before he had time to react, unsheathed it, and drove it into his chest. The soldier stared in horror as Ronin ripped the sword out of his body, spraying blood into the air. With one swift kick to the chest, he knocked the soldier over the side of the cart.

"Help! Help," the driver screamed.

Ronin held the blade out. Kari slid her bindings on its edge, freeing her hands. She took the sword, then cut his and Ina's bindings.

"We have to move," Kari ordered. Other soldiers quickly descended from their carriages, rushing toward them. Kari leaped over the side of the cart. Her legs buckled. They gave way as she hit the ground, collapsing to her side. She was still weak from the poison.

Ina landed beside her, face-first in the grass, while Ronin dropped to his hands and knees. He was shaking and unsteady as he helped them up. All three reeled from the poison's effects. Any prolonged fighting wasn't going to end well.

Two soldiers drew their swords as they approached. Kari hated killing. Every time she killed someone, it felt like the memories of their lost potential would haunt her. She could see the faces of everyone she'd ever killed in her sleep; all the people who died because of her. Kari wished she lived in a world where killing wasn't a regular occurrence. She never wanted to hurt anyone again. But these weren't people. They were murderers. They'd sold their morality, their humanity, to be subservient to the orders of a genocidal Guardian. They looked at her like she was a monster, so she would no longer defend her existence with mere words. Instead, she would do it with the edge of a sword.

Kari stood beside Ronin. The pair rushed forward at the first two soldiers. The first, obviously an inexperienced fighter, swung wildly at Ronin. He sidestepped, dodging the incoming strike. Carrying forward with his momentum, he rammed his elbow into the soldier's face. Without breaking his stride, Ronin dropped to the ground and kicked the soldier's feet out from under him. The soldier hit the ground, dropping his weapon. Ronin snatched up the sword, then mounted the soldier. With one quick slash, he opened the soldier's throat, pouring bright red blood onto the green grass.

The other soldier attacked, swinging his blade at Kari's head. She parried the sword strike and launched forward, driving her blade through his chest. He groaned as blood oozed from the wound. She pulled the sword out, and blood splattered her soft skin.

Her hands trembled. Killing was becoming easier. She gripped the hilt of the sword tightly, steadying her hands. But there was no time to reflect on it now. Enemy soldiers rushed toward them.

"Run!" Kari cried. She turned and grabbed Ina's hand, pulling her as they made a mad dash to the forest. The only hope they had of losing their captors was in the woods. There was nowhere to run in the open plains.

Behind them, the soldiers clattered, and their feet erupted in a stampede of thuds as they made chase. Their yelling and banging were slowly drowned out by the sound of galloping hooves against the earth. The forest was such a long way away. They weren't going to make it.

Damn her lack of foresight! Kari should have known better than to try to escape while her spirit energy had yet to return. She gritted her teeth. This was her fault. These soldiers were after her, and it was her shortsightedness that began the battle before they were ready. Their deaths would be on her hands. The situation called for it, however. She wasn't going to die here at their command.

"Down!" Ronin knocked them to the ground as a blade swung by their heads as the first mounted soldier passed by in a thunderous gallop.

They stood to their feet as horse-mounted soldiers quickly surrounded them.

"You should feel honored," Ronin cried out to the soldiers. "Today, you get to die by the hands of a Kitsuno Kai and one of the most powerful Shagin ever to live."

Was he bluffing or being arrogant? There was no way they could fight them all in their current condition. Kari tried to focus her energy. Damn it, she still wasn't getting anything.

The first cavalry unit charged forward. Ina dropped to the ground while Kari and Ronin rolled out of the way. One mounted soldier pulled out of rank, charging at the group. Ronin leaped up as the soldier slashed downward with his sword. Ronin dodged the strike and swung with his own, but the horse was too fast. He missed as the soldier galloped past.

"Get ready to run," Ronin said. He wiped at the sweat dripping down his forehead. Even though he was too weak to fight, he was still willing to do so for her. There had to be something she could do.

Ronin charged forward as another horse and soldier rushed toward them. The soldier readied his sword to strike, and Ronin did the same. He met the soldier's blow, his sword striking the soldier's wrist, lobbing off his hand. The man screamed, letting go of his reins. Ronin slashed at the horse, drawing blood across its chest. It reared back in pain, throwing the soldier from his saddle onto the ground. Ronin didn't stop. He charged forward into the line of cavalry, franticly swinging his sword. It was enough to scare the horses and riders alike, who quickly darted from his reach.

"Go!" Ronin screamed.

Kari hesitated. She couldn't leave him. Ina tugged on her arm, her eyes wide and filled with panic. Kari's nostrils flared. Ronin wouldn't die. He was too stubborn to do so.

Kari and Ina dashed into the opening Ronin made, running toward the forest. With every step, Kari's legs threatened to give under her. This was a horrible plan. They weren't going to make it. But if she was going to die, she wanted to die fighting.

A horse-drawn carriage rushed in front, stopping their advance. It was the driver from earlier. He leaped out of the transport, drawing his sword.

Kari jumped as an arrow struck next to her. She turned to face the archer. He aimed, releasing another shot. Yelping, she swung her sword. It hit the shaft of the arrow, knocking it out of the air.

She couldn't see Ronin, but a crowd of soldiers had surrounded where he had been before. Her heart raced to the point of breaking. Hopefully, he was okay.

Kari and Ina sprinted around the other side of the carriage, away from the sight of the archer. Now would be a perfect time to use her light powers and turn invisible. She didn't have any spirit energy, not even the slightest bit of an aura to protect herself.

Kari screamed as a blade swung at her head. She dove to the ground, avoiding the attack. The driver was back. Ina cried out and tackled the man, knocking him to the ground. Kari stood, ready to finish off the driver. Three more soldiers appeared from around the carriage, drawing her attention.

These soldiers were better equipped with thicker steel armor and wielding spears. Kari clenched her jaw. Could she truly fight without her spirit energy? These soldiers wouldn't hesitate to kill them, and she wouldn't be able to slice through their armor with her sword. She needed her magic.

"Get behind me," Kari ordered, grabbing Ina and lifting her. She would still defend her friend at any cost. Ina rushed around her as Kari faced her new opponents. The soldiers thrust with their spears. She parried, but a second thrust kept her from being able to follow with her own attack. Without her spirit aura, she couldn't afford to take even a glancing blow.

The three soldiers struck out with their spears, each thrust forcing Kari back. It was all she could do to defend herself. She parried strike after strike, but it was becoming more futile. What little strength she had was fading quickly.

Ina screamed as more armed soldiers appeared. One grabbed her, shoving her to the ground. The soldier raised his sword for the killing blow.

Kari had already lost one friend. She wasn't going to lose another.

"No!" she screamed. Using all her strength, she swung her free hand. A flash of light erupted from her fingers as a whip made out of solid light appeared in her hand. She slashed at the soldier. The whip struck his shoulder and traveled through the other side of his abdomen, cleaving him in half.

"Ahh!" Kari screamed as pain pulsated through her skull. Her light whip dissipated, and she dropped her sword and grabbed at her head. The exertion was too much in her weakened condition, the blinding pain forcing her to her knees. Her vision doubled, but Kari gritted her teeth. She couldn't lose consciousness. She had to save Ina.

The driver stood above her with his sword raised, but she couldn't move. Her strength was utterly gone. Her arms trembled as she attempted to raise them, but to no avail.

Kari closed her eyes as the driver swung his sword at her neck. But the blade never contacted its target.

Kari looked up. Standing in front of her was a tall, beautiful blonde woman in a flowy white dress. A pink symbol made up of a circle with an upside-down arrow surrounded by two dots adorned the back of her dress. Her bare arm was all she used to block the blade.

"What is the meaning of this?" she demanded, knocking the sword away.

The soldiers quickly dropped their weapons, falling to their knees in submission. The woman wasn't alone, either. More soldiers wearing shiny silver armor surrounded them. The same symbol that was on the woman's dress was also on the soldiers' armor—except it was blue instead of pink.

"This woman," the driver argued. "She killed my brother."

"And I would have, too." The woman's sapphire-blue eyes shot daggers. "She is to be my guest, and here you are treating her like another common prisoner. Were you going to kill her?"

"She's a Shagin monster."

Kari winced at the driver's words.

The woman's spirit energy exploded from her. Kari never felt anything like it before. The woman had to be immensely strong for Kari to be able to sense her aura like this.

The woman's expression hardened. She wanted to kill this man. Instead, she merely snapped her fingers.

Two of the silver knights surrounded the driver, seizing him by the arm.

"You should count yourself lucky I'm in a forgiving mood after that comment. The fact remains you have defied my orders, and you will be held accountable for your actions."

The two silver knights escorted the driver away without a further word.

"I'm so sorry about this." The woman turned toward Kari, her expression softening. She held out a hand, helping Kari to her feet. "I never meant for this to happen; you have to believe me. I thought it would be best to hire mercenaries to bring you here instead of using our own knights. I didn't want to tip off the Xianese to what we were planning."

Kari rubbed her eyes. "Ina, where's Ina?"

"I'm here," Ina hurried over and hugged her. She was bruised and cut, but unharmed.

"I am Ilyia," the woman continued. "It is a pleasure to finally meet you, Kari. This must be one of your retainers?"

"I suppose," Kari ignored the question. "Where's my brother?"

Ronin walked toward them, escorted by another woman. He waved, bloody but alive. The woman with him was just as strange as Ilyia. She wore thick orange-and-black clothing—padded armor most likely. A black mask revealed only her bright green eyes, red lips, and the scarred flesh surrounding them. Black and orange dyed rope and leather strips attached to the covering created the appearance of hair.

"By the gods, you're covered in blood," Ina exclaimed.

"It's not mine." Ronin smirked.

"This is one tough bastard," the masked woman said. "Poisoned, yet he still managed to kill seventeen armed soldiers."

"Artemis, if you think that's impressive, you should have seen Kari," Ilyia said with a smile. "Even with Aura's poison powder, she was still able to conjure her light whip."

They'd orchestrated this? "What do you want with me?" Kari asked.

"I told you, I want you to be my guest," Ilyia responded, holding out a hand for Kari to take.

"You're Shagin?" Kari asked, fixated on the Shagin insignia on Ilyia's dress.

"Yes, we are."

CHAPTER FOUR

"I don't understand," Kari said. She reached out to take Ilyia's hand, but stopped shy. "How can you be Shagin?"

This didn't make any sense. How could there still be Shagin living on the mainland? But they were Shagin, that much was clear. They had full mastery of their auras. Techniques only passed down through Shagin. People like Jiaorong and even Ronin could form spirit auras, so that others could learn Shagin secrets. But such mastery indicated more advanced knowledge than Jiaorong possessed. They had to be Shagin. Although, the true sign was their eyes. Shagin all shared vibrant eyes. They were distinct from the dull colors of other nations.

Kari recognized the name Ilyia. She was the last Champion of Shagin, the leader of the Furies. But anyone could claim a title. If she were indeed the Champion, she would wield the Champion's weapon, the Golden Rod.

"We survived." Artemis clenched her fists. She shook her head, correcting herself. "We ran. When all hope was lost, we fled and hid in the ruins of our people."

Kari didn't know what to say. Did they expect her to be angry they'd abandoned their sisters? It seemed like it would be somewhat hypocritical. Her mother had ran. All who survived had. The united armies of the Three Realms were brought down upon them.

"These two—they are your companions?" Ilyia asked, changing the subject.

"They are more than that," Kari said. She smiled at Ina, who returned the gesture. "Ina is my sister."

Artemis gave Ilyia a sideways look. Kari knew it would be hard to understand. Shagin were sisters, and the divide between Shagin and the rest of the world, forced upon them by the Guardian, would make such bonds between Kari and Ina unusual. But it was how she felt. She only hoped Ina shared the same feelings.

"We've been through a lot together," Ina added, stepping beside Kari. Her heart raced at her friend's support. "It might sound strange, but the bonds that we've formed is just as strong as blood. We've fought and bled for each other, and we will die for each other."

Kari closed her eyes, remembering the shared pain they went through together. Ina was the only person to stand by Kari from the beginning of their captivity in the harem. Ina never stopped believing in her. She even took a knife in the back from someone Kari once thought of as a sister.

They had come so far together, the three of them. In such a short amount of time, both Ina and Ronin had become Kari's closest friends. The bonds they shared through their struggles formed stronger than any she had with any others. Kari couldn't help but smile. "And Ronin is my brother."

"You are Shagin," Artemis sneered in disdain. She glared at Ronin, eyeing him. "You do not have a brother."

"Yeah, she does. Try to keep up." Ronin stepped toward Artemis, returning the glare. He did not appreciate being waved off by this stranger. Artemis either did not know who or what he was or was unafraid. In Xiang, the Kitsuno Kai were greatly feared. They possessed the power to execute anyone at any time. It was a mindset Ronin carried.

"We share the same father, and my mother raised him. We are siblings through and through," Kari said, stepping between the pair.

Ronin sighed, closing his eyes. His posture relaxed, and he backed down.

Ilyia placed a hand on Artemis's shoulder. The woman scoffed, but she let it go. "But they are not Shagin," Ilyia explained. "We do not consider the children of our fathers as our brothers and sisters."

"I do." Kari stared at Ilyia, her resolve unfaltering. Tradition be damned. Tradition had seen her exiled. She knew how she felt, and that wasn't going to change.

"Fair enough." Sheepishly, Ilyia shrugged. "I guess I should expect some of our traditions to be lost among the survivors. Although I suppose it is not such a terrible thing."

"Why did you bring us here?" Ina asked.

That was a good question. If they were Shagin, all they'd had to do was ask. Kari would have come. The situation was odd.

"Truth be told, you two were never meant to come, only Kari," Ilyia said bluntly. "With it being common knowledge Shagin were not only alive, but had also overthrown Xiang, we knew we had to take action to protect Kari before the Guardian sent his hunters after her."

"It was a good thing we intervened when we did. Your chancellor was already plotting your death, little one," Artemis added.

Kari winced. She hadn't been called a child in years.

"He thought it would be best to eliminate your friends along with you," Artemis continued.

"He agreed to turn you over into our custody for a price. We provided him the poison powder to nullify you. Apparently, it worked out verily well. We take the blame for your deaths, and he gets a lot of gold," Ilyia said.

How was this a good thing? Kari had lost her throne. Abdicating was one more choice taken away from her. The fears she had, the traditions she fought against, nothing was stopping them from returning.

But there was something else bothering her.

"If you are blamed, won't the Guardian come after you?" Kari asked. It seemed an odd choice to save her only to draw further attention to them. "After all, you are Shagin."

"The world doesn't know that," Ilyia explained. "And we plan to keep it that way for as long as possible, at least until we are ready to bring our sisters back."

"Bring them back?" Kari asked. Was such a thing even possible? The Guardian would never allow it. He would kill them if they attempted it.

"We've been working toward that goal over the past few years," Ilyia said. "Rebuilding our home and fortifying our defenses so our sisters can return. For that, we could use all the help we can get."

Kari grinned. They had a plan. If they could bring Shagin back to the mainland, Kari would help however she could. Shagin were doomed to die if they stayed on Mystikos. An all-female race exiled on an island would eventually die out. Bringing them back could mean their survival.

Kari scanned the carriages. The prisoners weren't Shagin. Why were they being taken into the Shagin Nation? Her smile faded.

"What about these other people? Who are they?" she asked, motioning toward the others.

"Criminals mostly," Ilyia said. "Some are prisoners of war. We are constantly trying to rebuild our home. For that, we need money. We've reached out to other nations, and they pay us to take their criminals."

"That's horrible," Ina said, placing her hands on her hip. "You can't just treat people like this."

Ilyia waved off her concern. "These people are murderers and thieves. They'd execute them or let them rot in prisons in their home countries. At least this way, they can come here where they might have a chance."

"A chance for what? To die?" Ina asked.

"We rehabilitate those we can. They are more than welcome to join us. Reformed prisoners and refugees make up most of our population. Those we can't help, we indenture. They work for us, serving whatever time sentenced, or seven years, whichever is shorter. We need all the help we can get to rebuild our home. Once they have worked through their punishment, they are free to go."

"This is wrong," Ronin said, rubbing his chin.

"You disapprove?" Ilyia's eyebrows arched. Maybe they had heard of the Kitsuno Kai after all.

"No, not at all. I don't care." Ronin waved his hand. "You said you rehabilitate them, whatever, that's fine."

"Then what's wrong?" Kari asked.

"I didn't think Shagin let outsiders into their territory, much less men."

That was true—Shagin were protective of their land and their secrets. They had to be. By decree, the Guardian forbade them from entering any territory outside of their land. When they went on Pilgrimage, they had to be careful not to be detected and identified as Shagin. The only protection they had from the cruelty of the Guardian were the secrets of their magic.

"We do it because we have no choice." Artemis glared at Ronin. "There are only four of us left."

"Five now," Ilyia corrected, placing a hand on Kari's shoulder.

Kari smiled in response. She might be an exile, but they still saw her as Shagin.

"We have prepared a private carriage to take us to Koruzeru. Come, there is much for us to discuss," Ilyia said.

"Does that mean we don't have a choice?" Ina asked. "Are we prisoners, too?"

Kari shot her a sideways glance.

"I didn't mean it like that," Ilyia said. "You are more than welcome to leave, although the surrounding area can be dangerous. I am offering you a haven. Please stay for a few days. At least until the Guardian is no longer hunting you."

"Koruzeru, that's the old capital," Kari said. "We'll be traveling into the heart of Shagin?"

"Of course," Ilyia said. "There is so much I want to show you."

The thought of traveling to her ancestral homeland excited and terrified her. She had studied the Purge. While the stories never went into detail, she knew enough about it to know she didn't want to see its remnants. But her mother had been born just through those woods. It was where, just a few decades ago, Shagin had lived and thrived. Now, the remaining survivors slowly died off on a small island hidden away from the world.

Those who fled the Purge knew it was only a stalling tactic. It had destroyed Shagin beyond repair. There were too few left to sustain a civilization. They fled, knowing their people would eventually die out. To escape the horrors of the Purge, they'd fled. Saving those they could was a bittersweet victory.

Shagin didn't give birth to males, and Mystikos was too far away from the mainland to go on Pilgrimage and return with a child. It meant the current generation—Kari's—would be the last.

Kari placed her hands on her stomach. Her generation wouldn't be the last—her daughter would be. Her stomach turned. Hopefully, the battle hadn't caused too much stress on her growing child.

Why did she care? She had thought about ending the pregnancy, but she had been too apprehensive about trying any herbal remedies. The Seed provided her body with natural resilience, which would make any attempt problematic if not outright dangerous.

Were her motherly instincts setting in?

Kari sighed. She wasn't sure she wanted them to. There was still time to end the pregnancy. Perhaps an abdominal massage would be enough. But if she followed through, would that doom her people? Every birth would be needed to rebuild what was lost. Either way, time was against her. She needed to make a decision sooner rather than later. For now, she was content pushing the pregnancy to the back of her mind.

Ilyia helped them board the last remaining carriage. Unlike the others, this carriage was enclosed with ornate black wood and red curtains. The remaining caravan stopped just before the Latari Forest and set up an encampment, while they went on ahead.

It would take them about nine days to travel through the forest to reach Koruzeru. Ilyia decided it would be best to travel alone as opposed to riding with the caravan. With their heavy loads and the number of passengers, it would take the caravan nearly twenty days to reach their destination.

The trees of the forest were massive, bigger than any Kari had ever seen. They were a good fifty feet wide and nearly four hundred feet tall.

"Impressive, right?" Artemis asked, noticing Kari's expression. "Some of the bigger ones are often hollowed out and used as homes."

"Wouldn't they rot?" Ina asked.

"We use enchantments to keep them alive," Ilyia added.

They traveled on the southern road from Sumar to Koruzeru. While the eastern route was the easier path, it went through the city of Saburta. Saburta saw some of the worst atrocities committed during the Purge. It was where the Elders had surrendered to appease the Guardian, and the genocide began.

Days passed as they traveled through the forest, stopping only to rest or camp for the night. Ilyia returned Kari's seed pouch. With it, she could grow fruits and vegetables to eat. While this meant they didn't need to stop to forage for food, it was still a good idea to let the horses rest. In the evenings,

Artemis would disappear into the forest and return with game for dinner.

Kari stretched as she stepped out of the carriage. It felt good to extend her legs. They felt cramped and restless after riding for hours.

They had stopped in a small clearing in the forest. Lush green grass was a welcomed reprieve from the fallen leaves and detritus they were used to seeing. The surrounding trees provided ample shade.

Kari slipped off her shoes, then wiggled her toes in the grass. The forest was fantastic—from the massive trees to the smell of timber and vegetation. Even the moist soil added to the scent.

Her ears perked up. A stream ran beside their campground. The clear water coursed over rocks, spilling into pools before running to the next. A fallen tree covered in moss guarded the creek, arching its way from one side to the other, leaving it unimpeded.

She smiled at the life surrounding her.

Warm rays of sunlight broke through the canopy of the trees, illuminating the forest. Kari collapsed onto the grass. She outstretched her fingers, curling into the soil to feel it all. The woods were alive and healthy, and she felt one with it.

"You look happy." Ilyia sat next to Kari.

"How can I not be?" Kari leaned back, flopping onto the earth. She folded one arm behind her head, draping the other over her face to shield it from the rays of sunlight.

"Is it that bright?" Ilyia asked, noticing her squint.

"No, she's just protecting herself from her mortal enemy, the sun." Ronin folded his arms across his chest, his grin spreading.

Kari chuckled. "I do tend to burn easily."

"And what of you?" Ilyia asked, clearly noticing his ghostly appearance.

"I prefer the shadows," Ronin responded.

"Mom never had this problem," Kari said, sitting upright. "Is this something we get from our father?"

Ronin nodded. "He burned like roasted duck over a flame."

Kari grimaced. That was some analogy. "I wish I could have met him at least once," she mused, pushing the mental image away. "Or even just seen a portrait."

"I think your skin is beautiful," Ina said. She dropped behind Kari, draping her arms around her shoulders.

Kari's heart fluttered. What was this feeling? Ina's embrace, her words, sent shockwaves through Kari's body. They were friends. Now that friendship seemed to be growing ever more potent. Perhaps there could be more to their friendship.

Kari shook the thought away. She didn't know how Ina felt, and she would not risk their friendship by revealing her burgeoning feelings. It was a crush—one that would go away in time.

They started setting up camp for the evening while Artemis returned with a wild boar to roast. Ilyia seemed annoyed at the large kill.

"It's wasteful," Ilyia scolded. "I told you to stick to small game. We lack any method to keep the extra meat fresh."

"Maybe so, but it's delicious." Artemis winked. "Tell me you don't want boar meat. We could wake up to fried bacon in the morning. Besides, we should be celebrating our sister."

"We are the protectors of this forest," Ilyia said, her hungry eyes on the meat as it hung over the campfire. "At least until our sisters return. It is ours to take care of."

"It's just one pig," Artemis said, poking at the roast with a stick. "Their numbers have grown wild. What's the big deal?"

"The forest has to remain healthy. If everyone thought the same—that one life doesn't matter—then the forest would be deprived of life."

"A little dramatic, don't you think?" Artemis shot back.

"I don't know," Kari said. "I agree. Even when I fight, each life I take feels like a momentous decision. I hate killing. But I only do it because I have to."

"Yes, how dare those people make you kill them," Artemis joked. "They forced your hand."

Ilyia shot her a look. Artemis grumbled, but shrank in submission.

"It's not as easy as that," Ina said. She placed her hand on top of Kari's. Her fingers felt smooth and gentle. "You don't know what we've been through. Kari did whatever it took to keep us safe; we both did."

"I don't know. Sometimes, people deserve to be killed," Ronin said, popping his wrists.

"Can we not talk about this?" Kari asked.

Ronin rolled his eyes, but he stayed silent.

"Sure, what do you want to talk about?" Ilyia asked.

"I know." Ronin perked up. "What are you doing on the mainland?"

"Besides trying to rebuild our home?" Ilyia asked. "We are the Furies. It is our job to protect Shagin at any cost. We trained our entire lives to fight. Yet, we failed. Now, we have a chance to redeem ourselves."

"Why did you fight in the Sovereign War?" Kari asked. It was something even the survivors on Mystikos wondered about. "The elders refused to get involved. Why go against them?"

"Why did we turn renegade?" Artemis licked her lips. "Are you familiar with the Cavalian Civil War?"

"Not intimately," Ina said, glancing at Kari.

But Kari knew. The Cavalian Civil War was the start of the Sovereign War. Shagin children growing up post Purge were taught the lesson.

"History is lost to those under the Guardian's rule," Ilyia added, shaking her head.

"The nation of Cavalia was divided into five tribes. Over time, the five tribes developed different belief systems and religions with the Mylians worshiping the Triune gods,"

Kari explained. "They believed it was their sacred duty to convert the other tribes, using force if necessary."

Ilyia met Kari's gaze, and she nodded in approval. "The Triune Concordant dictates everyone in the Three Realms should worship the Triune, or the nation could lose its sovereignty."

The Concordant established the governments of the Three Realms—the Niwendian Empire, the Kingdom of Adgul, and the Terran Union. It also banished Shagin from leaving the Latari Forest on fear of death, and the Concordant was amended to codify their extermination.

"So, the Mylians went to war with the other tribes?" Ina asked, listening intently.

"They did, and it was a bloody war." Artemis clapped her hands together, leaning forward as if she were telling a ghost story. "Each side was hellbent on exterminating their enemies."

"The problem was the Concordant also forbids war and any acts of aggression," Ilyia said, sounding far more solemn than her compatriot. "It's what drew the Guardian's attention. He gathered the armies of Terra together, then marched on Cavalia.

"Most assumed he would end the fight. Instead, he sided with the Mylians. He demanded the surrender of the other tribes, or he'd order their extermination. When they refused, he went to work.

"He utterly destroyed the Koroks. It was genocide. People slaughtered, their homes razed, their culture destroyed. But it worked. The other tribes surrendered, and they were forced to assimilate to the Mylian way of life."

"This wasn't the first genocide committed by the Guardian," Artemis said. "History is full of people who refused to submit to his tyranny. They ended up wiped from existence. Most of that history is lost to the ages."

"When the Sovereign War started, it was in response to the Korok massacre," Ilyia said. "Nations finally demanded independence from the Terran Union."

"My teachers said Shagin manipulated the other nations into fighting," Ina said. "In school, it was always referred to as the Shagin War."

"Lies." Artemis kicked up grass and dirt.

"The Sovereign Alliance offered Shagin freedom from the oppression of the Triune Concordant for our help," Ilyia said. "The Elders feared the risk wasn't worth it, that the other nations wouldn't keep their promises. But it was an opportunity we couldn't pass up, even if it meant betraying the Elders.

"Unfortunately, we lost the war. As the Sovereign Alliance crumbled and nations began suing for peace, they needed a scapegoat—us."

"I was just a kid when it happened," Ronin said. "But I remember it well. At the start of the war, Eanna was so scared as Xiang stayed loyal to the Guardian. She was afraid someone would discover she was Shagin, then come for Father and me. It got to the point where she wouldn't leave the house except at night when people couldn't see her eyes as well."

"I didn't know that," Kari said.

Ronin nodded. "Father spent time traveling. He was a general, you know? Fought in the war. I think it pained him as much as her. I spent a lot of time with Eanna in those days. She taught me all sorts of things—like spirit energy and such."

"She was a traitor," Artemis snapped.

Kari's heart skipped.

"Artemis," Ilyia rebuked.

Ronin's eyes narrowed, his hands twitching.

He leaped at Artemis. Seizing her by the throat, he slammed her onto the ground, pinning her arms with his legs. His hand shot toward his kodachi, drawing the curved blade from its sheath.

Ilyia caught his arm, stopping him from attacking.

"Ronin," Kari screamed.

His eyes cut toward Ilyia, whose sapphire eyes glared back.

"I'm sorry," she said, releasing his arm.

He grunted and stood, releasing Artemis. With a quick flash of steel, his sword disappeared into its sheath, hidden away under his coat.

"Those were Shagin secrets," Artemis said, sitting upright.

"Artemis, that's enough!" Ilyia placed her foot on Artemis's chest to force her down. "Do you understand?"

"Yes, Miss," Artemis mumbled.

"As for you..." Ilyia turned toward Ronin.

He waved her off. "Won't happen again." He smirked, stalking off toward the stream.

"Is he always like this?" Ilyia asked, raising a brow at Kari.

"If only you knew," Ina said.

"I'll talk with him." Kari headed for her brother.

Ronin stood silently, watching the water. He didn't respond or move as she approached. Kari stood by him. What was she supposed to say?

"I was only two when my father began seeing your mother," Ronin said, breaking the silence. He still did not turn toward her.

"She's your mother, too," Kari said, reaching for him.

When he scoffed, Kari recoiled. "My mother died during childbirth. For ten years, Eanna raised me as her own. Father was never around, and our servants were afraid of me."

"Even as a child?" Kari asked. Ronin sneered.

"They were afraid of Father, who wanted me to be tough and fearless," Ronin said. "He restricted the servants from taking care of me. Even tried the same with Eanna, but she refused to obey mindlessly. You have her smile, you know."

Kari wanted to reach out to him, to embrace him, but could she? He never seemed the type to appreciate physical touch. Still, he was in pain. That much was clear. "I'm sorry. It sounds like you had a difficult childhood."

Ronin shook his head. "It wasn't."

They stood in silence, studying the stream as it ran through the forest. A leaf floated down, landing in the stream. The current grabbed it, rushing it through the stones. It bobbed and weaved along the water's path, meeting everything along the way. It bounced on rocks, spinning as it moved. Each collision threatened to derail the leaf's path, but the water did not stop, and neither could it.

"Come on, you two." Ina approached. She draped her arms around the pair, pulling them toward her. Ronin scoffed, but he didn't resist. "You should come eat. It's been a long day. Tomorrow will be even longer."

Kari clenched her jaw. They would be in Koruzeru tomorrow, and she would face the new path the Fates had placed her on—one that took her back to the ruins of her people and their possible salvation.

CHAPTER FIVE

THEY FINALLY ARRIVED AT Koruzeru, entering through the western gate. A large wooden wall constructed from logs surrounded the city. Five roads fed into it from the gates located to the north, east, south, west, and northwest. A multitude of buildings made from wood and stone comprised the city proper. Towering jagged cliffs ran the length of the northeastern shore. Builders constructed houses and structures into the cliffs. The southeastern bluff overlooked the Arddean Sea.

"We've rebuilt most of the western side of the city," Ilyia explained. The restored buildings lacked the decorative posts, framing the sides, which were so prominent in Sumar. Remnants of the posts were still present on some. It appeared the reconstruction lacked the same decorative flair and architecture of old. "We've also built up the area surrounding the Temple of Lasan. You're aware of this temple, correct?"

Kari nodded, but she was apprehensive about visiting. Both the occurrence of the Cataclysm and the creation of the Seed happened there. That temple housed her legacy—one of darkness and death—and it was hers alone to bear.

They followed the winding dirt road into the city. People lined the streets, cheering as the group entered. The carriage stopped in front of a wooden building shot through with stone accents between the different levels. Since the decorative framework was still intact, the structure must have somehow made it through the Purge.

After they descended from the carriage, a knight climbed aboard and took the reins. He led the horses to the nearby stables as the crowd rushed to surround them.

"Lady Ilyia, thank you for your blessing."

"Welcome back, Lady Ilyia."

Ilyia held out her hands. "Please, please, thank you for your support, but these weary travelers need their space and rest. If you would be so kind as to give us some room, there will be plenty of time to sit and talk tomorrow."

It was hard to tell what the people cheered for, but the crowd parted without much fuss. An older woman stayed behind. She dropped to her knees, then held out a loaf of bread.

"Thank you, Lady Ilyia. You have given new life to these old bones. Hope for my family as well. I can never repay what you have done for us. Please accept this as a token of my gratitude. I know it is small and not befitting of someone of your stature, but it is all I have to give."

Ilyia took the bread, then helped the woman to her feet. "It is I who should be thanking you. This loaf of bread represents so much more. I will cherish it. Tonight, I will break bread with my sisters. Thank you."

Smiling, the old woman departed. Ilyia handed the bread to Artemis, then motioned for the group to follow her.

"That's quite a welcome," Ronin said. Was it cynicism or jealously Kari detected in his voice?

"I must gather Chaska and Aura. No doubt they will want to meet you," Ilyia said. "Artemis, can you take them to their quarters? Kari, after you've settled, please accompany Artemis to Lasan."

After she agreed, they followed Artemis on foot as they headed toward the inn. More knights and mercenaries marched past them. The knights wore silver glittery plate armor with the Shagin symbol decorating their backs. The mercenaries, on the other hand, wore a mismatch of various armors and clothing, making it easy to tell them apart.

"Why are there so many soldiers?" Kari asked. The sight of so many armed guards made her uneasy.

"This is our sacred home. You understand this, little one?" Artemis asked. Kari nodded. But that made the presence of so many outsiders odd. It was one thing to allow strangers into Shagin, but this was Koruzeru. How could Artemis be so hostile about her mother teaching Ronin, but welcome this? "The Guardian already destroyed it once. The soldiers are for added protection. It is a precaution—in case the Guardian returns to raze the city. Not to mention that we need help to keep watch over the prisoners."

"You house prisoners in your sacred city?" Ina asked, raising an eyebrow.

"We use them to help rebuild what was damaged. Some concessions are necessary for survival. Isn't that right, little one?" Artemis asked.

Kari only nodded. She understood all too well what necessity would drive someone to do. She had made sacrifices when facing the Tian brothers. It made sense for the Shagin to carry the same mindset, especially since they emphasized survival at any cost.

Artemis opened the door to the inn. "We have a room prepared for you. You'll have to excuse the cramped space. We'd only expected one of you. The keeper will take care of any needs."

It was a tiny room with only one bed and a cushioned chair.

"Where will we sleep?" Kari asked.

"I'll take the chair." Ronin dropped onto its red cushion with a thump.

"I guess that leaves the bed for us," Ina said. "Which side do you want?"

Heat radiated in Kari's face. Why did Ina's question embarrass her so? She'd shared beds with other girls. Kari fixated on Ina. She knew the butterflies in her stomach fluttered purely because it *was* Ina.

"It won't matter," Artemis said, breaking the silence. "We'll be able to secure better accommodations soon. At most, you will have to put up with this for a night or two."

"I guess we can switch sides each night if you want," Ina said, sitting on the edge of the mattress.

"There's a washroom at the end of the hall," Artemis said. "I suggest you get settled. Afterward, I'll take you to Lasan."

Kari nodded. She already missed the warm baths of the palace. They had become one of her favorite luxuries. With no hesitation, she headed toward the washroom. She undressed, then climbed into the bath. Grimacing at the lukewarm water, she hurriedly washed, wishing it were hotter. Still, it was nice to get cleaned up.

Kari stepped out, dried off, then redressed in her dusty silk ruqun. The dress showed signs of wear after their journey. The ends were frayed and unraveled, and the seams had rips. She would have to acquire new clothes soon, or she would be wearing silk rags.

"Are you ready?" Artemis asked.

"I am," Kari said. She held up the ends of her skirt. "Is there a place to get a change of clothes?"

"I'll see what I can do," Artemis said. "For now, let's meet with Ilyia and the others."

"I'm coming with you," Ina said.

"You are not Shagin," Artemis shot back. "You are not allowed in our temple."

"Then I will wait outside," Ina said, standing her ground.

"You don't have to come," Kari added. She appreciated her friend's concern, but she feared offending Artemis. Besides, if Ina saw the temple, she might ask its origin. What would Kari say then? She couldn't admit she was the Bearer. The secret behind the Seed was too shameful to share. "Why don't you rest here with Ronin?"

"We should both come with you," Ina said. "There is strength in numbers."

"You're suspicious of us?" Artemis laughed. "I like you, kid."

"You agree with me, Ronin. Right?" Ina asked, turning toward him.

"Of course not," Ronin said, slouching in his chair. "I'm staying here. Go if you like. I haven't felt right since being hit with that poison powder."

"The effects can linger for a week or two." Artemis shrugged, folding her hands behind her head. "Sorry about that, but we had to make it look convincing to extract you without a fuss."

"We'll be okay, Ina," Kari said. Truthfully, apprehension at going alone filled her with dread. Like Ronin, she, too, still felt weak, and her spirit energy had yet to return. She would feel better with Ina's company, but she didn't want to come across as fearful of her Shagin sisters.

"Please, let me come with you. I'm worried about you," Ina said, clasping Kari's hands in her own.

"I suppose there's no harm in coming," Artemis said, scratching the back of her mask. "You just won't be allowed inside the sanctuary."

Relieved, Kari felt a weight lift from her shoulders.

The Temple of Lasan was to the southeast of the city on the bluff overlooking the sea. Artemis led them to the coast. An embankment ran down from the cliffs down to the beaches.

The roar of surf crashing against the shore struck Kari's ears. It had been so long since she'd seen the ocean. Joy overcame her, and she took off running for the shore. The blue water beat against the sandy beach as dark storm clouds rolled in from the horizon. It was just like home. Kari threw off her shoes before darting across the sand and into the surf.

The cool water washed over her feet before retreating, pulling sand from under her toes. Closing her eyes, she breathed in the crisp air.

"I don't think I've ever seen you this happy," Ina said, catching up.

"It's been ages since I've seen the ocean. I grew up on an island, you know. Can you swim?" Kari asked.

"Not really," Ina stammered. "I can get out of the water if I fall in, but that's about it."

Kari grabbed Ina's hands. "I can teach you!"

Ina stared at the waves as they broke upon the shore. "I don't know. What if we started in a slow-moving puddle?"

"Come on." Kari pulled Ina into the water. "Look, it's not deep here. You can probably reach for a good bit."

Ina let out a yelp as the cold water splashed up to her waist. She wrapped her arms around her chest, shivering. "Does the cold not bother you?"

"You don't notice it once you're fully in the water." With a grin, Kari dove under the waves. The liquid washed over her face, rejuvenating her. She broke through the surface, then slung her wet hair out of her eyes. "See? It feels great."

"If you say so." Ina laughed. "Here, I think you missed a spot." Ina splashed her.

Kari laughed and grabbed Ina's hand, pulling her forward. "If we go out a little farther, we can float in the waves."

"You should get out of the water," Artemis called from the beach.

Kari's smile faded. "Why? Is this not allowed?"

"No, I just don't want you to find anything."

"Find what?" Ina asked. They sloshed through the water as they made their way back to the shore.

"Bodies," Artemis replied, averting her eyes.

"What?" Ina placed her hand over her mouth.

"We tried to collect as many as we could while we repaired the city. We've pulled a number of our fallen from the water. But there is always the chance there are more still out there."

Kari shivered in the wind, folding her arms in front of her. She'd been enjoying herself. How could she have forgotten? The extermination of her people had happened here, yet she'd been acting like a child playing at the beach.

Ina wrapped her arms tightly around Kari, probably sensing her shift in mood.

"Sometimes, it's good not to think about the tragedies of the past," Ina murmured, stroking Kari's hair. "We all need time to enjoy the little things, or we risk being swallowed by despair."

"Thank you," Kari said, gazing into her friend's dark eyes. Ina knew all too well about despair. When they'd first met, Jiaorong had just murdered Ina's fiancé—on their wedding day. Sometimes, it was easy to forget how much pain Ina carried.

"Let's go, you two," Artemis said. "We need to get you into dry clothes."

"How bad was it?" Kari asked.

"Are you familiar with the Battle of Koruzeru?" Artemis asked. Kari shook her head. She only knew it was the last defense of Shagin, and it had fallen surprisingly fast, but the survivors had lost the details. If anyone did know, they didn't talk about it. "I was injured and missed the battle itself, leaving Ilyia alone for the defense. The city was surrounded. We blockaded the gates and waited for them to attack, but instead of moving in to engage us in open combat, they gathered more of their armies around the western entrance. We couldn't escape by land or withstand the sheer numbers of the entire world crashing down upon us.

"They had a blockade of ships off the coast. We never put much stock in naval warfare. On land, our spirit energy gives us the advantage. But on water, we drown as easily as anyone else."

Kari knew how easily, too. She had almost drowned in her fight against Jiaorong.

"We had fishing boats, but no warships. If we had tried to flee to Mystikos and they pursued us, we would have lost.

So, Ilyia came up with a plan. The naval blockade was small, but she knew more ships were coming. Time was against us. We loaded our fishing boats with as many warriors as we could fit, and we sailed up to their warships. Our warriors boarded their ships. If we could take them, we could flee and protect ourselves from anyone who dared to give chase.

"But it was a trap. Once our warriors had boarded, they set fire to their own ships. The smoke signaled the remainder of their fleet, which waited where we couldn't see beyond the horizon. So many of us drowned beyond these shores. We tried to save as many as we could, but they had waited for us where the water was deep. If it had been closer to the shore, our casualties wouldn't have been so severe.

"We made the fatal mistake of pulling warriors from the eastern gate to help rescue those in the water. Their armies stormed the gate, and it fell quickly. Soon, the other barriers fell as well. It was chaos. Their armies and navies bombarded us from all sides. And we scattered, trying to recover from our botched attempt to steal their ships.

"The city fell in less than a day," Artemis said. "Come on. We'll meet with Ilyia, then get you dry clothes."

Artemis led Kari and Ina to the top of the bluff to the Temple of Lasan. The people they passed smiled in greeting. They seemed genuinely happy Shagin had returned to the city. It was a welcomed reprieve.

Lasan was large and wide, with two great wings extending from the main body of the temple. The temple itself consisted of three floors and a basement. At the center was a large dome with a smaller one behind it. Like the other older buildings, elaborate posts framed its corners and windows.

They entered through the grand double doors into an antechamber. Double stairs flanked them on either side.

"Ina, I have to ask you to wait here," Artemis said. "This is Lasan. We do not permit outsiders in the sanctuary."

Ina cocked a brow at Kari, but she nodded. "I understand."

Kari followed Artemis inside. The massive room was mostly empty. Two rows of pews sat close to the entrance with a stage and podium in front. A balcony overlooked the sanctuary. A large spiral staircase on the far side led to a third-floor door. A statue of the goddess Nebura overlooked the room. Her midsection started above the top-floor doorframe, her arms extending downward with open hands on either side of the railing.

Ilyia and two other women waited inside. They rose as the duo entered.

"What happened?" Ilyia asked. "You're soaked."

"We stopped for a swim," Artemis said. Ilyia grimaced, shooting Artemis a look.

"I'm glad you made it," Ilyia said, turning her attention to Kari. "Chaska, Aura, this is Kari."

"This is Kari?" Chaska exclaimed. Her short black hair paired well with her amethyst eyes. She had a tattoo of two red arrows on one side of her face. "Tis wonderful to finally meet you! Do you know how long tis been since we've met another sister?"

"Sorry for the poison powder," Aura, a petite woman with pink hair and blue lapis eyes, said. "I tried to make something that wouldn't be too nasty. The full effects should wear off in a couple of days."

"I can't believe you all are real," Kari said. "This is too good to be true. I've been so alone."

"Since your banishment?" a voice asked.

Kari's heart jumped.

A young man descended the spiral staircase. Each step he took was fluid, but his feet hitting the steel stairs made no sound. "Please excuse my rudeness, but I could not wait any longer for an introduction."

"Kari," Ilyia said. "This is Seignior Vipin."

"The pleasure is all mine," Vipin said. From behind the podium, he smiled.

"How do you know I was banished?" Kari narrowed her eyes, her heart pounding in her chest. Did he know? He couldn't.

"Because you are the Bearer of the Seed, are you not?" Vipin said.

Kari took a step back. He knew what she was? Shagin would never be so reckless as to reveal the identity of the Bearer. The Seed was created upon the apocalyptic splitting of the Three Realms into pocket dimensions. The old world was annihilated in the Cataclysm. It was believed, if the Seed fell into the wrong hands, a second Cataclysm could occur. This had to be a trap.

Ilyia held out a hand toward Vipin in an apparent stop gesture. "It's okay, Kari. We knew who you were the moment we heard about you. It's the only reason they'd send a young Shagin to the mainland. You can trust us. No one else knows. We will protect you. Vipin is our ally; you can trust him as well."

"If you knew, you shouldn't have brought me here," Kari said, scanning the sanctuary for an escape. "I should be banished and in hiding."

"Like you and your brother, some traditions need to be put to rest," Ilyia said, placing a hand on Kari's shoulder. "If we are to save Shagin, we'll need all the help we can get, which includes you as well. We'll have to do our best to keep you secret and safe from those who would desire the Seed."

Kari scrunched her brow, gaze shooting between Ilyia and Vipin. "You've lost me. Why did you call him seignior?"

"Vipin is the one who saved us from the Purge," Ilyia said. "We are the Furies—or what's left of them. He helped us escape the destruction of Koruzeru, and he is the one who has put us on our path."

Kari gritted her teeth. The Furies were a council that oversaw Shagin warriors. They were the generals who betrayed the Elders. The Elders decided to keep Shagin out of the Sovereign War. The Furies turned renegade, then led half of Shagin's fighting force into battle. Their actions served as justification for the Purge.

"But if you are the Furies—and if you are Ilyia, the last Champion of Shagin—shouldn't you have the Golden Rod?" Kari asked, sounding more accusatory than she intended.

Ilyia smiled. "But I do."

She held out her hand, and a golden light shot forth from her palms. Kari gasped when it materialized into the shape of a glittering golden staff. The solid gold had leather wrapped around the end, and the tips of the rod formed round pommels.

"That's..." Kari's words trailed off. Shagin had long believed they'd lost the sacred item after the murder of their people. But there it was, still in the hands of its proper wielder. Ilyia truly was the Champion of Shagin.

"I understand your hesitation," Ilyia said. The staff glowed yellow before it disappeared within her hand. "Hopefully, that will belay any doubts."

Kari nodded. "You said Vipin put you on your path. What path is that?"

"We are rebuilding Shagin. One day, we will bring our sisters back to the mainland and pay for our mistakes," Aura said, staring at the ground.

"Vipin will lead us to a new age. We will bring the Guardian to justice for his crimes, then save Shagin from extinction," Ilyia added.

"How?" Kari asked. "How could one man accomplish that?"

"Because he is a supreme being with ultimate power," Artemis said. Vipin descended the aisle toward Kari, his footsteps soundless. "That is what he is, little one. A god made flesh."

"Not quite," Vipin said. He held out a finger, touching Kari on her forehead. In an instant, her weakness and fatigue vanished, and her spirit energy rushed back. "I am but a man, just with unique abilities."

"What did you do to me?" With spirit energy, one could heal and regenerate wounds, even heal others, but never that fast. It took time and effort. What he'd done was instantaneous, and it hadn't felt like spirit power.

"I know you women have a lot to discuss, but would you mind joining me? I don't think a simple explanation will suffice. I think I'll need to show you." Vipin held out his hand for Kari to take.

"It's okay," Ilyia said. "We'll be here waiting."

Kari wasn't sure if she should trust them. These four women were Shagin, but they were still strangers. They were so different from the Shagin on Mystikos. These women were warriors. They were the Furies, after all. Kari remembered the name all too well from her studies. They were renowned for their battle prowess and served as leaders of Shagin's warriors.

Kari took Vipin's hand. His skin was icy cold. It sent shivers down her spine. He led her up the spiral staircase, then into the third-floor chamber. Blue stones decorated the floor of the round room.

"This was once the Chamber of the Seers for your people," Vipin said. "I know you don't trust me. You have no reason to. I am unknown to you. Everything must be strange to you. I wish the transition would be easier, but there was no other way."

"Artemis said you were a god." Kari studied the strange man. He chuckled at her puzzlement.

"I'm not a god, but I'm not human anymore either," Vipin began. He walked over to a nearby table. He picked up a handful of sand, letting it trickle through his fingers. "For one thing, I can't feel. Everything is so distant to me. It's part of the tradeoff, you see. I transcended my humanity in exchange for near-limitless psychic abilities."

"You can read my mind?" Kari hugged her arms around her chest.

He smiled. "Only if you let me. It would be rude otherwise." When he held out his hands, the sand floated off the ground and levitated near him before settling into a bowl on the table. "I can move objects and instantly heal others with my mind."

"Your skin is so cold."

"That's because I'm dead. I had to die to achieve this," Vipin said. "It means nothing can kill me, so that's a nice perk."

"Why?" Kari asked. "Why would you do this to yourself?"

"I am a Korok."

Kari could do nothing but gape at the young man. The Koroks had been wiped out by the Guardian, which had led to the Sovereign War. It had to be why the Furies trusted him. He was like the Shagin.

"I was only twenty-one when the soldiers took away my world—my wife, my son, and my daughter. Just a few years later, when I saw it happen again, I knew I had to do something. This was the result." His expression seemed sad. "I'm sorry I couldn't save your people. The transformation took longer than expected."

Kari wiped at the tears in her eyes. He understood more than anyone else ever could. Even Ronin couldn't grasp the severity of the Purge. He still partly blamed her mother for taking her and fleeing—for abandoning him.

"We are at the point where I can finally make a difference." Vipin eyed the ceiling. "My powers are still forming. I died in this city, and now I can't venture beyond it. I want you to help us. I plan to create a shield around Shagin to protect it from danger. When I do that, we can bring your people back.

"Once we've saved Shagin, we can finally bring justice to the Three Realms. The Guardian has committed crimes against humanity. He repeatedly used his power to commit genocide. Now, war has been waged against the Three Realms once more. We can put an end to the Guardian's reign of terror. Peace and balance can be restored to the world. Hopefully, we can end this war before it engulfs us all."

CHAPTER SIX

"I DON'T TRUST THEM," Ronin said, lying on the bed with his arms over his head.

"Do you trust anyone?" Ina responded. Ronin grimaced in response.

"Maybe we should hear them out?" Kari said. She sat on the bed next to Ronin, already hot in her new clothes. She had changed into a thick velvet dress, navy and black with silver trim. It was a similar cut to what was worn on Mystikos and the rest of Shagin, though more cumbersome. The main dress was sleeveless with multi-layered vents on the skirt. She'd foregone the matching bolero since she was already sweaty.

"Didn't we already do that?" Ina asked. She rummaged through the pile of clothes Artemis had brought earlier. All heavy thick velvet and cotton, they were nothing like they were used to in Xiang. Shagin warriors typically wore thickly padded clothing in the case their auras failed. The quilted cloth armor supplied extra protection. By the looks of it, it was mostly what the Furies had to wear.

"You didn't meet Vipin. I think we can trust him." Kari felt a bit guilty. She had chosen the prettiest dress from the lot, leaving Ina with only tunics and clothes fit for a warrior. Despite his bloodied and torn clothing, Ronin had refused to change. He still wore his black coat, along with the tattered light blue sash of the Kitsuno Kai.

"I think we should go home," Ina said, holding up a thick brown tunic.

"Remember when the High Chancellor tried to have us killed, then usurped the throne for himself?" Ronin asked, grinning. "Good times."

"Then we take the throne back," Ina protested, throwing the tunic on top of the others she had rejected.

"With just the three of us?" Ronin asked, sitting upright. "He has the armies of an entire empire on his side."

"Well, if you're just going to naysay every idea, why don't you come up with something?" Ina snarked, snatching a blue tunic off the floor.

"We go to Mystikos, settle down, and enjoy life. If we get the urge to fight Cai Ren and his armies, we'll have Shagin on our side. Can't lose," Ronin said.

"You know I can't go back home," Kari said. She'd been banished. If she stepped foot on Mystikos, her presence would endanger everyone there. To protect the Seed, no one could know its whereabouts. At least, that was the idea. "Besides, the Shagin would never fight that battle. There's too few of us left, and most aren't warriors."

"Ronin, do you mind turning around?" Ina motioned to the tunic she held.

"Actually, I do," Ronin said, refusing to move.

Kari shot him a look. Grumbling, he turned his back toward Ina.

"What do you want to do, Kari?" Ina asked, tossing her tattered silk ruqun to the ground.

"I want to stay here. I think we can do actual good here. They seem genuine in their desire to make things better. Just look at the people in the city. They seem to be much happier now. Vipin and the Furies have brought tranquility to this city. We can bring this to the entire world. Imagine it... a new age of peace across the Three Realms."

It might merely be idealistic thinking on their part, but it was worth fighting for the goal. At the very least, they could save Shagin. Bringing the Guardian to justice for his crimes could wait. Besides, the Immortal Warrior had finally perished. The current Guardian, Legato, hadn't ordered the Purge, though he still supported it. At the time, he had been the Sage of Terra. He'd carried out the Immortal Warrior's order without pause, so he was just as guilty.

"If that's what you want, I will stay by your side," Ronin said.

"You're more like a puppy dog than a wolf," Ina scolded as she fastened the blue tunic.

"What did you say?" Ronin jumped up, facing Ina.

"You do whatever she says without question," Ina said.

Why were they fighting? Kari wondered.

"I'm sorry, Kari. I'm all for bringing peace to the world, but something is not right about this," Ina continued.

"What do you mean?" Kari asked. How could there be something wrong with bringing peace?

"This Vipin—the people around here think he's a god."

Kari sighed. So that was the issue.

"I asked him about it," Kari said. "He's not proud of it, and he was honest about it. He can't control what people think. Besides, essentially, that's what he is. His power is not based on spirit energy. It has no limits."

"Don't you think that's odd?" Ina asked.

Admittedly, his source of power was a bit odd, but it was no different than an enchantment. He'd merely found a way to enchant his body at the cost of his life. "I know the Shagin don't share the same gods as everyone else, but won't whatever gods you believe in be upset about you passing this guy off as a god?"

"It's a goddess," Ronin added. "Well, sort of. They worship the Fates, and the goddess Nebura is a fallen Fate, but not really. It's complicated."

"He's not perfect, but at least he's doing something." Kari thrust her hand through her hair. "I just think we should stay here for a little while longer—try to get a better feel for them. If they are what they seem, I wouldn't want to spend the rest of my life regretting not helping them."

Kari met Ina's eyes. Couldn't Ina see how much this meant to her? Kari could save her people or do nothing and let them die.

"Fine," Ina reluctantly agreed. "I suppose there's no harm in staying for a few more days. It's not like there's a whole lot of places for us to go."

"We can go fight an army if you're still interested," Ronin jabbed.

Kari sighed. In a few months, she wouldn't be able to travel freely. They would need to solidify their plans for the future. As her pregnancy progressed, she would have to take better care of herself.

Did this mean she had made her decision? Was she willing to carry the pregnancy to term?

She pinched her brow. "There is something I need to tell you."

"Of course, what is it?" Ina asked.

Kari stared at the wall. She was late, and the doctor had confirmed she had a happy pulse. "I don't know if I have the words."

"Whatever it is, we are here for you."

When Ina took Kari's hands, heat flashed through her face.

"Agreed," Ronin added.

Kari closed her eyes. This would be so much easier if they weren't here. "I'm pregnant."

What would they think? Say? Silence fell upon the room, one that seemed never to end.

"Who's the father?" Ronin asked.

"Don't be stupid," Ina snapped.

"Oh," Ronin muttered, averting his eyes.

Ina pulled Kari closer, embracing her. "We'll be here for you no matter what. What are you going to do?"

"I don't know," Kari stammered. She squinted. "I think I'm going to keep it."

What would they think of her if she did? What did she think of herself? She still wasn't sure if she could ever love her little one, but she would try. Besides, she had a responsibility to help rebuild her people.

"Are you happy?" Ina asked.

"I think I am." Kari stared into her friend's dark eyes.

"I'll be there to help you with the baby," Ina said.

Kari's heart fluttered. Ina was genuinely kind to make that offer. "It does mean we'll need to find a permanent home soon, at least for the time being."

"Of course," Ina replied. "We'll need to take care of you and the baby. Ooh, we could go shopping for baby clothes."

"I don't think there are any shops around here," Ronin said. He came closer, settling his arm around Kari. "You'll have my support as well."

There was a knock on the door, followed by it squeaking open, ending their conversation.

"I hope I'm not intruding," Ilyia said, entering the cramped room. When her gaze fell on the pile of rejected clothing, she smiled.

Ilyia's white-and-pink dress, while being the same cut as Kari's, was made from cotton and appeared considerably cooler. With the strength of her aura, Ilyia must not feel the need for thicker garments.

"Kari, I was wondering if you would join me?"

Kari accepted the invitation. They headed toward Lasan, where a crowd had gathered.

"The festivities will start soon. In the meantime, there is something you should see," Ilyia said, leading the way through the mass of people.

The crowd roared. It was a sight unlike any Kari had seen. People rushed up to them, all pleading.

"Please help us."

"Heal us, mistress."

"We're not worthy of your grace."

Kari instinctively recoiled as people touched and groped at her. These people were sick—lepers, paraplegics, while others were missing limbs. Some simply coughed or carried unknown illnesses of which Kari was afraid to guess.

"Please let us through." Ilyia grabbed Kari's arm, forcing their way through the crowd.

"Make way for Shagin," a man cried out.

Ilyia and Kari broke through the beggars, hurrying up the steps to the doors of Lasan.

"Have patience. Your trust will be rewarded this day," Ilyia said, addressing the crowd.

Kari followed Ilyia into the temple.

"Who are those people?" Kari asked as the door closed behind them. "They looked so sick."

"Most are," Ilyia explained. Vipin stood in the center, studying the statue of Nebura. "They've all come so Vipin can heal them."

Vipin faced them. "Some have traveled for weeks, even months. Some even come from Pasonia. Word of our exploits grows daily. It is both a welcome sign and worrisome. If we grow too large, the Guardian will come before we're ready."

"We hold these festivals once a month," Ilyia said. "It allows plenty of people the opportunity to come and be healed."

"It must take quite a while to heal them, even with your powers," Kari said.

Vipin smiled. "Not at all. I can heal the entire crowd at once."

"We spend the rest of the time celebrating Shagin," Ilyia explained. "When the new age comes, people will not fear and hate us as they once did."

Kari jumped when a loud bang rang out.

"I suppose I should get out there before they tear the door down," Vipin said, heading toward the sanctuary doors.

"Please wait for us to begin," Ilyia called. "I want to show Kari something first."

Vipin inclined his head as he left the sanctuary.

Kari followed Ilyia up the spiral staircase, then into the Chamber of the Seers. Ilyia continued over to the far side of the room, then knelt.

"If you ask anybody, any Shagin, they will tell you this room was the highest point in the temple," Ilyia said. She held up a finger, gesturing around them. "Any maps or blueprints of the temple will show you the same. But there is a secret only the Elders and a select few know. Come stand next to me."

Kari did as told. With her index finger, Ilyia traced the Shagin emblem on the ground. She gave it three taps. Kari nearly fell as the floor underneath her shifted and rose. They now stood on a translucent platform, which ascended to the ceiling.

"Ilyia, is this safe?" Kari asked, gaping at the rapidly approaching ceiling.

"Just you wait." Ilyia stood, wrapping her arm around Kari.

Kari's head contacted the ceiling, but it did not hit. Her head went through, followed by the rest of her body. Soon, she stood in a new chamber. It was smaller than the one below it, but bookshelves and different-sized tomes filled it. There was a desk and chair at one end with a bed in the center.

"Welcome to Shagin's best-kept secret." Ilyia beamed. "Welcome to the Chamber of the Bearer—your chamber."

Kari stared in disbelief at the many books. How did she not know about this? Did anyone on Mystikos even know?

"We kept detailed journals on each Bearer, including their former lives and what little we know about them after they were called. Which, for most, we know next to nothing. Everything the Shagin knows about the Seed and its power is here. There are research documents; books on theories; lists of all the Bearers; books on Dante, its creator;

anything you could ever want to know about the Seed is in this room."

Kari's eyes widened. "Isn't this dangerous? What if someone discovered this room and tried to use the Seed for their desires?"

"It is dangerous," Ilyia confessed. Her smile faded, replaced with a solemn expression. "But it's more dangerous for the Bearer not to know her power. Whenever a new Bearer was called, they were given three days to hide away in this chamber to study before they were banished."

"Three days?" Kari mumbled. "I didn't even get three hours."

Ilyia's brow furrowed. "I'm sorry. That must have been difficult for you."

Kari stared at the bed. "Is this to be my permanent quarters?"

"No, not at all." Ilyia laughed. "This chamber is yours to do with as you please. If you choose to sleep here, you are welcomed to, but I have no intention of forcing the matter. I do think you should familiarize yourself with what you carry. I would say to take your time and explore the tomes to your heart's content, but if we wait any longer, we might miss the festivities."

They descended the platform the same way they'd entered the chamber, then made their way out of the temple. Vipin had moved the crowd away from Lasan. Kari breathed a sigh of relief. She appreciated the breathing room, glad she didn't have to fight her way through it again.

Ilyia went to join Vipin while Kari sat on a grassy hill, overlooking the masses. While she liked seeing everyone so jubilant, the size of the crowd was a bit overwhelming.

The attendees thanked Shagin, singing praises to them and Vipin. The crowd loved them, and it was easy to see why.

Kari grinned. It had been so long since she had been this happy. Seeing so many joyous smiles was a great reminder of the kindness within people's hearts.

The crowd gathered around Vipin. The families of the sick and wounded had helped them gather for this moment. They came together, and now their trust and hard work would be rewarded.

This was why the Shagin had been welcomed back with open arms. They had found a way to cure people of their ailments and prolong their lives.

"Are you ready?" Vipin asked. The crowd cheered in response. "Okay, let's begin."

A bright burst of blue light shone from Vipin. In an instant, everyone was healed. Arms and legs grew back, lepers had clean skin, and the sick and the dying were relieved.

Kari's smile grew even wider as everyone roared in appreciation. She couldn't resist any longer, and she joined in the thunderous applause.

Vipin held up his hands to silence the crowd. "I know what a lot of you have said about me. It is a rumor that has been spread by my very own people—that I am a god. But I am *not* a god. I am merely a man. But I promise you this—I will help bring a new age of peace throughout this world. So long as you trust me, I will always protect you. I promise you that no harm will befall you. You will be under my protection."

It was strange. Vipin, the dead man, seemed to have so much life in him.

"He's remarkable, isn't he?" Ilyia approached, then sat next to Kari on the grassy hill. "When I first met him, I couldn't believe how big his heart was. During each day I am around him, I am reminded of what kind of person I want to be."

"Is it always like this?"

"Not always." Ilyia ducked her head. "Unfortunately, some of what we do is not pleasant. We have captured several villages from the Torredins. Some have joined us willingly. Others, not so much. That is where the Furies come in to play. We do the necessary work to further our cause. If we can avoid fighting, we will, but we live in a cruel world. To protect life, sometimes you have to fight and take life. It's one of the ironies of the world we live in. This new age will fix that."

Kari understood. She had taken her fair share of life. It wasn't pleasant, but it had been necessary for her survival in the harem. "What do you expect this new age will bring?"

"A world full of peace, justice, and love." Ilyia kept her gaze on Vipin. "This world isn't fit for people like me. I have no intention of being a part of it. But if I can help fight against evil—one last crusade, one last battle—I will do so."

"I wish I could help, but I don't want to fight," Kari murmured. While she loved Ronin, she did not want to become like him—immune to suffering, a killer with a stone-cold heart. "I've already taken enough life."

"You misunderstand me. We have more important plans for you, my dear." Ilyia stood, then reached for Kari. "Come with me. I will show you what your purpose will be in this new world."

Kari allowed Ilyia to pull her up, then followed her. Ilyia led her outside the western gate to a large clearing before handing her a handful of seeds.

"These people have barely any food to eat. Vipin might be able to protect them from dangers and heal their inflictions, but even he cannot feed them from nothing." Ilyia motioned to the open field. "But you can. The plant masters of old used to provide us with a nearly unlimited supply of food. With the power of the Seed to draw from, think of what you could accomplish. Do you think you can plant this field?"

Kari took a deep breath. She had never managed anything quite this big before. But if this were what the new age needed, she would give it everything she had.

Kari dropped to one knee. Closing her eyes, she placed the seeds into the soil, the gentle breeze moving through her hair. She exhaled, the soil of the earth beckoning her. It yearned for her.

She poured all of her energy into the seeds. Sweat dripped down her brow as rows of fruit trees and vegetable bushes erupted from the ground. As her strength began to falter, she stumbled, but she had to continue. Ilyia bent, placing her arm around Kari in support.

The vegetation grew, budded, and blossomed. Plump morsels appeared in the foliage. In a single moment, she had taken a handful of seeds and planted a field full of adult plants, ripened fruit, and fully formed vegetables.

She collapsed onto her back in the green grass, gazing up at the deep blue sky. With a weak smile, Kari closed her eyes as she tried to catch her breath.

"That was incredible." Ilyia settled beside her. "With enough practice and training, you could feed everyone."

"This is your plan for me?" Kari laughed tiredly. She wouldn't have to fight *or* kill again. "To help feed people? I quite like the sound of that."

"I am extremely jealous of you," Ilyia said. "I've gotten old. When I met Vipin, we were the same age. He stayed young while I got older. One day, I will turn to dust, and he will continue without me. You, on the other hand, will stay young and pretty forever."

"I can still be killed," Kari said. That was how the other Bearers had died. The exact nature of their deaths was a mystery, but the Bearer eventually reached a point where they stopped aging. They didn't die, at least not by natural causes. The only way for a Bearer to die was if they were killed. Kari wasn't sure if that was a blessing, at least not the way it had been described to her while she was growing up.

It sounded lonely to have to watch loved ones grow old and die while she lived on. Rumors that some Bearers eventually killed themselves to end the loneliness persisted through the years.

Kari placed her hands on her stomach. Sickness filled her. She would have to watch her little one grow and die. Throat burning, she realized she didn't know if she could do it.

"You look so sad. What's wrong?"

Kari had just told Ronin and Ina. Telling someone she had only known for a short time seemed wrong. After all, the father of her child was her rapist. It was almost too painful to admit. But if there were anyone who *would* understand, it would be Ilyia, another Shagin. "I'm expecting."

"Expecting what?" Ilyia asked, arching her brow.

"A child," Kari said, her voice quivering. "I'm going to be a mother."

Ilyia laughed.

"Why is that funny?" Kari asked, venom dripping from her words.

"What do they teach Shagin these days?" Ilyia asked, shaking her head. "You are the Bearer of the Seed. You can't get pregnant. From what I understand, your cycles will eventually stop. Is that what all the fuss is about?"

"Not just that," Kari protested. "I saw a doctor who said I have a happy pulse."

"What is that supposed to mean?" Ilyia asked in confusion. "Xianese superstitions? If you don't believe me, wait a few months and see."

A tear slid down Kari's cheek. Yet another choice was being taken from her. "Never?"

"I'm sorry," Ilyia said. "They don't call it a curse for nothing."

"So, I truly will be alone."

"Not anymore." Ilyia placed a hand on her shoulder. "Vipin will live forever. Two lonely gods roaming the earth—one brings order and healing, and the other feeds the hungry."

Kari's heart skipped. Was that why they'd brought her here?

"Is that my true purpose? To be a partner for him?"

"No, I didn't mean that," Ilyia said. She lifted her hand. "I honestly don't want to think about it. I just don't want him to be alone."

"You care for him?"

"He is my lover." Ilyia averted her eyes, a frown forming. "We were supposed to be together forever. But I can't live up to my promise."

Kari and Ilyia walked back to the inn. Ina, Ronin, and Artemis stood outside.

"Ilyia, Chaska and I are ready to move out," Artemis said, approaching them. "We should be back in a few days."

"Understood." Ilyia sighed. "If we are to complete our shield, we will need dalium. Not far from here, we believe there's a town with a hidden stash. Unfortunately, it is controlled by the Guardian."

"Why do you need dalium?" Kari asked, glancing between them. "What kind of shield is this? I thought Vipin's power was your shield."

"Do you honestly believe we would risk the safety of our sisters on a metaphorical shield?" Artemis asked. "When we bring our sisters back here, we need to ensure the events that led to the Purge never happen again."

"It's an energy barrier," Ilyia explained. "There are tunnels that run under Koruzeru. They were used to create the enchantment separating the Realms into pocket dimensions. Using Vipin's magic, we can utilize the residual energy in those tunnels to create an energy barrier. Potentially, it could surround not just Koruzeru, but the entirety of Shagin. We wouldn't have to fear another invasion. However, we need more dalium if our enchantments are going to work."

"Securing the dalium won't be easy," Artemis said with a smirk. "It's secured in the Torredins garrison. The task is fit for a Fury."

"I don't want any loss of life," Ilyia scolded.

Artemis rolled her eyes. "Yes, Miss."

"If you need to infiltrate their base, you should let me come," Kari said. She wasn't sure if she genuinely wanted to, but she could at least help ensure no one died. "I can use my light powers to bend and refract light, effectively turning myself invisible. I could easily sneak in without being detected."

"No offense, little one, but I'll handle this my way," Artemis said, pointing to her chest. "I don't need you slowing us down."

"No," Ilyia said. "I like this. Kari's powers could be beneficial in retrieving the dalium without resulting in any loss of life."

"Kari..." Ilyia took her hands. "I know you are not a Fury, but I would like you to accompany Artemis and Chaska. I know you have your reservations about our cause, but believe me when I tell you I want nothing more than for you to join us. It's only fitting. We are your sisters. As the last Shagin, we should stay together. We could use your help."

"I will come with you to help in any way I can." It would be an opportunity to learn more about them and their goals before making a decision.

"We should come as well," Ina said.

"Agreed," Ronin said.

"No offense, but you two would just slow us down," Artemis said. "In the event things go to hell, we can't afford to babysit."

"Then we will leave Ina behind," Ronin said. Ina scowled. "I have fought my fair share of battles."

"We do not need a killer in our ranks." As if out of nowhere, Vipin appeared behind them. "I mean no offense, but I can smell the blood on you."

"Yes, I find it quite rejuvenating for the skin." Ronin grinned wolfishly. He was intentionally antagonistic. Hopefully, that wouldn't come back to haunt them.

"Let me be blunt," Vipin said. "I trust Kari as Shagin, and Ilyia has more than vouched for her character. I also trust Ina. She seems more than willing to question our ethics. That is a noble quality to have. However, I don't trust you."

"Odd coming from a man who could heal me back to my full strength, but who has instead elected to keep me under the effects of that poisoned powder, which came from your order. Trust goes both ways."

Sighing, Vipin placed a finger on Ronin's forehead. "I'm sorry. I nearly forgot. Is that better?"

Ronin grumbled under his breath, but refrained from speaking aloud.

"Our destination is not far from here," Ilyia said. "It is the town of Anuatu."

"Anuatu?" Kari asked. "That's where my mother was from."

"Take this." Ilyia handed her a golden skeleton key.

"You're giving it to her?" Artemis asked, her jaw dropping. "Really?"

Kari clenched her jaw, deliberately ignoring the woman.

Ilyia shot Artemis a glare before returning her attention to Kari. "There is a door that's isn't a door. If you use this key, it will open a portal to a place outside of space and time. You'll find the dalium there. Look for a door with gold trim."

Kari clutched the key. She could do this—infiltrate the garrison, retrieve the dalium, and prevent any loss of life, all while critiquing the intentions of the Furies. Drawing a deep breath, she readied her resolve.

CHAPTER SEVEN

KARI WAS AMAZED BY the sheer beauty of Anuatu. It was a town built around and on a three-tiered cliff. The Sinnu River ran through it, forming a double waterfall at the cliffs. It fed two pools, one in the middle and one at the base. The pool at the bottom poured into the caverns where the Sinnu River disappeared from the surface, then proceeded underground toward Koruzeru.

Everything centered on the river. Houses and other buildings had been built into the cliff face. A singular bridge at the top connected the two sides of the town while the remainder surrounded the pool.

Kari couldn't contain her smile as she gawked at her mother's home. It was more astonishing than anything she had ever seen. Although she wished she could have taken a few of the tomes from her chamber, doing so would have been too dangerous. She wanted to learn all she could about the Seed, but there would be time for that later. The beauty of Anuatu was enough for now.

Kari, Artemis, and Chaska sat at a table at an outdoor café, the remains of their lunch scattered on the surface.

The passing people didn't pay attention to them, even with weapons strapped to their sides.

Ilyia had insisted Kari carry something for defense. She believed Kari would feel more comfortable with a jian, a one-handed straight sword. Truthfully, Kari preferred a jhuma, a tradition Shagin sword, or a kodachi like Ronin carried. Neither Artemis nor Chaska wielded traditional Shagin weapons. Artemis had a straight sword strapped to her leather belt, whereas Chaska carried a double-sided voulge, the blades wrapped in leather casings. The soldiers had given them odd looks as they entered the town, but nobody bothered to stop them. Obviously, they didn't believe three women were a threat. The soldiers probably assumed they needed the weapons for defense while traveling.

Artemis motioned to a building carved into the stone cliff face at the base of the waterfall. Two flags, bearing the symbol of the Guardian, flew outside the building. They were Torredins, foot soldiers of a madman.

"That's where we need to go."

The building had all the architectural highlights of a traditional Shagin building—wood and stone construction, a square roof, and elaborate framework decorating the front. The building stood out amongst some of the newer developments, which lacked the decorative flair and possessed higher, angled roofs. The Torredins had massacred everyone here and stolen their heritage to use it as a base for their hatred. Kari bit her lip.

"Looks like they are utilizing it as some sort of garrison for their troops," Chaska added, taking a bite of her meal. Stuffed inside large leaves, duck meat mixed with onions, tomatoes, and chilies. It had been roasted until brown, and it looked tasty. Kari's dish was more simple—baked fish served over rice.

"We're not here to fight," Artemis reminded them. "We sneak in, find the dalium, and get out. That's where you come in, little one, if you're up for the task."

"I'm ready," Kari said, puffing out her chest. She wanted to get out of the heat as soon as possible. Ilyia had insisted Kari wear padded armor for protection. Her dress was from Ilyia's wardrobe. It was the same cut as the velvet dress, but much more cumbersome. Red with a velvet exterior, it had layers of padded cotton lining the interior, meant to protect from oncoming blows.

If Kari were this hot in the summer heat, she could only imagine how Artemis felt. In her black leather mask, which didn't seem to have any breathing room, she had to be dying. Add to that, she was garbed in fitted padded cotton armor that covered her arms and long pants, all in black. Kari wasn't sure how the woman hadn't passed out from heatstroke.

Chaska looked the most comfortable. While her clothing was just as padded, her blue top was sleeveless and cut low in the front, revealing her cleavage. Her full skirt was just as revealing. Slit on the sides, it only covered her upper thighs. She'd strapped a stuffed fox to her side. Her outfit seemed highly impractical for a warrior. Then again, if she were as strong as Ilyia, she didn't need the armor. Besides, their goal was to avoid fighting.

Artemis leaned across the table, whispering, "I don't like this, but it is Ilyia's decision to make, so listen up. If you use your powers, you should be able to sneak in undetected."

Kari nodded her understanding. Her heart skipped, and her pulse raced. How could she have been so stupid? She'd forgotten to tell them a huge detail. Hopefully, they wouldn't be too mad. "Is this a bad time to mention I can't see when I'm invisible?"

Artemis buried her face in her hand, stifling her laughter. "That's sort of an important piece of information unless you think daftness will secure our objective."

"Kari isn't used to strategic thinking," Chaska said, placing a reassuring hand on Kari's arm. "Tis all right. New plan. For now, we'll observe the garrison. We'll wait to make our move until tonight after everyone is asleep."

"I suppose," Artemis said. "That was our original plan. Although we could just skip all the waiting and take the garrison by force."

Chaska cut her eyes toward her.

"It was just a suggestion." Artemis held up her hands in defense.

They finished lunch, watching the soldiers. Kari missed the food of Xiang. The rice, noodles, and seared meats of Xiang were far tastier than the roasted fish and duck on bland, crunchy rice that was popular here. She poked at the dry and overcooked fish. Even the food on Mysitkos, which was mostly fish and whatever vegetables they could grow, was better than this. Or maybe she had simply gotten used to the cushy palace life. Kari blushed as she realized just how pampered she had been for the past few months.

"I heard about your coup in Xiang," Chaska said. "Impressive work."

"It wasn't a coup, not really," Kari said. The reminder about her actions in Xiang embarrassed her, though she wasn't sure why. The thought she'd intentionally set about to overthrow a kingdom was both untrue and seemed unscrupulous.

"Tis not what we've heard." Chaska smiled at Artemis, who merely sighed in response. "You infiltrated their harem, forged an army, drove the younger brother to murder the elder, and then slew him in a one-on-one duel for control of the empire. Tis a story of legends."

"It wasn't like that at all." Kari didn't want to talk about it. Everything the Tian brothers inflicted upon her, as well as her struggle for survival, were memories she would rather bury deep within her mind and never think of it again. "What's with that stuffcd fox?"

Chaska took the small toy off her belt, then hugged it close to her chest. As she stroked its head, she stared deep into the toy's eyes. "I was a mother once."

Kari's heart sank. She knew the story without Chaska even having to say it. Artemis placed a hand on her comrade's shoulder.

Chaska gazed up at the sky. "Tis odd. I left to fight a war to help make a better world for her. But when I returned, she was gone. Just like everyone else."

"I'm so sorry."

"What would you know of the Purge?" Artemis asked in disdain. "Were you even born?"

"Just barely," Kari replied. The Shagin Purge was an extremely sensitive topic for the surviving Shagin on Mystikos. She'd heard about it from her mother and teachers, but it was always with a sense of vagueness. Nobody ever talked about it in detail, only said the Shagin were brutalized and exterminated. Even still, the horror was conveyed to the younger generation.

The survivors on Mystikos were a mixture of Shagin on pilgrimage, trial, or those rescued from the homeland. Kari could always tell who had lived through the Purge and who was lucky enough to have been absent during the atrocities.

Whenever the Purge was discussed, those who had been victims, who lived through it, would simply stare off into the distance. In their eyes, the horror and despair in their memories were obvious. It had always sent a cold shiver down her spine. She would often lay awake at night, wondering what it must have been like for those who struggled for life. Now, she had the chance to talk with two women who not only lived through it, but had also stayed behind in hell and were still fighting for heaven.

"I was only a few months old when the Purge began," Kari added. "My mother, Eanna, lived outside Shagin with my father and Ronin. When the Purge began, she took me and fled to Mystikos with the others."

"What do they teach you about Furies and the Renegades?" Chaska asked. "At the time, we were ridiculed and ostracized for our actions and beliefs. Do they still blame us for what came to pass?"

"Nobody blames you for what happened." Kari didn't want to tell them the truth. She could see the pain in their eyes. It was the same pain she had seen in the survivors. But the other Shagin *did* hold them responsible for the Purge. The consensus was that if the Furies hadn't turned renegade and fought in the war, the Immortal Warrior would have never turned his army on them.

Chaska smiled. "That would be a lie." She held up her necklace. A teardrop-shaped sapphire dangled from it. "This is a memory stone. We all have one."

Artemis showed hers off as well.

"What is that?" Kari asked.

"Memory stones are exactly what they sound like," Artemis said, rolling the stone between her fingers. "They hold the memories of others. Their entire memories and consciousness are stored in the stones. The ones we wear are merely for looks. They are empty because when they were gifted to us, we gained the memories of our fallen sisters."

"Why? Why would you do that?" Kari asked, her eyebrows furrowed.

Artemis gripped her stone, her knuckles turning white. "Someone's entire life is stored in these stones. Certain prisoners found a way to seal their life stories so future generations could understand what happened and never forget. When someone with spirit awareness touches the stone, the person's entire life, memories, and emotions become yours. You don't simply know what they know. You *experience* it. Every moment, every emotion felt, every pain endured. It all becomes yours. We failed our sisters, but we will never forget them. We each have the memories of a fallen sister who was imprisoned and tortured due to our failure. We will not fail them again."

"I was lucky," Chaska added. She kissed the stone and released her grip on it, letting it dangle freely around her neck. "I gave my daughter to my mother when I left to fight. This stone is hers. Even though I never got to see my daughter again, I have, in a sense. Through my mother, I experienced the joy she felt as she watched my daughter in their final days. I've also seen how my daughter died. I can still hear her final cries as her murderer's blade drove into her tiny body. I've seen the face of the man who killed her, smelled his breath as he tortured my mother. I've felt every pain he inflicted on her."

"That's horrible." Gasping, Kari held her hand to her mouth. What these two women had endured was beyond nightmarish.

"The worst part was still to come," Chaska continued. "My mother loved me with all of her heart, at least until the Purge started. I felt that love turn to hatred and disgust. Every time she thought of me, every waking moment, she blamed me for the death of my daughter. Twas rage that filled her heart. She wished I had never been born, so her daughter wouldn't be responsible for what happened."

"Our home turned into hell." Artemis sneered. "Imagine piles of corpses—nonstop torture and rape. We lived through it twice. That is why we do what we do. We cannot rest because the spirits of the dead will not allow us to. All that we can do now is forge a world where atrocities like the Purge never happen again."

"Do you regret it?" Kari asked. "Fighting, I mean. Do you regret fighting in the war? Taking the lives you did?"

"Never," Chaska said, shaking her head. "Our only regret is that we didn't try harder to convince the Elders to fight."

"The Guardian had already committed genocide against the Koroks, and it wasn't the first time," Artemis explained. "It was always a possibility he would do it again. That was why we fought. The Guardian was immoral and wrong, and he deserved to be stopped.

"I fought the Immortal Warrior myself." Artemis pointed to her mask. "He did this to me. Afterward, he left me for dead. I regret not being stronger. Not being able to kill the bastard myself. Not stopping the genocide that was to come. The Immortal Warrior was evil, and I rejoiced he died. His successor and those who follow him are just as evil. What we do is not always pleasant, but we do it in the name of peace and sanity."

"Could Vipin not heal your scars?" Kari asked.

"He could, but I don't want him to," she answered. "The person I once was died long ago. When our work is finished and we have peace at last, I plan to join her."

Kari averted her eyes. Suicide was Artemis's answer? It wasn't just the other Shagin who blamed the Renegades for the Purge; they blamed themselves as well. They carried no hope for themselves—only hope they could restore balance and justice to an insane world.

"Come on," Chaska said. "We've got work to do."

The trio stood. After they left the restaurant, they headed into the streets. Kari looked at the town and its occupants with new eyes. She remembered the numbers. Every twelve years, a census was completed. There had been 541,732 Shagin before the war. Only 5,222 survived. It was a harrowing apocalyptic figure. But in the past, it has only been a number. She had grown up with other survivors, but they never talked freely about the Purge. Now, everything seemed so much more personal.

She'd still been a child when she left Mystikos. It was only natural for the adults to shield her from the truth to protect her innocence. But she'd never fully understood. It was only now, in exile, that she felt truly connected to her people.

"Thief!" an old woman cried from a nearby market stall. She held onto the wrist of a small boy as he frantically tried to get away from her, a loaf of bread clutched in his other hand.

"Tis a shame." Chaska closed her eyes, expression pained. "Corporal punishment is usually the standard for stealing. The poor hungry child will be beaten or worse."

"We can't let that happen." Kari started toward the incident.

Artemis grabbed Kari's shoulder, yanking her back. "That's not why we are here."

"Isn't it?" Kari asked with a scowl. "I refuse to let atrocities go unpunished."

With a smirk, Artemis finally nodded.

"Guards," the woman shouted. "Someone, get the guards!"

"If there is an issue with this boy, I will handle it," Kari said to the woman. Anger and rage flared inside her like a volcano ready to erupt. "He tried to steal this bread, yes? How much does it cost? I will buy it for him."

"Money isn't the point anymore," the woman said, slamming her fist down on her wooden stall. The bowl of silver coins on the top rattled. "If he isn't punished, he'll steal again. We'll see how quick his hands are with one less finger."

"That's insane! He was just hungry." Not too long ago, she had been this boy. She remembered those days all too well. Living on the streets with Suying, stealing what little food they could just to survive. Even as a songstress in a teahouse, theft was sometimes necessary simply so they didn't starve. The Guardian's soldiers would permanently punish a child for trying to live? Not on her watch. She would kill any bastard who tried to harm this boy.

Kari placed her hand on the hilt of her sword. "Remove your hand from this child before I do it for you." The viciousness emerging must come from her father's side.

"What did you say?" The woman released the boy, who took the opportunity to run off with his bread. She glared at Kari with dull grey eyes. "Wait a minute. I know those eyes. You're a Shagin. Hey, everyone! It's a Shagin!"

The woman had no proof, but she happened to be right.

"How many?" Kari's knuckles turned white as she clenched the hilt of her sword, but she did not draw the blade. Artemis and Chaska stood back, observing. "How many women have you accused of being Shagin simply to get rid of them?"

It was not uncommon to accuse women of being Shagin to eliminate them—if a woman had too much power, was too pretty, or slept around. Heat radiated through her face. Kari would not stand for this.

"What's going on?" A few soldiers ran up to them.

Kari shot Artemis and Chaska a threatening look, warning them to stay back. She wanted to handle this on her own—needed to. Her people had tried to appease their aggressors, only to be wiped out. For too long, she had felt powerless as she struggled to appease those who wished her harm. She'd sacrificed her body and spirit to survive the Tian. But she wasn't helpless anymore.

"I am Shagin," Kari declared. On a collective gasp, the soldiers drew their weapons.

"Do you know what the penalty for being Shagin is?" one soldier snarled. He stood poised with his sword raised, ready to strike.

"It's death," Kari replied, stalking toward him. She would not show fear. "Death for being born. But why kill me now? Don't you want to know what I do? Don't you want to know if there are others?"

"What do you want, monster?" The soldier backed away while still pointing the tip of his sword at her.

"I've come to bring peace. I want to speak with whoever is in charge of your garrison. And I want you to take me there now. If you do that, I won't bring war." Kari's words were far harsher than she'd intended. However, to gain their attention, she needed to demonstrate strength. In submission, Kari held out her arms.

The soldier eyed her up and down, but he did not move from his defensive position. "Get her weapon," he told his comrades. They hesitated, eyeing her warily.

"Would it help if I turned my back?" Kari asked, turning around with her arms still outstretched. She twisted to see the soldiers. This was either the bravest or dumbest idea she'd ever had. They could stab her before she could react. Kari readied her aura, facing forward again.

Kari nodded toward Artemis and Chaska, signaling they should stay back as the soldiers gathered their courage and finally approached to relieve her of her weapons. Two soldiers flanked her, gripping her arms and leading her away. From behind, a soldier shoved her toward the garrison. Clearly, now that she was weaponless and held in place, they finally felt bold. They took her inside the stronghold, where even more soldiers waited.

The soldiers inside studied her quizzically as she was escorted to a round table. She pulled free from the soldiers who held her. They jumped back, placing their hands on the hilts of their swords. Ignoring them, Kari took a seat at the table and waited.

She scanned the room while around thirty soldiers gaped at her. Most appeared frightened. All seemed ready to kill her.

The door opened, and a grizzled old man dressed in scale armor entered. He marched right up to the table, then took the seat across from Kari.

"So, you are her," he said. The soldiers surrounded the table. They were inept soldiers faking their fortitude now that their commander was here. "I am the general of this garrison. Let's get right to it. Why have you come here?"

"I am here to negotiate your surrender," Kari said, clasping her hands on the tabletop. The commander reared back, laughing. She narrowed her eyes. Despite her throwing herself into the net, he still thought he was in control. It didn't matter, though. What mattered was that she changed his mind. "The crimes of the Guardian are numerous and shameful. We will make a better world, a world built on compassion and justice. We are extending an offer for you to rescind your loyalty to your corrupt ruler and join us instead."

"We?" the general asked, raising an eyebrow. "There are other Shagin?"

"Yes," Kari said flatly.

"You speak of justice, but you've brought war. Your army already captured Sumar. And you confirmed our worst fears—the Shagin have returned to ravage the world again. I am not amused. We've all heard the rumors of what happened in Xiang. I take it you're from there?"

This man understood nothing. This land belonged to Shagin. It was the Torredins who had stolen it from the people they'd murdered.

"Join us," Kari said. Maintaining neutral was crucial. She had to give him a chance. The reason she was here, after all, was to prevent any loss of life. Kari clenched her jaw. "We do not want to fight. We want peace. But if you stay loyal to that monster, we are prepared to fight."

"Is that a threat?" The general motioned to his soldiers. They drew their weapons. "I will protect this world from the monsters. I do commend your bravery. You are surrounded, trapped with nowhere to run, and we have your weapon. Sadly, monsters like you cannot be allowed to live so long as you threaten this world."

"Please don't do this. This is your last chance to surrender." Kari didn't move, calmly eyeing him.

"Kill her."

The soldiers rushed forward with their weapons at the ready. Kari raised her hand, focusing her spirit energy. A blinding flash of light emanated from her palm. Her light whip shot out and struck the general, instantly decapitating him. She spun her whip in a circle, hitting the approaching soldiers. Blood sprayed through the air as her magic effortlessly tore through flesh and bone. Their bodies collapsed to the ground, lifeless.

Kari closed her eyes, bowing her head. It hadn't had to go this way. If only they would have listened to reason. Such senseless losses of life. These soldiers had aligned themselves to a regime of genocide and madness. They'd showed no remorse, and they'd paid the price.

"Die, monster!"

Kari's eyes shot open as a soldier with a spear charged forward.

"Ugh!" he shouted as a long blade shot through his skull, halting his advance. The blade retracted through a hole in the wall, and the soldier crumpled into a heap.

The door flew open, crashing against the wall with a bang as Chaska and Artemis rushed into the building.

"Meet my Shadow Sword," Artemis said, holding out her weapon. "The blade can extend to any length."

"So, that's the power of the Seed." Chaska stared at the heap of bodies surrounding Kari. "Impressive."

Kari's face reddened. She didn't feel proud of the carnage surrounding her. But she finally understood what she wanted to fight for—a better world. To do that, the

Guardian and his Torredins needed to face justice for their many crimes against humanity.

"I guess we're done with diplomacy?" Chaska asked.

"I've had enough of placating others," Kari said, averting her eyes from the dead. Shagin had attempted to submit to the Guardian. They'd surrendered and laid down their weapons. In return, they'd been murdered. She was tired of death. But docility and passivism only beget pain and suffering. She had seen too many people die already. No more. "We've moved beyond that."

"You know this means we just declared war on the Guardian, right?" Chaska asked, removing the leather coverings from her double-bladed voulge.

"We're already at war," Kari responded, her resolve like steel.

"What do you think?" Artemis asked, cleaning the blood from her sword.

"I don't know," Chaska said. "You think the three of us can take this town?"

A wicked smile flashed across Artemis's masked face. "Damn right."

CHAPTER EIGHT

"WE STILL NEED TO find the dalium," Chaska said, placing a hand on Artemis's shoulder. "The last thing we want is to be routed by a larger force without it."

"We won't be," Artemis growled, pulling away.

"Artemis and I should focus on the fight." Chaska addressed Kari. "You can locate the dalium, then join us afterward. You still have the key, don't you?"

"I do, but won't you need help?" Kari asked. The last thing she wanted was to leave them shorthanded. She wasn't sure if she should feel grateful or insulted. It was either a vote of confidence on Chaska's part to put Kari in charge of finding the dalium... or else the other woman was trying to get Kari out of the way so the Furies could go to war.

"Go, find the door. We'll handle the guards," Artemis said. Her tone said it more than her words. Even behind her mask, her eyes showed the spirit and rage of a warrior. Her aura gave off a killing intent. Arguing with her was pointless. With Artemis's resolve, they had nothing to fear. Kari gulped, knowing she wouldn't want to stand against the warrior woman in her state.

Kari nodded, leaving Artemis and Chaska to fight.

Kari ran through the building, searching for the door with the golden trim. Three guards descended upon her. Focusing her energy, she lashed out with her light whip, slashing though the first guard. The second rushed into striking range, thrusting his sword at her.

Kari focused her spirit aura, batting the blade away with her forearm. Apparently, she'd grown stronger since the weapon hadn't even scratched her skin. She struck back, swinging her whip at the man. When she sliced into his chest, blood began to spurt as he fell.

The third soldier retreated, trying to maintain his distance. Kari flicked her whip, extending it with her power. He raised his sword to parry. The light whip sliced through the metal blade, carving into the side of his neck. He gurgled as he crashed to the ground.

Killing and fighting had become too easy. She was much stronger than when she'd fought Jiaorong. At the time, she had been afraid she would lose herself to the violence—that her heart would harden and she'd see murder as an everyday occurrence. That fear was no longer present. Hesitation no longer plagued her.

She continued through the building, making her way down a flight of stairs. There it was—the wooden door with golden trim. Her assignment was far easier than she'd thought it would be. Kari retrieved the key from her pocket, then inserted it into the lock. When she twisted the key, blue light erupted from the cracks in the door. What was behind this door was a mystery. She couldn't hesitate now. Taking a deep breath, she gathered her courage. She threw it open, resolutely marching through the blue light.

She stood inside a massive stone room. The ceiling had to be at least a few hundred feet high, and the room was just as wide. A statue dominated the center. On the far end, a box rested on top of an altar.

If she could get that, she could leave. When she rushed across the room, her footsteps echoed against the stone walls. She darted past the statue, hurrying toward the altar.

Something struck the back of her head. Pain shot through her skull, and she screamed. Vision doubling, her knees gave out, sending her skidding across the cold floor. A stone thunked beside her. Gingerly, she prodded the back of her head. Her fingers came away dry—no blood, which was good. At least her aura had been strong enough to withstand the strike. Even still, she couldn't take too many blows like that without being sent to premature death.

Kari's eyes widened as two boulders flew toward her. She scampered to her feet. Diving out of the way, she crashed to the ground as the rocks whizzed past, colliding with the far wall and erupting into stone shards.

Kari returned to her feet, focusing her energy. She formed her whip again as she stared her opponent down.

The statue stepped forward, flexing its arm. Seemingly at its command, chunks of stone were ripped from the floor and levitated. At its gesture, the stones shivered in the air before coming to life and rushing at Kari.

She dove, then rolled underneath the first few boulders. The ones still to come changed course as she moved. Kari grimaced as a flying stone shot for her face. She struck at it with her whip, tearing a gash into the boulder and throwing it off course. It collided with the ground, the force of which sent shockwaves rumbling through the floor.

Rolling underneath another stone, she slashed at a third with her whip, tearing it in half. She had to destroy the statue before it killed her. It was far away, farther than her whip could reach.

She cleared her mind, transforming her whip into an arrow. In her other hand, she made a bow. She flexed the bow, aiming the statue. When she loosed the shaft, it streaked across the room in a blinding flash. The arrow flew between the floating rocks. It struck the statue center mass, tearing a hole in its chest. The levitating boulders fell in a simultaneous thud that shook the ground.

The statue swayed, but it did not fall.

It raised its hands to the ceiling, facing Kari. A low rumbling sound echoed. Her heart nearly stopped. That sound...

Her eyes shot up to the ceiling. Giant stone blocks began raining down. Kari ran, dodging each block as it crashed to the ground. Two stone blocks fell on either side, threatening to crush her. She dove between them as they crashed into each other.

The two blocks erupted, rushing toward her. Kari screamed as the hail of stones pelted her, sending her spiraling to the ground. Her body ached as she forced herself to her hands and knees. Another rock erupted from the ground, colliding with her face. The force of the impact lifted her. She collapsed and rolled onto her back, gripping her face as blood trickled from her nose.

Kari's eyes widened as more rumbling erupted in the chamber. A boulder hurtled from the ceiling. There was no time to dodge. Lashing out with both hands, she fired a blast of light energy at the boulder. It shattered, erupting into pieces. She made a light barrier to shield herself from the rain of stones.

Her chest heaved from the exertion. She couldn't take risks like that again. Light blasts were powerful, but wasteful. Kari could already fill her energy failing, her aura weakening from the effort. She had to be more careful about her energy usage.

Kari rolled to the side, then returned to her feet. Wiping the sweat from her brow, she faced her enemy.

The statue tilted its head in response.

Kari's knees buckled as the floor buckled and broke free. Pieces shot upward, launching her toward the ceiling and threatening to crush her—no time to think. Jumping off the platform, she plummeted a hundred feet to the ground below. She gathered her energy into her aura, rolling as she landed.

Kari leaped to her feet, then rushed toward the statue. She raised her whip, ready to strike. The figure waved its hands. Stone blasted from below, coating its body in rock armor. Kari's whip collided against its neck, tearing through the rock, but not enough to end the fight.

The statue leaped forward in a surprising display of speed for a creature made of rock. It reared back and landed a stone-fisted blow to Kari's face, which sent her spiraling.

It stood over her, landing blow after blow against her. Yelping, Kari convulsed with each blow. Her defenses were failing, each strike inflicting more and more pain. She refused to be beaten by this creature.

Kari launched her whip, wrapping it around a large stone. When she pulled it toward them, it struck the statue in the back of its head, knocking it off her.

She rolled to the side, then slashed at the statue. The whip struck its neck, leaving a gash in the stone. The statue swayed from the blow, but it did not falter. It raised its arm toward Kari.

"Ahh!" She sliced at its arm, and the whip cracked in a blinding flash of light. It tore through the stone, severing the statue's arm from its body.

The creature's head turned, tilting toward its fallen limb.

Kari's grip tightened around her whip. She swung at the creature's neck, lobbing off its head. The statue stopped, standing motionless.

Kari sighed. Her whip dissipated. Hunching over, she rested her hands on her knees. She'd done it. It was over. Her chest heaved as she struggled to catch her breath.

The statue stepped forward. Kari clenched her jaw. The sculpture took another step, raising its remaining arm.

Damn it! Why won't it die?

The statue paused, its headless body seeming to stare through her. A creaking noise emanated from its body. It lurched forward, then crumbled to dust.

Smiling, Kari dropped to her knees. It was truly over.

The chamber had been turned to rubble from the battle, though the altar still stood. She needed to hurry. This place might only exist outside of reality, but it was still made of stone. There was no telling if it could withstand the stress of the battle, and, if so, for how long. She didn't want to be buried in it, lost forever.

She headed over to the altar where the wooden box sat safely in its place. She had never seen dalium before. This substance was not from their world, but its magical properties were immense. She undid the fasten, then lifted the lid.

"What is this?" The box was full of jewelry. There was no dalium—no dust to be found. Had she done all of this for nothing? Sighing, she closed the box. Regardless of the contents, this was her treasure, her trophy. She wasn't going to leave it behind.

With the box in tow, she headed for the door and back into the building.

Artemis and Chaska waited on the other side. There was no way they'd finished, nor found the door that quick. She'd barely had enough time to find the portal and retrieve the jewelry box.

"Did you get it?" Artemis asked, staring at her prize.

"This was the only thing in there," Kari responded, handing it over to Artemis.

"What happened to you? Are you all right?" Chaska asked. She pulled Kari over to her. Examining her bruised face, she pawed at Kari's cheeks and skin.

"There was a statue in there, a living one," Kari explained, trying to escape from Chaska to no avail. "It attacked me."

"A sentinel?" Artemis asked in disbelief, her hairless eyebrows arching. "There was a sentinel in there? You fought a sentinel?"

"I guess you are tougher than we thought." Chaska grabbed Kari's nose and moved it from side to side, examining it as if were broken.

"Ow!" Kari winced.

"Your nose doesn't look broken, and I don't see any permanent injuries. Your spirit energy tis strong," Chaska said, releasing Kari.

"It was all for nothing. All I got was this." Kari pointed to the box in Artemis's hand.

Artemis opened it, and her mask bulged as a smile crept upon her face. She licked her lips. "Oh, that's clever."

"What is?" Kari asked.

"A key that turns a random door into a portal, a sentinel to attack anyone who is not allowed in, and, if you make it past that, you have a box filled with junk. Only someone who knows what they are looking for would see it." She rummaged through the contents, then picked out a single gold ring. "Here it is. Hold out your hand."

Kari took the ring from her, staring at the trinket in the palm of her hand.

"Do you feel it? Reach out with your spirit awareness."

Kari closed her eyes, concentrating. The ring tingled in her hand. "What is this?"

"It's an interspatial ring. Ilyia has one. It's how she can summon the Golden Rod as she does. Put it on, and I'll show you how it works."

Kari slipped the ring on her finger. It was too big, sliding up and down with ease.

"The ring is enchanted. Think of it not as a ring, but as a storage chest. Any item you can lift, you can store in the ring. Here, focus your spirit energy into it, then imagine its contents filling your hand."

Kari did as she was told. Almost immediately, the ring reacted to her spirit energy. It shrunk in size, fitting perfectly around her ring finger. A glowing yellow blob of energy formed in her hand. It slowly took shape, forming into a small bag.

"Tis it," Chaska said, taking the bag. She opened the bag, pulling out a handful of the golden powder like grains of dalium. "This is a lot of dalium. It might be enough to complete the modifications to the array."

Chaska let the dust rain back into the bag before drawing it closed. She handed it back to Kari.

"Go ahead and store it away, then let's get going," she said.

Kari focused her energy. The bag glowed before fading away into the ring.

"How do you feel after fighting that sentinel?" Chaska asked, offering her hand for support.

"I'm fine." Kari waved off the gesture. Now that the fight was over, she felt much better. "My energy's already coming back. That's one of the benefits of being me, I suppose. My energy recovers fast. What about the soldiers left in the town?"

"They're all dead," Artemis said with a wicked grin.

"All of them?" Just how powerful were these women? The Furies were legendary in their fighting skills. It was why they served as generals, but to capture an entire town in such a short amount of time—it was unthinkable.

Artemis shrugged. "I guess a few could have fled."

CHAPTER NINE

"WHAT HAPPENED HERE?" ILYIA asked, glaring at her subordinates. Chaska folded her hands behind her back and bowed her head, unable to look Ilyia in the eyes. "I see you disobeyed my command and started a private war."

"We did what had to be done," Artemis said, standing her ground. "We *are* renegades, right?"

Ilyia narrowed her eyes, her lips curling into a scowl. Kari couldn't let them take the blame for something she'd started. She had to take responsibility for her actions.

"Ilyia, this is my fault. I instigated the battle," Kari said, stepping beside Artemis. "I decided to liberate the town. It's my mother's home, and I couldn't let it stay in the hands of Torredins."

Sighing, Ilyia pinched her brow. "While I understand your eagerness, this may draw the Guardian's attention before we are ready."

Artemis gave Kari a sideways smile, and Chaska nodded in appreciation. Even with their approval, a wave of uneasiness washed over Kari. Ilyia was right. Kari's actions could bring the scorn of the Guardian upon them. It was something to be mindful of in the future. However, any risk was worth it to free her mother's home.

"Then we must hurry with our preparations," Chaska added, breaking free from her submissive posture.

"We either killed or drove out most of the soldiers," Artemis said. She raised her arm, then scratched the back of her mask.

The strength of the Furies was genuinely frightening to behold. In such a short amount of time, they'd fought a force of armed soldiers. Even with only two women, they won with little effort. "We captured about twenty others. When they saw our strength, they surrendered without much of a fight."

"If only they had listened to reason," Kari said, bowing her head in reverence. "We had no choice."

Ilyia's cocked a brow. "You force a confrontation. When they don't listen, you slaughter them. Then you have the audacity to say it's their fault you had to kill them? If you had stuck to the plan, no one would have died."

Kari's eyes fell. Ilyia was right. This was her fault.

"Tis a tad harsh," Chaska said. "All three of us fought. Twas for the best."

Ilyia rubbed her forehead. "We don't have the numbers to control another territory effectively." Stopping, she peered into Kari's eyes with a smile. "Kari, since this was your decision, and this is your mother's home, I am appointing you as Archon of the town."

Kari's heart jumped. "Me? Why me?" Was this a vote of confidence or punishment?

"Yeah," Artemis agreed, stepping forward and motioning with her arms. "You can't seriously put a child in charge of a town."

"She is no younger than we were when we first became warriors." Ilyia placed a hand on Artemis's shoulder, clearly meant to as a calming gesture. She turned her attention back to Kari. "You were empress of an entire nation. Surely you can handle one town."

This was a test. Ilyia *was* holding her responsible for her actions. "Tradition dictates a separation of powers. The Furies lead the warriors, and the Archons lead the towns."

"I understand." Kari sighed. That was tradition. The five councils that governed Shagin maintained separation, but those councils were long since gone. Not even the survivors on Mystikos had revived them. Still, it was a great honor. It showed Ilyia's trust in her. Kari took a deep breath, then nodded. "I'll do my best."

"That still leaves the prisoners. What should we do with them?" Artemis asked. So far, they had locked the prisoners in the upper-floor dungeon of the garrison. It was only a temporary solution, but they didn't have the personnel to guard them in Anuatu.

"You should direct your question to Kari," Ilyia said. "She is the Archon now."

Still, it was a decision Kari didn't know if she could make. Why must Ilyia pressure her to decide the fate of their prisoners so soon? Kari pursed her lips. Again, it seemed the lives of others were placed in her hands. What did justice look like in this situation? These were the Guardian's soldiers, Torredins, as they were known... but that wasn't necessarily true. Kari rubbed her hand through her hair. Not all soldiers who served the Guardian were Torredins. Only those who pledged unswerving loyalty to him obtained the title. So they could not all be held accountable for the Torredins' crimes.

"We should treat them the same as any other prisoner," Kari said. Even if they weren't Torredins, they were still under the command of the Guardian. As such, they could be held responsible for aiding a genocidal madman. But if such an act could only be just if they were allowed to defend themselves. "They should stand trial. If they are found guilty, they should help rebuild Shagin. When they've completed their service, they will be released."

Regardless of their title, they served a barbarian who destroyed this land. It was only fitting they help rebuild it. They would have to ensure the trial was as impartial as possible. As Archon, she would oversee it.

"Not bad, little one," Artemis said approvingly.

They supported her decision. Kari breathed a sigh of relief. At last, she had done something right.

"Miss," a knight said, approaching the group. He snapped to attention, then knelt. "We found something you might want to see."

Ilyia motioned for the knight to stand. He stood, then handed a silver ring with a red gem to Ilyia. She held it up to her face. Lips forming a scowl, she examined it.

"So, I see," Ilyia said, squeezing the ring in her fist. "It looks like this is a task for the new Archon. I trust you can handle this?" She held out the ring toward Kari.

"What is it?" Kari asked, taking it. Its cool metal was light in her palm. The ring had the symbol of the Guardian etched on either side of a ruby gem.

"It is the ring of a Torredin bastard," Ilyia replied, her gaze bouncing between Artemis and Chaska. "Specifically, the ones who served faithfully during the Sovereign War. It's a reward for those who achieved special commendations during the Purge."

"Torredins who committed genocide. They're still here?" Kari couldn't believe it. The foot soldiers of the Guardian—the army that answered directly to him, the group that led the extermination of her people—they weren't just stationed here. They were living in her mother's town.

"Tis long been known the Guardian gave land to certain loyalists following the Purge, so tis possible several could reside in the town," Chaska said, shaking her head.

This was terrible. How could those responsible for murdering Shagin now live in their former homes? They'd profited from the death of Shagin. Stolen their land. It was barbarism at its worst.

"I will not stand for this," Kari said, balling her fists. Her knuckles turned white. "How dare these men reside in the place where they massacred so many? I want these Torredins found to stand trial for their crimes."

"Are you sure you're up for this task, little one?" Artemis asked, placing her hands on her hips.

Kari's muscles relaxed. Could she do this—find the Torredins? She had no experience as an investigator. However, if other people could do it, she should be able to, but it didn't matter. If she gave it her all, she could succeed. She wouldn't stop until she did.

"I am," Kari replied.

"I'm trusting you to find the Torredins," Ilyia said. "If we leave them in the town, they could sabotage our efforts."

"Understood." Kari's heart fluttered. It was a tremendous responsibility, one fit for a leader. She had never sought to lead others, yet, somehow, she always found herself doing so. The Furies were counting on her. They trusted her with this task—a task of the utmost importance—that showed their confidence in her. They would not suffer failure, so neither would she.

"The former earl of the town will be the most likely way to find them. I will bring him to you at once," the knight said before departing.

"As the new Archon, you take him to the main hall," Ilyia said.

Kari gritted her teeth. Ilyia wanted her to show strength and determination. It was what Kari lacked in Xiang. Now, the fate of her people rested on her resolve.

"Sit on the throne. It will give you an air of authority."

The group bid her farewell, leaving Kari alone with her thoughts. She waited for the knight to return with the town earl.

The Torredins had massacred this town, and all like it. What must it have been like living here? So many years ago, the Torredins had torn through here, ripping families from their homes. Hunted down Shagin. Women and children had been taken away to an unknown fate.

Kari closed her eyes, shaking her head.

That wasn't true. Their fate was known to all. Certain death had awaited them. But death by what means? In the latter days of the Purge, bounties had been placed on Shagin. The traitors offered so much money per Shagin found that it had set up some Torredins for life.

Kari was but a babe when the horror of the Purge took place. She'd lived in safety and comfort with her mother, far from the violence and murder. Her mother had fled to safety when the Purge began—hidden away on Mystikos. Kari was glad, but felt guilty all the same. Other children hadn't been as lucky as her. Soldiers had shoved and pushed, terrified and corralled them, before executing them all.

Kari balled up her fists. It wasn't *fair*. Life wasn't fair. Why did these barbarians feel the need to strip Shagin of life and dignity? They attempted to deny them of their humanity. In the process, they'd lost their own.

"Kari!" Ina ran up to her, then threw her arms around Kari's neck. Ronin casually walked behind Ina, scanning their new surroundings.

Kari closed her eyes, melting into Ina's embrace. Why did this feel so right?

"How was the trip here?" Kari asked when Ina released her.

"Not bad," Ronin replied. Yawning, he stretched his arms.

"Not bad?" Ina asked, shooting him a sideways look. "You spent the entire trip purposely antagonizing Ilyia."

"Well, if she didn't annoy me, I wouldn't have," Ronin shot back.

When Ina rolled her eyes, Kari smiled.

"This place is so beautiful," Ina said, staring at the double waterfalls. "So, this is where your mother was from?"

"Yep," Kari said, beaming.

"I heard stories from Eanna about this place." Ronin tilted his head, watching the water crashing into the bottom pool. "I can't believe I'm finally stepping foot in here."

Ronin shrugged, turned, and started walking away.

"Where are you going?" Kari called.

He didn't bother turning back around. Just held up a hand, then waved. "I'm going to take a nap."

Kari scoffed. What was with him?

"Don't mind him," Ina said, interlacing her arm with Kari's.

"I don't think he means anything by it," Kari added. Ronin was always a bit odd, especially around others. He carried a laid-back demeanor, but his eyes were quick and caught the smallest detail. It made it difficult to understand what he was thinking.

"How are you doing?" Ina asked, eyeing her up.

Kari raised an eyebrow.

"After the battle, I mean. You don't think it was too much strain?"

Kari sighed. "I guess I haven't had the chance to tell you. I'm not pregnant after all."

"That's good news." Ina smiled. "Isn't it?"

Kari shook her head. "I'm not sure. You see, I can never get pregnant. I'm sterile. It is just one more choice taken away from me."

"I'm sorry." Ina clasped Kari's hands in hers. "But you still have a choice. You can adopt whenever *you* feel ready. And I will still be by your side."

Kari smiled softly, pulling Ina's hand toward her face. Ina's skin was soft and delicate. Kari wanted nothing more than to place a tender kiss on the other woman's fingers. "Thank you," Kari whispered.

"What are friends for?"

"Miss," the knight said. He approached, followed by another man. Kari released Ina when the knight shoved the man forward. "I've found the earl."

She expected it to take longer, but at least it meant she could finish this. Even though she'd hoped for more time to prepare what she was going to say, she supposed she'd have to make it up as she went along like everything else.

"Good," Kari replied, cementing her resolve. "I'm ready for this."

She said goodbye to Ina, then motioned for the knight to lead the way to the town's main hall as the earl followed behind. Kari cut her eyes toward the man, who merely grumbled in return.

The main hall was small, especially compared to the massive throne room of the Hall of Heaven and Earth. It was rather dull, too, with the only decoration a red rug across the stone floor.

Kari took her seat as the knight forced the earl to kneel before her. Gritting his teeth, he relented, raising his head to gaze at her. Her emerald-green eyes met his brown ones. It wasn't right to make him kneel. He might have been an earl under the Guardian, but he wasn't a prisoner like the others. With any luck, the man would serve as an ally.

"You don't have to kneel," Kari said, motioning for him to stand.

"You're in my seat." The man sneered.

She had to show strength and authority.

"I'm the new Archon," she said, dismissing his words. Crossing her legs, she slumped in her new throne. She had to present herself as confident and in charge, despite her true feelings of inadequacies. "You might have missed it, but this town is no longer under the oppression of the Guardian."

"So, you are our new tyrant?" the earl asked. He tried to stand to his feet, but the knight forced him back down.

Kari waved the knight away. He scoffed, but took a single step back. Sighing, she clasped her hands in front of herself. "I am not a tyrant."

"Is that so?" the earl almost shouted, rising to his feet.

"What is your name?" Kari asked.

"Ryder," he replied. He turned his head, eyeing the knight before cutting his gaze back to Kari. "You captured my town, enslaved my people, and now you demand my name?"

"Your people are not slaves. Why don't you see that?" Kari asked. She uncrossed her legs. Leaning forward, she moved closer to him. "I freed you from the Guardian's control."

Wildly, Ryder swung his arm around. "The Guardian kept us safe from the likes of you. He gave us peace while you bring us to war. You are a monster who deserves to die."

"You no longer have the right to speak to me," Kari said with a flick of her sleeve. She leaned back in her chair, frowning. Just like the Torredins, he had sacrificed his humanity to satisfy the Guardian. Still, Kari would give him a chance to redeem himself. It was only fair. "There are Torredins in this town. I want you to identify them for me."

"Why? So, you can murder them?" He scowled.

"They must be tried for their crimes." Kari slammed her fist onto the arm of her chair. She wasn't a murderer. Instead, she merely sought to right what had been wronged so many years ago. "They are barbarians who willingly serve a genocidal maniac. When they didn't refuse his order to massacre my people, they gave up their humanity."

"I won't do it!" Ryder shook his head, throwing his hands into the air.

"You will do it, or you will face the same punishment," Kari said more harshly than she'd intended. Could she do it? Hold him responsible, too? Kari tried to shake the thought away to calm her spirit, but her resentment was too inflamed. Even though she hadn't lived through it, the Purge was still a sensitive topic.

"The men have families. Whatever they did, it has been nearly twenty years since. That's a lifetime ago," Ryder said.

A lifetime ago? How many lives had they ended? Did murderers think time would erase Shagin memory?

"How many families did they butcher? How many lives were destroyed? How many hearts broken? So many people murdered by their hands. Time does not forget genocide. Now tell me their names!" Kari's anger choked her. She wanted nothing more than to lash out at him for daring to excuse the genocide of her people. All he had were excuses for why those responsible shouldn't face justice—shouldn't be held accountable for their actions.

"I respectfully decline," Ryder said, mockingly placing a hand over his heart.

"All you have to do is write down their names," Kari protested. Why couldn't he comply with her simple request? Fearing the Guardian's wrath, the world succumbed to his whims and murdered her people, yet this man could find the courage to protect the murderers. He was a hyp-ocrite.

"No." He shook his head, marching toward her. "You hate the Torredins for being loyal to the Guardian. You will have to take me first. Like them, I, too, am loyal."

"I could," Kari said, her voice trembling. She didn't want to do this, but anyone who shielded and protected murderers was just as guilty. There had to be a better way. What could she do to show the differences between her and the other Shagin? Kari nodded. "I understand the need for impartial justice. If you stand with the Torredins, you will represent them during their trial. Will that satisfy you?"

"It's a start," Ryder said.

"Then you are dismissed," Kari said. If she were forced to be around the man who defended the genocide of her people for much longer, she was afraid she would lash out. Harm him. She hated feeling this way, which only made her hate stronger.

Grabbing the earl, the knight shoved the man toward the door, his feet scuffing on the stone floor. The knight stopped, twisting back toward Kari.

"That still leaves them free to roam, ready to form a counterinsurgency against us," he said.

Kari rubbed her chin. She didn't have any other options. Although it would make her a hypocrite, too, the Torredins had to be found, even if she were hesitant to call for it—she had to.

"Then go door to door. Someone has to know something."

CHAPTER TEN

The town gathered for the trial of the Torredins, which Kari held at the bottom waterway. It was a beautiful summer day, which made her more hesitant. To ensure justice was both fair and impartial, she needed to bury her feelings. Hopefully, the inclusion of Ryder would ensure impartiality by giving a unified voice to the Torredins.

In the brief time she'd had, she'd rummaged through the records to identify as many Torredins as possible. Following the Purge, The Immortal Warrior had granted seventeen men parcels of land for their service, located in Anuatu. While their names weren't listed in the records, the town had conducted a census only a year after, which indicated the families that had moved immediately after the Purge. Cross-referencing that and known military records, correspondences, and the town annals made it possible to identify the most likely candidates who were still living there.

So far, she had identified eleven of the possible seventeen. She was aware the other six could have been killed, fled, or simply moved away. Her uneasiness, however, came from discovering all eleven still had their ring from the Guardian. It meant there was at least one more Torredin left in the town. Kari would not stop searching until she found the last one who so carelessly lost their prize for genocide.

As it stood, she still needed to decide the fate of those she had captured. They deserved a speedy trial. Beside the Torredins, she had to consider the other prisoners they had caught while retaking the town. She could disposition them at the same time.

The knights brought the eleven Torredins to the front, forcing them into seats and taking up posts behind them. The remaining soldiers they'd captured when they took back the town sat to the left of the Torredins. She'd ordered the prisoners to remain unshackled since she believed in the practice of innocence until proven guilty—at least until after the trial.

As promised, she'd allowed Ryder to serve as their advocate. Standing in front of the prisoners, he faced Kari. The remainder of the townspeople sat behind the Torredins. Her rule as Archon had just been announced, but word traveled quickly. This would be her first public appearance. It seemed as most of the town had gathered for the trial to see their new ruler in action.

Kari took a deep breath. The crowd made her uneasy, but she shored her confidence. She had stood before the court of Xiang—now the lives of others were placed in front of her.

Clearing her throat, she straightened her posture. A hush fell over the audience. Fear apparent, the prisoners stared up at her.

"We are gathered for the trial of these Torredins before us," Kari said as loudly as she could, while still using a measured tone, so those in the back could hear her. "They are accused of committing crimes against peace; for participating in a war of aggression to subjugate and eradicate Shagin; for participating in war crimes that include the murder, torture, and rape of Shagin; and for the participation of genocide against Shagin. What is their plea?"

"Not guilty," Ryder said, motioning to the accused Torredins. "Some of these men aren't even Torredins. They are merely soldiers. The law of the Guardian dictated what happened. The events of the Purge are regrettable, but these men should not be held responsible. They were sworn to fulfill the law, and that's what they did."

Kari clenched her jaw. If they would simply take responsibility for their actions and show remorse, she could forgive them. They had acknowledged their role—indirectly—in the genocide, but they refused to accept responsibility for their crimes.

"So, you acknowledge the accused had roles in committing these crimes, but you still insist on their innocence?" Kari asked. "The accused cannot participate in genocide, then retroactively absolve themselves of their actions. These men—and these men alone—are responsible for what they did."

"This is a façade," Ryder interrupted. He held up a finger as if he were making a grand point. "How can you be an impartial judge? As a Shagin, you are part of the injured party. You've already made up your mind. Besides, as stated, the law was clear. You're attempting to redefine the law *after* the so-called crimes were committed simply to justify this sham. There is no justice in a court without law."

The crowd murmured in agreement. Kari forced herself not to roll her eyes. How could anyone argue they didn't know genocide was immoral... *and* have an entire crowd agree with them?

"Prohibitions against the genocide of my people might not have been codified into law," Kari said, swallowing her anger. She needed her rancor to fight for her fallen sisters, but any outbursts would simply prove Ryder's point that Shagin were the real monsters. She waved her hand, dismissing his point. "But basic human decency indicates that genocide, murder, torture, and rape are not only wrong, but also immoral. You cannot argue ignorance of that widely agreed-upon fact."

Ryder stalked forward, wildly swinging his arms. He looked unhinged, yet the crowd didn't respond to his outburst. Not faltering, Kari fixed her gaze on him. She wouldn't hesitate, nor would she fail again.

Scowling, Ryder planted his feet. "You argue against indiscriminate murder, yet you want to kill these men for no other reason than serving on the wrong side of your war," he said, motioning toward the Torredins. "These men have families. The crimes you speak of were committed nearly twenty years ago. Yet, if you murder these men, you will be the one committing similar crimes *today*."

Ryder continued. "And what of the other soldiers here?" Fire and anger filled his expression, fitting for a loyalist to the Immortal Warrior. "They are merely men performing a job to secure their livelihoods. These men are not the criminals you have accused them of being. They are prisoners of war, and they should be treated as such under the Articles of Aggression."

"The law you cite is the Guardian's." Kari shook her head. "It has no bearing in Shagin. The accused willingly serve a man who continues to commit crimes against humanity. He has ordered genocide on more than one occasion. Swearing allegiance to him accepts culpability in his atrocities, which is a crime."

Kari exhaled. She had to show strength. Her weakness in Xiang had led to Cai Ren's betrayal. Then, her lack of strength and conviction ended with her being dethroned and Xiang in chaos with the threat of a civil war. She couldn't afford to show weakness now.

"I have heard your pleas. After you make your final case, I'll make my decision about the fates of the accused," Kari said. However, Ryder *was* partially right. She *had* already decided what action to take if the Torredins refused to show regret for the Purge. But she would still give them this one opportunity to repent before deciding on their sentences.

"Only three of these men are actual Torredins. The rest were simply soldiering under the command of an army loyal to the Immortal Warrior. It is not right to lump them together." Ryder's fierce defense made sense for a man who was the earl of the town just a few days ago. It would have been his job to protect his people from outsiders. Despite his heated words, she'd bet he was merely fulfilling his duty without actually believing in his words. Kari had to remember that. "Anyone who served under the Guardian would have done the same."

"The Guardian murdered my people," Kari said. Her heart raced, her breaths choppy. Listening to Ryder defend genocide disgusted her. Supporting the accused was one thing, but the act itself was indefensible. It was time to end this. She needed to decide their fates. In the time leading up to the trial, she'd agonized over her decision. It weighed on her. Yet, for her fallen sisters, she couldn't delay.

"These men are the foot soldiers of a tyrannical genocidal maniac. They fought a war meant to erase my people from existence. Half-a-million Shagin—innocent people—were murdered for a crime we never committed. Shagin have always been treated as subhuman, forced to live in exile from the rest of the world. The Guardian spouted a nonsense excuse in his order to eradicate us, and the accused followed the command of a madman. A Torredin is a soldier under the Guardian's command. The accused men fit the description. Justice must be served to deter others from committing such evil acts. Throughout history, the only proven constant is that humanity will always repeat the worst of its atrocities."

"If you condemn these men, you leave their children fatherless, their wives widowed. How can you justify that?" Ryder spat, standing his ground.

"How can they justify genocide?" Kari responded. Even if they had been conscripted, they'd still chosen to comply with the wishes of a tyrant. Resisting, even if it meant facing the Guardian's wrath, would have been the moral action. As for the men's families? They knew the horrors their loved one had inflicted, yet they still supported them. In her opinion, that meant they, too, endorsed genocide. Kari could not tolerate those kinds of people living in the new age she sought. "They could have resisted evil or refused to follow. Instead, they chose to commit evil themselves. For those crimes, I sentence the accused to death by hanging. Their estates shall be seized for reparations, and their families banished from Shagin."

An uproar came from the crowd as the Torredins started a hushed conversation amongst themselves. Kari narrowed her eyes, having expected more of a reaction from the men.

"You'll banish the families without any supplies or assets?" Ryder asked, his eyes wide and his mouth agape. "That's a death sentence in itself."

Kari scoffed. She'd been banished from her people. It gave her perspective while allowing her to grow and experience new cultures. "I was banished in much the same way, and I survived. They will have to find a way like I did."

"They will die," Ryder protested.

"My decision is final," Kari said, raising her hand. "This court is dismissed."

After the crowd departed, the knights escorted the prisoners to holding cells to await their punishment. Still, there was more work to be done.

Kari didn't want to rest until the remainder of the Torredin bastards were found and brought to justice. She could return to her research notes to see if she missed anything, but exhaustion crept over her at the thought.

If she wanted to find the last one, she'd need Ronin's assistance. As a Kitsuno Kai, he'd led investigations before. And he could perceive the truth, even a fact hidden in lies.

It wouldn't be difficult to convince him. He always seemed willing to help her. Finding him would be a different story, however. He and Ina came with Ilyia and Aura to Anuatu, but his ghostly presence made knowing where he was at any given moment hard to discern. He could come and go as he pleased without much notice.

Leaving the monotony of her research for another day, she headed into the town to find him. The Furies said they hadn't seen him, which wasn't too unexpected. He didn't play well with others.

After an hour, Kari gave up her search, but the thought of returning to her documents filled her with dread. Instead, she decided to get some rest before returning to the courthouse.

Kari opened the door to her quarters. Stretched out on the couch, Ronin had his arms folded behind his head. Surprised at the sight, she paused. Ronin was rarely still, usually scurrying about in search of his next project. Ina sat on a chair next to him.

"The last place I looked," Kari said.

"Of course." Ronin didn't bother to sit up. "Once you find what you're looking for, why keep looking?"

"Ronin," Kari said, getting straight to the point. "I need your help."

"So I've heard," Ronin said, moving to a sitting position. Unblinking, he stared back.

"I need your help to find the Torredins hidden in town," Kari said, sitting next to him. "The knights found most, but a few still elude us."

"I'm not interested," Ronin said, then yawned.

"What do you mean? These people murdered Shagin, and they should be brought to stand trial."

"Kari, you can't do that," Ina protested. "You're killing these men."

"I'm not killing them," Kari said. She refused to. They weren't worth her effort.

"You gave the order," Ina said.

Kari's heart skipped. Taking a deep breath, she tried to slow her breathing and racing pulse. She had done that.

"It's justice," Kari said. Their sentencing was merely the consequence of their actions. "They committed genocide, and they have to be held accountable."

"But you're not going to watch?" Ina asked.

Kari wrinkled her nose. *Watch?* What kind of person would want to watch others die?

"There's no need," she said.

"Odd, isn't it, how quick and easy it is to order someone's death, yet you can't even bring yourself to watch the act you decreed?" Ina said, shaking her head. "It's like you know it's wrong."

"I have no desire to see someone die," Kari corrected. How could Ina not see the need for justice over what these men did? "The atrocities of the Purge must never happen again. If punishment is not adequate—if justice does not meet the crime committed—then the pattern of hatred and death will continue. Others won't feel the need to stand against the next genocide. Consequences have to be had for the participants as well as those who commanded it."

"I can understand holding the Torredins accountable for their actions, but what you've done to the other soldiers is slavery."

"No, it's justice," Kari insisted. Apparently, Ina didn't understand the concept of justice. She was blind to the rigid black-and-white morality where anything even remotely hinting at the cruel nature of the world was evil. The truth was the world was gray. Morality was gray. Sometimes cruelty and evilness must be met with actions that could seem cruel and ruthless on the surface but were meant to prevent more evil from occurring. Ina was too idealistic to see that. "They aligned themselves with a regime that destroyed my home, and they should help rebuild it as penance."

"That's your idea of justice? I thought justice was about restoring balance," Ina said.

Kari wanted to share in Ina's idealism, but she was jaded. She had witnessed to the truth of the world. It was not kind or caring, nor did it not concern itself for civility or niceties. Justice had to be severe to restore the balance of evil men.

"Is it not?" Ronin asked. Kari breathed a sigh of relief at Ronin's support. "They would be rebuilding what was destroyed. That's restorative."

"It's still slavery. They have no choice in the matter," Ina said, her voice filled with the same fire as Ryder's.

Kari gritted her teeth, hating to see her friend like this.

"It's servitude, not slavery," Kari said. Slavery implied there wasn't any hope for release, but the men would only serve limited sentences. It was a fitting punishment for their crimes.

After their sentence was up, they'd be released. Why couldn't Ina see that? If they were slaves, they would never earn their freedom.

"Oh, I agree." Ronin moved, propping his legs on her.

Scowling, Kari knocked them off. He grunted, but he didn't attempt to replace them.

"They committed a crime, so they should serve their sentence. It's only seven years. Of course, I would have killed them. However, your actions will alert the Guardian of your presence. I will not aid in your death."

"And this has nothing to do with your feelings toward Vipin and the Furies?" Kari asked, rising.

"I won't lie—I hope they all die painful deaths," Ronin said with a smirk.

"I won't be a part of this, and I can't believe you two would," Ina said, storming off.

"Hey, I think this entire situation is stupid," Ronin shouted, stopping her in her tracks.

"You think what we're doing is stupid?" Kari gritted out. Rage flashed through her, heating her cheeks.

"No, just the way you are acting," Ronin clarified.

Lips pursing, Kari flexed her hands, temper building.

"Ronin, that's enough," Ina chastised, glancing at Kari.

"No, I want to hear this," Kari said, not feeling as sure inside as she sounded. "You think I'm stupid?"

"Childish, stupid, imbecilic—take your pick," Ronin said.

Kari glared, angry and hurt.

He studied her, a gentle sigh escaping his lips. His posture relaxed. "The Guardian knows who you are. No doubt, he will be searching for you to either confirm your death or kill you himself. You should lay low. This little stunt of yours will only attract attention. If you were smart, you would heed my advice and move on. I can protect you a lot easier if you go into hiding."

"We're trying to save my people. If the Torredins are here, they could stop us," Kari pleaded. "The fate of Shagin relies on our success. How can you not see this? You would condemn us to death simply for your grudge?"

"Don't you dare accuse me of that," Ronin snarled. Launching himself up, he grabbed her by the shoulders and pinned her to the couch. "I don't give a damn about your politics. But I have sworn to keep you safe, and that's what I will do."

"This isn't political." Kari winced as his fingers dug into her skin. "This is basic human decency. My people will die."

Frustrated, Ronin released her. "My decision is final. Go find someone else to help you."

"I don't need you to protect me," Kari said. A part of her knew he was right. The Guardian would come again. Without the backing of Xiang, he would send assassins this time. But she refused to show fear. She could make a difference—Kari could feel it in her core. With the Furies on her side, the Guardian should be the one afraid. "Just look around at what I did. I freed our mother's town."

"At what cost?" Ronin snapped.

"Her humanity," Ina replied.

CHAPTER ELEVEN

Kari stormed off, slamming the door on her way out. The nerve. Ronin had never acted like that toward her, not since finding out they were siblings. Perhaps it was his true nature after all.

Kari rubbed her shoulders. She didn't need help. Ilyia trusted her to find the Torredins, so she would.

"Family squabble, eh, little one?" Artemis leaned against the nearby wall, her arms folded across her chest.

Kari turned up her nose. "Why do you keep calling me that?"

"Well, have you seen yourself?" Artemis leaned forward, then pinched Kari's cheek. "You're just so tiny and cute."

Kari swung at Artemis, who moved out of the way.

"And you're so sensitive, too." Artemis laughed.

"What do you want?" Kari growled.

"I thought you could use some help finding the remaining Torredins," Artemis said.

"You don't trust me to do it?" Kari asked.

"Oh, no, not at all." Artemis winked. "But just think how good you'll look in front of Ilyia if you find them. No one even has to know I was here."

Kari closed her eyes. The woman was trying to manipulate her, but Kari wouldn't fall for her games.

"Thanks, but I can handle this on my own."

"Okay, but without any leads, you won't go very far." Smugly, Artemis cocked a brow.

"I do have leads," Kari lied.

"Really? You do?" Artemis laughed. "And here I thought you'd exhausted all of your efforts."

"I'm going to see a lead now." Kari stomped past her.

"Oh, then you won't mind if I tag along," Artemis said, trailing her.

"You don't have to," Kari insisted.

"But what if you need help? There are all sorts of scoundrels, just waiting for their chance, who are willing to take advantage of a child like yourself."

"I'm not a child," Kari protested.

"Good, then you won't mind me coming with you."

Kari clenched her teeth, storming off with Artemis in pursuit.

"Just where are we going?" Artemis asked, matching her pace.

Kari had no idea, but she knew who would. "I'm going to see Ryder."

Ryder had been appointed earl of the town right after the Purge. Her knights searched his house, but they'd found no evidence of the other Torredins. He had to know more, though. She would have to make him see the necessity of bringing them to justice.

Kari and Artemis approached his residence. Two small children played outside—a blonde girl and a boy with messy brown hair. They ran around each other, swinging a package around as if it were a sword.

"I'm looking for Preston Ryder," Kari said. The two kids froze, eyes on her.

The boy stepped toward Kari. "That's Father."

"May I speak to him, please?" Kari asked, bending to the boy's level.

He darted into the house without another word.

"I see you found some kids your age to play with," Artemis joked.

Kari rolled her eyes.

She approached the girl, who plopped in the dirt by the package. They shared a smile.

"I know you. You're Shagin, aren't you?" the girl asked, her golden braid glistening in the sunlight.

"I am," Kari replied. How could anyone look upon someone as sweet and innocent, yet see a monster worth killing? It wasn't human. Yet, children just like her were killed in the Purge.

"That's so cool. When I grow up, I want to be Shagin, too." The girl grinned.

Kari laughed. She didn't want to crush the girl's hopes, though it was nice to see someone her age look up to

Shagin. "I wish it were that simple, though I'm sure you would have made a fine Shagin."

"Too bad you can't," Artemis cut in.

Kari glared at the woman.

"I know what happened to them," the girl said.

Kari averted her eyes. No child should be faced with such horror.

"They were killed by the Guardian. I don't understand why. Momma said it was because you don't believe in the gods."

"That's part of the reason, though it is more complicated than that," Kari explained. She wasn't sure how much she should tell a child.

"I don't understand. Talus says, 'do not kill'. Why would his prophet kill you for not following his teachings? It doesn't seem right."

Because Torredins are hypocrites, Kari wanted to say, but she knew better. It was best not to challenge the girl's worldview. Artemis opened her mouth, but Kari held up a hand to stop her. This girl didn't need Artemis's jaded input.

"It's because everyone is flawed. We make mistakes, and we're not always consistent with our beliefs," Kari explained. "Did your mother teach you about Shagin?"

"She did," the girl said, staring at her hands. "I was born blind, but Momma took me to Koruzeru to see this wonderful man who gave me sight."

"Vipin," Kari said. Shagin and the Koroks could accomplish so much by working together. Still, it made her uneasy to attribute Vipin with Shagin. But Kari supposed they were now the same. "He is wonderful."

"If the Shagin did that for me, they can't be bad, can they?"

Kari sat next to the girl, taking her tiny hand. "We're not bad. We're the same. Everyone is the same. We all share the same blood, the same hopes and dreams. We all want a better future."

"Shagin gave me one," the girl solemnly said.

Pride filled her at the girl's open heart, but she changed the subject. "What's that?" she asked, motioning to the package.

"Take a look." The girl grabbed the package and ripped the paper off, revealing a jhuma, a traditional Shagin sword. The small curved blade bounced sun rays off the girl's golden hair.

"Isn't she a beaut?" Artemis said, staring at the sword.

"What do you need this for?" Kari asked. If the children hit each other with the package, the blade could have torn through the wrapping and cut them. How could their parents be so reckless?

"To fight the Guardian if he ever comes back," the girl said.

"You should leave the fighting to the adults." Kari picked up the sword. It was heavy in her hands, more so than she remembered swords to be.

"The Guardian didn't care during the Purge. He killed children along with everyone else. I have to be able to defend myself. And I will kill all the bad guys." The girl took the sword from Kari, her young eyes flickering with an emotion that left Kari cold.

Kari stared at her now-empty hands. How could violence be the solution? Yet, it was needed for defense and protection.

"Promise me that you'll never use it," Kari said, gaze fixated on the weapon. "Please, promise me you'll give that to your parents."

The girl nodded. "I promise. But what if something bad happens again?"

"I won't let it," Kari said. "I promise."

The door to the house opened. A scowling Ryder exited.

"Claire, go inside," he ordered. He glared at Kari. "May I help you?"

"I was hoping you would invite me in so we may talk."

Begrudgingly, Ryder motioned her to follow him.

"Artemis, please wait out here," Kari said. She needed tact and discretion—not snide comments—to win over Ryder.

"As you wish," Artemis said.

Ryder scoffed as Kari kicked off her shoes before entering his house. She followed him into the dining area, then took a seat at a round table.

"May I ask you something?" Kari asked.

"Haven't you done enough?" Ryder replied, sitting across from her.

Kari sighed. It was her turn to ask the questions. She remembered how Ronin had interrogated her during her time at the harem. He'd spoken with authority and directness, actively leading the conversation. It was something she needed to mimic now. "I've been led to believe you moved to the town following the war."

"I wasn't the only one," Ryder said. He picked up a pipe from the table and lit the end, puffing out smoke. "I don't understand the meaning of this visit. Your knights already visited earlier this morning. I will not stand for this sort of harassment against my family or me."

"I'm going to be blunt," Kari said. Ronin had been confident of his statements. His directness had caused her to falter at the time. She needed to use the same tactic to catch Ryder in a lie or a half-truth, as was most likely the case. "Are you a Torredin?"

"If I were, do you think I would tell you?" Ryder snickered.

Kari blushed. It had been a dumb question. She shook her head, trying to return her focus.

"My people were murdered. I want to find those responsible—need to hold them accountable for their actions."

"The man responsible is dead," Ryder said, blowing smoke at her. Coughing, Kari swatted at the billowing cloud as it washed over her face. "The Immortal Warrior died, and the new Guardian isn't to blame."

"He upholds the same laws passed by his predecessor," Kari said. "The Torredins followed the commands of the Immortal Warrior and slaughtered my people."

"As you said, they were following his commands," Ryder said. The way he chomped on the end of the pipe reminded her of a cow chewing on cud. "They are not responsible."

"They could have refused," Kari protested. "They could have resisted! They were told to commit genocide, and they did."

"It was decades ago." Ryder rolled his eyes.

"Seventeen years," Kari corrected. It was the same argument from him, again and again.

Ryder sighed. "What do you want from me?"

Kari leaned forward in her chair. "I'm trying to help you. Please, if you'll just tell me where I can find the remaining Torredins, I'll leave you and your family alone."

Resignation stole over his expression. The sooner he told her what she needed to know, the sooner she and her knights could stop harassing him. He knew it. "I don't know. I've heard rumors, but that's all they are."

"I'll take whatever you can give me," Kari said.

Sighing, he set his pipe down. "A group was last spotted fleeing to the southeast. I believe they were headed toward Koruzeru. If you hurry, you might catch them before they arrive."

"Why would they be going to Koruzeru?" Kari asked.

"I can't say," Ryder hedged.

The band of Torredins wouldn't get away—not on her watch. She hated the idea of killing, always had, but to save lives, she would do what she must. She refused to let the Torredins murder indiscriminately. They would pay for their hatred.

"Why didn't you tell the knights about this earlier? We could have stopped them sooner."

"As I said," Ryder replied. "They are only rumors. Besides, these people were my neighbors, my friends. How could I turn on them?"

Kari tilted her head. "So, you would be culpable in their crimes?"

"I can't control the actions of others, only my own," Ryder said.

He had helped, at least as much as he felt comfortable doing so. It might not be as much information as she desired, but it must have taken a lot for him to deliver it. For that, she was grateful. "Thank you. I will notify the knights right away."

"May the gods be with you." Ryder stood, then offered his hand out for her to shake.

Kari stared at it. It was so unusual to shake hands. In Xiang, bows were the standard greeting. Other parts of the world preferred more intimate greetings, such as the touching of hands. Shagin formally greeted each other with hugs. It was strange becoming accustomed to the different greetings.

Kari's eyes widened. She seized his hand, pulling it closer to her face. Tan marks of a missing ring were present. Kari dropped his hand, digging in her pocket.

"What the devil are you doing?" Ryder asked.

"I believe this is yours." Kari held up the Torredin ring so Ryder could see it.

"You are mistaken." Frowning, he folded his arms across his chest.

"We'll see." Kari grabbed ahold of his hand. He resisted as she forced it open, then slipped the ring onto his finger. It slid into place with ease and covered the tan marks—a perfect fit. "You're a Torredin."

"Damn, you're perceptive," Ryder said, yanking his hand back.

Rage flared. Why he had been so adamant about defending the Torredins became clear. He'd tried to justify his actions. How could he? "You're coming with me to stand trial like the rest of the Torredins."

"No, I am not," Ryder said in a matter-of-fact tone. "You're going to let me go."

Kari narrowed her eyes. "Why is that?"

"After your sham of a trial this morning, I feared this might happen. So I captured two of your Shagin sympathizers, and I poisoned them. Only if you let me go will I disclose their location. If you don't, they will die."

Kari gritted her teeth. "You are a Torredin bastard." She readied her aura to fight. Ryder had given up his humanity to be nothing more than the enforcer for a genocidal Guardian—just like the others.

"I won't let you take me," Ryder said, inching away from her. "What happened to your people was a shame, that's for sure. But this trial of yours is only for show. You've already made up your mind to kill us."

"You're not giving me a good reason to change my mind," Kari snarled, advancing on him. She wouldn't show fear. Instead, she'd be brave and demonstrate her strength.

"I didn't lie, you know." Ryder held up his hands as he pleaded. "The Shagin event was a lifetime ago. I've changed so much since then. I was only doing what was commanded."

"Do you think that absolves your crimes?" Kari spat.

"Daddy!" Claire darted into the room, rushing toward Ryder. "Please don't hurt my daddy!"

"Claire, get out of here," Ryder barked.

Kari's energy waned. The little girl who had her sight restored was his daughter. "I don't understand. How could you help execute Shagin only to rely on us to heal your daughter?"

"I would do anything for my daughter," Ryder said, kneeling to embrace Claire. "Even turn to the enemy for help."

"You're a hypocrite," Kari said, lowing her defenses. "But if you come with me, I promise you will face fair justice."

"At the end of a noose?" he asked, looking up at her. "I know what fate awaits me if I tell you their location."

"Then, you should know what awaits you if you don't." Kari balled her fists. Part of her wanted to submit to her anger, but she had to be better than him. "If there is any humanity left in you, I should be able to talk you down. If I'm wrong, I will kill you."

"Die now or die later? Those are my only options?"

"No," Kari said. She was not a murderer, but justice could not be forsworn. "Face justice in a trial or face summary execution now."

"Not my daddy, please," Claire begged, wrapping her arms tighter around her dad.

"Your father helped hunt down and exterminate my people. Even now, he holds two innocent lives in jeopardy. He must stand trial." How could the girl defend him? Claire idolized Shagin. Vipin had even restored her sight, yet she would stand with her father? The Guardian corrupted and twisted Ryder into a vile creature capable of murdering innocents to escape justice for his crimes of genocide. Now he had corrupted his daughter. This barbarism had to stop.

"My daddy's a good guy—he wouldn't do that," Claire said, cheeks tearstained. "He's not a bad guy like you."

Kari's heart stopped. She wasn't bad either, merely seeking justice. But through the eyes of a child, justice could seem cruel.

Ryder placed a gentle kiss on Claire's forehead. "Fine, I will go with you." He rose. "Please, just leave my family out of this."

"I promise." Kari nodded.

"Before I tell you where they are, just know you won't get away with this," Ryder threatened. "The Guardian's hunters are coming."

"I will deal with them when they come," Kari said. "Now, where are the ones you poisoned?"

"In my back room. I'll take you there."

Ryder led Kari into a rear room. Two girls about her age laid prostrate on a bed. Kari rushed over, then placed her fingers on one's throat. She was unresponsive, but she had a pulse. Slow and weak, but there.

The other girl moaned, eyes fluttering open. At least one was conscious.

"Am I going to die?" she asked, coughing.

"No," Kari said. "I won't allow you to die."

"Lying doesn't ease the fear." The girl slumped, her eyes closing.

"Why? Why would you do this?" Kari glared at Ryder, who merely sighed in response.

"Simple," Ryder said. "I knew if I couldn't elude you, I'd need a way to escape. You can either save them or capture me. Not enough time for both."

Kari gritted her teeth, light emanating from her fingertips. "Or I could just kill you." It was all she seemed to be suitable for these days.

"Could you? With my children in the next room?"

Kari's aura faded as her muscles relaxed.

"As I thought." Smugly, Ryder's lips twisted. "Make your choice."

Ryder darted out of the room. He slammed the door shut, leaving Kari alone with the two girls. She wouldn't let him get away with this, but, right now, saving these two girls was more important.

Kari's mind raced. The girls were pale and sweaty with weak pulses. There were simply too many poisons that could cause this. How would she begin to counteract its effects?

The conscious one moaned. Her eyes rolled back, her head flopping to the side.

"Damn it!" Kari rushed over, finding her pulse. So weak. She didn't have much time left to live.

Killing was so much simpler. Whenever Kari's enemies stood before her, it took nothing to end their lives—but saving a life? Where did she even begin?

She had become death. It had been her first thought when faced with the Torredins. She couldn't solve this problem with violence and death—only life.

Kari could save them.

She placed a hand on each of the girls, planning to link her life energy to theirs. They would live off her, at least temporarily. But it was dangerous. The only way to harness the power was to kill the host. But she wouldn't need to fully harness hers—just share it. In theory, it should work.

Kari took a deep breath. She could do this. Save a life by any means necessary.

When she extended her aura over the two girls, they glowed a brilliant blue. Time to open the channels of her life energy. Her aura turned green as her energy fused with theirs.

Kari fell backward, hitting the floor. Her body shook and convulsed, her arms violently spasming. She heaved, expelling her stomach's contents. Her vision began to blur as the room around her spun faster and faster. Before long, all that was left was a black empty void.

She was falling. Beneath her, the void whirled as it sucked her into nothingness. Lights spun and sprang from the hidden wells deep beneath the emptiness, launching to furiously circle above her like vultures before exploding in a flash.

The void reached out, consuming her body. All that was left was her mind—her essential existence. But not even that was off-limits. The darkness bored into her skull, her thoughts pouring into the vast emptiness surrounding her. She tried to cry out at the excruciating pain, but she couldn't make a sound without mouth or voice.

She knew her body was here with her, but she couldn't find it, couldn't think, couldn't breathe. The pain seeped into her mind as it attempted to purge all that she was.

She fell faster. Flames appeared as if from nowhere, licking at where her face should have been. She was indeed in hell. Oh, how she longed for the coldness of heaven, for the sky above. The fire spread across her imaginary body, destroying the last traces of her existence. Heat seeped into her mind, threatening to consume her very essence. Part of her wanted them to take her—to end it finally. But she couldn't allow it. It was more than her life at stake.

An eternity passed before everything went silent. The room faded back into reality. Or maybe she'd disappeared. At this point, there was simply no telling. But the chamber wasn't the way she remembered it. The now-white walls bled red as the ceiling melted into the black floor. Three guerrilla-shaped shadows stood a few feet away. They seemed to watch her as she laid on the floor. Two serpent-like creatures writhed their way along the reforming bed.

Kari screamed as loud as she could, but nothing escaped her throat. Escape—she had to escape! Head spinning, she watched as the two serpents slowly morphed back into the two girls.

Ilyia, Artemis, and Chaska hovered above her.

"I was worried about you, so we came looking," Artemis said.

"Kari, are you all right?" Chaska asked in concern. "We tried to heal you, but without Vipin, healing someone who had nearly exhausted their life energy was difficult."

"I'm okay," Kari said. She scanned the girls. Both were sitting up, watching her, too. They were alive. Kari shivered. She was drenched in sweat. Her pants felt as if she had been dunked underwater. She placed her hands on the wet patch, then brought it to her nose. She had urinated on herself. "Some hero I am."

"What are you talking about?" Artemis asked, kneeling beside her. "I have never seen such bravery."

Ilyia crouched on Kari's other side. "What you did was very foolish and dangerous, but two people are alive because of you."

It had been a trap. The Torredins had expected Kari. They wanted her dead, and it didn't matter who they hurt to achieve their goals. Ryder was a Torredin. He would pay for this.

CHAPTER TWELVE

"Good job, little one, on routing out the remaining Torredins. They might have escaped, but at least they are no longer in Anuatu," Artemis said, wrapping her arm around Kari's shoulders.

She blushed. It didn't feel like a job well done. If she had indeed succeeded, the Torredins would be facing justice for their crimes during the genocide.

Artemis examined her. "Looks like you need a drink." Releasing her, she held out her hand for Kari to take.

"I'd rather have tea," Kari replied, taking Artemis's offered palm.

"What you don't drink?" Artemis led the way down the road.

"I never gained a taste for alcohol." Kari stumbled behind Artemis as the woman half-dragged her down the road toward a tavern.

"That's all right." A wicked grin flashed on Artemis's masked face. "Come on. I have a drink I'm sure you'll enjoy."

Kari's heart nearly beat out of her chest at Artemis's mischievous grin, but she did not resist being led inside. Chaska already waited, waving them over to her table.

"Rum for me and a Green Apple Thunder for the Archon," Artemis called to the barkeep, who nodded in reply.

"Do you think they have tea?" Kari nervously asked.

"Try this before you switch to your boring tea," Artemis said as the barkeep placed a mug of rum and a bottle of clear liquid on the table.

Kari's hand hovered near the bottle as she glared at the liquid.

"Stop being a child and drink it," Artemis scolded.

Kari blushed and seized the drink, placing it against her lips. She took a sip, expecting the cool liquid to burn the back of her throat, but it didn't. It tasted like sweet candy, with none of the ill effects of alcohol.

"This is good," Kari smiled. She had anticipated Artemis to haze her by giving her the most potent drink imaginable. "Doesn't taste like alcohol at all."

"That's because it doesn't have much in it." Artemis winked. "Perfect for a little one like you."

Kari scoffed, but she didn't relinquish her drink. She took another sip, trying to ignore Artemis.

"We wanted to see how you were holding up after your ordeal," Chaska explained. Kari mulled it over. Where to begin?

"Hey," a tall blond man suddenly shouted. He stood atop his chair, then continued. "Hey, everybody. Listen up. I just wanted to make an announcement. I appear to have misplaced my money, but that shouldn't stop us from having a good time. You see, I once wrestled a bear to submission, saving this town from an almost-certain mauling. So, I think everyone should just buy me a drink."

"Looks like the drunks have come out early," Artemis said, rolling her eyes.

"Sit down, you drunk bastard," the barkeep called.

The man grumbled before dropping into his chair.

Kari shifted her gaze to the table and her half-empty bottle. "Do people who drink always behave this way?"

"I find those who drink like that tend to be trying to forget." Chaska eyed the man. She shook her, returning her attention to Kari and Artemis.

"It's desperation," Artemis added.

"Back to my question," Chaska said, taking a dainty sip from her mug.

Kari shook her head. "I can't bring myself to attend the executions. I could condemn the Torredins, but I can't watch the life leave their eyes. I have killed before, but never with words. It's unsettling."

"That's what I was afraid of," Chaska said. "You have a sensitive heart."

"Don't waste your tears on those barbarians. Torredins don't have any humanity." Artemis slammed her empty mug down on the wooden table.

"They are the enemy, but are we to feel no remorse over the loss of life?" Kari raised her eyebrows.

"Ina's naivety is getting to you," Artemis said, lounging in her chair.

"I guarantee the death you gave them was merciful compared to what they did to us." Chaska folded her hands. "Stay with us long enough, and you'll begin to understand the cruelty they inflicted on our sisters."

Kari fiddled with her now-empty bottle. Chaska was right. At least Kari thought so. She shook her head. Still, killing the enemy just because they were the enemy didn't seem right. Kari shook away the thoughts with a sigh.

"Excuse me," she said, rising. "I'm going to see about another drink."

When Kari approached the barkeep, he smiled.

"My lady, care for a repeat?"

Kari shook her head. "Do you have any tea?" Tea was refreshing, and it helped her think clearly. She hated to admit it, but Artemis was right. Even after one drink, her head felt slightly fuzzy.

"Not in here, my lady."

Kari sighed. "A repeat is fine." So long as she didn't turn out like that drunk man, she supposed one more wouldn't hurt.

"While you're buying, care to buy me a drink?" the drunk asked, approaching Kari. She gritted her teeth. It was like a curse—think about him... and he showed up.

"I think you've had enough," Kari said flatly.

"Oh, don't be like that." The man eyed her up and down. "Say, you're awfully pretty. My name is Falcon. What's yours?"

"Are you telling me you don't recognize the Archon?" the barkeep interrupted.

Falcon held up his hands in defense. "You're the Archon? I mean, I knew that."

Kari grabbed her new bottle, then turned her back on Falcon. "I must return to my friends."

Falcon darted in front of her, halting her retreat. "What's the rush? We got you a drink. At least tell me something about yourself. Where are you from?"

Chaska stepped between Kari and Falcon. She placed her hand on his shoulder and pushed him out to arm's length. "You should leave before your drunken stupor infects us all."

"Fine, fine," Falcon said, stepping away from Chaska. "You could at least buy me a drink first."

Chaska shot him a look, and he skirted back in fear. "Come on, Kari, ignore this fool."

"Kari, eh?" Falcon said, turning toward the tavern door. "That's a beautiful name. I'll remember it."

Chaska shook her head as Falcon departed the tavern. "Tis no one more foolish than a drunk."

Kari nodded her agreement, then turned to head back toward their table. Chaska caught her arm, pulling her close.

"We haven't had much time to talk, just the two of us," Chaska said. "I fear this may be the only chance I'll have."

"What did you want to talk about?" Kari winced as Chaska's fingers dug into her wrist.

"Let me be blunt," Chaska said, staring intently into Kari's eyes. "What are your intentions?"

"My intentions?" Kari asked, raising an eyebrow.

"I envy your power," Chaska said. "You can do great things, yet you hide behind the façade of a meek girl."

"I don't know what you are talking about," Kari said honestly.

"Fine." Chaska blinked, releasing Kari's arm. "Keep up the charade. I only hope when the Fates show your path, you have the dedication to act."

"I won't let you down," Kari said. What could Chaska mean?

"See to it that you don't," Chaska said.

Kari and Chaska rejoined Artemis, and they finished their drinks. The conversation remained lighthearted. Kari was glad they could finally talk about things outside of their pain. They discussed different applications of magic and how it played an integral part in Shagin life. Mystikos and the future of Shagin, once they were restored on the mainland, was also explored at great length.

"What's your next goal as Archon?" Chaska asked.

"I don't know," Kari responded. "Honestly, I feel a little odd being named Archon. I'm not even a matriarch." She placed a hand on her stomach. "I can never be one."

In Shagin society, only women who had undergone pilgrimage and returned as mothers could be named matriarchs. Although it was customary for only grand matriarchs who had experienced multiple pilgrimages and given birth to more than one child to be given the honor. It was thought that only matriarchs who had faced the struggles of pilgrimage to ensure Shagin's continued survival were dedicated enough to be Archons and lead the people.

Kari could never be a mother. She had been upset when she thought Jiaorong took away her choice. Relieved when she'd discovered she wasn't pregnant, though sad for having lost the ability to choose. Now guilt and shame mixed with those emotions. It was yet another choice taken away from her by force.

As a child on Mystikos, she'd never thought she would see the day when she would be able to go on pilgrimage herself. It was forbidden for any Shagin to leave the island. It didn't change the fact she'd often fantasized about a future where she could hold her little one in her arms, one that would never come.

She'd played with a baby doll when she was a child. It was a little rag doll made from scraps of cloth that she used to dress up and care for. She'd sung lullabies to her baby, the same way her mother would sing to her. Something she would never get the opportunity to do for real.

Sighing, Chaska placed her hand on Kari's. "You might not have a little one to call your own, but you will be the mother of a new age. That is what matters."

Kari smiled. "Thank you." It was a sweet sentiment.

Screams erupted from outside the tavern, permeating through the wooden walls. The barkeep dropped the bottle he held and ran from the bar, slamming the door shut behind him. Kari glanced at Artemis and Chaska as they were left alone in the tavern.

"What's going on?" Kari asked.

"Only one way to find out," Artemis said, jumping to her feet. "Come on!"

Heat radiated from the door, and the trio darted out into the street. Smoke and flames blazed from the nearby buildings. Falcon stood near the water, his blond hair billowing in the haze. Draped in a black cloak over black armor, he had a longsword strapped to his side.

"I was beginning to think you would never come out of there," he said, his grin malicious. He held up a copper medallion etched with circular blue markings. "I am Falcon, and this medallion is who I am."

Kari recognized it. It was the same symbol as the Torredins—the symbol of the Guardian. Kari balled her fists. "What is the meaning of this?"

"I'm on official business, sent by the Guardian himself. Once it is complete, I'll be on my way," Falcon said, gripping his pendant.

"You might be talking, but you haven't said anything of meaning yet," Artemis snarled. She raised her fists, ready to fight.

Falcon licked his lips. "I think that might be fun, testing my skill against yours."

This wasn't good. The man was looking for a fight. Even with three of them, he acted like he was the one in control.

"Did you set these fires?" Chaska demanded.

Falcon cut his eyes toward her, his smile fading. "Not personally, though it was my idea."

"Why?" Kari asked.

Falcon ignored the question. "You are the fugitive from Xiang—Kari. Is that right?"

Kari's heart skipped. "I am."

"I want you to know I have no personal feelings of hatred to you or your companions. Nor do I care about what happened here. I'm simply here to do a job and get paid. And while you think you have the advantage with your numbers, standing before you is one opponent you have no hope of defeating. What I would like is for you to come with me willingly. We'll leave with no fuss. And I promise no harm will come to you while in my custody. Or if you cannot come peacefully, we'll be forced to make a mess."

Kari had no intention of going with him, which meant they'd fight. She had defeated Jiaorong, and her powers had only grown since then. This man was delusional if he thought it would be easy.

"I'm not going. Go back to your guardian. Inform him that, one day, he'll have to answer for his crimes."

Falcon twirled the medallion in his fingers. "And the negotiations break down."

Chaska drew her sword. Falcon held out a hand, grin flashing. He flicked the medallion up and then snatched it out of the air, pocketing it.

"I heard about how you helped that kid the other day. It moved me deeply. But it got me thinking about children in general. So, I took that boy and a few others I could grab, and I had them imprisoned somewhere in this burning town. Now, you three are welcome to fight me and let those children burn to death, or you two can leave Kari and me to ourselves."

"You must think we're fools," Artemis said, her knuckles clenched until they were bloodless.

"I think you three are formidable foes. But I hope you're foolish ones. So... what's it going to be? A town, and everyone in it, is currently being reduced to ash. Missing children need to be rescued."

"Go." Kari glared at Falcon. What kind of fiend would burn an entire town to get to one person while going so far as to threaten children? The act defined cruelty and barbarism, which fit the guardian and his followers. She would make him pay. "Find the kids and save them. I can handle him."

"I'm not leaving you, little one," Artemis protested.

"You've seen my power, so you know what I can do. You have to save as many people as you can," Kari insisted.

"Artemis," Chaska pleaded, grabbing hold of the stubborn warrior's hand. "We have no choice but to leave Kari. Let her act on her power."

"Fine, but we'll be back. Don't die," Artemis ordered. She and Chaska ran into the burning town, leaving Kari alone with Falcon.

"How magnanimous of you," Falcon said, rolling his eyes.

"People are going to die," Kari shouted. "Do you think this is some sort of game?"

"People die every day," Falcon said dismissively. "And for someone so concerned about innocents dying, you sure left a fine mess in Xiang."

"What do you mean?"

"You don't know? After you usurped the throne, then abandoned it, you left a power vacuum. Xiang has fallen into multiple factions. It is currently tearing itself apart in a civil war. Innocent people are dying because of you."

"That can't be." Frozen, Kari stared at her hands. She was supposed to make it better. What had happened? How had she failed?

"It's true," Falcon said, stretching his arms back behind him. "Now, I'm here to capture you so you can face justice for the crimes that *you* committed."

Kari wiped away the tears forming in her eyes. "I told you... I'm not going. Draw your weapon." She swung her arm, and her light whip materialized. Poised to strike, she held it aloft.

Falcon laughed. "I won't be fighting you. Athena!"

The wall of the nearest building erupted into fragments, and a woman leaped out. Kari's heart nearly stopped. That leap was impossible. The woman had blonde hair, like Falcon, but she was garbed in glittery silver armor, a shield in one hand and a massive two-handed claymore sword in the other.

Kari dove out of the way of the claymore. The massive blade slammed into the ground, leaving a crater in its wake. She rolled onto her feet and swung her whip wildly at Athena, who pushed it away with her shield.

Damn. This had been Falcon's plan all along. He now had the upper hand, so why wasn't he attacking, too?

She lashed out with her whip. Athena blocked the attack with her shield, charging forward. Kari jumped back as Athena swung her blade at her head. It missed with only inches to spare. Kari gritted her teeth.

Athena wielded her heavy sword with the speed of a one-handed sword. How was she so strong?

Kari spun her whip around and lashed out. Athena blocked the attack, but Kari didn't let up. She struck again and again, but Athena blocked each blow with her shield.

"Athena," Falcon called. "Notice the way she fights. She's trying to keep you at a distance. Those wide swings of hers won't do much good up close. I don't think she has had much practice with that whip. If you keep close, she'll falter."

Kari squinted, hardening her jaw. Athena merely stared, emotionless.

But then she raised her shield, holding her sword, ready to strike.

This was no good. As long as Athena had that shield, she would have the advantage.

Kari swung her whip. Athena pushed Kari's weapon aside, darting forward. Kari whirled her arm out to slash at Athena, but her shield cut off the attack before it could hit its mark.

Athena thrust her claymore in an arc, too close for Kari to parry. She focused her spirit energy, transforming her whip into a shield. The woman's heavy weapon struck the construct, shattering it.

Kari screamed as the blade hit her. The force of the impact lifted her off her feet, sending her spiraling backward. She struck the ground, tumbling until she managed to stop herself.

Waves of pain pulsed through her body. She placed a hand on her stomach where the sword had struck. Warm blood oozed between her fingers. The wound wasn't life-threatening. Her spirit aura had seen to that, but she couldn't take another blow of that magnitude.

Kari struggled to her feet. Her arms shook as she lifted herself off the ground.

"She has a spirit aura," Falcon said. "But even auras aren't invincible. Enough strikes, enough force, and she'll fall."

Who were these people? This was unreal. How could such strong fighters serve the Guardian? With Athena's power and his knowledge of spirit energy, she no longer felt as confident.

"Give up before you die," Athena threatened, raising her sword. "You're outmatched."

"Fuck you!" Ronin appeared as if from nowhere, leaping at Athena.

His first kodachi forced Athena to jump back while deflecting the blade with her sword. Ronin's arm moved so fast it seemed to blur as he aimed the other curved sword, pointing the blade at Athena's neck. His quickness meant she didn't have time to raise her shield.

The clang of metal echoed amongst the roaring flames. Falcon had joined the fray. His longsword blocked Ronin's much shorter weapon.

"You must be the Kitsuno Kai." Falcon smirked.

Ronin responded with a roar. He rushed his opponent with a fury of slashes. The onslaught forced Falcon backward, but he fended off each attack. Falcon's eyes narrowed as Ronin's blade flashed toward his head.

Falcon stepped forward, evading the attack, then gut-punched Ronin with the pommel of his sword. Ronin hunched forward on impact. Falcon lifted his sword and brought it around Ronin, striking him in the back.

Ronin screamed as blood sprayed into the air. He crumpled, his blood staining the grass.

"Disappointing," Falcon mocked. "I expected more from a blue wolf."

Enraged, Kari reformed her whip and charged Falcon. Athena intercepted, bashing Kari with her shield and sending her crashing down alongside her brother.

"Ronin," Kari muttered as pain raced through her body. She reached out, grasping at Ronin.

Groaning, Ronin lifted his head. Kari breathed a sigh of relief. He was alive.

"Kari," Ilyia called, sprinting toward the group with Aura.

Falcon sighed. "They just keep coming."

Ilyia held up a hand. A golden glow erupted from her palm, forming the Golden Rod. "You'll regret coming here."

Ilyia charged Falcon. She struck out, but he jumped back from her first swing. She slashed downward at his head, but he sidestepped. Breathing hard, Ilyia spun around, swinging her staff with all of her might. Seeming almost bored, Falcon raised his sword to block the attack.

An earth-shattering boom erupted from the clash. The staff shattered the sword into thousands of fragments, sending Falcon spinning through the air. He hit the dirt, but rolled right to his feet.

"An enchanted weapon?" Falcon said. "I should've known."

Ilyia leaped up, then swung her weapon downward. Jumping out of the way, he reached under his cloak and drew a curved dagger.

He ran at Ilyia. Grabbing her, he wrapped his free arm around her and stabbed her in the back of the neck. She cried out as he continued to slash into her tender skin.

Aura rushed the pair, staff at the ready. Falcon released Ilyia, darting backward. He seemed rattled, holding tight his spotless dagger which failed to pierce through Ilyia's aura.

"Athena, we're leaving. The tides have shifted. We're not winning this fight."

"Do you think we will just let you leave like that?" Ilyia huffed, tensed to attack.

"Think it through. A burning town. Trapped kids about to die. And only two people searching for them. Let us go, and save the kids. Pursue us, and they die. If they do, that's on you."

Falcon and Athena didn't wait for a response. They turned tail, dashing through the streets of the burning town.

"Cowards!" Ilyia yelled.

Kari returned to her feet, then limped over to Ronin. Much like her own, his wound wasn't as bad as it seemed. His spirit energy, while not as strong as hers, had saved his life.

"I'm fine," Ronin grumbled as Kari helped him up.

"Ilyia, the children," Kari said, heart in her throat.

"I know. We'll find them."

Ilyia bandaged Kari and Ronin as Aura joined the search for the missing children. The silver knights arrived, helping the townspeople put out the fire.

"Who were those two?" Kari asked.

"That man said his name was Falcon, right?" Ronin asked, rubbing his wound. "Falcon the Outlaw? Leader of the Thunder Five?"

"What is the Thunder Five?" Kari asked.

"A group of bounty hunters—or more like paid killers—under the Guardian's employ. They've garnered quite the reputation in the underworld." Ronin banged one fist on top of the other. "Damn it. I've never lost a fight until recently. It was one thing for Jiaorong to defeat me, but now to have this honor-less killer best me?"

"Are you implying Jiaorong was honorable?" Rage flashed in Kari. "Do you know what he did to me?"

"Didn't you kill him? I would say you are even."

"What?" Kari balled her fists. How *dare* he!

"This Falcon was toying with us. Did you see it? He wielded his sword with his left hand, even though he was righthanded."

"How could you tell?"

"He drew his dagger with his right hand. When he was in trouble, that's what he fell back on. How do you not notice these things?"

"We searched everywhere for the missing kids," Artemis said, sitting next to Kari. "There was no sign of them. We did find the boy. He was with a group of townsfolk who had fled into the forest. Said he was never abducted."

"Falcon lied to us?"

"See, no honor," Ronin said.

Kari shot him a sideways look.

Artemis placed her hands behind her head. "While we were drinking, they warned the townspeople of their plan to destroy their homes. A band of warriors forced the townspeople to flee into the forest. They were gone by the time we found them."

"This is a disaster." Ilyia walked over to the group, shoulders hunched "Kari, do you see the cruelty of the Guardian? It's a taste of what he is capable of, him and his ilk."

"How many people died?" Kari asked.

"Hard to say." Ilyia rubbed her hand in her hair. "In the attack, maybe not many, but it doesn't matter. Look at this place."

Smoke and ash surrounded them. Most buildings had collapsed, and the few that hadn't looked damaged beyond repair.

"These people are without homes, food, resources. They won't last long like this." Ilyia kicked the ground, sending soot flying in the air. "What happened?"

"I think this is my fault. The Guardian is after me," Kari started, but Artemis placed a hand on her shoulder.

"No, little one," she said. "If the Guardian knew of our existence, he would be after all of us."

Ilyia sighed. "What's done is done. Let's focus on what we do now."

"How far is Koruzeru from here?" Kari asked.

"Just a few days," Artemis said. "Why do you ask?"

"These people need a home, so we give them one."

Ilyia smiled. "I like it. Artemis, round up the Furies. Try to convince as many of these people to follow us to Koruzeru as you can. We won't make them come, but we do offer safe passage and refuge."

"Yes, Miss."

CHAPTER THIRTEEN

Kari watched from atop of the wooded hill as the caravan from Anuatu arrived in Koruzeru. It would be difficult to find all the homeless safe shelters, but at least it gave them extra hands to rebuild.

"It's a shame what happened to Anuatu," Ronin said, sitting next to Kari underneath a shade tree. Rays of light shone through the leaves and branches.

"At least we saved as many as we could," Kari said. The crowd marched through the city gates. Most were on foot, carrying what little belongings they had left from the fire. "And we can give them a new home here in Koruzeru."

"Now, will you finally admit I was right, and this entire crusade was nothing but a foolish delusion?" he asked, folding his arms across his chest. Rage flashed inside her at his words.

"How can you say that?" Kari asked. If anything, it only proved the Furies were right. The Guardian and his Torredins were evil that must be resisted against. If they continued, if they went unchecked, more people would suffer and die under their tyranny.

"You have eyes, but you fail to see. You brought the destruction on yourself." Ronin rolled his eyes, shaking his head.

"I can't believe you are so full of yourself that you would believe I caused what happened." Could he not see she had fought this with all of her might?

"I guess they haven't told you, have they?" Ronin asked.

"Told me what?" Kari asked, stomach sinking.

Ronin reared his head back, bellowing in laughter. "The prisoners, the people you sentenced to death, they escaped in the fire. I wouldn't be surprised if Falcon freed them first, then had them set Anuatu ablaze."

"That can't be." Her rage turned to fear as a wave of anxiety washed over her. Face reddening, her eyes burned as she blinked back the forming tears.

"I guess your new friends don't tell you everything," Ronin said, standing. "You should've listened to me and left before instead of going with those imbeciles."

"Those *imbeciles* are my sisters," Kari yelled, gnashing her teeth.

"And I am your brother," Ronin shouted.

Or so he claimed. No brother would behave like this.

"If you want to stay here, fine, that's your choice. But when you're ready to stop being a fool, you can leave with me."

"I'm staying with my sisters," Kari said, her resolve unwavering

Ronin nodded, licking his lips. "I'm gone. I won't stay here to watch you die. Falcon will return for you. Even if we stop him, the Guardian will just send an army after you."

"Then go," Kari spat venomously. "I will not run and hide."

"See you around." Ronin turned, stalking off without another word. He passed Aura and Ina, who stopped to stare as he stormed by.

"What was that about?" Aura asked.

"Nothing," Kari said, wiping at her cheeks as tears streaked them.

"Didn't sound like nothing," Aura said.

Ina offered her hand. Kari took it, but she didn't know what to say.

"I think he hates me," she finally muttered.

"Oh, Kari," Ina said, hugging her. Something about Ina's embrace just felt right. "He doesn't hate you. Siblings fight. That's all."

Kari shrugged. "What are you two doing out here?"

"We were talking about the barrier. I want to understand your goals better since I know how much this means to you," Ina said.

Kari's heart lifted. Ina was trying to understand. She had finally seen what Kari did.

"I just don't understand why you went through all that trouble for a bag of sand?"

"I told you. It's not sand," Aura corrected. "It's dalium."

"You say that like I should know what it is," Ina said, placing her hands on her hips.

"Dalium contains natural magical properties," Kari explained. "It's used to create enchantments and power spells."

"I thought your spirit energy did that," Ina said.

"Spirit energy is different." Kari smiled. It had been such a long time since she was able to talk about magic so openly. Even with Ina and Suying, she'd never gone into detail for fear someone might overhear. Magic wasn't forbidden in Xiang, but most of the world still feared it. "Everyone has spirit energy. With the right training, anyone can learn to harness it to form an aura. Then there are cantrips like my plant magic—special abilities unique to certain people. Spirit energy powers cantrips. But spellcraft is completely different.

"Spellcraft is ritual-based, and it's the most powerful form of magic. Spirit energy acts as the catalyst and controls the spell, but dalium powers it."

"Is that what we're doing? A spell?" Ina asked.

"Not quite," Aura said. "Spells are powerful, but only provide a temporary effect. And since dalium doesn't naturally exist within our reality, we want something a little more permanent."

"An enchantment?" Kari asked, her ear perking up.

"Exactly," Aura said, smiling. She traced patterns in the area. "I'll weave the dalium into an object with my energy."

"Jiaorong," Ina said. "His sword was enchanted."

"That bastard," Aura said. "That probably belonged to Shagin. Every Fury carries an enchanted weapon. During the war, we had tried to lay siege to Valceem, but we couldn't break through the wall. I think he was a captain then, but he led several guerrilla-style battles against us. Even fought off a Fury. I'm impressed, little one. He had quite the reputation for being a good fighter."

"What are we enchanting?" Kari asked, turning the subject away from Jiaorong.

"The array." Aura's eyes widened in delight.

"You can't," Kari protested. How could they be so reckless? "The array created the Seed and caused the Cataclysm. Countless people could die."

"You worry too much," Aura replied, waving off her concern. "We've studied the array. It didn't create the Seed. The array simply harnesses energy. That energy was used to form the Seed. We have to modify it to harness its power to create our barrier. Hence the dalium."

Kari breathed a sigh of relief. So they did understand.

"Do you want to see it?" Aura asked, holding up the bag of dalium.

"See what?" Kari asked.

"Our work," Aura said. "The array. I figured you would want to see it. After all, it was used to create your power."

Kari nodded.

Aura led Kari and Ina down into the basement of Lasan to a back room. She stopped at a corner, then knelt. Using her finger, she drew the Shagin symbol on the stone bricks. When it glowed yellow, the stone turned translucent.

"We have secret chambers hidden throughout," Aura explained. "With a little spirit energy and the right know-how, they can be unlocked."

They phased through the stone, then descended a ladder.

Kari expected darkness to meet them in the tunnels, but a series of glowstones were positioned at the bottom of the ladder and interspersed along the tunnel walls.

"Impressive, isn't it?" Aura asked. "These tunnels make up the array."

"This is massive," Kari said. As she touched the nearby wall, it glistened with a hint of gold from her touch.

"It's responding to your spirit energy. The walls are infused with dalium, making the array one giant enchantment," Aura explained. "I couldn't even begin to imagine the amount of dalium used to create it or the sheer willpower of the enchanter."

"Where do all these tunnels go?" Kari asked, focusing down the seemingly never-ending tunnels.

"Throughout the city," Aura said. "We don't know the actual design used, but the overall shape is a circle that encompasses all of Koruzeru. Some of the tunnels even extend outward into other cave systems, with some branches stretching for miles beyond the city walls. Though we don't know why. As far as we can tell, the array only impacts Koruzeru."

Aura knelt and poured a line of dalium on the ground, forming it into a spiral shape. The powder glowed as it infused into the ground.

"What are you doing?" Kari knelt beside her.

"The array pulls energy from a source, stores it, and amplifies its effects. The person who created it was a genius," Aura said as she made other circular shapes with the dust. "Our modifications will help us harness the power from the array so we can channel it into the barrier. It's a delicate process. In all honesty, we don't fully understand the array or how it works. We know enough to activate and harness it, but the slightest miscalculation could have dire consequences."

"More dire than its original use?" Kari asked, her brow furrowing.

"Possibly. It was created to pull life force from the area, so we could accidentally trigger the array, extend its range, or just simply break it so it doesn't work."

"The array is evil, just like the Seed." Kari averted her eyes. "It killed nearly half-a-million people to create the realms, not to mention the countless lives lost in the Cataclysm."

"It's not evil, and neither is the Seed." Aura smiled and stood, dusting off her trousers. "They are tools, nothing more. It is how they are used that determines their nature."

"So, how much more dalium is needed before the array can be activated?"

"Hard to say." Aura shook the bag in her hand. "What's left of this should be enough to finish the modifications. After that, we might have some leftover, but I doubt it will be enough to power the barrier we wish to create. We will need a lot more energy."

"I would like to help," Kari said. "If I can find more for you, I will do it."

"Thank you." Smiling, Aura sat the bag down on a nearby workbench. "Vipin and Ilyia are constantly trying to find more sources of dalium. When Shagin fell, our sisters went to great lengths to hide our reserves. We couldn't risk it falling into the wrong hands, because once it's gone, it's gone. Nebura brought dalium over with her, and the supply in our reality is nearly depleted."

Kari left Aura's side, wandering around in the dim tunnels. They reminded her of home. Leading up to her trial, she had studied the tunnels of Mystikos, even explored parts—always guided, of course. It was the purpose of the trial to present hardships and self-discovery for Shagin children to reflect on the person they wanted to be—who they saw themselves as. It was how they chose their names.

So much had happened on her trial. The tunnel had collapsed, killing her friend. Kari exhaled, placing her hand on the jagged stone wall. It shimmered at her touch. It was terrific the tunnels had held up for two thousand years. The enchanter must have been extremely powerful and gifted to manage such a feat. Dante the Splendid was more than skilled. He'd split the world into three pocket dimensions, forming the Three Realms. The array was a powerful tool. Scorch marks from its activation were still present on the rocks, as clear as the day they were made.

"Don't wander off too far." Aura and Ina approached her. "I would hate to lose you in this labyrinth."

"Sorry, I was just thinking about home." Kari blushed. She had gotten lost in the tunnels at home, and she'd only found her way through luck. It would be embarrassing for that to happen here.

"It must be hard for you, being torn from your home twice in one lifetime," Aura said.

"I've only ever thought of Mystikos as my home," Kari replied.

"Still, you must have friends you left behind in Xiang," Aura said.

Kari nodded. "There were a few. Though my closest living friends are with me."

"Do you have anyone close?" Aura asked, folding her arms around her chest.

"What do you mean?" Kari asked.

"Anyone special," Aura clarified. "A lover perhaps? I know about what happened with Jiaorong, but did you have anyone you cared for?"

Kari darted her gaze over to Ina before returning her attention to Aura. "No, there was no one."

"What about you?" Aura asked, raising a brow at Ina.

"Not anymore," Ina replied. "I was betrothed, but he was murdered by the former emperor of Xiang, and I was forced to join the harem."

"Jiaorong," Aura said, biting her lip. "He was quite a bastard."

"What about you?" Kari asked.

Aura shook her head. "Never."

"Never?" Ina responded. "Not even a passing relationship?"

"No." Aura's lips tilted on one side. "It is difficult with my powers. I create toxins, whether I want to or not. As a result, all of my bodily fluids are poisonous to some extent. Even touching the sweat on my skin could be fatal."

"I'm sorry, that must be difficult." Kari had long lamented her light powers for their very nature. She could only begin to imagine the frustration and remorse brought on by powers that prohibited physical contact. "I guess not all cantrips are beneficial."

Aura sighed. "Don't feel sorry for me. I don't. I have made peace with my fate for some time."

"What about medicine?" Ina asked. "Surely, there is some sort of medicine or remedy that could neutralize the toxicity?"

"It's magic. I doubt that any nonmagical remedy could help," Aura said.

"My father was a doctor in Xiang," Ina added. "He used to say everything was possible with enough knowledge."

"He sounds idealistic." Aura clicked her tongue, turning her head. "The real world doesn't work quite so nicely."

"He devoted himself to the study of medicine, and he was greatly respected in our community," Ina clarified.

"What happened to him?" Kari asked. Ina never spoke about her father. She would only occasionally talk about her sister or betrothed.

"What makes you think something happened?" Ina asked.

"You've just never mentioned him is all," Kari responded.

"He got sick. His body shut down, and he perished," Ina said, her face falling. "My mother tried to keep his practice running, but it was no use. My sister, Emiko, volunteered for the harem to support us. She rose in rank to the status of Head Matron, but the same disease that took my father claimed her as well."

"Then you should know all too well that not everything can be solved with solvents," Aura said. "Magic is the best source of knowledge."

Ina smiled. "I aim to prove you wrong."

"Do you mind if I wander around on my own?" Kari asked.

"I don't know," Aura said. "You might get lost."

"My trial took place in the tunnels of Mystikos," Kari explained. Hopefully, she wouldn't get lost as she had then. Of course, she wasn't going to tell Aura that. "I won't go far. This was where the Seed was made, so I want to know more about it."

Aura nodded. "Okay, but take a glowstone with you."

Kari grabbed one of the stones, not that she needed it, and headed into the dark. Her powers could illuminate far more than the glowstone could. Still, it was best to relieve Aura of her misgivings and comply.

Kari wandered through the tunnels. The walls glistened as she passed, responding to her energy. She'd never seen anything like it before. Even without focusing her energy into an aura, the walls still reacted to her. They were that sensitive to magic as she passed.

She stopped, examining a stick poking out from the bottom of a wall. How had that gotten there? There were no other signs of vegetation. No twigs or leaves to be seen. There were wooden beams here and there, supporting the walls and ceiling, but nothing to justify a small stick like this.

She bent to get a closer look, but it was too dark to see. Holding out her hand, she willed a brilliant flash of light from her fingertips. Forming the light into a ball, she allowed it to float above her head, illuminating the tunnel.

Kari gasped, placing her hand over her mouth. It wasn't a stick. It was a bone—someone's forearm jutting out from the stone wall. The fingers were outstretched on the ground. How had it gotten here?

Kari pulled on the bone, and more of it phased through the stone wall.

Who was this? How had they died?

Kari placed her index finger onto the wall. Her finger tingled as she drew the Shagin symbol. Like before, it glowed yellow, and the solid wall became translucent.

Kari closed her eyes, taking a deep breath as she stepped through to the other side.

A scream pierced her lips, echoing in the chamber. Bodies piled upon bodies, decayed to the bone, lay strewn about in the hall. The one belonging to the arm had a spear jabbed through her rib cage. Skeletons were heaped on top of each other, some appearing no larger than children, some even small enough to be toddlers and babies.

Tears streamed down Kari's face. Her only thought was *why*.

Aura and Ina phased through the wall behind her.

"By the gods," Ina muttered, turning her head away. She covered her mouth as if she were about to vomit.

"Come on, Kari," Aura said, reaching out to her. "You don't need to see this."

"What kind of barbarian could do this?" Kari asked, burying her face in Aura's covered shoulder.

"Now you've seen the horror of the Purge firsthand," Aura said. She turned back to the wall, then quickly drew the Shagin symbol. "It is a hard sight, one I wish you didn't have to see. We found other mass graves like this. Evidently, we missed one."

Aura helped them back through the wall, leading them out of the tunnels.

"I'm sorry you had to find that," she said, escorting them to the inn. "I'll let the others know so that we can give our sisters a proper burial."

"That'll be nice," Kari said. She still couldn't get the sight out of her mind, nor the stale smell from her nostrils.

She wanted to help them with the burial, but she didn't want to experience that again. The sight of death was too much to take. At the very least, she could serenade their fallen sisters once a proper burial site was ready. She would compose a song for them to take to the Fates.

Kari took a bath in an attempt to remove any lingering smells from her skin, then returned to her room. It would be night soon, and she was ready to sleep after the day she'd had. Already curled in bed, Ina read a book on medicinal herbs Aura had found her. She was serious about trying to find a cure. Kari was glad her friend had finally found something to focus on in Shagin. Ina was a brilliant young woman, and if she were studying to help Aura, perhaps she would be willing to stay in Shagin indefinitely. Kari liked the thought of that.

Kari took off her dress, then changed into a loose-fitting nightgown as she climbed into bed next to Ina. She didn't have time to get comfortable before a couple of knocks on the door caught her attention.

"Hey, little one," Artemis called. "Open up."

Kari opened the door. Artemis laughed upon seeing her. "The sun's still up. What—is this your bedtime?"

"What are you doing here?" Kari asked, rolling her eyes.

"Put your clothes back on. Ilyia wants to see you," she said.

"What about?" Kari asked, arching her eyebrow.

"It's supposed to be a surprise, so just act like I didn't tell you," Artemis said, winking. "She wants to make you a Fury."

"Me a Fury?" Kari asked, stunned.

"That's exactly how you should act when she tells you," Artemis laughed. "You no longer have a town to be Archon over; we might as well begin rebuilding the Furies. After what you've been through the past few days, she thinks you're ready."

"I understand," Kari said. "Give me a moment to get dressed."

Once she had changed back into her clothes, she followed Artemis into the Temple of Lasan. Ilyia and the other Furies sat in the pews near the front altar.

"I would like to make it official," Ilyia said, bouncing from the pew. "I want you to join us. To join the Furies."

Kari never thought of herself as a warrior. She still didn't, but this group of women battled to make the world a better place. At least, that was their intention. The people she had killed still haunted her dreams. She could see all of their faces. The thought of their futures being ended by her hand, all of that possibility, it was an overwhelming burden. How could a better future be forged if it meant ending the destinies of others?

Still, she agreed with their end goal. The reign of the Guardian had seen murder and genocide, and it had to be opposed. The first Guardian, the Immortal Warrior, had conquered the Three Realms through force. He had declared himself the supreme master of the three worlds. In a time of chaos, he'd risen and established stability to the realms, but he'd maintained it by force and domination.

It seemed slightly ironic Vipin and the Furies were determined to forge this new world through force, too.

Was this right?

Kari wasn't sure. The question raced through her mind. She understood their anger and passion. Their people had been hunted down and murdered by the Guardian and his armies. Kari agreed the evil of the Guardian had to be opposed, but were they going about it in the right way?

"I'm unsure." Kari dropped her gaze to the floor, unable to look Ilyia in the face.

"What is there to be unsure about?" Ilyia asked. She reached out, then tilted Kari's head up until their eyes met. "Our people deserve justice. Do you not want to see justice prevail? If we don't act, these atrocities will repeat. We have a moral responsibility to prevent that from happening."

Chaska held up a hand to stop Ilyia. "I understand. You are young, and you have a gentle heart. Tis the violence and the killing, yes?"

Kari nodded.

"I can relate to that," Chaska said, briskly rubbing her hands together. "When I first started fighting, the thought of killing made me sick. The first time I took a life, I couldn't sleep for weeks. I was told that I would get used to it after a while, and I did. But every life is precious. Each one we take is a monumental decision made in a split second. But we fight to protect. We don't do it because we want to, or because we enjoy it, but to keep others safe."

"Exactly," Aura added. "We sacrifice our innocence to protect the sanctity of others."

"Sacrifice our innocence to protect others," Kari repeated. "I think I understand. When I fought the Tian brothers, I did terrible things. I killed people, and I sacrificed my body to protect my friends. I didn't have a choice, but I did it to help, not to harm."

"Then you see why we do what we do?" Artemis asked.

"Yes, I think so." Kari's battles with the Tian had taken a toll on her. She still felt the effects. These women had sacrificed so much to help others. Chaska had lost her child. They'd all surrendered their innocence to become warriors for the greater good. Their sacrifices were noble. If anything, she envied their convictions. She lacked any such certainties about her actions.

"And truthfully…" Ilyia added. "There are only four of us, Kari. We could use your help. You have the power to make a difference."

Kari didn't know if she could willingly give up what little naïveté she had left. However, she realized it was past time for her to grow up and accept her responsibilities to not only her people, but also to the world. "I think I'm ready. I want to join you."

"That is wonderful news," Ilyia cheered, clapping her hands.

"Welcome to the Furies, little one," Artemis said.

Chaska threw her arms around Kari. "Finally, we can bring an end to this chaos. Together."

"Before you can be fully considered a Fury, you must do one thing." Ilyia picked up a wooden box from off the pedestal. She lifted the lid, revealing eight sapphire stones resting in indentions within the fabric-covered inside. "You must choose a memory stone."

"No," Artemis said, her eyes widening in what Kari could only call horror. "It's too soon."

"Yeah, Ilyia." Chaska tsked, placing her hands on the box as if to take it away. "You can't possibly expect Kari to choose one without any preparation. She has already taken a big step simply by joining us."

"I know this is a risk," Ilyia said, pulling free from Chaska. "But if we want Kari to understand our plight, she must live through the nightmare the same as we did. If anything, her sharing her life energy with two people, managing to keep both alive, has proven the strength of her mind, body, and will."

Kari clenched her jaw, nerves starting to swirl. "The stones . . . I would gain the memories of someone who survived the Purge?"

"No, not a survivor," Aura murmured. "Remember, everyone who couldn't flee or wasn't on pilgrimage died. These belong to the fallen."

"It's more than memories," Artemis said, cutting her eyes toward Ilyia. Swallowing nervously, she continued in a haunted, hollow tone that didn't sound like her at all. "You will live through the person's entire existence in an instant. Everything they were, everything they felt, will infiltrate your mind. All of their thoughts, their memories, their experiences—in a single maddening flash, you will drown beneath them all. Their joy, their pain, their death. Their character, their morality; their sins, strengths, and weaknesses; their entire life—and death—will be yours."

Kari would experience mortality. Not just a death, but also the moments that led to it. Not many living souls could say they knew what it felt like to die. How had the others experienced this and still maintained their sanity?

"You don't have to do this," Chaska said. "Tis not a choice to be made lightly. There were six of us to start. Once we used our memory stones, we lost the other two. They couldn't handle it, and they ended up committing suicide."

Fighting and killing weren't choices to be made lightly either. If Kari were going to do that, she needed to know what it was like to go through it—to die. Heart in her throat, she reached out to the box of stones. Her shaking hand stopped just shy of its edges.

"Will it hurt?" It was such a strange question to ask. Of course it would hurt to be violently murdered.

"Yes," Ilyia said coldly.

Kari closed her eyes. The people she'd killed—she needed to know what they'd felt. Was she the monster she feared? Her beliefs and endeavors seemed to be right, but killing was killing no matter what side one claimed. But was she truly a good person? The latter question haunted her the most. The only way to find the answer was to experience the blade from the other end. Without a doubt, she'd know then.

Kari took hold of one of the sapphires, then lifted it from the box. The stone felt weightier than she'd expected. She closed her eyes, but nothing happened.

"You have to activate it first," Aura said.

"What?" Kari asked, peeking from beneath her lashes.

"You activate it with your spirit energy," Ilyia explained. "You have to charge it in much the same way you would spirit charge a weapon. Once you do, the stone will grant you the memories of the fallen."

"Who was this?" Kari asked, examining the blue stone in her hands. Cold dread seized her mind. Could she do this?

"That was Carina, daughter of Sen," Aura said, fixated on the stone Kari held. "Be prepared. None of our sisters died a quick or painless death."

"We're pushing her too soon," Artemis scolded. "Kari is just a child."

"But this is the only way to know." Kari squeezed her eyes closed, clutching the gemstone. In just a moment, it would be over. Kari could survive the mere moment—it was the aftermath of living with the memories and what they might prove about her for the rest of her potentially extremely long life that she wasn't quite so sure she could handle. Trembling all over, she poured her energy into the stone.

A bright blue light emanated from the stone as her aura engulfed it.

So far, so good.

Until it wasn't...

The scream that ripped from her throat didn't even sound human. It felt as if it shredded her vocal cords, but the anguished, broken sound continued to claw its way out.

Hurtling the stone across the room as if it suddenly turned into a hot coal, she convulsed, body jerking wildly out of her control. As if beat by invisible fists, she tripped and stumbled until she crashed to the floor. Grabbing fist-fuls of her hair, she yanked and twisted, pulling out clumps as her limbs seized.

Her screams never stopped, the metallic taste of blood filling her mouth and choking her. The frantic shouting of the Furies barely even penetrated the horror Kari continued to endure.

"Help her."

"Quick, before she hurts herself!"

"Get her somewhere safe."

The world spun around Kari. Nothing made sense. She pounded the stone floor with her fists until they were scraped and bruised. When a hand tugged at her arms, she instinctively shot a blast of light at its owner without realizing it. Unable to stop the horrors trying to unfurl in her mind, she repeatedly slammed her head into the hard floor, not even pain or dizziness able to break her free. Someone tried to restrain her, but she yanked away and bashed her forehead again and again until blood poured down her face, blinding her to the outside world. But not to the one inside her mind. Oh, no...

Violently, she fought against the magical tendrils slithering into and slashing at her brain. They demanded entrance, worming their way into every crevasse, taking her over, assuming ownership. Refusing wasn't an option. Still, she attacked herself, gouging into her skin with jagged fingernails as if she could claw the magic out.

"Stop her, Ilyia!"

"What do we do?"

"This was too soon."

"I know, Artemis! Don't you think I know that now?"

"She's dying."

"No, she's going to end up killing herself."

Kari screamed until pain and darkness were the only parts left of her reality. Her world faded until she became nothing more than a wail piercing the night.

Soon, even that noise dwindled away.

Kari vanished, lost in another person's memories.

CHAPTER FOURTEEN

CARINA, DAUGHTER OF SEN

Memories from the Stone

STRANGE HOW THE ACTIONS of so few can have such a drastic effect on so many. Today, I heard the elders have already sent word of our surrender to the Guardian. His coalition marches closer toward us with each passing day. The nations, which just a few months ago were locked in battle, are now united in their hatred of us. We—*Shagin*—are the scapegoats. Historically, we have always been considered the 'others'. Now, they blame us for the war. Us. We didn't even fight—choosing to stay neutral. Yet, they say we bewitched the other nations into battling each other.

They can't be that stupid, can they?

My hand trembles as I write a letter to my friend, Enki, explaining why she needs to leave Saburta to stay with me in Shurada. If someone intercepts this and reads it, I'm afraid of what will happen. Will they see my fear and apprehension as an insult to the "greatness" of the Immortal Warrior? I am due any day, and I am afraid of what this will mean for my daughter. What will happen to us? Will we lose our sovereignty? Will our elders face their tribunals? Will we be forced to pay retributions for the cost of war?

All I can do is hope. Hope and pray.

I am not a soldier. Not a leader. I am not a priestess. Not the bearer. I am simply a baker. They would have no interest in me or my little one. At least I have that thought to fall back on.

Ten thousand. Ten thousand renegade soldiers defied the elders to fight in the war. And now, those ten thousand have brought the war to the half-a-million people of Shagin. Once again, Shagin will pay for the actions of the foolish few.

The coalition forces have passed through the Latari Forest, and they will meet with the Elders and warriors in Saburta. Apparently, we will lay down arms, then accept whatever repercussions deemed fitting for our "crimes." The idea is laughable. We did nothing, yet here we are with the entire world descending upon us. It is utter madness.

I am fleeing Shurada, heading for Shiimti.

They are slaughtering us.

The stories coming from Saburta are beyond nightmares. It is less than a three day's journey on foot. At any moment, I expect the soldiers to pour over the hill. I don't have any money to travel, and the roads are packed with fleeing women. I tried telling Enki not to take the streets—that they would be easy prey for the coalition—but she would not listen. *I'm sorry, Enki. If I ever see you again, I will tell you I am so deeply sorry.* But I must do what's best for my little one, which is I escape into the wilderness. I can survive long enough to make it to safety. I will survive, and I will bring my child into this world.

***

Drip. Drip. Drip. The maddening metronome of the cave runoff is the only sound I hear. It is a blessing—better the sound of water drops than the screams of the dying. It has been seven days since I left Shurada, and my daughter is already a day old. She is the most beautiful thing I have ever seen.

Her cheeks are squishy and soft, and her tiny hands are so delicate. She is the personification of innocence and perfection. But outside of this cave, there is an endless army that wants her dead.

The soldiers found the group I traveled with as we made our way through the forest. I ran as hard and as fast as I could, and it triggered my contractions. A modern woman is not meant to give birth in a cave.

I could hear my companions die as I fought through the pain, praying to the goddess they would not find me. So far, the Fates have been on my side. I just wonder how long that will be the case.

I love my daughter more than I could ever imagine. But I dread when she's awake. Her soft, gentle cries for essential nourishment and comfort could kill us. Why did she have to be born now? Why now during these times?

A single tear falls from my eyes, landing on my daughter's face. Her skin is warm and moist as I wipe away my joy—turned into grief.

I don't know what madness waits for us outside these cave walls, but the stories I've heard are nothing short of hell. Word reached my former companions that Shiimti is unreachable. The rumors now are that the elders are preparing a last line of defense, the last Shagin resistance at Koruzeru.

It's strange to think we've already been pushed back that far. The capital is on the shore. It will be a long and challenging journey with both a newborn and my body being so sore. I lost a lot of blood during childbirth, and I am uncertain if I can make the journey on my own. But that is my only hope for my daughter and me. The Guardian's army has effectively trapped us here in our own home.

In the past seven days, I have seen forests piled with bodies of all ages. They are mutilated, stripped, and disfigured. I will not allow that to happen to my daughter. I will not let it happen to me. The soldiers are scouring through the forest. If I stay here, we will be found and killed. I will have to wait until there is a break in their ranks before I head farther east to the capital.

I will fight through the pain, the same as I did during childbirth, and I will bring my daughter to safety.

Placing a tender kiss on her forehead, I silently beg, *Please be a good girl for Mommy, and don't make a sound. Our lives depend on it.*

Why? Why did we come here?

Koruzeru has fallen. Chaos and confusion were her undoing. Just a few months ago, the Shagin warriors were the most feared group in the war, now the bulk of our army has been defeated with little effort.

I huddle with my daughter in a cold dark cabin, the charred ruins of what was once considered a charming family home. Holding her tight in my arms, I dare not let her go for a moment. I have seen the bodies of other children lying prostrate in the dirt among the mounds of the dead. Some are no older than my daughter. At least one was cleaved in half.

I can't bring myself to even look at my little one anymore. Every time I do, I see the smile upon her face, and I love her even more. Then I remember the sights I have seen, a road lined with corpse after corpse; the once-clear blue water of the Latari River dyed red; the rows of severed heads neatly lined up on the city walls—not as a warning, but as a sport—and I wish she didn't exist.

Caring for her is a burden I cannot bear.

I love her so much.

She whimpers in my arms. I'm holding her too tightly, but I find it impossible to loosen my hold.

I jump as the door opens. Zayenda enters, then closes it behind her.

"Where have you been?" I ask. "You've been gone far too long. I thought they had finally captured you."

"They almost did, but I gave them the slip." Zayenda smiles reassuringly.

I hold my daughter even closer to my chest. If Zayenda let her arrogance get away from her and they followed her back here, my daughter's life is forfeit.

"Don't worry. I made sure no one followed me." Zayenda walks over, then strokes my baby girl's cheek. "I would never do anything to place this precious one at risk."

We had only known each other for a couple of weeks, but we had already become fast friends. It was the atrocities around us that brought us together, but the sisterhood of Shagin that bound us to each other.

"Hope isn't lost yet," she says. "Shagin from all over the world, anyone on pilgrimage, they've returned."

"Why would they do this?"

"They know there is no chance of fighting or repealing the armies of the world, but some have organized a smuggling network. They have used a series of boats to help those fleeing escape."

"Escape to where?"

"I'm not sure, but there is an underground cavern that runs underneath Lasan. They've used the system of underground rivers and caves to bypass the blockades. The next trip will be in three days. If we can survive until then, we will live."

***

The time has come for us to make our escape. This will be our greatest challenge yet. We have spent the past few weeks living on limited food. With our bellies empty and a newborn with us, we will venture out into the frosty winter air, hiding from those who relentlessly hunt us.

I fear the worst. Those who have been captured by the Guardian's soldiers have been brutalized beyond belief. Rape, rape, and more rape. Shagin are raped or tortured or both. The horrors are never-ending.

If we fail, we will die. I do not fear death at this point. Instead, I fear the cruelty that will befall us before then.

But mostly, I fear never knowing who my daughter will be. I fear she will die without a name, so I have sinned. I have named her Ninti, the lady of life. It might not be who she is, but it is how I know her. She is life among the death that surrounds us.

I wrap Ninti in my cloak, choosing her warmth over mine. If she stays warm, she will hopefully remain quiet.

"Are you ready?" Zayenda asks. She holds a large wooden staff fashioned from a fallen tree branch. It will be our only defense if we are caught. Honestly, I wish it were a small dagger. If caught, I feel the best defense would be a quick death by our own hands rather than the barbarism that would befall us.

We head out into the dark streets. The ruins of the once-beautiful city smolder around us. Our surroundings become more dilapidated with each passing night. It is only a mile from here to the temple, but that mile might as well be a hundred. The soldiers who patrolled the streets are fewer at night, but when the enemy consists of nearly all of the world's nations, fewer is a relative term.

We dart into the bushes next to the road, a ditch filled to the brim with the bodies of our fallen Shagin sisters, and the stench of their decaying flesh assaults my nose. At least the guards are easy to spot. They carry lanterns and torches, making them bright targets in the starless night. We just have to wait for them to pass, then we can continue our way. We'll need to be quick, or we run the risk of being left behind and having to wait for the next trip. There is no telling how long that might be.

The soft cries of Ninti pierce the silent night air. She stirs and paws at me, her little body shivering in the cold.

"What was that?" The soldiers turn in our direction. They know we are here.

Zayenda tugs at my shoulder, motioning to the pile of corpses behind us. Without a sound, she drops to the ground and rolls into the morbid heaps. Holding Ninti close to me, I follow suit.

"I know I heard something over here." The soldier holds his torch over the mounds.

Ninti squirms as she sees the light. She looks around as her tiny mouth opens. Before she can cry, I expose my breast and press her tight against me. Without fuss, she latches on and begins to feed. All that I can do now is hold my breath as the soldiers examine the bodies for any signs of life.

A soldier steps closer to Zayenda. He draws his sword, then squats mere feet away from her.

"Bring that light over here," he demands.

Zayenda closes her eyes, lying perfectly still. I envy her. While my heart races and my body trembles, she appears calm. If they were to look at me, there is no way they wouldn't notice the tiny infant feeding at my side.

The soldier stares intently at the corpses. He's looking right at Zayenda. A smirk appears on his face as he raises his sword. He stabs it into the body next to her, then uses it to prop himself to his feet.

"What a waste of time. It was probably just a rat. Let's go."

Once they are gone, we emerge from our hiding spots. Zayenda glares at me and Ninti, who has fallen back asleep.

"I'm sorry," I start, but she raises a hand in protest.

"It couldn't be helped. The innocence of your little one is bound to bring risks, but it will be worth it when we are safe."

"Thank you for understanding."

Zayenda doesn't respond. Even in the darkness, I can see the whites of her eyes as they widen and stare past me. She doesn't say anything—just walks forward.

The corpse of a woman is propped against a pole. A metal wire runs through her nose, hooking her to the wooden post. Her body has been torn apart, impaled time and time again beyond counting. They used her for sword practice by hooking her like an animal, then stabbing her to death.

"What monsters." I'm not sure if I am speaking or Zayenda.

"We can't stay here. We have to move," Zayenda hisses.

We quickly make our way through the city, but the nightmare never ends. The streets are filled with the atrocities committed over the past few weeks. Blood and body parts line the roads; the stench of death is all around. Shagin lay where they were killed. Some have their organs ripped out, lying beside them, while others are naked, signs of rape and torture evident. Some women have been stripped and bound to chairs or posts to make it easier to rape them repeatedly.

The nature of humanity is to use and abuse each other. Barbarism and brutality are our intrinsic natures. Perhaps it would be better to die than to live in a world where such cruelty not only occurs in such droves, but is also allowed and ordered by the so-called guardian of humanity.

Zayenda opens the door to what was once a tavern. My heart nearly jumps out of my chest at the sight of an entire squad of soldiers. They stare at us. This is it—we've come to our doom. Tears begin to form in my eyes. My daughter will die here. I will die here.

"Well, come in and shut the door," a young captain demands. "You're running behind. The boats have already begun to depart."

My strength departs me as I drop to my knees. "You're going to help us?"

"Yeah," the captain replies. "We're not all evil. Some of us have hearts."

Tears stream down my face as I begin to sob uncontrollably. "Thank you."

"Have many others made it tonight?" Zayenda asks.

"Quite a few, yes." The captain reaches down to help me to my feet. "There isn't time to waste. The voyage is treacherous and long. Escort them down."

One of the men opens a trap door, then begins to lead us into the cavern.

The front door to the tavern crashes down. Soldiers march inside. We've been found.

"Run," the captain yells. "We'll hold them off!"

We sprint down the dark tunnels faster than I knew my legs could go. It will be only a matter of minutes before the soldiers catch up. There is no way the small group of men can hold back the sheer number of soldiers.

We finally reach the underground docks. Twenty or so women stand around a singular boat full of passengers.

"We'll come back tomorrow," the woman helming the boat says. "Our other boats didn't make the journey here, but we'll return. Just wait patiently. We'll dock on the other side, then come straight back for the rest of you."

"That won't be an option," the man who led us down here says. "The enemy is coming. We're compromised."

Panic and fear quickly descend upon the group.

"What are we going to do?"

"You have to take us with you!"

"Fill up the boat!"

"We're going to die!"

The helmswoman signals for the boat to take off as other women start trying to force their way into the small vessel. She begins knocking them back into the water. "The boat can't take the weight. I'm sorry."

"At least let us die with some dignity." A warrior jumps up, then slams her legs into the ground. Rocks and stone race up to her arms and engulfs them, magically forming tentacles from the rubble. "We'll kill as many of those bastards as we can to buy you time."

Zayenda backs against a wall, her mouth agape at the realization we're trapped. This is it—this will be our deaths. I stare down at Ninti. Her eyes are open. She blinks at me, a soft smile forming on her face.

I will not let this be the end.

Holding Ninti above my head, I begin pushing my way through the crowd. They shove back and nearly knock me off my feet, but I ram even harder. One woman grabs my shoulder and tries to pull me back, but I elbow her in the lip and break her hold. Without thinking, I finally tear through the crowd and launch myself into the water.

Air is instantly knocked from my lungs as I submerge into the icy water up to my chest. I hold Ninti as high as I can as I hurry after the fleeing boat.

"Please wait," I call. "Help me!"

The helmswoman doesn't even look back. "I can't. I'm sorry. There's no room."

"Just take her. Please," I cry out in desperation.

The helmswoman turns her head, wide-eyed. She reaches out, and I hand her Ninti.

"Thank you," I sob.

The helmswoman stays silent. She stares at Ninti before pressing her to her chest. She looks back at me as tears begin to slip down her face.

"Her name is Ninti. Please take care of her."

The helmswoman nods in understanding. "She'll have a good life. I promise you."

I watch as Ninti and the boat fade into darkness. She's gone. I'll never see her again, but her memory will live on in my mind. I can die peacefully with the knowledge that my daughter, my little one, will grow to reach adulthood. I just wish I could see it.

***

I survived the night, though I'm not sure how. The soldiers grabbed me from the water, but it's hazy. What I do remember is the beating that followed, along with the sight of the young captain who bravely helped us. He was still alive when they lead us out of the cavern. They made us watch as they peeled his flesh off with broken pieces of tile. I can still hear his screams when I close my eyes.

I wrap my arms around my chest as I try to stay warm. I thought for sure I would die from the cold. Now I must endure this. They've repurposed the Temple of Lasan into a prison. Our most sacred place is where they plan to kill us.

Zayenda hasn't spoken a word since we were captured. She is my cellmate, but at least we will die as friends.

My thoughts linger on my little one. I pray to the goddess she survived the journey. If some of the boats didn't make it to the cavern, I can only imagine how much more difficult and dangerous the voyage will be while being pursued and with a vessel full of panicking women.

I have to tell myself Ninti made it. That she is safe. It is the only way I will maintain my sanity in this nightmare.

They plan on torturing us before they kill us. It's what they've done to the other Shagin prisoners they've captured so far. Those are the options—a brutal, but relatively quick death in the city, or torture and rape in the temple.

***

I am so hungry. I haven't eaten since my incarceration. They feed us, but I cannot bring myself to eat meat. They aim to prove we are the monsters they believe us to be, so they feed us the flesh of our fallen.

I am to die here anyway. There is no escape, so it might as well be by starvation. It seems just as good of a way to die as any other.

***

Another woman was raped to death last night. It was across the hall from my cell, and I saw it happen. A group of soldiers beat and used her until she died from exhaustion.

The soldiers take what they want from us. They pull us from our cells to slake their urges, whether rage or lust.

Sometimes, it is torture. Other times, it's rape. Usually, though, it is both.

I place my hand to my now-bald head, running my fingers over the deep lacerations that were left from the blade used to shave off my hair. They left me with no dignity. The warrior from the cavern didn't survive being captured that night. Though she did kill wave after wave of soldiers until their numbers overwhelmed her. She vanished in a sea of hatred and swords. I wish I could have joined her.

"Get up." A soldier opens my cell door, then drags me to my feet. I don't have the strength or the will to resist.

Soldiers gather a group of Shagin, leading them deeper into the temple. I trip, then fall to the floor. Not having the energy to catch myself, I slam face-first into the stone.

"Get on your fucking feet." The soldier kicks me in my side, yanking me up.

"Why..." I whimper.

"Why?" The soldier strikes me across the face. "You're nothing but monsters. You're not even human. You be-witch men, then you steal our children and take them off into the forest to be raised in your demon cult. You fucking baby stealer. You're a monster—you deserve so much worse than we can ever do to you."

He shoves me into the back of one of two lines. At the front of each column is an officer with a sword.

"First to a hundred wins," one officer says to the other. After they shake hands, they force the women in front to kneel. They take their positions behind their prey. "Ready, steady, go."

They swing their swords, decapitating their first victim. Soldiers quickly force the next in line to their knees while the officers rush in behind them. After a quick slash from each, two more bodies hit the pile.

These bastards are killing us from behind. They don't even dare to look us in the eyes before they murder us. Cowards.

There are twelve more women in line behind me, and the two officers seem to be matching pace. If they keep this up, I am sure to die. I will die for sport, for their amusement.

More heads roll as the officers make their way down the line. With each swing, they start to become sluggish. As they reach the midpoint, their once-instant kills become less clean strikes and more rough hacks. Becoming weaker, it takes them multiple swings to make it through bone.

As they approach me, I do not fear their blade. I welcome it. My sisters' severed heads share the same peaceful expression. Finally, they are at rest after this horrific ordeal. The Guardian has ordered all Shagin to be killed. The prolonged deaths we are being exposed to serve no purpose other than to satisfy their amusement. In this place, death is a certainty. I just want it to end.

The next woman smiles as the officer readies his sword to kill her. What is she doing? I can feel her energy rising as her aura strengthens.

The officer's blade thuds against the side of her neck. Blood spurts, but the wound is shallow. Her spirit aura is too strong for the weak officer.

"You'll have to do better than that," she mocks.

He swings again, but the result is the same.

"If you're going to kill me, I will make you pay. You will lose." She laughs almost maniacally.

He swings again and again. Each strike digs a little deeper, but she doesn't die. The other officer advances to the end of his line.

No. Damn her. She's ruining everything. I am supposed to die here—I need to. Let it be quick and by the blade of a sword.

The officer hacks away. Her eyes roll back into her head. With one last swing, he decapitates her.

Finally, it's my turn.

I drop to my knees before the soldier has time to kick them out from under me. Closing my eyes, I bow my head, waiting for the sweet release of death.

"Finished!" the other officer cries. "I win."

No.

I was supposed to die.

Please finish your line. Please don't make me go back to my cell. Don't let them visit me again.

They took Zayenda this morning. I don't know why. At this point, what does it matter? They've inflicted every nightmare imaginable on us. The only thing we can hope for now is a quick death.

I am in hell. A nightmare that never ends.

The guard throws a piece of meat through the cell doors. Its intoxicating aroma fills the room, and my mouth begins to water. I have not eaten in weeks. Can barely stand at this point. Any fat on my body has withered away, revealing only bone.

I know I shouldn't eat this meat. This is a person, but I can't fight it anymore. The hunger is too much. I bite into the gritty and chewy morsel, but it's delicious nonetheless. How can I think that? Tears stream down my face as I take another bite. I am a monster.

What have I done?

I devoured the meat; I cannibalized one of my Shagin sisters. Why didn't I just let myself starve?

A soldier opens the door to my cell, then tosses Zayenda to the cold stone floor. She's a bloody mess. Her breasts have been cut off, as well as the muscles from her legs and arms. They didn't even bother to bandage her.

The soldier lets out a boisterous laugh. "I hope she tasted good. If you want, you can always have another bite."

My heart nearly stops. I ate my friend. I knew her, yet I still ate her.

I collapse to my hands and knees next to Zayenda.

Her eyes flutter as she struggles to open them. Her mouth doesn't even move as she tries to speak. "Love… love." Her eyes close, and she loses consciousness.

***

I stare at Zayenda's body. I had taken off some of my remaining clothes and torn them into strips to bandage her, but it wasn't enough. Her body had grown too weak from the abuse we have suffered. She died in the night.

I am all alone now.

"Look at them." Two soldiers stop at my cell door. "They look like feral beasts."

"This is their true nature. See that? This one ate her friend."

"They are monsters."

"Watch this." The soldier takes a vial out from his pocket, holding it up so I can see it. "Shagin, I want to make a deal with you. Everyone here is going to die. There is no escaping that. But do you see this? This is poison. You can take this and end your suffering. You will simply go to sleep." He motions to a woman in the adjacent cell. "But I'm going to torture her to death in a most unpleasant manner. Have you ever heard of vivisection? Of course not. I'm going to cut her open and play with her organs, keeping her alive as long as possible. Hours, maybe days. Alternatively, you can take her place, and I will give her the poison. The choice is yours. You have until tomorrow to decide."

This is what I want—a quick and painless death.

***

"Have you made your decision?" The soldier smiles. He knows what I want. He knows what I am going to choose.

They think we are monsters, but it is they who are. I want nothing more than a quick and effortless way out, but I will not give them the satisfaction of being right. I will show them the strength of the Shagin spirit. I will set aside my wellbeing for someone else. This is the strength I will leave my little one. I will show them the power of love, and I will die with dignity with one small victory for my dying people.

"Torture me."

CHAPTER FIFTEEN

Kari opened her eyes. The darkness of her room was all around her. The quiet still of the night sent shivers down her spine. She covered her eyes, her hands shaking.

They were watching her. The eyes. They were everywhere—the eyes of the forgotten.

She pulled the covers over her head. They would go away if they couldn't see her. This didn't make any sense. Why was she afraid? She wasn't a child with childlike fears anymore. Logically, she knew there was nothing in the dark, but that wasn't what she believed anymore.

Her hands shook. Her entire body shivered, not from the cold, but overwhelming emotion. She had to be perfectly still. Even the slightest movement would alert them to her presence. She could almost feel their ghoulish hands hovering over her legs. She wanted to scream for help, but who would hear her? The damned would.

They haunted her. The memories of the dead, the souls of the victims—they wouldn't let her rest. They needed her to join them, to embrace the darkness.

Her body spasmed as she struggled to catch her breath. This was how she would die. She would stay hidden until death took her, and she would join the fallen.

She laid there, still and motionless, until the morning light eventually broke through her bedroom windows. Safe in the light—yes—but, even with it, she couldn't bring herself to remove the blanket from her head. She didn't want to see another day.

This agony was endless, and it would not let her rest.

"Kari, you've got to eat. It's been three days." Ronin's voice reverberated through the blanket.

Kari shot up to a sitting position, throwing the covers off. She hadn't even heard him enter the room. His pale ghostly skin mirrored the souls of all those he had killed. Ronin was dead inside, too. He was just waiting for the right executioner. They all were.

"Why are you still here?" Kari asked. He said he would leave her. He'd *said*. Now, he stayed, and she didn't deserve him to.

"Did you think I cared for you so little I would leave you?"

"Care for me?" Kari couldn't understand. Even though they were siblings, they had only known each other for a brief time. It was hardly long enough to know each other. "But I am a stranger to you."

Ronin sighed. He walked over, then sat on the edge of her bed. Instinctually, she recoiled. "I can see Eanna in you. Our mother was kind and gentle. I miss that about her. At any rate, it's good to see you responsive, but you need to eat to keep up your strength. I've brought you some pork buns."

Ronin tore open one of the buns, then sat it on the table next to her. The smell of the meat, its aroma, filled her nostrils. Her empty stomach growled in response. Juices dripped from the savory pork.

Kari's eyes widened. It was happening again. The cycle of death and destruction, it would always repeat. The world was doomed. *She* was doomed.

"No!" Kari grabbed the bun, hurling it across the room. Grabbing her head, she closed her eyes as she tried to fight off the memories. "I can't. I can't. I *can't*."

"What's wrong?" Ronin reached out to her. Kari scrambled backward, then hugged her knees to her chest.

"I ate her. I ate Zayenda. I didn't want to. I didn't know." Kari stared at her hands. Foreign tears ran down her face, splashing in her palms. "No, it wasn't me... Was it me? Am I her?"

"You're not making sense," Ronin said.

"Who am I? Am I a good person?" Kari lunged at Ronin, seizing his hands. "Kill me. End it now. Take your sword. Drive it through me now."

Ronin placed his hand on the hilt of his weapon, pulling away from Kari. His dark eyes met hers. They were eyes filled with death. He just needed to add one more life to the darkness.

"You're finally up," Artemis said, entering the room.

"What did you do to her?" Ronin launched up from the bed, seizing Artemis by the throat and slamming her into the wall.

"No! Stop," Kari screamed, covering her head with the blanket again. "I can't take it! Not another life! I just can't!"

Ronin snarled as he released Artemis.

"She's adjusting," Artemis explained.

"I know, you've said it before." Frantically, Ronin paced across the room. "Undo it. Whatever you did, change it back."

Artemis sighed. "There is no going back. Right now, her mind is still trying to process the new memories. Eventually, she'll come to terms with them and be able to accept her new normal."

Ronin shook his head. "Fuck you."

Ronin was usually more stoic. Kari had never seen him like this. Was this his true nature? The wolf hiding inside his mind?

"I'm going to find Ina." Ronin stormed out of the room, slamming the door shut behind him.

"Your brother is quite the character," Artemis said, sitting next to Kari. "But he is right. You need to eat something to keep up your strength."

"You said I'd accept this?" Kari asked as her eyes watered. "How can I ever accept everything that happened to her? Artemis, how can people be so cruel?"

"I'm sorry." Artemis clenched her jaw, averting her eyes. "It was too soon."

"Is this the true face of humanity? Are we inherently evil? We use and abuse each other. There is no point to any of it."

"That is why we fight," Artemis said, balling her fist, turning her knuckles white. "We can reshape the world. By doing so, we can make sure that atrocities like the Purge never happen again."

"Never again," Kari said. They could begin anew. A new age would dawn, and they would helm it. The sacrifice of innocence—she understood it now.

Days had passed. The line between her and Carina became more apparent. She was starting to see where she ended and Carina began. Even still, the memories were still there. Everything was hers to bear. Kari had lived a second life. It had happened in a moment. But who else could claim to have lived two lives beside Shagin?

It wasn't her life, but that didn't change the way she felt. She had been Carina. Carina's life, her memories, her experiences, they felt just as much Kari's as her own.

Kari stayed in the Chamber of the Bearer, studying the Nasu Codex. The codex was the book detailing Shagin's knowledge of the Seed. There were individual tomes written on different Bearers, even books that went into unusual theories and in-depth analysis of the Seed. Still, the Nasu Codex was the most comprehensive manuscript detailing information on the Seed and the Bearers.

Kari had learned more about her powers and history in the past few days than her entire life living on Mystikos. The elders of Shi Zinni Village were newly appointed, following the Purge. It was possible they did not know the information. Kari stared at the list of Bearers. Nine stretched over fourteen hundred years back to Calista the Outcast, the founder of Shagin and first known Bearer. At the bottom of the list was, "Hikari, Daughter of Eanna, called at age thirteen," scribbled in red ink.

The Seed was death—created from death—and served as the anchor point for the enchantment separating the Three Realms. She was death—she had *become* death—killing her enemies without mercy, overthrowing tyrants and killing barbarians who threatened peace and tranquility. Carina was dead—she had died because others viewed her as an outcast, as someone who threatened their way of life.

They were all the same. Everyone was the same. Killing out of fear, to protect themselves from a perceived threat—real or imagined.

It was so ironic how death preserved life. No one could live without killing or having someone else kill for them. They killed and ate to live. They killed and defended to live. Were anyone's hands clean of blood?

An endless war came, and the enchanter, Dante the Splendid, created the Seed. He killed his people to harness their power and separate the Three Realms, nearly wiping out all life. He'd done this to preserve peace and end a war without one.

So many people had died, and she had killed so many.

Kari—no, Carina—had been murdered. She was tortured and died, cut open and played with as if she weren't human. But all living beings felt pain, joy, and sadness. Even plants responded to touch and would release pheromones when damaged in an attempt to ward off predators.

Everything wanted to live, yet nothing could—at least not for long. Life was short, fleeting, and precious.

Kari stared at the codex. Nine names, including hers, comprised the Bearers.

"*Calista, Daughter of Nebura—Year of Birth 627 AC—Year of Death 83 NA*

Ai, Daughter of Jingyi, called at age 24—Year of Birth 59 NA—Year of Death 330 NA

Daphne, Daughter of Narissa, called at age 20—Year of Birth 310 NA—Year of Death 330 NA

Diana, Daughter of Narissa, called at age 17—Year of Birth 313 NA—Year of Death 833 NA

Xiuying, Daughter of Xuan, called at age 15—Year of Birth 818 NA—Year of Death 1028 NA

Fiorella, Daughter of Flannan, called at age 23 —Year of Birth 1005 NA —Year of Death 1317 NA

Urania, Daughter of Thera, called at age 12—Year of Birth 1305 NA—Year of Death 1317 NA

Mhairi, Daughter of Nilam, called at age 34—Year of Birth 1283 NA—Year of Death 1373 NA

Hikari, Daughter of Eanna, called at age 13—Year of Birth 1360 NA"

There was the Tragedy of Narissa. Daphne, Daughter of Narissa, was called as Bearer at the age of twenty. She was the eldest of two daughters. She refused the destiny the Fates called for her. A Bearer's life was too much to endure, so she'd killed herself, driving a dagger into her heart upon confirmation by the seers. The curse was then passed on to the next Bearer. Diana, Daughter of Narissa, was then called. Narissa lost both of her daughters on the same day. Diana accepted her fate, pledging to ensure no one would have to endure the curse again. She became the longest living Bearer, not dying until she was five hundred and twenty years old.

There was Urania, Daughter of Thera, the youngest Bearer, called at age twelve. She had yet to undergo her trial, but she'd been allowed to record her name, becoming a full sister before her banishment. The ship meant to take her to exile on the mainland capsized. Urania drowned—too young to die.

Being the Bearer meant a live of solitude. Unable to form longterm connections and relationships and isolated from her sisters. With all, the most probable cause of death was speculated to be suicide. The Bearers struggled to live with the curse inflicted upon them, and they chose to end their lives.

Would that be her fate?

She wanted it to end—wanted everything to end. Even her face felt heavy. She wished to sleep and never wake up.

Kari closed the codex, then picked up the butcher's knife she'd stolen from the inn. It was such a tiny thing to feel so heavy. So strange.

After she left Lasan, she walked down the streets of Koruzeru. The buildings she passed seemed so much taller than she remembered. They dwarfed her, towering over her. Even the buildings that had been rebuilt still showed signs of the carnage inflicted within. Scorch marks here and there, collapsed stairs, broken boards. Those in pristine condition were a lie. They might look pretty and strong, but they had been the location of so much death and decay.

Kari stared at the knife in her hand, her face reflecting from the silver blade. The pain had to stop, but it never would. She would have to live with this pain for the rest of her incredibly long life.

She pressed the edge of the blade against her throat. It wouldn't be the first time her throat was slit. Only this time, Ronin wouldn't be there to save her. The metal of the knife dug into her flesh. She didn't want to die, but she was tired.

How could she live the rest of her life with this pain? The memories would last forever. She just wanted it to end.

"You won't do it," a voice said from behind her.

Kari tore the knife away from her throat, turning to face the stranger. He was a young man with brown hair tied into a ponytail with his bangs hanging in front of his face.

"Who do you think you are?" Kari asked, hiding the knife behind her back.

"I'm sorry, I don't mean to be presumptuous." The young man smiled, holding up his hands in defense. He had a similar facial structure and eye shape to her. He must have been following her for some time, tracking her from Xiang. "My name is Warren. I've been following you for a while; I just don't think you'll go through with it. Taking your own life, I mean. You're stronger than you think you are. When you realize it, you'll put the knife down."

"You've been following me?" Kari said, more accusatory than inquisitive. She gripped the knife.

"Not literally." Warren shook his head, smirking. "I've been following your legend. You've accomplished a considerable number of things. You're sort of my hero."

"You're from Xiang?" Kari already knew the answer. She just wanted him to confirm it, confirm he was spying on her—an agent of Cai Ren, no doubt. Even now, he would not rest until she died. No one ever rested until death.

"No, but my mother is," Warren corrected. She was positive he lied.

"What do you want?" Kari narrowed her eyes.

"Mainly, just to meet you," Warren said. He reached behind her, then took hold of the knife. She wanted to stab his hand. Instead, she released her hold on the blade. Why would she do that? Why give up her only escape? "And to help shake you out of your apathy. Your friend, Ina, I don't know where she's at, but she needs your help. She's going to die today unless you can save her."

"Is that a threat?" Kari pulled away from Warren.

"No, I am only here to help you. One way or another, you will find the motivation to channel the pain you're feeling into fiery passion. You will do remarkable things. I just want to lessen your suffering along the way. If I can."

"How do you know any of this? And just who are you?"

"I snoop. As for who I am, I am a specter, the last bastion of hope for a dying civilization." He turned, waving as he strolled away. "We'll meet again, you and I."

Such an odd man. He seemed to be not too much older than her, but there was something ancient in his eyes as if he were a veteran soldier. His cryptic speech and vague warnings were frivolous. But still, checking in on Ina was a good idea. Just to be safe.

Kari rushed through the city, heading toward the tavern. She breathed a sigh of relief when she spotted Ina with her back to the far end of the adjacent wall. She was safe.

A group of men rose from their tables, their chairs sliding and skidding across the wooden floor. Kari clenched her fists as they surrounded Ina. Her eyes widened. Ryder was with them, standing in the middle of the group.

Had Warren been right?

"Ina," Kari called, hurrying toward them. The men turned to face her, but they did not release Ina. "Are you all right?"

"Kari," Ina cried, peering through the men. She tried to push her way through the men. One grabbed her shoulder, shoving her against the wall. Ina whimpered, and Kari scowled.

"Well, look who it is." Smiling, Ryder motioned for the men to part and allow Kari to pass.

"Kari, you have to run," Ina said as Kari stepped forward.

Kari shook her head. She inched her way through, stretching her hand toward Ina. "We're going."

Pain shot through Kari's neck and head from a blow. Kari fell to the ground.

"You're not going anywhere, bitch!"

The men pounced on her, and Kari gasped for air. They were going to kill her. Warren led her to a trap, to her death. She closed her eyes as a fist rained down upon her. Kari didn't bother to channel her spirit energy. It didn't matter. Whatever they did to her, it didn't matter so long as Ina was safe.

A fist struck, watering her eyes and sending pain through her face. She was stepped on and kicked from all directions. Her sides ached and throbbed as each foot impacted. A kick to the gut knocked the breath from her. She crumbled, holding her stomach. A boot to the face sent shockwaves through her entire body as she seized on the ground.

"Do whatever you want to me, just leave Ina alone." Blood poured down Kari's face from her broken nose. It would be over soon. She just wanted it over.

"Don't worry. We will," Ryder snarled. Mounting her, he punched her in the face, repeatedly striking her. She winced and groaned as each fist shattered bone, rocking her head back and forth.

"Ahh!" she screamed as her cheekbone gave way from the blows. She wrapped her arms around her head, her body spasming, and sobbed.

"Stop, this isn't right." One man grabbed Ryder by the arm, pulling him off her.

"Get off me. This bitch is going to get what's coming to her. She threatened my family. Because of her, our homes are gone!"

Ryder pushed the man back as other men grabbed at the dissenter, then pulled him away. Rearing back, Ryder punted her in the side.

"Oh!" Kari grabbed at her now-broken ribs as she panted for air.

"Look, she's not even fighting back," the man protested, pointing at her. "Are you even sure she's the one?"

"You're right, I never thought a Shagin would be this weak," another man said, releasing his hold on the dissenter.

They couldn't stop now. She wanted them to finish it. End it. They couldn't make her go back to her room. If she did, the shadows of the dead would continue to visit her. It was her turn to join them.

Just let it all end.

"I... am," Kari said, struggling to get the words out. Her body was broken and bloodied. "I... am... Shagin."

"What did you say, bitch?" one man screamed.

Kari gripped her sides, forcing herself to sit upright. She stared at the men. "I am Shagin. Kill me. Go on! Do it!"

Ryder lifted Kari off the ground by her shirt. He pulled out a dagger, pointing the blade at her chest. Slowly pressing the tip into her, he drew blood.

"You can't do this," the dissenter protested, grabbing Ryder's arm, preventing him from impaling Kari.

The men grabbed at the dissenter again, snatching him back. Smirking, Ryder slid the blade deeper. Kari groaned as the knife hit bone.

"Do you know who this bitch is? This is the monster who destroyed our homes and conquered Xiang. My father died on her gallows! Now, I'm going to cut out her heart. We'll see what color this beast bleeds."

The dissenter broke free, grabbing the blade of Ryder's dagger. "I won't let you do this. The fight's over. She's incapacitated. She can face justice, but this is wrong."

"Let go!" Ryder yanked the blade free, causing blood to spray into the air as the edge sliced through the flesh of the man's hand. He grimaced and dropped to his knees, holding his bleeding palm.

"You're going to die, just as you deserve." Ryder held the knife up to her face.

Kari closed her eyes. Warren was right about her. She wouldn't have killed herself because she didn't have the courage. But she could allow them to kill her. They could release her and end the pain.

"Kari," Ina cried out.

"Shut your mouth." A man grabbed Ina by the hair, slinging her against the wall. "Monster lovers will reap the same punishment."

"I said, leave her alone," Kari screamed. Her spirit aura flared up. Planting her feet, she effortlessly tossed Ryder off her. Light erupted from her hand, forming her whip. She slashed at the man attacking Ina. Her light whip sliced through his body with ease.

Blood splattered, dripping down the wooden wall. Drops of blood dotted the room. It seemed she had become death again.

Kari shrieked. She dropped to her knees, then clutched at her head. Tears mixed with blood as they both poured down her face. She sobbed, broken. What had she become?

"Take your men and leave," Ina told the dissenter. "Please."

He nodded, rising on shaking legs. "Come on. Let's go while she's letting us."

The men stared in horror at the carnage that had unfolded. They did not argue with their comrade.

"We have to kill her," Ryder pleaded. But the men didn't waste any time. They grabbed Ryder, pulling him away as they left the tavern, leaving Kari and Ina alone.

Ina wrapped her arms around Kari as she cried. "I'm sorry, Kari. Why didn't you fight back?"

"If I had, I would have killed them. What would I be then? What am I now?" Kari buried her face in Ina's chest.

"Oh, Kari." Ina held her tight.

Kari pulled free, gazing into her friend's eyes. "Would you kill me? Please?"

CHAPTER SIXTEEN

Kari laid in her bed. She was so tired of lying around. But everyone else was so adamant she rest, even though she didn't need it. Vipin had healed her wounds. It wasn't her body they were worried about, though. It was her mind.

Ina had told them about what had happened in the tavern, and about how Kari had asked to die. Vipin had sent the Furies to look for the group of soldiers who had attacked them. She wished he hadn't. It didn't matter what happened to them now.

Kari remembered everything. She had been the one to kill them. She had killed so many. Why was life so fragile? In an instant, it could be ended. Shattered. Like a broken mirror whose shards crashed to the ground into millions of pieces, the death of a single person broke more hearts than could ever be counted.

Chaska was driven by death. Her child's death forced her to fight harder. It was a never-ending pain for her. The hatred she must feel had to be more intense than the brightest star. She was justified in her hatred.

Carina had loved her daughter so much. Even in the end, she only wished for Ninti's happiness—that and death.

Kari placed her hand over her eyes. She couldn't think—didn't even know what she wanted. One moment, she wanted to die. The next, she didn't. Nothing made sense. She hated the world. Hated people. She hated herself.

How many lives had been broken because of her? It was an endless cycle of pain and hate.

"You look too grim," Ronin said, the blood of all his victims dripping from his lips.

"I think I need to get out," Kari said, shaking the image from her mind. "I think I need to feel the earth again."

"Last time you went out, you tried to get yourself killed," Ronin reminded.

Would he care if she died? Would anyone? He had killed so many. So had she. Would one more life make a difference?

"Am I a prisoner now?" Kari asked, venom flowing from her voice.

"No, but I won't abandon you. Especially now." Ronin stood, then grabbed his long coat. With one graceful motion, he spun the cloak around himself, slipping his arms into the sleeves. He reached out for Kari. "Shall we go?"

Smiling, Kari took his hand, climbing out of her bed. They headed into the fresh evening air.

Kari found a quiet place under a tall tree. She took off her shoes, then wiggled her toes in the grass. The sky was so blue. How had it gotten so blue? The world just kept turning. She could feel it under her feet.

The cosmos was so infinitely big. They were on this tiny blue dot, adrift in the vastness of the universe. The Fates weren't watching them, or, if they were, they didn't care about the actions of humanity. They were stories told on the whispers of the wind. Nobody cared about their pain or their struggles.

Shagin were nearly extinct, yet the world kept turning.

She recognized the woman who took Ninti, or she almost did. There was only a little over five thousand Shagin left. Kari had a friend, about her age, who was the daughter of Ninti. Perhaps they were the same person. Maybe the helmswoman misunderstood what Carina said.

Warm tears streamed down Kari's face. Ninti had made it. She was alive. If only Kari could see her again. Maybe one day, she would find a way to return to Mystikos for one last goodbye.

Kari envied Carina. Holding her baby had filled her with so much joy and wonder. Kari would never have that feeling for herself, but at least she'd gotten to experience it secondhand. That was more than any other Bearer got. But it wasn't enough. She didn't want a child right now, but one day, once the pain had subsided, she might. She wanted a little one to teach—to show how to live a better, nobler life than she had.

"There you are," Ina said, running up to them. "Did you hear? The Furies captured that group of men who attacked us. Well, most anyway. Ryder and a few others eluded them."

"Is that good?" Kari asked. They all knew what fate awaited them now. They would be killed. It would add more blood to her hands.

"I don't know," Ina said. "They have been sentenced to death. What's going to happen to them isn't right. They should face justice. I honestly believe that. But do they deserve to die? I just don't know."

"They would've killed you." Ronin shook his head, cutting his eyes toward Kari. He didn't want her to hear Ina talking about this.

"Justice? It's such an odd concept. I don't think I understand it." Everyone seemed to be seeking justice for something, but what was it? How could justice be intertwined with vengeance and bloodshed? "Does anyone deserve to die?"

"We don't have to talk about it right now," Ronin said, taking Kari's hands in his.

"I'm lost." Kari pulled away from Ronin, turning her back on her friends. "I'm so lost, you know. My compass is broken. I can never be found."

"You are still you," Ina said, stepping to face her. "You are still a good person at heart."

Love. It was what Zayenda told her before she died. A message to Carina. It gave her hope, courage, and determination. It was that same determination that allowed her to spare a sister from a torturous death.

Ina had stood by her side for so long. Her dark eyes stared into hers. Kari reached out, brushing Ina's hair behind her ear.

"Thank you for being there for me," she said.

Ina smiled. The corners of her lips curled gently upward, and her eyes gleamed. "I will always be there for you, the same way you've been for me."

Kari's heart raced, and her legs trembled. Her hand fell, brushing against Ina's shoulder. Her smooth, soft skin sent ripples through Kari's body. "Thank you," she whispered.

Kari closed her eyes. She wrapped her arms around her friend, then pressed her lips against Ina's. Her mouth was soft and tender. Kari's heart was right at last. Everything was right. She kissed Ina.

Ina pushed her away, putting her hand to her mouth. "What are you doing?"

"I…" Kari averted her eyes.

"You didn't even ask me." Ina scowled. "After everything that happened to me, everything Jiaorong did to us, why did you think that was acceptable? How could you do that to me? You know I had a fiancé. I don't even like women."

Kari buried her face in her hands. "I'm sorry." Why? Why had she done that?

Tears streamed down Kari's face. Ronin reached out to her, but she recoiled from his touch. She couldn't take this. All she wanted was to be anywhere but here.

Kari darted toward the forest, running as fast as her legs would carry her.

"Kari," Ronin called.

She didn't stop. Darting into the woods, she kept running. Branches and leaves nicked her, but they didn't slow her. She focused her spirit energy into her aura, strengthening her muscles to carry her farther and faster. Each step she took was a step closer to relief and freedom. Kari ran until her lungs burned, her muscles ached, and her spirit energy waned.

She was alone. The only sounds were birds. She collapsed in the underbrush. Would the forest claim her? *Could* it claim her?

She really was lost.

She stood, then walked to a nearby tree. With a simple touch, branches sprouted and vines descended. Grabbing the vine, she pulled. Could it support her weight? Kari gazed through the forest canopy at the sky above.

Goddess, what was left for her to do?

Kari dropped to her knees, a soft breeze wafting through her hair. She fell onto her back, draping her arms over her eyes.

Her mind was blank, yet tumultuous. A cacophony of incoherent thoughts occupied her mind. Leaves rustled, tree branches swayed, and clouds soared through the blue sky. She watched clouds float by. It was bright, and she was forced to squint.

How could she have been so foolish? Ina was her best friend, but Kari had ruined the friendship with her stupidity. Kari had been wrong about a great many things. It seemed she was never right. All she wanted was to go back to the way things were before. But time passed her by.

Kari wasn't sure how long she laid there before the rustling of leaves alerted her. She didn't want to move or open her eyes. All she wanted was to be left alone.

"Kari," Ina said, rushing over to her. "Are you all right?'

They'd found her. Ronin's doing, no doubt. Kari didn't move or take her arms off her eyes. She didn't want to see anyone. "I'm fine. I'm sorry for what I did."

"It's all right," Ina said, kneeling beside her. "I know things are difficult for you now."

"You shouldn't be running off by yourself," Ronin said, walking over. "You made a mistake. Move on."

Uncovering her face, Kari sat up. "I'm so sorry."

"I forgive you." Ina took Kari's hands, then helped her up. "We're friends, and we always will be. We'll move forward as if that never happened."

"Thank you," Kari said, nodding as tears formed in her eyes.

"It was a good kiss." Ina grinned. "I wish I were attracted to women."

Laughing, Kari rubbed her eyes. "You are a great friend."

"Come on," Ronin said, glancing around the forest. "We should return to Koruzeru."

A rustling of leaves alerted them that they weren't alone. Kari turned to see two familiar people marching toward them. Falcon and Athena were here.

"What do you think the odds are of running into you here?" Falcon asked, drawing his sword.

Kari retreated. She couldn't do this. Not now.

Ronin grabbed Ina's arm, pulling her behind him. Drawing his swords, he stood poised, ready to strike.

"There are two of us and only three of you. Since our last fight went in our favor, I wouldn't hold it against you to go ahead and surrender before one of you dies." Falcon switched his sword to his right hand. Kari narrowed her eyes. Ronin's assessment was correct.

"I see math isn't your strength. I expect nothing less from a simpleminded killer such as you," Ronin said, planting his feet.

"Scathing." Falcon smiled. "It's good to know your skills aren't the only thing that's dull."

"Falcon, do you want me to take the assassin, and you take the two girls?" Athena asked, raising her large, two-handed sword.

"No," Falcon replied. He eyed the trio, his gaze bouncing between each until finally stopping on Ina. "That one doesn't have a weapon. Judging by the way she's trembling, I don't think she's a fighter. And Kari, surprisingly, looks ready to run as well. No, I'll take all three. Just keep them from escaping."

"You arrogant bastard!" Ronin charged at Falcon with both his swords, ready to attack. His feet kicked up grass and dirt with each step.

Ronin swung with his right hand as he thrust his left at Falcon. He sidestepped the thrust, parrying the cut with his longsword. Falcon drove the tip of his blade into Ronin's chest.

Kari's heart skipped. Falcon was too strong. Ronin couldn't win.

"Ahh!" Ronin roared, jumping out of reach. His aura protected him, preventing the stab from piercing more than just skin. Kari couldn't watch.

Falcon didn't wait for Ronin to regain his footing. He lunged at Ronin.

Wildly, Ronin swung with his right hand, halting Falcon's charge. Falcon spun his sword around Ronin's slicing blade, then struck the back of his hand. Ronin yelped, dropping his sword as blood trickled down his fingers.

Kari's gaze darted back and forth from the battle to the ground. What could she do? What *should* she do?

Ronin jumped back, trying to get out of reach of Falcon's longer blade. The man thrust his sword at Ronin's leg, nicking his thigh with the tip of his blade.

Ronin winced as blood trickled out of the wound. He was outmatched. This fight would be his last. Falcon would strike again and again, chipping away at Ronin's aura until nothing was left. Kari balled her fists. Her vision tunneled, and her head spun.

Ronin lunged forward, slashing at Falcon's head with a downward strike. Falcon stepped back as the blade cut through the air in front of him. He brought his sword down on Ronin, slicing through his chest.

Screaming, Ronin faltered, dropping to a knee.

Falcon followed up with a thrust to the chest, sending Ronin spiraling to the ground. Warm tears streamed down Kari's cheeks. Her brother lay defeated at the feet of her enemy. If it weren't for her, none of this would be happening.

Ronin groaned, rolling onto his hands and knees. He gripped his sword tight, turning his knuckles white. "I will beat you!"

He couldn't. Kari could feel it. His spirit energy was failing.

Falcon readied his sword for the death blow, a thrust into Ronin's back. "Persistent dog."

"No!" Kari screamed. She fell to her knees as tears poured down her face, falling to the detritus below. "Please stop. I can't take this anymore. Please don't kill him."

The battle stopped as all eyes fell on Kari. Ina dropped to her knees, then wrapped her arms around Kari.

"It's going to be okay," she whispered.

How could she say that? People had died because of her, and now her brother was on the verge of death. Falcon wouldn't stop until she was captured. The Guardian wouldn't stop until she was dead. Her resistance only meant more people would be harmed and die for her life.

She had witnessed so much death and decay, both through her eyes and Carina's. How could the world be so cruel?

"It's not," Kari responded, covering her face with her hands. "It's never okay. Everyone dies. It never ends. Make it stop."

"Is this a trick?" Athena asked, raising an eyebrow.

"I... don't think so," Falcon responded, lowering his weapon. He stared at Kari as she sobbed into Ina's shoulder.

"We're not done!" Ronin screamed, trying to force himself to his feet.

"Stay down. I don't want to kill you." Falcon sheathed his sword, approaching Kari.

"You bastard!" Ina stared up at Falcon, shooting daggers with her eyes. "Why won't you leave us in peace?"

Falcon ignored her, kneeling next to the pair. "I have a job to do, and I can't stay my sword until it's complete. Will you be my prisoner?"

Kari gripped Ina's shirt. She could end this. It was all she wanted, so she nodded.

"Thank you," Falcon said, inclining his head. "You are far braver than I, and I will keep my promise to you. Athena, gather the others. We need to move out."

Athena disappeared into the forest. Falcon walked over to Ronin, then took out a handful of gauze and bandages from beneath his cloak.

"Let's get you fixed up," he said.

"Go to hell," Ronin spat. He grabbed his swords. When he forced himself to his feet, blood oozed from his wounds. "Our fight isn't over."

"Ronin," Ina scolded, motioning to Kari. He grimaced, but he did not drop his guard.

His and Kari's eyes met. "Please, I've made my decision. This is what I want."

Ronin gritted his teeth, then threw his weapons to the ground. "Fine. Give me the damned bandages."

"Yeah, I don't think so anymore," Falcon responded, stepping back from Ronin.

"Please, allow me to bandage his wounds." Ina outstretched her hands toward Falcon.

"Very well." Falcon tossed her the supplies.

Ina rushed over to Ronin, immediately starting to treat his wounds. Falcon approached Kari, then offered her his hand.

"Please, give me your hand," Falcon said.

Kari shook her head. She stood on her own. "I am fine. Thank you."

"No, it's...um...for your shackles," Falcon stammered. He swallowed hard.

"Oh." Kari blushed, holding out her hands.

Falcon bound her hands and feet in metal shackles. Once Ina was finished with Ronin, he did the same to them as well. Falcon was busy collecting their weapons—Ronin's swords and Kari's seed pouch—when Athena returned with a group of soldiers.

Ryder and some of the men who attacked Ina were with them. Kari sighed. She had agreed to this—had agreed to go to her death. Part of her wanted it, but the rest wanted to fight. It didn't matter either way. The world would go on without her.

"This will prevent you from using your magic," Falcon said, placing a metal collar around Kari's neck. When he rubbed a small brush around the end of the collar, the metal fused, sending an icy chill through her body. The tingle of her spirit energy faded away.

"It's a long journey on foot through this forest. These two will just slow us down. We only need the girl," Ryder said, drawing his jhuma. Rage flashed through Kari. How dare he use a Shagin weapon?

"I can't let them go. They'll give away our position. If we leave them chained up, they'll die of exposure," Falcon argued, placing a collar on Ronin's neck.

"And what's your point?" Ryder swung his sword through the air with an audible swish. "We should just kill them and be done with it."

"I gave my word," Falcon said, his eyes narrowing.

"Like that matters," Ryder said venomously.

Falcon ran his hand through his hair. "You don't know me, and I don't answer to you. And I don't like being told what to do. It makes me violently angry. So, while they are in my custody, all three are under my protection. No harm will come to them. If anyone tries to, they will answer to my sword. So, shut up and do what I say. If you have a problem with following my orders, feel free to eat a dick."

"Tough talk coming from a criminal," Ronin growled. "You are nothing more than a hired brute."

Falcon grimaced.

"He doesn't mean it," Ina spoke up.

"No, the first chance I get, I will kill you," Ronin said, smiling.

Falcon snickered. "You know, if it weren't for your energy shield, at least three of those strikes I gave you would have been lethal, not to mention that you wouldn't have a hand right now."

"Falcon," Athena called. "If you are done, we should move. We don't want those other fighters following us."

"Agreed," Falcon said. "Let's go. We have a long journey ahead."

CHAPTER SEVENTEEN

THEY STOPPED TO MAKE camp for the night near a stream. The soldiers set up a tent for Kari, Ronin, and Ina, then chained them to the middle support beam.

"We have to escape," Ronin said, pulling on his restraints once they were alone. The links rattled with each tug, but they did not falter. He kicked at the support beam, causing the entire tent to shake. "If we wait until almost everyone is asleep, we should be able to flee into the forest with minimal effort."

"No," Kari responded. She placed her hands on his shoulder, stopping his attempt to break free. "I can't run from this anymore."

"They will kill you," Ronin protested. Jerking his shoulder free, he began pulling even harder against the chain.

"Kari, I know you are going through some things now, and death might seem appealing, but you don't want this," Ina said. She shivered in the frosty air. Even with their tent, it would be a chilly night without proper clothes and blankets. The Latari Forest was filled with hot days and cold nights. "And what about us? Should we die, too?"

"No, I don't want anyone to die," Kari said, dropping to her knees. "I'm just so tired."

Kari rubbed her forehead. She wanted to rest, but no one would ever let her.

The flap to the tent opened. Falcon entered, along with two other soldiers. They handed a plate of food to each prisoner.

"Eat up," Falcon said. "We have a long hike tomorrow. You'll need your strength."

Kari stared at her food, the smell of the roasted meat filling her nostrils. Her mouth watered. She picked up the venison, then brought it to her mouth.

Zayenda.

Kari dropped the plate to the ground. It shattered upon impact. She placed her shaking hands to her face. "I can't. I can't. I just can't." She sobbed as streamed poured down her face.

"What's wrong?" Falcon asked, kneeling to pick up the broken pieces.

"How dare you feign concern for us!" Ina scolded. She pulled Kari tight to her chest.

"I'm not." Sighing, Falcon motioned at one of the soldiers to finish cleaning up the mess.

"Leave us." Ronin clambered to his feet, glaring at Falcon. "If you come in here again, I will kill you."

Falcon ignored him, still crouched next to Kari and Ina. "She needs to eat."

"Why, so she doesn't slow you down as you escort her to her execution? Or is this her last meal?" Ina asked venomously.

"Look, I don't know what fate awaits her when we arrive at Justia, but it's been a long day. Tomorrow will be even worse. She'll need her strength," Falcon said, taking Ronin's plate away and sliding it closer to Kari.

"I can't. I won't," she repeated, pushing the offending item away. "I won't consume life to sustain my own."

"It's the meat?" Falcon asked, eyeing her dinner.

"Do you have anything else that's not meat? Bread, vegetables, fruit, anything?" Ina asked.

But even those were was alive. Plants, while not possessing the same level of consciousness as animals, were just as alive. They could respond to touch and damage. How was eating them justified? Kari sighed. She had to eat—she knew it. Perhaps a vegetarian diet was the best option.

"I think all we brought were cured meats for roasting," Falcon said. He glanced at the other soldiers, who shook their heads.

"She can grow them with her power," Ronin said. "But I don't think you are brave enough to unleash her energy to allow this."

Falcon scowled at Ronin. He took hold of Kari's hands. "Can you do this?"

Kari wiped her eyes, then nodded. "I'll need my seed pouch."

Falcon gestured for one of the soldiers, who left after his instructions.

"Sir, you can't be considering this," the other soldier said. "She could kill us all! This is a terrible decision."

Kari's heart skipped.

"It might be, but it's my decision to make." Falcon took a small brush from his pocket, then held it against Kari's collar. "I'm trusting you."

He motioned with the brush, and the collar snapped apart. A rush of energy flooded Kari's body.

The soldier returned with the seed pouch. He chunked it at Kari.

Falcon undid Kari and Ina's shackles.

"You look cold," he said. "We have a fire out here if you want to warm up."

Ronin held out his hands. "Undo mine, and I will personally throw you in that fire."

"You're not invited." Falcon pointed at him, smirking.

"This is why you don't have friends," Ina said.

Falcon and the soldiers left the tent, leaving the friends alone.

"He's a coward," Ronin said.

"No, you're just hyper-aggressive," Ina said.

Kari placed a seed on the ground, pouring her energy into it. A fruit-bearing tree sprouted, growing plump oranges. She plucked one, then began peeling its skin.

What was wrong with her? What had she become?

Kari hurried over to Ronin. She grabbed his shackles. "I won't let you two die with me."

"Good, free me so we can escape," Ronin said.

"You can. I won't be going," Kari said. Forming a key with her light powers, she then unlocked his shackles. "I can't flee from this forever. Instead, I will make my case before the Guardian and let the Fates decide the outcome."

"Don't be naïve," Ronin scolded, rubbing his wrists.

"He's right," Ina said. "I think these people are well beyond reason. For what purpose would you stay? To die?"

"No," Kari said flatly. Honestly, she wasn't sure, but she needed to see this out. "I hate them. Every single one. I need to know if that is all I have left—if there is more to me than hatred."

"Hate is good," Ronin said. "It means you haven't forgotten what they've done. Remember the Purge, and what they did."

"Where does justice lie? In vengeance? In balance? In bloodshed? How can we build a future with bloodstained hands?" Kari asked, staring at her own.

"Blood is on their hands," Ronin said, taking hers. "They murdered countless innocence. They deserve nothing more than the same fate."

"I think you are right," Kari said, pulling away. Was that the universal truth? Violence and hate could only be met with more violence and hatred? "And the cycle continues until everything is dust."

"Don't be so grim," Ina said.

"I need to know what true justice is—need to know who I am and what I deserve," Kari said.

Ina averted her eyes, and Ronin stared. They didn't have the answers she sought. No one did. Perhaps some things couldn't ever be known. Kari pulled apart her orange, then plopped a slice into her mouth. The fresh juice and pulp danced with her tongue. She could live like this, without meat.

They ate in silence, then slowly drifted to sleep as the night waned on. They were each given a single blanket they had used to cover the hard ground. Ronin and Ina fell asleep quickly, tired from the day's hike. Kari, on the other hand, tossed and turned, unable to get comfortable. She was cold. She had spent so long sleeping in warm, soft beds, so it was odd to have to sleep on the ground with minimal coverings again.

After a few hours of being unable to fall asleep, she left the tent in search of the fire. At least it would be warm and away from Ronin's snoring.

"Couldn't sleep?" Falcon asked as she walked over. He was alone on a log by the campfire, poking the firewood with a stick.

"No," Kari responded, sitting next to him. "You?"

"I don't sleep much these days." He turned a log over, and sparks flew as the crackling heat engulfed it.

"Why not? If you don't mind me asking." Kari folded her arms across her chest. She would do anything for one of

Ilyia's padded shirts right about now. It didn't seem right for the day to be as hot as it was with the night so cold.

Falcon sighed. "Lovers' quarrel."

"About what?" Kari stared into the flames. She used to roast fish with her mother over a fire like this. Her heart quivered. She had killed a living creature, cooked its flesh, and then consumed it—tearing into its body with her teeth. If the roles were reversed, if it were an animal doing that to a human, it would be nightmarish.

Kari shook her head, trying to dislodge the thought. What would it feel like if she placed her hand in the fire? Would she feel anything at all? She pressed her palm to her forehead, but the idea would not leave her.

"You should try to get some rest," Falcon said, scrutinizing her. "Sleep would do you well."

"I can't," Kari said, shivering. "It's too cold."

"Sorry, we didn't exactly pack our supplies thinking about keeping you comfortable at night." Falcon glanced around the camp as if to make sure no one was watching. He took off his black cloak, then draped it around Kari. "This should help."

"Thank you," Kari muttered. Him being kind made no sense. "Why are you letting me roam freely? Aren't you afraid I'll escape?"

"No," Falcon said, shaking his head. "I know you won't. I know that look in your eyes. You've resigned yourself to death. At least part of you has."

Kari averted her eyes. How did he know her thoughts? What made him so perceptive? "You don't know what I've been through."

"I know you were a concubine," Falcon said, poking at the fire. "I'm sure you went through hell. Why else would you topple an empire?"

"It's more than that." Kari examined her hands in the flicker of the firelight. "I don't know who I am anymore."

"No one but you knows that." Falcon tossed his stick into the fire. It crackled and charred as the flames licked up around it. "Don't let who you were define who you'll become. You are you—at this moment. That is all. Set your sight on who you want to be and strive to be that person, and that is who you will become."

Kari sighed. It was like this man had been talking to Ina. They were both idealistic and naïve.

"And who do you want to be?" she asked. How dare he try to lecture her? Just who was he?

"Have you heard of the Thunder Five before?" Falcon sighed, rubbing his lip. "We are all criminals. We are out-laws who hunt outlaws—a killer, a pirate, a deserter, and a thief. And I am a murderer. The first person I killed, she... we all strive to be better than who we were."

"Better?" Anger and rage flooded Kari's tone. "You burned down my mother's town, and your foot soldier tried to murder innocent people when I confronted him!"

"I had nothing to do with Ryder's plot," Falcon protested. "As for the town, I gave the people plenty of time to escape."

"An escape to where?" Kari asked, venom dripping from her lips. "All of their possessions, food, and money were destroyed. You simply gave them a slower death."

"I..." Falcon stammered. "I didn't think about that."

"How did someone like you become a Torredin anyway?" Kari asked, flicking her sleeve and shaking her head.

"I'm not a Torredin," Falcon said, tone matter of fact. "I may work for the Guardian, but I don't blindly follow him. A lot of his rules are pretty dumb. Just let people be, and they'll be happy."

Kari scowled. Just who was this man? "So, why do you do it?"

Falcon shrugged. "I can help people while putting dangerous, unrepentant criminals away."

People like her. Or, at least, she was deemed to be a dangerous criminal for merely existing. How could she repent for living?

"What will you do with me?" Kari asked, her face dropping.

"That's not for me to decide," Falcon replied, grimacing. His eyes bounced from her to the ground and back again. "I am simply here to do a job and bring you to Justia."

Kari met his light blue eyes. They were coated with blood, just like hers. "Can I ask you something?"

"You haven't held back so far," Falcon wryly said.

"How many people have you killed?"

He puffed out his cheeks as he exhaled. "Too many."

"Do you feel remorse?" Kari folded the cloak around her, crossing her arms across her chest. It was more for protection from the truth than the cold.

"Sometimes," Falcon responded. "But I have to remember, while in a battle, that it's them or me. I choose me."

"And what about the people in the town you burned? They weren't threatening you," Kari said, her brow furrowed.

"Maybe not currently, but they are still members of a hostile state. They were my enemy, and I treated them like such." Falcon closed his eyes. "Besides, I evacuated the town after you killed the few soldiers we had there to maintain peace and order. No one died because of my actions."

He was lying to himself. Kari wanted to feel proud and boastful for knowing that, but all she felt was sorrow for his delusions.

"You left those people without shelter or food. If we hadn't helped, many would have died," Kari said. Was she just as deluded? She had killed so many people. Had lost count of the number of bodies she had accumulated. She would like to believe each life ended was vindicated, but was that the case?

"I don't have to justify my actions to you," Falcon snarled. Kari jumped at his outburst. He sighed. "I'm sorry if I snapped. I realize I might have fucked up at the town. I didn't think it through. So what made you want to overthrow Xiang?"

"I didn't overthrow it," Kari snapped. He was trying to change the subject, but it was one she didn't want to talk about. "At least, I didn't intend to. I was a songstress forced into the emperors' harem. I did what I had to do to survive."

"If you were a songstress, know any good songs?" Falcon stared up at the sky.

Perhaps he picked up on her apprehension. Either way, she was relieved. She could finally return to being the songstress, if only for a moment.

"Only the best." Smiling, Kari gazed into his eyes. Her heart skipped as his blue eyes stared back at her. Why did his gaze affect her so? Ignoring her racing heart, she began to sing.

"Once upon an endless night,
Where lovers meet within twilight.
Bathed in the ocean
Craved for devotion
Fingers interlaced in a tight embrace
Fade away in the dark without a trace
A touch so sacred
Forever awaited
Memories of lips so tender and sweet
Just another night and I'll live for your heat
A spirit so young
A song unsung
A story, an unending endeavor
My heart beats for you forever."

"Wow," Falcon said, resting his hand on top of hers. "That was amazing. I've never felt this strongly about a song before."

"It's one of my gifts," Kari explained. "I infuse my voice with spirit energy to heighten emotions."

His touch was warm and kind, but painful at the same time. Still, Kari welcomed it. If only it were Ina's hand instead. She clasped his tighter. It was odd how the simple act of human contact made her feel so alive.

Falcon blushed and shot to his feet, leaving her alone on the log. "You should get some sleep," he said. "You can keep my cloak. Use it to stay warm." He hurried to his tent.

Kari gritted her teeth. Damn. She'd done it again. How could she repeat her mistake so soon? She closed her eyes. He wasn't Ina, yet, for a brief moment, Kari had held her—she'd held her lover's hand.

The next morning, they packed up camp and headed out before the sun had even risen. She was tired, exhausted even, but not able to sleep.

The group of soldiers marched in a single file line through the forest. Kari, Ronin, and Ina were sandwiched between Falcon and Athena.

Athena had glared at their lack of shackles, but she didn't say anything. She rested her massive sword on her shoulder as they marched.

"I can't help but notice we are lost," Ronin said, following behind Ina.

"We're not lost," Athena retorted, shoving him to move faster.

"We're headed south, but there's nothing that way but the coast," Ronin said. "Do you have a ship waiting for us?"

"No," was Athena's only reply.

"Then, we're lost."

"Your allies would anticipate us heading west to the mountains. Instead, we are heading south," Falcon called back.

"I'm pretty sure that didn't make any sense," Ronin said, smiling. "Unless you're stupid. In that case, carry on."

"Would you shut up?" Athena shoved Ronin again.

Laughing, Ronin rattled the shackles, which had been placed back around his hands. "You two are so tough, keeping me chained up. Of course, I would be frightened of me, too."

"Ronin," Ina said, exasperated. "Please stop antagonizing them."

"Why? Do you think they might kill us?" Ronin asked, winking. "Oh wait, they are already marching us to our deaths."

"You sleep with this guy?" Falcon asked Kari, pointing toward Ronin.

"What?" Kari blushed. "He's my brother!"

"Oh..." Falcon's face reddened. "I thought... I mean, you don't... Are you sure you're related?"

"I guess you don't know everything," Ronin mocked. "You are a blind fool who follows his master's call without question."

"Better that than an assassin," Falcon barked.

"This coming from the mercenary." Ronin smiled. "Just thinking about killing you brings me so much joy."

Falcon scoffed.

They continued hiking, eventually arriving at a circle of twelve stones. Etched in each stone was a strange rune that glowed a dull blue.

"What is this?" Ina asked, eyeing the circle.

"It's an Aeolus Gate," Falcon responded. He held up his medallion. "When used in conjunction with an Aeolus Medallion, we can instantly teleport to any other gate."

Kari's heart sank. "What's on the other side?"

"We're going to Justia. That's where we are meeting Gabriel," Athena said.

"The Sage of Terra?" Ina asked. There were three sages, one for each of the realms. Each sage was the ruler of their realm, answering only to the Guardian.

Falcon faced Kari. "Gabriel is a good man. An honorable man. If you plead your case and explain your actions, he will be just."

"Do you not know what you just said?" Ronin asked. "You do know why you were sent after her, right?"

Falcon shrugged. "She killed the emperors of Xiang."

Ronin laughed. "You are a blind fool."

"She's Shagin," Ina said bluntly.

"Motherfucker!" Falcon screamed, kicking the ground.

"We still have a job to do." Athena grabbed Falcon by the shoulder. "This doesn't change anything."

"The fuck it doesn't," Falcon said, spinning on his heel. "Do you know what we just did?"

"How did you not know?" Ronin asked. "Isn't it obvious she's Shagin? You even knew about Xiang, but not this?"

"There are three worlds we operate in. We just found out about Xiang when given this assignment." Falcon clenched his jaw. "I never thought Gabriel would be a part of this. I never imagined we would be either."

"Steady your resolve," Athena demanded. "Think of Arwyn and Hector. We must follow this through."

"How can we?"

"I knew you were too soft for this assignment," Ryder said. "Some bounty hunter you are."

"You piece of shit, you fucking knew!" Falcon grabbed the man by the throat. He drew his dagger ready to strike.

Kari's heart pounded. No more bloodshed. No more death. Her breathing raced. She had to stop it. Lashing out with her light whip, she wrapped it around Falcon's arm and prevented him from killing Ryder. Falcon's head jerked toward her as Athena and the other soldiers readied their weapons to attack.

Kari stared at Falcon, her resolve no longer wavering. "Not for me."

Falcon's eyes narrowed, but he nodded. Kari dissipated her whip, then held her hands up in a submissive position.

"Stand down," Falcon told his men as he sheathed his dagger. He faced Kari. "Don't resign yourself to death. You are better than that."

"I'm not," Kari said. Falcon didn't know her. He didn't know what she had done. How could she begin anew with everything that had transpired? Taking a deep breath, she stepped into the circle of runestones. "I'm ready."

Only a small group could go through at a time due to the space limitations of the ring. Kari and Ronin were to enter first, escorted by Falcon and Athena. They had to cram together to stand within the circle.

The stones whirred as a purple light erupted all around them. The sound ceased, and the light faded. The forest was gone. Instead, stone walls met them. Kari's chest tightened. She would find her fate here.

"Athena, take the medallion and bring the next group." After Falcon handed her the pendant, she stepped into the circle of runestones.

They whirred to life as purple light shot forth from the runes. When it faded, Athena was gone.

Kari gazed at the stones. She had never seen magic like this before. According to Shagin, teleportation was impossible. How could the Guardian have perfected it?

Her eyes widened. What was this? On the far side of the circle, etched in stone, was the Shagin symbol. She darted her gaze to each stone. They weren't random symbols at all. They were words—written in the ancient Shagin language.

"This is stolen magic!" Kari shouted, pointing at the gate. "This is Shagin magic!"

"What?" Falcon asked in confusion.

"The symbols are Shagin," Kari said again. "My people created this."

"No," Falcon said. "The Immortal Warrior created the magic tied to the gates. Only he knows how they work."

Kari shook her head. She pointed to the Shagin symbol. "Look, there. That's the word for *Shagin*. It means *outcast*. Beside it, there's the symbol for *together*. Then, *united*, *wind*, and *lovers*."

"Can you read what it says?" Ronin asked, stepping beside Kari, his brow furrowed.

"Give me a moment," Kari responded, kneeling to get a closer look at the symbols. "I can't speak the old tongue, but I can read it... somewhat."

"Shagin don't use these." Ronin knelt beside her, running his finger over the blue symbol.

"No." Kari shook her. "I've never seen anything like it before. But the words are Shagin."

"It has to be a coincidence." Falcon rubbed his chin. "The Immortal Warrior created these nearly two thousand years ago."

Light shot forth from the runestones as Ina arrived with the next group. Kari didn't budge as they walked past her. She continued to study the stones as Athena went back for more of the soldiers.

"I have to know what this says." Kari paced around the circle, examining each symbol.

"We can wait until everyone is back, but then I'll have to take you to your cell," Falcon said, grimacing. "I'm sorry, but that's the best I can do for now."

Kari nodded. She motioned to two of the symbols. "I believe it's a poem. These two say *Lover's Ballad*. I believe that's the title of the piece. If you follow it around from there, it says, '*Fly on the wings of the wind, united together, outcasts no more.*'"

"What does that mean?" Falcon asked.

"Honestly, I don't know." Kari shrugged. Legend stated it was the Triune gods who cursed Shagin to bear only female children, but the ancient Shagin wrote the Immortal Warrior was the one to curse them in an attempt to make them sterile. He'd withheld magic and knowledge from his people. Perhaps he'd stole this from Shagin, then hid its origins.

The Immortal Warrior hated Shagin for their worship of Nebura and the Fates. He demanded all nations worship the Triune gods. Shagin openness to spread knowledge infuriated him. His myths stated the Triune once ruled the Realms, but the spread of magic led to the people revolting against the gods. It was nonsense. If they were indeed gods, how would magic have mattered?

It would make sense for him to steal Shagin teleportation magic. He had banished Shagin to the Latari Forest. Even in the old days, it was a crime worthy of death to be Shagin caught outside their territory. These gates would have made enforcing his reprehensible laws near impossible.

Kari gritted her teeth. It seemed every ill that befell Shagin was connected to the Guardian.

"Everyone is here," Athena said after about her eighth trip through the gate. "We should get moving. Legato will be cross if we don't have her imprisoned soon."

Kari swallowed hard. Her time was up. It wasn't the unknown fate awaiting her that weighed heavy on her heart, but the knowledge she would never discover the truth of the Aeolus gates.

Falcon and Athena replaced the shackles and collars on Kari and her friends. The bounty hunters wanted it to look like they were at least following protocol. Kari didn't fight it. She had come willingly this far, so there was no point in resisting now.

They followed Falcon up a spiral stone staircase. By the looks of the walls and dimly lit hallways, sparsely illuminated by candles, they were in some sort of fortress. Their footsteps echoed through the stone corridors before they stopped at a large metal door. Falcon knocked three times, and a young soldier opened it.

"More heads for your collection?" The soldier smiled.

Falcon rolled his eyes. "I have the prisoners the Guardian wanted."

"Good." The soldier stepped aside so they could enter. Expansive cells filled the long room. They were barren, except for straw and hay lining the floors. Grabbing Kari's arm, he half dragged her to a cell at the far end of the dungeon. He slung her in before ushering Ronin and Ina in as well. After he slammed the iron door, he locked them in.

Kari stared through the bars. She was on her own now, locked in a cage while waiting to die.

"Whatever happens, I want you to know I have the utmost respect for you," Falcon said before he and Athena departed.

A smile crept across Kari's face. What little good his words did still filled her with warmth. She had lived a good life. Others saw the light in her core, and she had helped those she could. Closing her eyes, she collapsed to her knees. She drew a deep breath, exhaling slowly. No matter what happened, she was ready.

CHAPTER EIGHTEEN

FALCON

"Falcon, what are you doing?" Athena asked, trailing behind him.

"I have to talk to Gabriel. He needs to know she's Shagin," Falcon said, storming through the fortress halls. As Athena tried to catch up, he didn't break his stride. He had to hurry. If Legato acted first, there was no telling what would befall Kari and her friends.

"You think he doesn't?"

"He would have said something. He wouldn't go along with this. It's not right."

Falcon and Athena marched toward the courtroom, where two guards stood watch outside the wooden doors. They regarded them as they approached. The guards stood with arms crossed, their spears resting on the wall next to them. Falcon scoffed. Some guards they were.

"We need to see Gabriel," he demanded.

"The war council is in session. No one is allowed in," a soldier explained.

"Does it look like I care?" Falcon asked, pushing him aside.

Athena grabbed Falcon's arm. "You can't just barge in there."

"Why, what's the worst that could happen?" Falcon pulled away, then reached for the door.

"They could kill you."

Falcon stopped. Sighing, he retreated. "You're right."

"There is nothing more that we can do," Athena said. "It is best that we forget about this ordeal lest we forget about the children."

Falcon gritted his teeth. This was bullshit. Gabriel got them into this mess. If he hadn't sought them out, they wouldn't be stuck working for that bastard Legato. Falcon clenched his fists, turning his knuckles white. His weakness caused this. Now, the lives of his friends' children were being used as leverage against him.

"Fuck it." Falcon whirled and kicked the door in, sending it crashing into the wall.

The men in the room gaped as Falcon charged in. The guards rushed in after him, drawing their swords. Falcon rolled his eyes. They couldn't even be bothered to grab their spears.

Gabriel rose from his seat at the center of the table. He was a tall, muscular man who towered over his generals. His dark skin matched his even darker eyes. Based on his stature, he looked as if he could rip apart anyone with his bare hands. His foes called him Gabriel the Demon. In battle, he could fight like a possessed beast, but, outside of the action, he was an intellectual, reasonable man. Falcon needed Gabriel to utilize his wits now.

Gabriel held out a hand for the guards to stop. "What do you think you're doing?"

"I was going to ask you the same thing," Falcon retorted.

"You insolent whelp. You should know your place," one general screamed, banging a fist on the surface of the table.

Falcon held up his middle finger. "Hush, the adults are talking."

"Athena, you are levelheaded. Please explain what is going on," Gabriel demanded.

"I'm sorry, I can't control him," she said.

Falcon shot her a dirty look, but he quickly turned his attention back to Gabriel.

"Did you know?" Falcon demanded.

"Did I know what?" Gabriel asked.

Falcon gritted his teeth at the feigned ignorance.

"The girl you sent me after—Kari—did you know she was Shagin?" Falcon asked.

"I was hoping you wouldn't find out." Sighing, Gabriel rubbed his bald head.

"You son of a bitch," Falcon muttered.

"That's treason," a general shouted out.

"Wouldn't be the first time," Falcon said.

Athena buried her face in her hands.

"Legato thought it was of the utmost importance to eliminate her quickly. She had already toppled one nation. Time was against us," Gabriel explained.

"How can you agree with this?" Falcon asked.

"There is more to this matter than you are aware. Besides, it doesn't matter if we agree. The Guardian decreed it so. As such, I must follow. You do as well." Gabriel's voice boomed in the war room.

"Like hell I do. If you are given a bullshit order, you tell him to go fuck himself." Falcon glared, waiting for the man to justify his obedience.

"I'll have your tongue cut out for that remark," a general yelled.

"You'll die trying," Falcon responded, not taking his eyes off Gabriel.

Gabriel blinked, then smiled. "Tell me, Falcon, what would you sacrifice for your convictions?" he asked. "Would you die for them?"

"If need be."

"Athena, do you agree with his assessment?" Gabriel asked.

"I agree with his sentiment," Athena said. "Though, as usual, his actions are reckless. I do not believe that defiance is defensible in this cause, given the circumstances."

Falcon shot her a look. "Thanks."

"I see," Gabriel said, rubbing his chin. "After considering your position, I have decided to follow through with my duty."

"You motherfucker." Falcon reached for the hilt of his sword, but Athena grabbed his arm. She jerked it, stopping him from drawing his weapon.

"Legato is meeting with the girl as we speak. He wants her moved to the tower immediately. However, I will postpone her transfer, effectively granting her a stay of execution until the morning. That will give her time to get right with her pagan gods. Will this satisfy you, Falcon?" Gabriel asked.

Falcon gritted his teeth. "Fine."

"Sire, she is too dangerous. She should be killed now," a general pleaded.

"They brought her here without incident; one night should make no difference. After all, we must be merciful," Gabriel said, smirking. "And Falcon, an interruption like this will not happen again. Is that understood?"

"It is." Falcon pivoted, storming from the courtroom.

The guards slammed the door shut as Falcon rushed toward the dungeon.

"You need to stop and think before you act," Athena scolded, hurrying to catch up.

"What are you talking about?" Falcon stopped, scowling. "That went great. I knew Gabriel would help."

"What conversation were you listening to?" Athena asked in disbelief.

"Gabriel gave us an entire night, and he asked me what I was willing to give up," Falcon explained. "He expects me to do something tonight, and this gives him plausible deniability so he can disavow us if we get caught."

"You *are* a blind fool."

KARI

Kari fiddled with the straw as she sat on the cold stone floor. Ronin had searched the cell for any weaknesses, but when he hadn't found any, he'd decided to rest and bide his time. At least, that was what he said. The guard had left them alone in the dungeon, which meant they were free to talk openly.

"We should prepare for the worst," Ronin said, straightening from his lounging position.

"What do you mean?" Kari asked. She didn't like that statement. Instead, she wished she could ignore it. Perhaps pretend it never happened.

The prison entrance opened, and a man in golden armor flanked by an entourage of soldiers entered. The man had grey hair that juxtaposed his still-black beard. He stopped within inches of the cell, his gaze bounced from Kari to Ina.

"Which one is Kari?" he asked.

"I am," Ronin said, jumping to his feet.

The man glowered, his hand moving toward the arming sword on his hip.

"I am Kari." Kari rose, then approached the cell bars.

"Thank you." After smiling at her, he motioned to the ground in front of the bars. "Now, sit."

Kari did as instructed. The man followed suit by crouching on the other side.

"Do you know who I am?" he asked.

Kari shook her head. "Should I?"

"I am Legato, Guardian of the Three Realms."

Kari's heart jumped. This was the Guardian? The man who'd sent Falcon after her... who called for her death?

"Do you have it?" Legato asked.

Her chest tightened. He knew. "Have what?"

Kari met his blue eyes. How could he look at her, but still see nothing but a monster?

"Leave us," Legato barked toward his men. Without a word, the guards departed. "Now that we're alone, we can talk freely. But I warn you... do not toy with me, or else I will kill your companions. Do you have the Seed?"

"How do you know about that?" Kari asked.

"My predecessor knew all sorts of secrets—ones you could only dream about. The Shagin filth are its keepers. The monsters have hidden it from us for so long, but their tactics have failed. You have it, yes?"

"I don't," Kari lied. "The Seed is a myth."

Legato smiled. "You do have it. At last, I finally found it. Tell me, where are the other Shagin filth hiding?"

"Go to hell," Kari spat.

Legato laughed. "If you tell me, I will make your execution quick. Otherwise, I will make it last for years."

"How can you call yourself a guardian?" Ina asked. "What did she ever do to you?"

Legato scowled.

Smiling, Ronin held up his hand to Ina. "You forget, he's not the Guardian. Without the Immortal Blade, you're not the true heir. What is it they call? Legato the Illegitimate?"

"I'm going to execute you tonight," Legato snarled, jabbing a finger at Ronin.

"No, you won't." Her brother grinned. "You need me and Ina alive. The information you need from Kari—if you kill either of us, you won't get it. You need us alive so you can torture us to get her to talk."

"Ronin!" Kari hissed.

"Why are you giving him ideas?" Ina asked, sounding horrified.

"He's right," Legato said. "I will torture these two until you tell me what I need to know. Let's skip the foreplay. How do I pull the Seed from you?"

"I don't have it," Kari insisted. She would die before she gave it up. All Shagin would die to protect it.

"Keep your secrets for now." Legato stood to his feet. "I'm having you moved to my tower. There I will find out everything I need to know."

He stalked toward the exit before pivoting toward Kari. "I think I'm going to cut out your pretty eyes." He left, slamming the iron door behind him.

"It's as I feared," Ronin said. "I swear on my life that we're going to get out of here." He paced around the cell, running searching hands over the wall and bars. "But first, we need to discuss the Seed."

"You know I can't!" Kari exclaimed. "The Seed must be kept secret."

"Oh, I'm sorry, I don't care," Ronin retorted.

"You should," Kari said.

"I don't know what this is about," Ina said. "But if Kari doesn't want to talk about it, she doesn't have to."

"Why am I the only voice of reason here? I know. Legato and Kari know." Ronin pointed at Ina. "The only person here who doesn't know is you, and there is no point in it."

"It's shameful," Kari whispered.

"More shameful than anything you did with the emperors?" Ronin asked.

"Stop that!" Ina demanded.

Kari buried her face in her hands. She didn't want to be reminded of the hell she went through. Not ever.

"Sorry," Ronin said, obviously noticing her change in demeanor.

"I'm sure when Kari is ready, she'll tell me," Ina added.

"Doubtful," Ronin said. "At any rate, it doesn't matter what she wants. We both need to be willing to do whatever it takes to protect Kari."

"I think we all want to protect each other," Ina said.

"It's more than that," Kari added. "I bear the Shagin curse. I am the Bearer of the Seed."

"What is that supposed to mean?" Ina asked.

Kari could do it. Ina needed to know. Kari's life was unimportant—only the Seed mattered.

"The Seed is an energy source," Kari explained. "It tore the world apart, forming the Three Realms and holding them in pocket dimensions. It's responsible for the Cataclysm, the apocalyptic event caused by the division that nearly wiped out all life, nearly two thousand years ago."

"By the gods," Ina whispered.

"The Seed holds the Realms apart," Ronin interjected. "But it can also merge them back together. Three worlds simultaneously crashing into each other. It would be the end of existence as we know it—a second Cataclysm."

"Okay...so what do we do?" Ina asked.

"Protect Kari at all costs," Ronin said. "If the Guardian finds a way to use the Seed, we're all fucked."

Kari squinted her eyes. "If I'm killed, the Seed will be passed on to another Shagin. You need to kill me."

"Not happening," Ronin said, stubbornness tightening his jaw. "I won't let you die."

A hushed silence fell. Ina wrapped her arms around Kari. "We'll protect you."

"I'm not worried about me," Kari said. "If he gets the Seed, everyone will die."

"You're being melodramatic," Ronin shot back. "Only half the population died in the first Cataclysm."

"That's not helping," Ina scolded.

"The Seed is more important than me." Kari stared into Ina's eyes. "Please kill me before he uses it."

The door to the prison creaked open. Falcon rushed in, holding a set of keys.

"Come on, you're leaving," Falcon said, opening the cell door.

"I'm not leaving," Kari said. "Legato knows what I am. He knows about the Seed. There is no place that will be safe enough. I have to see this through. I have to die."

"Kari..." Ina placed a hand on her shoulder.

"Okay, I don't know what this Seed is, but fuck it," Falcon said. "You want to live, right? Let's go."

"Kari, we need to go," Ina pleaded. "I don't want to die here, and neither should you."

"Please don't tell me what I should or shouldn't want to do," Kari said. Her death was the only way to protect the Seed.

"Fine," Ina said, jumping up. "You keep saying you don't know who you are, and you don't know what the world has become. Kari, you have to find out if there is more to life than hatred and death. You won't find those answers on the executioner's block, you'll only find death. I won't join you."

Ina stepped out of the cell, then stood behind Falcon.

"What's it going to be, Kari? We don't have time to debate this," Falcon said. "Life or death—it's your choice."

Kari averted her gaze. "Just go."

Falcon shook his head. "Come on. We need to be quick."

Falcon and Ina left. Ronin stayed with Kari.

"You should go, too," Kari told him.

"My place is by your side," he said. "I will support you in whatever you choose."

"Am I doing the right thing?" Kari asked, meeting his eyes.

"No," Ronin replied. "But the fool was right. It's your choice to make. Tell me that you understand the answers you seek can't be found here. You have to find them. If you stay here, you never will."

Kari nodded. "I know."

"Do you want to die?"

"I don't know," she said. "I don't think I do, but I can't live with this pain."

"Then overcome it," Ronin said. "It won't be easy, and it won't be quick. In some way, the pain might always be there. But you can control it. You can master it. You can beat it into submission. Or you can sit and let it beat you to death."

"I don't know what the point would be. Why would I want to live in this world? I have seen the true face of humanity. I have experienced our true nature that abuses and destroys each other."

Ronin sighed. "I understand I have little capacity for friendship. I am not the easiest person to be around. I don't have friends. I had subordinates and superiors, but never friends. You accepted me without question. You've helped me be better. If you feel like humanity is inherently evil, that the world is corrupt, then show them a better way."

"Show them? Is it that simple?" Kari stared at her hands. Was that what Carina had attempted? To show her torturers the face of love?

"Make it that simple," Ronin said. He stood, holding his hand out to Kari. "You told the fool you hadn't resigned yourself to death. Will you show that?"

"It doesn't matter what I do. The Seed threatens everyone. I have a duty to protect it."

"Then protect it, damn it!" Ronin screamed. "If you die, you give up. We can protect it. If you die, there is no hope. Save the world, protect the Seed. Make the world the place it should be. I don't like Vipin, but his shield idea could ensure the Seed's safety. What's it going to be? Death tonight? Or you can fight this bastard with every fiber of your being."

"I want to live." Kari took Ronin's hand, letting him pull her to her feet.

"Come on. If we hurry, we can catch up to them," Ronin said.

They ran out of the cell, then through the dungeon before opening the door. Falcon and Ina waited.

"She said if we waited, you would come," Falcon said.

"Thank you." Kari took Ina's hands.

"We should hurry before we are spotted," Falcon said. "Athena has your gear. She is waiting for us at the Aeolus Gate. We'll send you wherever you want to go."

The Immortal Warrior was long since gone. His successor should be held accountable for his actions, but their methods hurt innocent people. It was a complex issue, one that couldn't be resolved by simply overthrowing a tyrant. She had done that in Xiang, and now the empire was engulfed in civil war.

Was there a better way? Kari was uncertain, but how could an age of love be forged through violence? It didn't seem that simple.

Kari turned to Falcon. "You were right. It is who we try to be that determines who we are, and the actions we take shape our future. Thank you."

"Let me come with you," he said.

"No," Athena added. "This is as far as we can go now."

"Yes, you would only get in our way," Ronin said.

"We could use your help," Kari said. "The Guardian will pursue us. Can you slow him down?"

"I suppose," Falcon said. "But we can help hide you. It's foolish to go alone."

"She won't be." Ina placed a hand on Kari's shoulder. "We're going with her."

"We won't need to hide if we hurry," Kari said. The Furies had a plan to protect themselves from Legato, but there was no telling just how much more work the array needed before the barrier could be activated. "But Legato will be coming for me."

If he came with his army before they were ready, it would be a fierce battle. Even with the strength of the Furies and Vipin, they would be outnumbered. Numbers were Shagin's downfall during the Purge. They wouldn't be able to hold back his army.

Kari gritted her teeth, balling her fists. If he got his hands on the Seed, all hope would be lost. He would activate it and destroy humanity in the process, just to solidify his power.

She had been aware of her duty to defend the Seed, but to what lengths would she go to protect it?

"I'll take you to the other side," Falcon said. "Once I go back through, collect the thirteen runestones. It will prevent anyone from following you. If you need help, you can lay them out in a circle, and it will activate a gate. I'll be watching it. If you activate the gate, we'll be there."

She kissed him on the cheek, and he smiled in return.

"Good luck," he said, blushing bright red.

A wall of purple light erupted all around them until nothing could be seen through it. It faded away, and they were back in the Latari Forest.

CHAPTER NINETEEN

The streets of Koruzeru were just as busy and lively as ever. People stopped to smile as they entered the city. They had to hurry; they couldn't afford to be distracted now. The Guardian was coming, and time was against them.

"Welcome back, Lady Kari," a man cried out.

Kari, stopped in her tracks, beaming from the welcome. It was nice to be appreciated, especially after talking with Legato. Ronin nudged her.

"Wasn't there something we were supposed to be doing?" he asked.

"Right." Kari shook her head, trying to focus on the task at hand. "The Furies will most likely be in Lasan. We should hurry."

"Ah." Ronin leaned back, stretching. "The one place we can't go."

"You can enter the building," Kari explained. "You just can't enter the sanctuary."

"Let me rephrase that." Ronin winked. "The one place I don't want to go."

"We should get some rest first," Ina added. Sweat dripped down her red face. She had struggled to keep up on the hike. Without control of her spirit energy, there was no enhancing her muscles or endurance, and they had traversed through the forest in less than a day.

"I can't rest until I know we are prepared and safe from Legato," Kari said. She was tired from the journey, and she could only imagine how much more exhausted Ina had to be. Still, the Guardian was coming. They needed to prepare as soon as possible. If his hunters showed while she was busy resting, she could never forgive herself. "You two go on ahead back to your rooms. I'll notify Ilyia."

Ronin and Ina departed back to their quarters, leaving Kari alone to find the Furies. She headed through the streets of Koruzeru. She had to find Ilyia. Time was against them. Legato knew she was the Bearer, and he wanted the Seed. He probably thought he could consolidate his power by merging the Realms, but the only thing he would accomplish would be the deaths of millions.

Kari opened the door to the Temple of Lasan, entering the sanctuary. Artemis sat in one of the pews. She jumped up, staring at Kari as the door creaked closed.

"What happened? Where have you been?" Artemis scowled, rushing over to her.

"It's a long story," Kari said. "Where's Ilyia? I need to speak to her."

"The last time I saw her, she was in the Chamber of the Seers," Artemis replied, pointing up to the third-floor balcony.

Kari darted up the steel spiral staircase to the chamber. Her footsteps echoed on the steel steps as she climbed to the third floor and the base of the statue of Nebura.

Kari reached the balcony, then opened the large decorative wooden door to the chamber. Ilyia stood from the blue marble floor, stones and sticks strewn around her.

"We were worried about you," she said, rushing over. She took Kari by the hands, examining her up and down. "I'm glad you are safe. When you disappeared, I feared the worst."

"Thank you for your concern."

Ilyia embraced Kari, then kissed her forehead.

"I'm so sorry. Artemis said she thought it was too soon for you to experience a memory stone." She released Kari, rubbing her eyes. "Of course, it's not a matter of being ready. No one is ready to experience what you went through."

"I agree." Nothing could prepare someone for the experience. Still, part of Kari was glad she had, while another would do anything to go back and refuse the offer.

"It is necessary to understand our plight," Ilyia said.

That much was true. Kari understood far better than she ever had. The atrocities committed in the name of the Guardian and his gods were beyond belief. And if they didn't hurry, they would only repeat.

"I met the Guardian," Kari said with a frown. "He knows about the Seed. Worse, he knows I have it."

"That can't be." Ilyia stared, wide-eyed. "How could he know?"

Ultimately, it didn't matter how he knew. Whether it was a lucky guess or superior deductive reasoning, it made little difference. Shagin were alive. He knew about the Seed. And now he knew she was the Bearer. There was only one thing to do—protect the Seed at any cost.

"He'll be coming for me," Kari said. Justia was legions away. They had dismantled the Aeolus Gate, storing the runestones within Kari's ring. It would take time for Legato and his armies to march on Shagin. But the gates were small, easy to hide. Most likely, Legato had gates hidden throughout each Realm.

Kari's chest tightened. Time was against them. If Legato mobilized his forces, they wouldn't be able to use the gates. They were too small. He would send his hunters after her. Only this time, Falcon and the Thunder Five wouldn't be the ones sent. It would be those more loyal to the Guardian. Perhaps the Torredins this time—vicious and cruel. Or worse, the Guardian and his Sages.

Scowling, Ilyia rubbed her face. "It is sooner than expected, but we'll have to go ahead and activate the shield. I only hope we have enough energy to do so."

That was good. If the barrier were as strong as they hoped it would be, it should be able to protect them. Unless there was another Aeolus Gate within Shagin, then a barrier would be useless.

Kari wiped at the sweat forming on her brow. They had to succeed. Had to stop Legato. The entire world depended on them. But more than that, the fate of Shagin depended on it. They had to succeed to save Shagin.

They weren't alone. They had allies within the Guardian's ranks. Falcon would help them, at least she hoped he would.

"Falcon helped us escape. He's going to try to buy us some time. He might be able to help us in other ways, too."

"The bounty hunter?" Ilyia raised an eyebrow. "The one who burned down Anuatu?"

How could Kari explain this to her? His reaction to finding out she was Shagin proved that he wasn't an enemy, that and him helping her. Falcon might have burned down her mother's town, but that didn't mean he was necessarily evil. He was human, flawed, and fighting a battle. The man showed his cruelty and brutality to his enemies. He wasn't so different from her. Had she not condemncd her enemies to death? Had she not banished their families for merely loving her foes?

Her actions were seen as cruel and heartless by those she inflicted them upon. Maybe that was the nature of humanity. Humanity brutalized each other—dividing each other into *them* and *us*. The truth was there was no *them*—only *us*. Humanity was all the same. Capable of love and happiness, dreams, and ambitions.

Maybe even Legato was like that? Could he be reasoned with?

How could she get Ilyia to see? Kari rubbed her hand through her hair.

"He's not as evil as I thought," she finally said.

"Of course he is," Ilyia said, shaking her head. "Don't be fooled by a small act of kindness. They are vultures, preying on the weak. The only people we can trust in this world are our sisters."

If that was the case, then why rely on the knights and allow others to live in Koruzeru?

"What about all the people you've brought together and helped?" Kari asked.

"A temporary alliance. They are useful to us, that is all." Ilyia placed her hands on her hips. "The world turned its back on Shagin. They all watched as we were annihilated, and they either did nothing or they helped kill us."

"There are still good people," Kari argued. She had seen that with her own eyes, and Carina's. "There were soldiers and a young captain who sacrificed themselves to save us. They helped Carina. And Falcon saved me from the Guardian."

That was after he had captured her, but Ilyia didn't need to know that.

"And it wasn't enough," Ilyia said. "The people of this world are just as complacent as the Guardian."

It might not have been enough, but at least they had tried. The young captain and his soldiers had given their lives to help them. They might not have been able to rescue all of Shagin, but they saved as many as they could.

If Ilyia thought the entire world was complacent in the Purge, did that mean she was considering them guilty along with the Guardian?

"And will you bring them to justice, too?" Kari asked.

"Yes," Ilyia said coldly. "We will create a new age."

"You can't do this!" Kari yelled. "You can't condemn the innocent with the guilty!"

"There is no one innocent, not one," Ilyia spat. Sighing, she clasped Kari's hands in her own. "I should have been honest with you from the start. I was afraid you would think we were monsters if you knew the truth. We've modified the array, and we will be using it to create a shield that will protect Shagin."

They had been honest about the use of the array from the start. But why would she think they were monsters if they had modified it?

Ilyia averted her gaze. "We need energy. Lots of it. The dalium isn't enough."

"Couldn't you find more?" Kari asked.

"Possibly, given the time. But we always had a backup plan in case we ran out of time."

Kari's eyes widened as the thought donned on her. "You would need an energy source. The array was first used to steal the life energy from others. And you've gathered all the necessary components. All these people, they're living about the array, and you have just enough dalium to activate it. They're sacrifices! Everyone in this city. You plan on killing them and using their energy."

Ilyia's face became emotionless. She closed her eyes, tilting her head upward. "That is an unfortunate consequence. But as I mentioned, they are just as guilty as the Guardian."

"You can't do that!" Kari protested. "That's not justice—that's vengeance! If you kill them, how are you any different from the Immortal Warrior?"

Ilyia's eyes shot open. "Don't compare me to him," she spat. "I am trying to save lives. I am trying to create a new world where atrocities like those committed in the past never occur again."

"So *you* would commit- the atrocities?" Kari clenched her fists. She would stop them if she had to. The idea weighed heavily on her heart. Could she stand against her sisters? Surely, they would see the wrongness of their actions.

"This is why I won't be fit to live in this new world. Make no mistake, I am a monster. But don't delude yourself in thinking these people are innocent. The entire world stood by as we were slaughtered. If you allow evil to exist, you are just as guilty. These people are criminals and killers, and you have no right to mourn them. We will forge a new world in fire, and they will be the spark that brings peace," Ilyia said. "Activation of the array requires life energy; it's an unfortunate truth."

Kari's heart sank, and her body went numb. The array was designed to gather life energy. If they were modifying it to perform what it was initially capable of doing, that meant it was at some point modified to do something else.

Kari's mouth dropped, her arms and legs trembling. "You activated the array before?"

"What?" Ilyia asked with a crooked grin.

"The tunnels, there were scorch marks and signs of recent use." Kari gasped, her hand shooting to her mouth. "Vipin... You created him with it."

"Yes." Ilyia gritted her teeth. Kari dropped to her knees, fighting the urge to vomit. "I wasn't going to let the deaths of my sisters go unpunished. By murdering us, the Guardian created the god of vengeance who would judge the world."

Kari's emerald eyes shot daggers at Ilyia as tears streamed down her face. "But you brought people here, and you were in charge of protecting this city!"

"The Purge had already started," Ilyia said, her own tears starting. She turned her back to Kari, covering her eyes. "There was no going back, no stopping it. I ensured it was over as quickly as possible, and that their deaths wouldn't be in vain. Each Shagin the Guardian killed only made Vipin that much stronger."

"You're mad." Kari wiped her face as she rose. "If he's so powerful, why do you need a shield?"

"To protect us from the second cataclysm." Ilyia spun around, launching a puff of white smoke into Kari's face.

Kari stumbled back as smoke filled her nostrils. It was the same poison powder Cai Ren had used. She swatted at the air as her head spun from the poison.

"We... can't..." Kari stammered. She had to fight to protect the Seed, so she focused her energy. Her aura was present, but unstable. If she didn't find a way to end the fight quickly, she wouldn't last long.

Ilyia leaped forward, summoning her staff. Kari intensified her energy into her hand. A blast of light erupted from her fingers, but her power was too unstable to form into her whip. Ilyia shielded her eyes from the light and charged forward, striking Kari in the gut with her staff.

Kari's eyes widened, and she howled as the force of the impact lifted her from her feet and threw her across the room. She rolled on the ground, clutching her middle as she tried to catch her breath from the impact.

Pain shot through her body as she tried to sit up. She screamed as blood trickled from her mouth. Damn it! Her ribs were broken, and she was losing consciousness. The room around her tilted and spun.

"It was the Cataclysm that plunged the world into the Age of Chaos and allowed the Immortal Warrior to seize power and reshape the world as he saw fit. There is no easier way to create a new age than through the same power. Unfortunately, the array can't activate the Seed." Ilyia placed a foot on Kari's chest, forcing her down. "But all we need is you."

CHAPTER TWENTY

KARI STIRRED AS SHE blinked the world into view. Her head and shoulders ached. She laid in a cushiony bed within the Chamber of the Bearer. Her arms were outstretched and bound tightly to wooden posts mounted to the head of the bed. Her feet were tied, then strapped to a similar post at the foot. Three large ropes ran the width of the mattress, across her body, and bound her to it. There was no slack in any of the bindings, and her movements were restricted entirely.

"I hope you're comfortable," Ilyia said, noticing Kari waking.

"Go to hell," Kari spat back.

"I meant that most sincerely," Ilyia said, bowing her head. "It was too soon. Artemis was right. Everything was too soon. I had hoped that giving you a memory stone would help you see the necessity of this. If only we had more time, you would agree with us and help us save the world."

"Save it?" Kari asked, raising her head. "You're going to destroy it."

"Our methods may seem cruel, but we will be creating a new world," Ilyia said with a flick of her sleeve. "You have nothing to be afraid of. We won't harm you, and the ritual won't kill you either. We need you alive. Your power to grow and control plants will help us rebuild after the Cataclysm."

Kari didn't care about herself. "Do you have any idea how many people are going to die?"

Ilyia nodded, sitting on the edge of Kari's bed. "I do, and it's a thought that weighs heavily on me. But do you understand how many people we will be saving? Generations upon generations will thank us for our actions."

Kari shook her head. "And what of our sisters? They won't allow this."

Ilyia's face fell, and she stared at the nearby bookshelves. "The unfortunate truth is, with the Guardian knowing you are the Bearer, time is no longer on our side. I'm afraid they won't be inside our shield when we merge the realms. Goddess forgive us."

"What you're doing is unforgivable," Kari said, scowling. "Innocent people are trying to live their lives, and you will murder them."

Ilyia leaped to her feet. "I told you, no one is innocent."

"What about the children you are about to murder?"

"They are just as guilty as their parents who watched and did nothing as Shagin was destroyed. They will grow up to be just as cruel and corrupt, but if we create this new age, those who survive will grow up knowing what true peace and justice are. This is a mercy for them."

"You're deluded," Kari said, her head falling back on the pillow.

"Maybe. But that's for the Fates to decide." Ilyia turned, walking toward the lift. She knelt, then drew the symbol of Shagin on the stone floor, summoning the enchanted lift. Pausing, she twisted back to Kari as she began to melt through the floor. "I am sorry for our treatment of you. You're still our sister. The bindings are necessary. I'm afraid you might kill yourself otherwise. When this is over, I hope you will understand. Even if you don't agree, you will still work with us to create our new world."

Kari shut her eyes. She didn't want any part of Ilyia's plan. Unfortunately, it was a little late for that now. She had insisted on bringing the people from Anuatu here, and they would die because of her. Everyone would die.

Ilyia headed down the lift, disappearing beneath the stone floor, leaving Kari alone in the chamber. She had to get out of here. If she didn't, the world would end. It would be her fault.

She pulled at the bindings. Without proper leverage, she couldn't muster the strength to break free. She focused her energy on her body, but her aura didn't respond. The lasting effects of Aura's poison powder, she was sure. And they had taken her ring.

Damn it.

Kari gritted her teeth. There had to be something she could do. Everything was out of reach, and she couldn't move against her bindings. Only books and the shelves they sat upon were in the room. Nothing she could use to free herself. Kari lifted her head to get a better look at the small study desk in front of the bed. A knife and some rope rested upon it. By the looks of it, it was the same rope that bound her in place.

Ilyia was careless. She either underestimated Kari or simply forgot to take the knife with her. Either way, with it visible, she could reach it with her powers and free herself.

Focusing, Kari cleared her mind. She struggled with all of her might to summon her light constructs. Her hands and fingers tingled from the surge of spirit energy, but nothing formed. Her head spun and whirled from the effort.

She had to do this. She had to break free. In the field with Ilyia, she had used so much more strength than she thought she had to grow the plants. It had always been like that. Whenever she was sure she was at her limit, she always found a way to overcome.

She was the Bearer of the Seed, the anchor point for the most immense enchantment in human history. The power of the Seed split the Three Realms apart. It was a power source, a font of near-limitless energy she could draw from. If only she knew how.

Ever since she'd found out she was the Bearer, she loathed her existence, she hated herself, hated the legacy of the Seed. This temple, this chamber, these books were made to store her legacy, the legacy of her predecessors. According to legend, the first Bearer founded Shagin. It was her blood that flowed through their veins. She was the

Champion of the Goddess. She didn't run from the path the Fates made for her. She embraced it.

If Kari wanted to save the world and prevent the merger, she would need to do the same.

It was the life energy of countless people sacrificed to create the Seed energy she would have to draw upon to save lives.

Kari reached out her right fingertips toward the rope binding her left hand, taking a deep breath. She could do this. Kari closed her eyes, focusing all of her energy into her fingers. Her head spun and throbbed from the exertion.

Kari groaned. Countless lives depended on her. She couldn't stop. If she failed, so many more would die—her mother, Ronin, Ina, Ninti.

"I won't let that happen!" Kari yelled, her eyes shooting open.

A blinding flash of light erupted from her fingers. It tore through the rope tied around her left hand, freeing her.

She gasped and struggled for air, clutching at her heaving chest with her free hand. Her shoulder and muscles ached from being outstretched for so long. She'd done it. There was no stopping now.

Using her free hand, she untied the rope on her other hand. She couldn't see where the lines around her torso and legs were tied, and she didn't have the strength to blast through each one. Kari's gaze darted toward the knife on the table in front of her.

She could do this. She had just enough strength left.

Kari moaned as she swung her arm out toward the knife. Light erupted from her hand, forming into a whip. The whip wrapped around the knife, and she swung her arm back. Kari's head throbbed, and the whip dissipated. The knife hurtled toward the ground, clattering against the stone floor.

"Ugh!" Kari clenched her fingers, curling them in frustration. She couldn't give up now. She had to escape.

Both of her legs were bound to posts. Without proper leverage, there was no point in trying to break them free.

The three ropes tightly held her in place. One rope ran over her legs, another her waist, and the last was tied just under her arms. If she could free herself from the top line, she could sit upright. She just needed to focus on one rope.

Once the top rope was cleared, the others would be easy—she hoped.

Kari wiggled and squirmed her arms, bending and twisting them under the rope.

"Come on," she groaned. After a moment, her arms popped free under the rope. Her new position restricted the motion of her arms, but it was still one step closer to being free.

The simple part was over. Kari grabbed hold of the top rope, pushing it up as she squirmed her way under it. Its tight bindings dug into her throat. Tilting her head to the side, she pulled the rope to her head. She groaned and gasped as it squashed her cheek and nose.

"Ahh," she whimpered as the rope pressed against her eye. Kari took a deep breath, pushing and pulling with all her might. The rope slacked as her head freed.

Gasping, Kari shot up to a sitting position. The ropes around her body must be tied under the bed. She leaned forward, then untied each of her legs.

Kari kicked and squirmed, breaking free of the bottom rope. She grabbed the rope around her middle, then pulled it down. Planting her feet on the bed, she kicked herself up. The rope passed over her hips, and she pulled each leg through.

Kari gasped. Leaping from the bed, she grabbed the knife from off the floor. She groaned as her head spun from the exertion of freeing herself. With the knife in hand, she headed over to the lift. She made the symbol of Shagin on the floor, but the lift did not activate. Kari gritted her teeth. Her spirit energy was still not back.

Closing her eyes, she focused all of her energy on her finger. It tingled in response. Again, she drew the Shagin symbol on the ground. It glowed, and she began to melt through the floor into the Chamber of the Seers.

Kari sighed. The room was empty. She was still weak, and her powers hadn't fully come back. But with the knife, she could at least defend herself.

But what was the point? Armed with only a knife and with her spirit energy locked away, there was no way she could fend off the Furies.

If she wanted to save the world, there was only one sure way to do it. She needed to die.

Kari's chest tightened.

She had taken so much life already, yet she wasn't willing to die to save it? She was a hypocrite. Her life was worthless compared to the lives of billions.

She had already died once, in another life. It had happened in these halls. Kari walked out to the balcony, staring at the chamber below. The pedestal in front of the empty rows looked so tiny and insignificant from atop the third-floor balcony. This temple, this sacred place, had been turned into a prison, a place of torture and death.

"Why?" Kari whispered. That was all she wanted to know—why it happened. How could humanity hate each other so? It was an endless war that led to the creation of the Seed, in hopes of a better world to come. Yet, this world was still filled with hatred and violence. "Why do we hate?"

The only peace her sisters who'd died in this temple found was in death. Carina wanted nothing more than to die a quick death like those of her fallen sisters. She was to rest forever.

Kari's body was numb. Her face was heavy. How many lives were going to end? How much death? The world was cruel.

Kari wanted to die. She didn't fully understand why, but she was just so tired. She couldn't fight this anymore—couldn't resist.

Her death could save the world.

She held the blade to her throat. Its cold metal felt cathartic against her skin. Her chest hurt, and she couldn't catch her breath. Rest was all she wanted.

Kari had her throat cut before, and it nearly killed her. She could do it again. Just lay there in a pool of her blood and drift asleep. It wouldn't be that easy. The pain she had felt was excruciating. Even now, the sharp edge of the dagger digging into her skin caused her to wince.

Kari dropped the blade, and it clamored against the stone floor. She couldn't do it. Kari didn't fear death. She welcomed it. She just didn't want to suffer. She didn't want to hurt anymore. If she could merely sleep and never wake up, she would.

There was nothing more for her here. She couldn't defeat Vipin and the Furies. If she fought, she would fail, and the world would suffer for it. Her weakness would cause the apocalypse. It was all too much to bear.

She had already endured so much. First the Seed, then Carina's life, and now the fate of the world. She couldn't face the dawn. Her heavy eyes demanded to be shut, and she hoped they would never open.

Kari placed a hand to her head. "Fuck my mind," she whispered to the nothingness around her.

She could leap from the balcony to the chamber below, but she could survive that, even without her spirit aura. She didn't have the strength to push the dagger through her body. It would hurt, and there was a chance she would survive, at least long enough for someone to find her.

She couldn't risk that.

A poison could work, but she would need something potent enough to finish the job. Unfortunately, she didn't have anything—not to mention her body was naturally resilient to poisons due to the Seed.

She stared back at the stone ceiling in the Chamber of the Seers. Just above this room was what she needed—rope. Kari could hang herself. She would need to make sure the rope broke her neck instead of merely asphyxiating her. Choking to death would be excruciating, whereas a broken neck would be fast. At least she hoped it would be.

"Stop it," she whispered, covering her eyes.

Kari shook her head, staring up at the statue of Nebura. She couldn't do it. She didn't want to die. At least she thought she didn't. She gazed into Nebura's eyes. Why? Why so much pain?

The goddess was beautiful. But that was all she was—a beautiful statue carved in stone. The fallen Fate who came to earth to save humanity in its infancy. Where was she now?

There was an inscription on the wall. Kari ran her hand over the words. It was the Song of Nebura.

> *Chosen by destiny,□*
> *She makes her own path,□*
> *Guided by*
> *The winds of change.*

If love was a weapon,□
None could surpass her.
Defying the Fates,□
She descended into
The plane of mortals.

Life radiated from her,□
Creating all living things.
Her task finished,□
She ascended into
The heavens.

Her journey complete and
Her quest fulfilled,□
Her life faded.
The Fates arranged
Her passing,□
But would not let her go.

Rewarded for her bravery,□
She was reborn as
The stars.

Kari's eyes watered, and her hands shook. What was left for her to do? Her eyes followed Nebura's torso to her extended hands, stretching out over the vast empty sanctuary.

Kari could take the rope, then tie it to the statue's hand. It would give her a large enough clearing and a far enough drop that it should break her neck.

"Shut up." Kari shook her head. Why was her mind trying to kill her?

She rubbed her hands over her face. There was nothing left for her to give. She had given so much of herself to others, and there was nothing left. What future did she have? She was an exile from her people, usurped from her throne, hunted by the Guardian, and hated by the world. She put a hand on her stomach. The Seed had taken so much away from her, and yet, the Seed would extend her life. She would live forever with this pain.

Unless she was killed.

Kari couldn't live another day like this.

It needed to end. She needed to die.

She wanted to die to rest forever.

Kari spun on her heel, then darted into the Seer's chambers. She activated the enchanted lift, impatiently waiting as it rose into the Chamber of the Bearer. Grabbing the rope, she hugged it to her chest as she descended again. She headed back to the balcony and jumped over the railing, landing on Nebura's open hand. She tied one end of the rope around one of the statue's fingers, then formed a noose with the other end.

The rope was heavy in her hands. There was no going back now. Gathering her resolve, she draped the noose around her neck. She stared at the ground below.

She wished she had a letter or something to leave for Ina and Ronin. They wouldn't understand. Kari didn't want them to be sad for her. She had finally found what she wanted. It was time to save the world. It was time to finally rest.

Kari closed her eyes, taking a deep breath.

"Goodbye."

Kari jumped.

In an instant, the rope went taut.

CHAPTER TWENTY-ONE

RONIN

RONIN CLIMBED UP THE side of the inn, slid open the window to Ina's room, and slowly slithered his way inside. He could have used the stairs and gone through her door, but that was what Ina would expect him to do. Besides, this was sure to give her a good fright.

Ina was too preoccupied changing into different clothes to notice him entering. Ronin didn't see the need. Even though his coat was torn and stained, he refused to change it. It was who he was, just like the fine silk ruquns of Xiang was who Ina was. Instead, she'd changed herself, compromised her identity, only to have a *clean* set of clothes. Ina finished tying a blue belt around her waist, then turned around.

"By the gods!" Ina jumped, grabbed her chest. "How long have you been standing there?"

A wicked grin flashed across Ronin's face. "Just a bit."

"How did you even get in here? I was facing the door the whole time."

"Window," he said. Shrugging, he pointed to the open window.

Ina gritted her teeth, her face reddening. She placed her hands on her hips, glaring at him. "What did you see?"

"Nothing worth seeing." Ronin's gaze cut over to the pile of clothes in the corner. "You should pack what you wish to take."

"You think we should go?"

Sighing, Ronin shook his head. "I don't put a lot of stock in the Furies' barrier. No offense to them, but..." He squinted his eyes, "Actually, fuck them. All it takes is one set of those runestones to be inside the barrier for it to be useless. Our best option is to run and hide."

"Run and hide?" Ina raised an eyebrow. "I never expected a fearsome Kitsuno Kai to suggest that."

"It's practical," he said, rolling his eyes. "There are only so many people we can kill before our swords whither and break."

Ina walked over to her dresser. On top, there was a set of beakers and vials, along with an assortment of materials such as herbs, roots, and stones.

"Are you still playing around with your medicines?" Ronin asked. He headed over, then picked up a vial containing a strange liquid. He held it up to his face, examining its contents.

"I'm not playing," Ina scolded, snatching the vial away.

Ronin's left eye twitched. "Last time I checked, you weren't a doctor," he said, malice pouring from his words.

"Do you think I learned nothing from my father?" Ina asked.

"Yes," Ronin said coldly. "But it doesn't matter. We should find Kari. The Guardian will come looking for us soon. We don't want to make it too easy to find us. Either we create this barrier now, or we run."

"You're not giving us a lot of time to rest," Ina said.

"Because Kari was right—we don't have any," Ronin said. "Pack what you want to take, just in case we have to leave quickly."

A sudden knock on the door caught their attention. Ronin's eyes quickly darted to the bottom crack, and he gripped the hilt of one kodachi. Only one shadow that he could see.

"Who's there?" Ina called, but there was no answer, only another knock.

Ronin motioned for Ina to stand back as he approached the door. He grabbed the handle, then threw the door open. A young man with long brown hair stood before him. Ronin's eyes narrowed as he examined the stranger.

His attire was odd. He wore a blue and black tailcoat with golden embroidery, similar to embroidery found in Xiang. The coat had puffy half sleeves with sleeves of a blue under-shirt extending from underneath. His pants were made out of thick white cotton, and he had a light blue scarf hanging around his neck.

Ronin couldn't determine from where he was from based on his clothes. He was a hodgepodge of different fashions and cultures.

"What's going on? Where's Falcon?" the stranger asked.

Ronin squinted. "Who are you?" he asked.

"Warren. I'm a..." He stammered. His voice was young, yet authoritative, and his eyes were sharp. He didn't seem to be much older than Kari, maybe nineteen or twenty by Ronin's guess. Yet, his dark eyes were that of a seasoned veteran. "Well, I know Kari."

He was lying. It was evident in the way he hesitated. There was more to this boy than he was letting on. His features were the only indication of where he was from. Like Kari, he was a hybrid of Xianesse and a western nation. There was no doubt about that. It could explain his odd choice in clothes.

"You're from Xiang?" Ronin asked. His hands hovered over the hilts of his swords. If he was from Xiang as Ronin suspected, he was most likely sent by Cai Ren. This boy was an enemy, and Ronin would not hesitate to end him to protect his sister.

"No... well... look, now's not the time for pointless questions. Time is against us," Warren said. He looked past Ronin, meeting Ina's gaze. "Where's Falcon?"

"He didn't come with us," Ina responded.

"What do you mean he didn't come with you? He was supposed to come with you."

Warren's voice rose, and Ronin's hands twitched. The man was Falcon's companion. Could he be a member of the Thunder Five? If so, was this all one big trap set by that fucker?

"Damn it, everything's going to hell!"

"I don't know who you are, but you're annoying, so if you don't give me some answers, I will kill you." Ronin gripped both of his swords, crowding into Warren's personal space.

"You won't," Warren replied. Ronin smirked, drawing his swords. Warren retreated a few steps. "They have Kari. You have to hurry."

"What are you on about?" Ronin asked. The stranger's eyes were stern and sincere. He was finally telling the truth. An unfortunate truth.

"Vipin and the Furies," Warren explained.

Ronin gritted his teeth. This wasn't good. He knew they shouldn't have trusted them. From the start, they were suspicious, flaunting their total disregard for Shagin etiquette and tradition.

"They captured Kari. You have to get her back!"

"Why would they do this?" Ina asked.

"It doesn't matter." Ronin averted his gaze. This was terrible, worse than being captured by that dog, Falcon. It was time Ronin admitted the truth. "We can't beat them; they are stronger than us. We'll need help before we can rescue her."

"There's no time," Warren said, his expression panicked. "They are going to use her to merge the realms, and wipe out nearly all life in the process."

"The Seed?" Ina's eyes widened. "They're going to use it?"

"Shagin would never," Ronin protested. At least true Shagin wouldn't, but these women had long ago abandoned their sisters to side with Vipin.

"You didn't know?" Warren clenched his fists. "They want to create a new world, and the best way to do that is to restart the old completely. They are going to activate the array to steal the life-force from everyone in this city to create their barrier. With the energy shield in place, they will be protected from the destruction when they use the Seed."

Ronin licked his lips. "Shit, that's a good plan."

"How do you know this?" Ina asked.

"How do you not?" Warren retorted.

How the man knew was a question of utmost importance, especially since Ronin did not. But that could come later. If the Seed were indeed activated, the results would be apocalyptic. That took precedent.

"If this is true, we need to move quickly," Ina said.

Ronin smiled. Finally, they agreed on something. "Are you going to help us?"

"I can't," Warren replied. Ronin cocked his head, staring him down. "I can't get any more involved than I already am."

"Are you scared?" Ronin asked.

"If that makes you feel better, then yes," Warren replied.

Fear no longer mattered. Countless people depended on them to kill the Furies. Most importantly, Kari depended on it. If the realms merged, her fragile heart would be unable to bear the burden of so many deaths.

"There are tunnels that lead to the temple. That's where they've taken her. That's where the ritual will take place. You do know how to enter the tunnels?"

"No," Ronin said, shaking his head.

"How do you survive on your on?" Warren groaned.

Ronin's smile grew broader. That was a decent retort. He was starting to like this kid.

"It's not like we've ever explored those tunnels before. We've only been in them once, and that was through the entrance in Lasan," Ina explained. "We've barely even been in this city."

Warren grunted. "I understand. Just come on, I'll show you where they're at."

They followed Warren to an old rundown shack near the eastern wall of the city. The inside of the building was burned and charred. Warren led the way inside to a small room. He lifted a trap door.

Ronin hated not knowing as much as this kid. Just who was he that he had such information? It was infuriating.

"Head down the tunnels," Warren said. "When you reach the fork, take the left path. From there, take two rights and another left. You should eventually come to a ladder that leads up to the basement of Lasan."

"Understood." Ronin crouched near the trap door, readying himself for the climb.

"Don't get lost," Warren warned. "You don't have time to waste, and I won't be coming after you."

"What are you going to do?" Ina asked.

What indeed?

"Leave this city."

"Coward," Ronin spat. How could the boy have such knowledge of things, how could he understand the threat, yet still refuse to fight? Warren looked fit enough. He had two arms, two legs, a strong jaw, and the eyes of a warrior. His cowardice made no sense.

Warren shook his head, heading for the door. "Good luck. We're all counting on you."

They didn't have time to dwell on this stranger's motives. They had work to do.

Ronin and Ina descended the ladder to enter the dark tunnels. The tunnels were dark and damp. Water dripped from the ceiling, falling off long stalactites and reaching down like claws to the stalagmites below. Tall stone pillars supported metal beams that ran the length and braced the roof of the tunnel.

"What's our plan?" Ina asked.

Ronin smirked. They didn't have much of one. "I plan to find Kari, free her, and hope she is in a condition to fight," he said. It wasn't a good plan, but it was all they had at the moment. "I think we can both agree we are mostly here for moral support. You're a dainty flower, and I'm outmatched."

Ina averted her eyes, but she didn't protest. She knew he was right. There was no point in arguing. A fight against the Furies would prove problematic. If he could avoid the conflict, that would be his preferred option.

They followed Warren's directions, traversing the tunnels. Any other time, Ronin might be mesmerized by the sights within. Glowstones were spaced periodically, giving off a hauntingly beautiful glow. They even passed a waterfall and an underground river. Still, his mind was fixated on the fight ahead.

He had mostly healed from his battle with Falcon. His spirit aura was getting stronger, but his body still ached. He had felt the strength of Ilyia's aura. It was overwhelming. He had never felt anyone else's aura, not even Kari's. He didn't know exactly what that meant, but he imagined she was immensely strong.

All four of the Furies would have spirit auras. Ronin clenched his fists. He knew the importance of an aura in battle. It was what gave him the edge in most of his fights. He was skilled, far more skilled than most, but his aura made him unbeatable. At least until he fought an opponent with an even stronger one—Jiaorong had dwarfed his spirit energy. It didn't matter what he landed against the man. Jiaorong merely brushed off all of Ronin's attacks. He had been like a dragon unleashed against a snake.

Ronin had nearly died in that fight. Now he faced four opponents who equaled or surpassed Jiaorong. And there was no telling how strong Vipin was. If this turned into a fight, it wouldn't last for long. It would quickly turn to a massacre.

"Damn it!"

"What's wrong?" Ina asked.

Ronin shook his head, but he didn't answer. If he lived through this, he would dedicate his life to cultivating his spirit energy and becoming stronger so he would never be put in a situation like this ever again.

It didn't matter if he survived this fight or not. The only thing that mattered was saving Kari and getting her far away from the Furies. He would worry about Legato later.

They reached the end of the tunnel. There was a ladder, but no opening. It was solid stone.

"I remember this," Ina said, stepping forward. "Aura used her energy to make the symbol of Shagin. You know, the circle and arrow thing. It made it so we could pass through the stone."

"That's clever." Ronin climbed up the ladder, then put his finger on the cool stone. He closed his eyes, summoning his energy into his index. Once he was satisfied, he traced the Shagin symbol onto the stone. Each mark shone a bright yellow under his touch. The stone became translucent, and his hand quickly passed through.

"Come on," Ronin said. "Be quick and quiet. We don't want them to know we are here if we can help it."

They both passed through, ending up in the basement of Lasan. Ronin peeked around the corner, but he didn't see anyone.

"I wish I had left you back at the inn," Ronin said, placing a hand on Ina's shoulder. "I can move quicker and quieter on my own."

"Why didn't you?" Ina asked.

"It's all part of my very horrible, definitely might kill us plan." Ronin smirked. "Worst-case scenario, I'll buy you time to get Kari out of here. But I think we both need to agree that we are expendable. The only thing that matters is saving Kari and stopping the merger."

Ina nodded. "I understand. The fate of the world depends on it."

Good, she wasn't as childish and naïve as he had feared.

The most likely place to perform the merger would be the sanctuary. It had plenty of space, plus they could imprison her in the Chamber of the Seers. Eanna had told him about the temple. It always fascinated him, even as a young boy. He knew it was forbidden for him to enter it, especially the sanctuary, but he had snuck in before on the night Kari had left with Chaska and Artemis on their mission to Anuatu. He'd explored the space, and now that knowledge would prove useful. He knew how to navigate through the labyrinth of halls.

Ronin led the way through the basement up the stairs to the second floor of the temple. The stairs leading to the vestibule would have probably been quicker, but they were more likely to run into someone there. It was best to avoid being detected until they found Kari. They rushed down the hallways on the balls of their feet, moving silently in the unlit halls.

When they approached the door to the sanctuary, Ronin motioned for Ina to stay back and be quiet. There was no telling if anybody was in there, at least not until they opened the door. At which point, they could be in for the fight of their lives.

He inched the door opened, peeking through the crack. Eyes widening, he felt his heart race at what he saw. Kari laid prostrate on the floor, a noose around her neck.

CHAPTER TWENTY-TWO

KARI

THE ROPE WENT TAUT around Kari's neck as she leaped from the statue's hand. A crack rang out in the empty chamber. The rope slacked, and she continued to fall.

Her spirit energy instinctively shielded her as she struck the ground three floors below, the impact of which knocked what little breath she had remaining out of her lungs. The stone finger she had tied the rope to struck the ground beside her, then shattered into pieces.

Stunned, she laid there, gasping for air. What had happened?

Coughing and gasping, she pulled at the rope around her neck. She sat upright, then tore the noose from around her throat.

"Why won't you let me die?" she screamed at the statue.

Tears fell from her face onto the rope in her hands.

A yelp erupted from her lips, and she threw the rope across the room. Burying her face in her hands, she cried.

Tears coated her hands and face, and her body heaved with each sob.

She was alive.

What more could she give?

Kari sat frozen on the stone ground, staring at the statue of Nebura. The door behind her squeaked open, alerting her that she was no longer alone.

Ronin and Ina rushed inside. Ina threw her arms around Kari while Ronin's pace slowed as he scanned the sanctuary.

"We found you," Ina cried. "Are you all right?"

Kari remained silent.

Ronin looked around the chamber at the debris on the ground.

"What is this?" he asked, his gaze stopping on the noose across the sanctuary. "Never mind. Come on. We have to get you out of here."

Ronin bent to help Kari up.

"I'm not going," Kari replied, refusing his help. She remained seated on the marble floor, unwilling to move.

"She's right. If we leave, the people of this city will die," Ina said, kneeling beside her.

Ronin snarled. "We agreed."

Kari shook her head, eying his swords. "No. I can't leave. I'm going to die here. I have to die. I need to die."

Ronin placed his hands on the hilts of his swords, retreating from Kari. "I won't let you. Whatever you are feeling, you can fight it. I will make you fight it."

"It's not just the way I feel," Kari said, her face falling. "I am the key they need to merge the realms. Billions will die. That's a burden I can't bear. You can't make me live with it. My life for everyone else's. It's the only way."

"Kari..." Ina reached out to her, but stopped shy of her and withdrew her hand.

"It's my life. I just want to die, end this pain, end this cursed existence. Please, just let me die."

"You're my sister," Ronin said, kneeling next to Kari. Closing his eyes, he wrapped his arms around her, embracing her. "I love you too much to allow you to just give up."

His embrace was odd and cold. He had never shown this much emotion. Kari wasn't sure what to make of it.

"Don't think of it as me giving up. My death will save countless lives."

"You're just scared," Ronin said, pulling away from her and gazing into her eyes.

"Fuck you," Kari said, pushing him away. "Don't tell me how I feel. You don't know what I've experienced. You don't know the pain I feel every waking moment of every day. I want it to end. If it doesn't, it will consume me, and it will continue to grow. They will use me to destroy everything. It's why I exist. I carry the deaths of billions every day. That's what the Seed is. The death of the old world. And they will use it to destroy the current. If that happens, I will kill myself. But I can prevent it by merely killing myself sooner."

"You bear it because you are strong." Ronin clenched his jaw and rose, looking down upon her. "You are stronger than you think."

"I've been here before...in this temple...in another life." Kari gripped the memory stone that hung around her neck. "I had a child taken from me. I was tortured, raped, and died. I saw everyone I ever knew and loved murdered. My current life runs in parallel. Only now, my death will matter. I can die on my terms. My death will save everyone."

"It won't." Ronin glowered. "It won't help anyone. They'd been planning this before they even knew about you. They have a plan to find the Bearer. If you die, the next Bearer will be called. Only they won't know of the Furies' treachery, and I won't warn them. I don't know where Mystikos is. Even if I could find it, the Bearer might be gone. The Furies would have a head start in hunting her down. If you die, you merely postpone the apocalypse, and you're passing that burden to someone else."

"Don't try to guilt me into living." Rage flared inside Kari. Her face reddened with heat. "I can't do this! I can't live like this. You don't understand."

Kari's hands trembled. Eleanor, daughter of Narissa, ran from her fate and her responsibility only for it to fall to her sister Diana. If Kari ran as well, who would be burdened by her fate?

Ina wrapped her arms around Kari. "I don't know what to say. I don't know how to make you stay. I suppose only you know that. I just want you to know I love you, and I am here for you."

Warm tears fell down Kari's face. Why was she crying? She closed her eyes, wrapping her arms around Ina in return.

Ina understood. After all, she had gone through her share of heartache back in Xiang. Her sister died, and the emperors came for her as a replacement on her wedding day. They killed her betrothed, then forced her into the harem. They were similar.

Ina stared at her. "You told me Shagin pick their names when they come of age. Why did you pick yours?"

"I took it from hikari, the word for light. It was in reference to my power and a promise to myself. I wanted to make the world a better place."

"You can't do that if you're not in it," Ina said.

"I know." Kari nodded.

"It won't be easy, but you can fight every day to live. We can find another way to stop Vipin, other than your death."

Kari stared at her friend. Her eyes moved to the silent Ronin. They could help her. They *would* help her.

"I think I want that," Kari muttered. "At least I do at this moment."

"Good, hold onto that feeling," Ina said.

"Then what are we waiting for?" Ronin asked, holding out his hand for Kari to take. "We need to move quickly. Escape is our only option."

Kari nodded, accepting his hand. He helped pull her up to her feet.

"I don't mean to repeat myself, but what of all the people in the city?" Ina asked, standing as well.

"I don't think we are in a position to help them," Kari said. Her heart sank. It was her fault. She had brought many of them here from the other town. Her chest tightened, and she struggled to catch her breath. They would die because of her.

"We are outmatched and outnumbered," Ronin said, clenching his fists. "Kari's in no condition to fight, and we can't afford to risk them capturing her. If we had the runestones, we could have those bounty hunters help us, and even teleport Kari to safety. But as it is, we'll have to flee on foot."

"We'll need to move fast. If they hit us with Aura's poison powder again, I fear we will succumb to them." Kari shut her eyes tight. She hated running. She hated dooming the entire city to die while she focused on her safety. Kari sighed. It wasn't her safety she had to focus on, but the safety of the Seed. "I'm still reeling from the last batch Ilyia hit me with."

"I almost forgot." Ina dove into her pocket, pulling out a small vial. "Here, drink this."

"What is it?" Kari took it from her.

"I was experimenting with different concoctions to function as a neutralizing agent for Aura. I wanted to help her get closer to people. I used powdered nahcolite crystals mixed with a small amount of dalium that I... that I stole... to counter the magical nature of the toxins. If I am correct, this should reduce the effects of the poison powder."

"I told you to stop pretending to be something you're not," Ronin rebuked.

"It will work," Ina said. "I think."

Kari stared at the vial in her hands. "Have you tested this?"

"Not exactly," Ina said sheepishly. "But what other options do we have?"

Kari nodded. With any luck, they wouldn't need to test its effectiveness. She pried the top off, then downed the liquid. It was chalky and tasted terrible.

"Give it a few minutes, and you should begin to feel more like yourself. I hope," Ina said. She pulled out another vial, passing it to Ronin. "You should drink some as well. Just in case we encounter them, it should protect you from the powder. I have one more if necessary. Though, I don't want to use it myself. If one vial doesn't reduce the effects, one of you can have the second."

"Hopefully, we won't need it," Ronin said. "I would hate to rely on untested remedies."

"It might be untested, but the logic behind it is sound," Ina said.

Ronin led the way down into the basement. They were just as quiet as when they entered. Kari still didn't feel any better, despite Ina's concoction. Hopefully, the medicine would take effect soon.

The basement sent chills down Kari's spine. She hated coming down here. The once-decorative doors had been replaced with iron bars. Remnants of torture and death were still evident in the cells. The entire basement smelled of blood.

The Furies had removed the torture devices and any other tools of death left behind by the Guardian's forces. But still, the memories were there. Kari had seen it at its worse. The temple had been repurposed to a killing ground. Even now, she could see the ghosts of those who died and those who had killed them.

"Stop," Kari said. She walked toward a cell door and stared inside, her eyes watering. The floor of the room was still stained with blood after all these years. "This is where it happened. This was where Zayenda died. This was my cell."

"Her cell," Ronin corrected, placing a hand on her shoulder

Kari cut her eyes to him, and he took his hand off her. "Of course." She bowed her head.

"We should keep moving," Ina said. She took hold of Kari's hand, trying to tug her along. "We can't afford to dally."

Kari rubbed her brow with her free hand, but she did not budge. "I just need a moment. Carina died not far from here. I have to see it."

Kari wanted to see the room with her own eyes. She needed to know it was real, that she wasn't crazy. Carina had waited in their torture chamber for hours for them to begin. It was another sister who was waiting for her death that gave her the memory stone Kari now wore around her neck.

Kari and Carina were sisters separated by time. If there was an afterlife, would Carina ever think about her? Would she be proud, ashamed, or apprehensive about sharing her life with her?

Kari shook the thought from her head.

"Kari, we don't have time," Ina warned, tugging on Kari's arm even harder.

"I know. It's just so real. How did this happen? There was no reason for such hatred to exist. Why couldn't we be allowed to live?"

"You understand," Chaska said, turning the corner and walking toward them. Ronin grabbed Kari's shoulder, pulling her behind him. "How can you understand? How can you live through this and not comprehend what we are trying to do?"

Kari pulled free of Ronin, then stepped forward. "I fully comprehend. The Fates know I agree the Guardian needs to be brought to justice. This world is corrupt and filled to the brim with hatred and death. It's got to change, but what you are doing will only bring more hate."

Kari's mind filled with all the faces of those she'd killed. She was hated by so many already—so many families, so many friends, hated her for her actions. Death, vengeance, it only brought more hatred. She had hated the Tian for what they inflicted on her, but, by causing their deaths, their mother hated her and took her own life in grief. The pain was never-ending.

"You're naïve and young," Chaska said. "The only way to create a world of peace is to force the change."

"People will die." Kari protested.

Chaska nodded. "It's an unfortunate truth. It will be a world of peace built on a foundation of blood. But there is no other way. Think of the world as a vase. It has been misshapen and damaged beyond repair. The only thing left to do is to start over. Destroy the old and create a new. Humanity is beyond redemption. They either assisted or watched as genocide was committed against us. There is no one worthy to redeem. So, we must begin again."

"So, you'll punish the entire world?" Ina asked, stepping forward. Ronin grabbed her, yanking her back.

"This isn't about punishment," Chaska said. "The only way we can repair the malice in people's hearts is to tear down the old constructs of the past. Worship of the Triune gods requires hatred to be spread. It dictates that all must conform to their beliefs or perish. This foul belief infects every living person, so that only evil exists in their minds. The entire world, all Three Realms, are corrupt. To save humanity, sacrifices have to be made."

Kari shook her head. "That doesn't make sense."

"And what of the other Shagin?" Ronin asked, venom dripping from his lips. "They're not here. If you go through with this, they'll die, too."

"That is our failing," Chaska said. "From what Ilyia said, we've run out of time. I'll forever regret the fate that befalls them. I have no intention of living past the merger."

"You're just going to commit this horrible atrocity, then escape by killing yourself?" Ina asked in disbelief.

Kari held up her hand to silence Ina and Ronin. She hurried over to Chaska, then took her hands. "I completely understand, and I agree a new age is required. But your actions will forever be unjustifiable, regardless of the outcome. You said everyone was corrupt and evil, and that's why you feel justified in creating chaos and death. But what of the children? Do they deserve to die, too?"

Chaska pulled her hands back. "Don't lecture me about this!"

"How many little ones will die?" Kari asked. "You lost your daughter, so you know the pain. And you would inflict that pain onto others? You will murder other little ones—justify it behind a veil of contrived righteousness?"

"And what would you know of the pain of losing a child?" Chaska scolded.

Kari wrapped her fingers around the memory stone hanging from her neck. "I thought I was pregnant, but the Seed took any hope of that ever happening away from me. Then there's Carina, who lost her daughter in the purge. She's not me. I know that. But I felt her pain, her sorrow. She would have done anything to protect her little one. Life is born, precious and innocent. Show me a newborn smile worthy of suffering and death."

Footsteps echoed against the stone floor, drawing closer. Ilyia, Artemis, and Aura rounded the corner, blocking their path to the tunnels. Ilyia glared at Kari. Artemis and Aura stood behind her, but didn't move.

Chaska stepped away from them, backing toward the other end of the hallway near the stairs.

They were blocked in.

"Ina." Ronin's eyes cut toward her. He drew his swords, stepping forward to confront Ilyia.

Ina grabbed Kari's arm and pulled her toward the stairs, but Kari held her ground.

"I'm not running," she whispered. "I'm not leaving him."

"Yes, you are," Ina said. "Fate of the world and all that, yes?"

Kari gritted her teeth. There was no time to argue.

"Stand aside," Ilyia barked. "You will be protected from the coming Cataclysm, but, if you resist, that protection will be withheld."

"I think I'll just kill you now, if that's all right," Ronin snarled.

"Run," Ina screamed, pulling Kari past Chaska and toward the stairs.

"Chaska, stop them," Ilyia yelled, but Chaska did not move.

RONIN

Ronin leaped at Ilyia, his swords ready to strike. Aura rushed forward, unleashing a puff of poison powder from her hands.

Ronin jumped back, out of reach of the poison's effects.

Smiling, Ilyia held out her hand. The golden staff materialized in her grip. "Artemis, inform Vipin to ready himself. Time is against us; we must merge the realms now." Artemis nodded before sprinting away. "Aura, take care of Ronin. Kill this Shagin wannabe. Chaska and I will handle Kari."

"Of course." Aura drew her sword, approaching Ronin.

"Let's go, Chaska!" Ilyia darted around the corner. Gasping, Chaska turned and ran after Kari and Ina.

Ronin smiled. Those fools. This was how he preferred it. He hated to admit it, but he couldn't kill them all at once. Their spirit energy was simply too strong, but he outclassed them when it came to skill. Kari could defend herself long enough for him to dispatch Aura. He'd kill them all, one by one.

"This should be fun." Ronin chuckled.

Ronin lunged at Aura, slashing with both of his swords. Aura parried the first attack. She leaped back out of the way of the second. Ronin lunged both points toward Aura, one aimed at her chest, the other her abdomen.

Aura deflected the thrust to her chest. The other sword struck its mark. Aura cried out, hunched over, and fell to her knees. Her spirit energy prevented a killing blow.

"Pathetic," Ronin screamed. He swung both swords at either side of her neck.

Aura held up her hand, shooting a puff of purple smoke from her palm.

Ronin jumped to the side, holding his breath. The powder burned his skin. His eyes watered and blurred. Aura launched another blast of smoke. Ronin rolled out of the way of the attack.

"Still alive?" Aura stood to her feet—a small stain of blood on her abdomen.

Ronin's legs buckled. This wasn't the same poison she used before. This would kill him. Ina had proved her mettle. Good girl. Her concoction was protecting him, but even with it, a full blast to the face would be fatal.

Ronin eyed Aura. She was planning something. He couldn't give her time to think.

"Ahh!" Ronin threw one kodachi at her. Aura parried it, but the blade spun and nicked her arm. Ronin charged forward. He grabbed her unarmed hand, yanking it down.

His palm sizzled, and pain shot through his hand and arm. Gritting his teeth, he released his grip. He swung his sword with a diagonal slash. She parried the attack, shooting another blast of poison at his face.

Ronin shielded his mouth and nose with his injured hand. He darted backward out of the poisonous gas. His eyes watered, and tears flowed down his face as he coughed uncontrollably. His body spasmed and ached. Dropping to a knee, he stared at Aura. She inched her way toward him with her arm outstretched.

Damn, that went to hell. He should have anticipated this. Her toxic abilities were too strong to remedy. He wouldn't last.

"You should have died by now," Aura cried. She rushed forward. Ronin's legs buckled as he struggled to his feet. She shot another puff of smoke at him. Ronin covered his face with his injured hand, spinning out of the way. Aura slashed at him with her sword. He winced as the blade tore into his side.

He stumbled onto a nearby wall. She rushed toward him with her sword poised, ready to pierce his skull. Ronin grabbed a handful of blood from his wound, then slung it into her eyes.

She cried out, wiping at the blood. With her advance halted, Ronin leaped forward and slashed at her face. Her eyes widened. She jumped back, but his sword struck, cutting the bridge of her nose and across her face, slicing through her eye.

Aura screamed, clawing at her face as blood poured from her wound. Ronin thrust his sword at her. He drove the tip into her screaming mouth, piercing the back of her throat. It emerged from the back of her neck. She collapsed to the ground, the sword still protruding from her mouth.

"Was that your best?" When Ronin pulled the sword out of her, blood sprayed into the air.

Staring up at him, she gargled on blood as it oozed out of her wounds and stained the stone floor. She clawed at his pant leg, coughing up blood. Arm going limp and collapsing to the ground, she ceased choking, her body going still.

Ronin fell to a sitting position. He dropped his sword, gripping the wound at his side. His left hand was blackened and blistering. He would have to hurry. Kari would need him. Ina's antidote only provided so much protection, and there was no telling if Aura had given any to Ilyia to use.

CHAPTER TWENTY-THREE

KARI

Ina half-dragged Kari as they dashed up the stairs. Why was she hesitating? Why was she resisting? Kari gritted her teeth.

They reached the top of the staircase, then entered the antechamber of Lasan.

"Can you fight?" Ina asked, stopping just shy of the main door.

Kari took a deep breath, focusing her mind. She was going to live—would prevent the merger. The Furies had to be stopped. "Yes."

The wall exploded and crumbled. The Golden Rod tore through the rubble, flying to Ilyia's hand.

"There is no escaping," Ilyia said as Chaska ascended the stairs behind her.

"Wouldn't be the first time you trapped your sisters to die," Kari retorted. Chaska's eyes narrowed.

"The Seed must be stronger than we thought for you to overcome the poison's effects already." Ilyia raised her staff. "I suppose any more poison would be useless against you. I'll just have to force you to submit."

Kari seized Ina's hand, darting toward the sanctuary. "Let's go."

Their footsteps echoed in the large sanctuary as they hurried past the pews toward the doors just past the podium.

Suddenly, a blinding flash illuminated the room. A bolt of lightning erupted from Ilyia's hand, then struck the ground. The stone floor exploded in a shower of debris, knocking both back.

Kari rolled, clutching her sides. The rolling thunder reverberated throughout the sanctuary.

Ilyia flanked them on one side, motioning for Chaska to take the other. Chaska stared at Kari, but she did not move.

Kari groaned as she returned to her feet.

"Chaska, why aren't you moving into position?" Ilyia asked, shooting her a look.

"I won't be fighting," Chaska said, folding her hands in front of her.

"What? You're siding with her?" Ilyia glowered.

"No," Chaska said, gazing into Ilyia's eyes. "I will observe—let the Fates decide who is right."

Ilyia sneered. "Fine. Just remember the outcome well."

Ilyia readied her staff while Kari focused her energy. Her aura was returning, but it was weak. It wouldn't be strong enough to take any blows from the other woman's weapon or her cantrip. Kari's fingers tingled, but her powers did not respond.

Kari narrowed her eyes, taking a deep breath. She could do this.

"Ina, get behind me," Kari said.

"No, I'm getting you out of here," Ina said, grabbing Kari's arm.

Kari tore free. "There is no running from this. We're trapped. We have to fight."

Ina closed her eyes and nodded as Kari stepped closer to Ilyia.

"Then let's see just how powerful the Seed is." Ilyia leaped high into the air, closing the distance between them in an instance.

Kari's eyes widened. She rolled out of the way as Ilyia slammed her staff down, obliterating where Kari had just stood. The stone floor had been reduced to dust and debris. It had shattered from the impact.

Kari launched a back kick, striking Ilyia in the gut. Ilyia stumbled backward with a gruesome smile. She swung her rod at Kari's head. Kari leaned back, and the staff rushed past her face within inches.

Kari heaved, biting her lip. What was Ilyia doing? She was staying outside of measure. She didn't want to kill her, only injure. Kari could use that to her advantage. There would be hesitation in the other woman's strikes.

Kari rushed forward, closing the distance between them. Ilyia gasped at the sudden move. Kari slammed her elbow into her face. Following through with her momentum, she thrust the flat of her other hand into Ilyia's neck. There was no point in striking with her fists so long as Ilyia's aura was strong, not unless Kari wanted to break her knuckles.

Ilyia planted her feet, slamming her palm into Kari's diaphragm. A blast of thunder and lightning erupted.

"Grahh!" Kari screamed. The electricity coated her body, lifting her off the ground and sending her reeling backward.

Kari slammed into the stone ground, smoke rising from her body. She whimpered and moaned as her skin tingled and burned from the shock.

"I'm surprised you still have fight in you," Ilyia said, smirking.

Ina ran over to help Kari to her feet. She groaned and shoved Ina to the side, standing on her own and glaring at Ilyia.

"You really would have made a good Fury." Thunder and light rolled in the sanctuary as Ilyia shot another blast of electricity.

The bolt moved faster than Kari could react. It struck her, branching through every inch of her body. She screamed, collapsing to her knees.

Kari gritted her teeth. She planted her feet and stood. If Ilyia was this strong, she could have saved countless lives during the Purge. "The Furies were supposed to protect Shagin. You were our Champion!"

"I still am!" Ilyia raised her hand. Electricity surged and crackled between her fingers. Kari focused her energy as she tried to catch her breath. She didn't have much left to give. A flash of lightning erupted from Ilyia's hand.

Ina screamed and sprinted toward Ilyia, tackling her, knocking the bolt off course. It whizzed by Kari's head, then blasted a hole in the wall on the opposite side of the sanctuary.

Kari rushed forward. She spun on her heel, striking Ilyia across the face with a spinning kick. Ilyia fumbled, but did not falter. Ina grabbed a large stone that had broken free from the floor.

Ilyia swung her staff downward at Kari.

She could do this. When Falcon fought Ilyia, he'd used her momentum against her. Kari clenched her fists. She would have to do the same.

Kari stepped to the side of the swing. She jumped into the air, her foot connecting with the rod, forcing it to the ground, and she sprung toward Ilyia. Kari focused her energy on her leg. She kicked with all of her might. Her leg collided with Ilyia's chin, sending her off balance.

Ina rushed forward, hitting Ilyia across the head with the stone. Ilyia spun, dropping to one knee. Her eyes cut toward Ina.

A lightning bolt shot forth from one finger, striking Ina. A scream broke free from her lips as she was knocked backward.

Kari ran forward, thrusting her knee into Ilyia's face. Ilyia caught Kari's leg. Electricity blasted through Kari's body.

"Ahh," she shouted, reeling from the attack. Ilyia stood, lifting Kari by her leg, then swung her, throwing her next to Ina.

Kari rolled onto her side, panting. Ina stared back at her. Neither moved.

"See, Chaska?" Ilyia said. "The Fates are on our side. Justice is with us."

Ina reached out, grabbing Kari. "The rear door. We can't beat her. Get ready to run. I'll buy you time."

Kari's gaze darted from Ina to the back door. She could make it. But even if she did, it wouldn't take Ilyia long to dispatch Ina and pursue her. Kari would have to be fast. Maybe she could lose her in the forest.

Ina crawled toward Ilyia. She cried out, forcing herself to her hands and knees. Ina didn't have an aura to protect herself as Kari did, and Ilyia's attacks had felled her. Ina gasped and sat upright on her knees.

"You still want to fight?" Ilyia asked.

Groaning, Ina made it to a standing position. "I don't want to fight, but I can't allow you to continue."

"How noble, but do you even know what you are suffering for?" Ilyia asked. "A new age will dawn. We will bring peace and justice to this insane world of ours."

"You cannot create justice through unjust means," Ina said. She stretched her arms out, stepping closer to Ilyia.

"Your age will be one built from death and insanity. I will stop you. Kari, run!"

Kari's heart skipped. Why was she still lying here?

"I was going to let you live," Ilyia said, raising the Golden Rod. "But I only *need* Kari alive. You can die."

Ilyia leaped into the air as before, her staff raised to destroy Ina.

What had Kari done? She had given up. She had given up on the world. Ina hadn't. Ronin hadn't. Carina hadn't. A new age would dawn, but it would be by her hands. An age made from peace. She would not give up.

She was the Bearer of the Seed. She carried the deaths of so many. But she bore more than just their deaths. She bore their lives, their hopes, their dreams. The promise of a better future, the same hope Ina wanted.

Kari would not let her die.

Kari shot to her feet and rushed past Ina. Ilyia's staff barreled toward her. Kari held out her hand.

"No!" Kari screamed. A blast of light erupted from her palm, blinding the room. The explosion sent shockwaves of energy coursing through the sanctuary, destroying every-thing in its path. Light tore through stone, leaving massive cracks and holes.

Ilyia shrieked, spiraling backward.

Kari faced Ina as the light faded. Spirit energy flowed through her body as her aura returned. "Thank you," Kari said. "Get somewhere safe. I'll handle her."

Ina kissed Kari's forehead. "Good luck."

Kari turned and faced Ilyia, who had already returned to her feet. Small cuts and bruises dotted her face and arms.

"So, you're not half-dead after all." Ilyia wiped the sweat from her brow. She raised the Golden Rod, poised to attack. "I will remedy that."

Kari swung her hand. A burst of light erupted from her palm, forming her light whip. "That staff belongs to the Champion of Shagin. The defender of our ideals."

"What do you know?" Ilyia rushed forward.

Kari slashed with her whip, but Ilyia blocked her attacks. Kari continued to flick her weapon. Ilyia blocked each attack, but could not get close. Kari had to keep her distance. Even with her renewed energy, she couldn't defend against the destructive capabilities of the Golden Rod.

Ilyia tried to flank Kari. She followed along, running forward, closing the opening and attacking along the way. Ilyia deflected each strike with her staff.

Kari's gaze darted toward the balcony. Artemis stood there, the Shadow Sword drawn, ready to enter the fray. Kari couldn't afford to fight both. She had to do something.

"You don't deserve to wield that staff," Kari said. "You are not the defender of Shagin! You betrayed us!"

"Every action I took was to secure our survival into the future." Ilyia knocked Kari's whip aside, creating an opening. She charged, ready to strike.

Kari allowed the whip to dissipate. She formed a bow in her other hand and an arrow in the hand that had held the whip. She loosed an arrow at Ilyia. The light arrow streaked across the sanctuary.

Ilyia knocked it aside with her staff.

"Tell that to our murdered sisters. You used their deaths to create Vipin." Kari loosed two more arrows.

Ilyia blocked them as well as she moved closer.

"What is she talking about?" Chaska asked.

"She's a liar!" Ilyia fired a bolt of lightning at Kari.

Kari formed her bow into a shield. The bolt struck the shield, shattering it in a thunderous cacophony. Kari was knocked back from the impact. She landed on her rear with a groan.

Ilyia rushed her with the staff raised, and Kari formed her own staff. Ilyia swung her weapon, but Kari knocked it to the side. She thrust her staff toward Ilyia. Ilyia parried, swinging at Kari's head. Kari rolled away.

She formed her whip, flicking it at Ilyia. Ilyia blocked the attack. Kari focused her energy, wrapping her whip around the Golden Rod. With a quick jerk, she tore it from Ilyia's grip.

Artemis leaped from the balcony, racing toward them. She thrust her sword, the blade's length shooting forward at Kari.

Kari kicked Ilyia away, facing the incoming blade. It was too late to dodge or parry. Kari braced for it to pierce her flesh.

Blood sprayed through the air.

"Grr!" Ronin screamed. He gripped the Shadow Sword tightly in his injured hand. The blade's point pierced through his palm. He forced the weapon down. Gripping it with his other hand, he prevented Artemis from retracting it.

Kari's eyes widened. She pulled the Golden Rod toward her. Gripping it with both hands, she leaped up and slammed it down against the Shadow Sword's blade. The metal snapped under the stress as the blade shattered.

RONIN

Ronin groaned. The piece of sword was stuck in his hand, which he held above his heart.

"What happened to Aura?" Artemis asked.

"Her? Oh, I wouldn't worry about her." Ronin smirked.

"You murderous bastard!" Artemis rushed toward Ronin, and he raised his kodachi to meet her.

Artemis's right arm transformed into a water tentacle. She slashed at Ronin's legs. The impact tripped him, tearing into his calves. She wrapped her water arm around him, preventing him from moving, then transformed her other arm and latched it onto his face. He grabbed at his throat as he struggled for oxygen.

"That's enough!" When Ina ran toward Artemis, the woman released her grip on Ronin and slashed at her.

"Don't make me kill you," Artemis warned.

"I'm not a defenseless child!"

Artemis raised her water tentacle, poised to strike Ina, but she didn't falter. She threw a handful of dirt and debris into Artemis's face. Artemis screamed, her arms transformed back to normal as she pawed at her eyes.

"Atta girl." Ronin cried. He jumped to his feet, then punched Artemis in the throat. Artemis gasped and clutched her neck, dropping to her knees. She stared wide-eyed at Ronin. When he hit her again, her aura faltered. He kicked her in the chest, sending her crashing to the ground.

Then Ronin groaned and collapsed, clutching his still bleeding side.

"Ronin..." Ina rushed over. "Are you all right?"

"I'm fine. What about Kari?"

KARI

Ilyia struck Kari with a bolt of electricity. Kari screamed and dropped the Golden Rod, but her aura absorbed most of the pain. She gritted her teeth.

Kari reformed her whip, eyeing Ilyia. Electricity surged and crackled around her.

"Be lucky I don't want you dead, or I would have stopped your heart by now," she gloated. "Why can't you see what we are trying to do?"

"I see what you are doing just fine," Kari said, forcing herself to stay upright. "Tell me. You said everything you did was for our survival. You were the defender of the city. Did you plan on creating Vipin before or after its fall?"

"What do you care?" Ilyia shot another blast of electricity. Kari formed a shield and blocked the blast, stumbling backward from the impact. "It was over. I wasn't going to let their deaths be meaningless."

Ilyia struck Kari with another shot of electricity.

Kari screamed, unable to stay upright. Her body smoked, her skin red and blistered from electrical burns. Her aura was fading, and she gasped for air. Ilyia stood above her. Electricity sparked in her hands.

"Let us end this," Ilyia said, readying to strike Kari with another bolt.

RONIN

Ronin snarled, but he didn't have the strength to reach them. He stared at the tip of the Shadow Sword impaled in his hand. If only he could use it.

He sneered. There was an idea.

"Ina, do you still have that last vial?" he asked.

"I do." Ina drew the vial from her pocket, then tossed it to him.

Ronin pulled the cork off with his teeth. He poured the contents into the wound in his hand.

"What are you doing?" Ina asked.

"I have an idea. It is a bad one, but I don't need this arm anyway." Ronin focused his remaining energy into the dalium mixture. He wasn't an enchanter, but he only needed this to work once.

He aimed his palm at Ilyia as lightning cascaded around her hand. He sent his spirit energy coursing through the dalium, charging through the broken tip of the Shadow Sword. The dalium activated, burning away his flesh. He screamed, and the veins in his arm ruptured and burst.

His arm shot forward, extending out like the sword.

Ilyia shot the blast of lightning at Kari.

Ronin's hand grew, tripling in size.

He struck Ilyia, knocking the lightning off course. It struck next to Kari, tearing a hole in the stone floor. She covered her head as debris and rubble hurtled through the air.

Ilyia was lifted off her feet.

"Ahh!" Ronin half screamed, half laughed. He slammed her through the spiral staircase into the opposite wall.

The wall collapsed around her. The statue of Nebura shook, crumbling to pieces from the impact. Stone and rubble rained down, crashing to the ground below. Dust billowed upward, engulfing the back half of the sanctuary.

Ronin's arm retracted. He shrieked, cradling what was left of his arm. The appendage was a bloody, charred stump, unrecognizable with bone protruding out in odd angles.

"Ronin!" Kari rushed toward her brother.

Ronin smiled. "That went better than I thought." Coughing, he sprawled onto his back.

KARI

Kari gaped at what used to be his arm. He needed medical attention. But even with it, there was little hope for his arm.

A rumbling sound drew her attention. Thunder rang out, exploding from the rubble as rocks and stone flew through the sanctuary. Ilyia hoppled from the ruins. Blood dripped from her face and arms. She limped forward. Her left arm was broken, and her explosive aura could no longer be felt.

"The Fates haven't abandoned me yet," Ilyia said, lightning crackled around her unbroken arm.

"Maybe not." Kari took a deep breath. Ilyia was strong. There was no denying that. Artemis had crawled onto her stomach while Chaska watched from in the corner. Kari didn't have much fight left in her, but maybe she wouldn't need any. "Artemis, Chaska! Did she tell you? She abandoned our sisters. Used their energy to power Vipin. She betrayed our people. She even helped ensure the deaths of our sisters would be quick."

"Shut your mouth!" Ilyia blasted Kari with a bolt of lightning.

"Grahh!" Kari screamed, spiraling to the ground.

"Don't believe this lying child," Ilyia spat, electricity surging around her fingers.

"The Fates have decided," Chaska said. She stepped in between Kari and Ilyia. "I knew, but I didn't know what I knew. I knew you used the array to power him. I think we all did. It made the most sense as to why he was anchored here. I always wondered. The ritual for Vipin would require you to prepare ahead of time. It was your strategies that failed in the defense."

"What are you on about?" Artemis muttered, her voice hoarse.

"Did we murder our people?" Chaska asked.

"Of course not! There was no stopping the Guardian. All I did was make sure their deaths mattered. So that our people could survive," Ilyia said.

"You provided him with information. Didn't you?" Kari yelled.

"By the goddess," Chaska said. She dropped to her knees. "What are you saying?"

"Artemis," Kari said. "You said the burning of the ships was a trap. Well, here is the mastermind."

Tears streamed down Chaska's face, and she buried her face in her hands. "My little one."

"What I did or didn't do no longer matters," Ilyia spat. "We had lost. It was over. Every action I took, I took to secure our future."

Artemis stared at Ilyia. She sat upright, then reached behind her head and unfastened her mask. She pulled it off, throwing it to the ground. Her head was burned and scarred beyond recognition. Where hair should have been, only lumps of brown flesh remained.

"Was it worth it?" Artemis whispered. "What have we done?"

"I..." Ilyia stammered. "Would you rather everything have been for nothing?"

Artemis looked into her eyes. "So, it's true. We are the monsters we've been fighting."

"What's true?" Vipin asked, appearing on the balcony. He levitated above the railing, gliding down to the sanctuary floor. "We will create a world where atrocities like the Shagin Purge or the fate that befell my people will never happen again." His eyes glowed blue. Kari was lifted off her feet, hovering in the air, her arms and legs immobilized. "Kari, are you ready to begin?"

CHAPTER TWENTY-FOUR

Purple light erupted all around them. The stone walls were torn apart, sending debris hurtling through the air. Bolts of lightning crashed through the ceiling, striking the ground, leaving craters in their wake. The roof crumbled into dust, revealing the swirling vortex in the charcoal sky. Ashen balls of energy streaked through the roaring clouds as they were drawn into the vortex.

Vipin had activated the array.

Kari jumped out of the way of falling stone. The howling wind whipped at her hair, sending dust and dirt into her eyes. In the chaos, she lost track of everyone else. The moment Vipin activated the array, the entire city turned into hell.

All she could do was stare in horror as the life-force of everyone in Koruzeru was pulled into the vortex. All of those people—thousands of lives—ended in a single fleeting moment.

Kari coughed as debris coated her. She shielded her eyes from the whirling wind. The sound of the vortex roared all around her. Thunder and lightning blasted from it, destroying anything in its wake.

Kari's heart skipped. Ronin was taking cover under what was left of the second-floor balcony. He was safe, huddled for protection, still clutching his arm.

A bolt of lightning clapped out from the vortex, striking the balcony. It exploded, sending stone raining down upon him.

"No!" Kari screamed. She was too far away. She couldn't save him in time. He couldn't survive the burial of stone and rubble.

The stones stopped, hovering just inches above Ronin. All of the raining debris around them froze in midair.

Vipin held out his hands, holding the mess at bay. With a single flash of his eyes, the wreckage disintegrated in an instant, leaving only a few remaining fragments of wall and the rubble on the ground.

The vortex glowed violet as the last of the life energy was consumed. It swirled and stretched out, engulfing and covering the entirety of Koruzeru in purple light.

Vipin held a crystal above his head. Electricity from the vortex sparked and latched onto the stone. It glowed, and the vortex spiraled down around to it in a cyclone of energy and color. The crystal absorbed the vortex, and the sky went silent.

The orange glow of dusk shimmered over the ruins of Lasan. The temple had been reduced to smoke and rubble.

"Vipin!" Ilyia cried out, hobbling over to him.

"It is done," he said, showing her the crystal. It shimmered a vibrant purple. "This crystal now powers our barrier. We are ready to begin the merger."

He reached out, then placed a finger on Ilyia's forehead. She gasped as her wounds healed, his power returning her to full strength.

"I wasn't expecting such damage to Lasan," Ilyia said mournfully. "It's a shame."

"A shame?" Kari screamed. "What about all the lives you stole!?"

"I fail to comprehend why you don't understand our plight," Vipin snapped, shooting daggers with his eyes. "Why don't you understand?"

"You need to understand that I'll never let you use the Seed," Kari said, meeting his gaze with her own. What was she prepared to do? What *could* she do?

Vipin rolled his eyes, holding up his hand. "Your compliance is not required."

Kari levitated off the ground, then floated toward him. She couldn't move. Her arms were frozen by her sides. Even her spirit energy was being blocked. She was helpless.

"Kari!" Ina cried, appearing from the debris, Chaska by her side.

"Vipin, please," Chaska called. She was bleeding from her leg, but appeared to be okay.

"Even you have lost sight?" Vipin asked Chaska. "What about your daughter? This will create a world where a tragedy such as that will never happen again."

"Only by killing countless other daughters," Kari yelled. She struggled against Vipin's control, but it was no use.

"There has to be another way," Chaska muttered.

"The Fates have decided," Ilyia declared, folding her arms around her chest. "As you said, this fight is over."

It wasn't over yet. Kari was chosen by the Fates to protect the Seed, and she would do so as long as she drew breath. She focused her energy. Her body tingled in response, but it wasn't enough to form a light construct.

"No more wasting time," Vipin said. He held up his hand as Kari floated over to him. "Let's end this."

Kari drifted over the ground, coming closer to Vipin. There had to be something she could do. Her spirit energy was there, but with her body frozen, she couldn't use it. That wasn't true. Energy didn't require her physical body to use. Her aura could be used to charge items, extending her power into them. It was usually done through touch, but that wasn't the only way. Vipin didn't use physical contact for his abilities. If he didn't need it, neither did she.

Kari focused her energy, extending her aura. Three leaves lay on the ground as she floated over them. She had to focus. Her muscles burned and throbbed at the effort. All she needed was her willpower to hold steady. The leaves twisted and aligned themselves with her thoughts. They were hers to use. Kari cleared her mind, pouring her aura into them. They launched up from the ground, hovering beside her.

"What is this?" Ilyia exclaimed, wide-eyed.

When Kari opened her eyes, the leaves shot at Vipin and Ilyia. Ilyia ducked out of the way. The leaf slashed at her face, cutting into her cheek. Vipin didn't move. He dropped Kari, who jumped out of his reach.

Two leaves stopped inches in front of his face, then disintegrated.

"Enough of these games," he bellowed, reaching toward her. The power of his mind froze her in place. "I wanted you to live through this, but I don't need you to."

"Think of your family," Kari said. "They wouldn't want you to do this. Think of how many more families like yours that you will be ending."

"Don't you dare talk about them," Vipin roared. His eyes glowed blue as an azure aura surrounded Kari. Crushing pressure followed. Her body felt as if it was being broken and squashed.

She groaned as the pressure increased. Lifting from the ground, she was thrown backward, slamming into the remains of a stone wall.

Kari coughed and moaned as she collapsed to her hands and knees.

"You know nothing of loss," Vipin said, stalking toward her. His face was stern and cross.

Kari gripped the memory stone around her neck. "I know nothing of loss? Are you forgetting what I'm wearing?"

"You only know loss through someone else," Vipin said, dismissing her pain. He waved his arm through the air, his psychic powers ripping the memory stone from around her neck and throwing it across the remains of the sanctuary.

Kari's gaze followed it as it landed before she turned her attention back to Vipin. "I've experienced my share of loss."

"Really? And what would you do if someone near to you died? Would you not hate the person who took them from you with every fiber of your being?" Vipin sneered.

"I can't answer that," Kari said, averting her eyes. It was the universal truth she had been exposed to—the endless cycle of hatred and pain. She had killed others for harming her friends. Now she was a hypocrite, decrying violence when she had spent so much time dwelling in it.

"Because you know I'm right," Vipin said. He glanced toward Ina. "What about Ina? If she died today, would you not vow revenge and seek to create a world where people like her would never die?"

"You'll kill people like her to create your world," Kari cried. "A world of peace cannot be forged with blood-stained hands."

"You didn't answer my question." Vipin raised his hand, lifting Kari to her feet. "Would you not hate the person who took her away?"

"I don't know." Kari averted her gaze. It was a question she could not answer. The truth demanded her to hate. When exposed to the worst of humanity, there were only two options. Either meet it with passive acceptance or meet it with hate—there were no other options.

"Tell me something, *little one*." Vipin smiled. "Do you love her?"

Kari stared at her. "I do."

"Good."

Vipin flicked his wrist. Ina's head spun as he snapped her neck.

"No!" Kari cried as Ina's lifeless body crashed to the ground. The world turned silent and still. Ina's body twitched, then nothing. How could this be?

Kari ran over to her friend. Ina's eyes were wide. Her neck and bone were twisted and bent with her head nearly entirely backward.

"Damn…" Ronin muttered, closing his eyes.

Chaska dropped to her knees, placing a hand on Kari's shoulder. Kari stared at Ina's body as tears streamed down her face. Nothing was right. Nothing would be right ever again. Kari placed her hand on Ina's.

Wake up. Please wake up.

It was no use. There was nothing Kari could do. No healing magic or linking life-forces could revive an-already dead person.

Kari paused at the thought, her jaw dropping. Tears streamed down her face.

Ina—her best friend—was dead, and it was all her fault. Kari narrowed her eyes as she turned to face Vipin. No, it was his fault!

Light erupted from her body, and her eyes glowed yellow. "Why? Why kill her?" She rose, facing Vipin.

"Good, now hate me with everything you are," Vipin said, a grin spread wide across his arrogant face.

Kari wanted to hate him. It was people like him, like Legato, like Jiaorong, who took everything from her, leaving her with only hatred and rage.

Kari launched her light whip at him. Vipin's eyes glowed blue, and the whip disintegrated. The blue aura surrounded Kari. She faltered to her knees as her body fell under the crushing weight of Vipin's power.

"Good, now you understand," Vipin bragged. He held out his arms. "Behold the inner you! Witness your rage! Embrace your vengeance! Hahaha! It did wonders for me!"

Kari gritted her teeth. She couldn't let him win. She planted one foot, struggling against the pressure of the aura.

"Muaah!" She managed to get to her feet. "I understand," Kari muttered. The overwhelming pressure was like stones piled up on every inch of her body. She clenched her eyes shut, blocking out the excruciating pain, and took a single step forward. "But... I refuse to hate you."

"I'm through with words. Now fight me," Vipin cried. "Show me the rage I feel. Show me how we are alike."

"No," Kari stubbornly said, taking another step forward. Her ankles felt like they would shatter under her weight. "We're nothing alike. We both looked into the void, but you faltered."

Ignoring the pain, Kari ran forward, charging at Vipin.

Vipin surrounded himself with his blue aura. When he held out his hand, Kari was lifted from her feet and shot backward.

Forming two large poles out of light, she thrust them into the ground, halting her momentum. Vipin grimaced. His eyes narrowed and his aura shot forward, striking Kari.

"Gahh!" she screamed. Her poles shattered, and she was sent reeling to the ground, landing with a thud. Blood erupted from her mouth. Kari grabbed her ribs. She was broken and beaten, but she would not quit. She couldn't let Ina's death go unchallenged.

She had to get closer, only then would she have a chance.

The blue aura engulfed her again, lifting her off the ground. With a flick of Vipin's wrist, Kari slammed into the stone floor. He raised her again, smashing her down a second and a third time.

Kari groaned. Her nose was bent and broken. Her aura exhausted. Her blistered skin had bruised and torn. She laid prostrate on the ground, her arms and legs limp.

Vipin lifted her, then levitated her toward him.

"Let's end this before I kill you," Vipin said, reaching toward her. "The new age dawns now!"

Kari stared, her vision blurry. Blood poured from her nose and mouth. He couldn't win. She had to protect the Seed.

Kari held out her hand, focusing all of her remaining energy. A blast of light erupted from her fingers. Vipin cried out, shielding his eyes.

He dropped Kari, who landed on her hands and knees. She shot up, running toward him. Vipin opened his eyes. They glowed bright blue, smoke erupting from them. Kari planted her feet, bracing for the impact.

The blue aura surrounded Kari.

"Ahhh!" she shrieked under the devastating force. Her bones cracked as they began to break. If she could truly call upon the Seed, she needed it now. She forced herself to stay on her feet, stepping closer to Vipin. Her ankles and legs burned and buckled, but she did not fall. She could not fall.

Her left arm shattered, blood erupting from her skin. Kari cried out, but she had come this far. Just—a—bit—further—

Blood poured from her body as she came within inches of Vipin. She reached out with her right arm.

"Why won't you quit?" Vipin asked, his eyes erupting in a violent burst of blue light.

"Because... I... need you... to know." Kari wrapped her arm around him. She pulled him toward her, then embraced him in a hug. Vipin's eyes widened at the gesture, returning to normal. "I understand. But I don't hate you. I forgive you."

Vipin's eyes erupted in a flash of blue light, sending Kari hurtling backward. She slammed into the ground, wheeling to a stop.

"What? How? Liar!" Vipin howled, his face contorting.

"You killed my best friend," Kari muttered, rolling onto her back. "That is something I can never forget. But I understand your pain. Hatred won't bring your family or Ina back.

It will only create more pain and hatred. You've spread your pain to me with the countless lives you've stolen today. That pain will only spread farther if you use the Seed. Hating the Guardian for what he's done only gives him more power over you. You are better than that. You can be free of him to make a better life, or you can submit to hatred and his rule over you. Either way, it won't bring your family back. You'll only take more families away."

Vipin's aura faded, and he stared at Kari. He held his head high. "You don't understand. You can only meet hatred with vengeance. *That* gives me power."

"I know a woman," Kari said. She struggled to sit upright, but her body collapsed onto the ground, finally giving out. She stared at the now-dark sky. This would be the last sky anyone would see if she gave up now. She had to continue fighting. Her strength was gone, her energy spent, and her only remaining weapon was her voice. "The bravest woman I ever met. Her name was Carina. She allowed herself to be tortured to death to spare another from the same fate. Her last thought wasn't for vengeance. She pitied those who hated her, and she only wished to show them the strength of love and unity."

"And it wasn't enough to save her," Vipin said, scowling. He walked toward her, glaring down at her.

"No, it wasn't," Kari agreed, unable to move. "But neither would hatred. Either way, she would have died. She couldn't control their actions, only how they impacted her. She controlled her own life, her own actions. She didn't allow them to change who she was."

"Are you saying I've allowed the Immortal Warrior to control my life?" Vipin asked, raising an eyebrow.

"Yes," Kari said. "Would you have become what you are if he hadn't murdered your family?"

"Maybe your right." Vipin sighed. "But I've come too far to go back now."

"I don't believe that," Kari said. "We are not defined by our past, but by who we are and what we do now. I'm not saying people shouldn't be held accountable for their actions, but you can't live in the past. You can always redefine yourself by what you do."

Vipin scoffed. "Do you believe that nonsense?" He outstretched his hand toward her. "I don't see how a world of peace can be made with such pacifism and nonsense."

"How can it be made with bloodstained hands?" Kari asked.

"Like so." When he motioned with his hand, she raised off the ground.

"Please stop," Kari begged.

Vipin smiled, placing his hand on Kari's forehead.

"Make me," Vipin grinned. "Show me the strength of your convictions!"

The sky rumbled as crimson clouds filled the air.

"You want vengeance for the cruelty committed against you. But what you don't see is that you're just as cruel—just as heartless."

Vipin's gaze pierced through to her core. The clouds spread and thundered until the entire sky was blood red and alive like a tiger's roar.

"You can stop this. Please," Kari pleaded. "How many people will look upon the sky with fear and horror? How many people will scream in terror as their world is torn apart? How many will cry out for vengeance?"

Vipin tilted his head, but he did not say anything. The sky opened as a burning ball of red and blue energy appeared through the clouds. Its strange flames licked the clouds, and the cacophony of noise only grew louder.

"If you continue, you'll make yourself the Guardian of this new age."

Vipin grimaced. He clenched his jaw as his gaze bounced between Kari and the red and blue ball. He licked his lips, then grinned. "You can be quiet now."

"I can't." Kari struggled to maintain consciousness as her vision doubled. The ball of fire in the sky grew as if it were approaching them. "The spirits of the dead won't let me rest. They're screaming out for you to stop. Can't you hear them?"

Vipin's eye twitched.

"Deep down, there must be some part of you that knows this is wrong," Kari muttered. "All you'll do is spread more pain to more people. Please, give us a chance."

"A chance to do what? Murder each other?"

Kari's vision blackened and tunneled. She didn't have much time left, but she couldn't give in now. "Think of the people. These beautiful, flawed, wonderful people. People have the capacity for good and evil. They have the potential for so much more—all they need is the right example to follow. You and I can show them a better way. Please don't give up on them. Don't give up on yourself."

Vipin sighed deeply, holding out his hand. He recoiled, his brow furrowing. Clenching his jaw, he placed his hand on her head. "This is over."

The blue aura surrounded her again. Kari winced, bracing for the pain. She gasped. The pressure never came. Instead, her bones were mended, her wounds closing.

Vipin released his grip on her, setting her gently on her feet. The ball of fire disappeared behind the crimson clouds, the rolling thunder ceased, and the clouds faded away.

He stared at her, unblinking. "You have shamed me," Vipin said. Kari gazed into his eyes. "Maybe you're right, or maybe it is nonsense. But I would like to find out. I would hate to go through this only to be proved wrong."

Tears fell from his eyes. He held up the crystal in his hand. "I have gone too far to begin anew, you know."

Vipin rose and walked toward Ina. "But I will give you a parting gift."

The crystal glowed. The energy stored within poured out, surrounding Ina's body. Her neck straightened, the color returning to her face. Ina gasped as life returned to her.

"Now show me the strength of your convictions. If you fail, know I shall return from hell to seek my revenge." Vipin smiled, closing his eyes. "I look forward to seeing the world you will create." His body cracked, deep fissures forming across his face and arms. He turned to dust, then blew away with the wind.

CHAPTER TWENTY-FIVE

KARI STARED AT WHERE Vipin had just been moments ago, her breathing raspy as she tried to process what she'd witnessed. What had just happened? Kari's gaze descended on Ina, who stirred as she fought to sit up.

"Ina!" Kari sobbed, running to her friend. She dropped to the ground, embracing her sister. "Are you all right?"

"I... I can't..." Ina grunted as she struggled to sit upright. "I can't move my legs."

Kari gazed at Ina's legs, but she couldn't see anything wrong with them. When Vipin healed others, he fully healed them. Unless—this was different magic—it was the power of the array. It brought Ina back to life, but what if it couldn't fully heal her? Kari gently cupped her hand over Ina's leg. Ina's eyes widened, and she shook her head.

"I can't feel it," she said with tears in her eyes. "What happened? I remember Vipin talking, then nothing."

What should Kari tell her? What could she tell her?

"I...You..." Kari stared into Ina's panic-filled eyes. If it had been her, what would she want to know? She took a deep breath, then resolved to tell the truth. "Vipin killed you, then brought you back."

"I..." Ina trailed off. Her eyes wandered around the ruined temple before settling back on Kari's. "Died?"

A single tear streaked down Ina's porcelain cheek.

"I'm sorry," Kari muttered, wrapping her arms around Ina. "He used the array to bring you back."

"Can he heal me? Where is he?" Ina asked, glancing around the ruins.

Kari shook her head. "He's gone."

Ina's eyes widened. "But I'm...paralyzed."

Kari looked away. What could she say to comfort her? Vipin had done this to Ina to hurt Kari. Guilt and shame flooded her. This was her fault. If she had listened to Ina to begin with, they could have left before this happened.

Kari gripped her head. "Ronin. Where's Ronin?" Kari frantically scanned the rubble. Ronin was face down on the far side of what was left of the sanctuary. "We have to help him. He's hurt."

Ina wiped the tears away from her eyes. "Take me to him," she said. "I can help."

Kari summoned her spirit energy, focusing her aura through her muscles, then lifted Ina in her arms and carried her over to Ronin. Kari sat Ina down before rolling Ronin over. He groaned, blinking at the motion. His face was paler than usual, and blood oozed from his mangled arm.

"We have to stop the bleeding," Ina said, pressing her hands against his wounds. "Kari, I need a sturdy stick and straps of cloth."

Kari did as she was told. After finding a stick, she took hold of her shirt, then ripped a long strip off from the bottom. Ina tied the cloth into a makeshift tourniquet around the rod before sliding it on his arm up near his shoulder. He winced as she tightened the tourniquet.

"We should leave this on until we can get him proper medical treatment," Ina said, tightly tying it in place.

"Shouldn't we loosen it periodically?" Kari asked. The tourniquet would stop blood flow to his arm, eventually killing it.

Ina rolled her eyes. "Only if you want him to bleed out."

"But couldn't he lose the arm?"

Coughing, Ronin gasped out, "I think the arm's already gone."

Kari's face fell. His arm had been reduced to a lumpy mass of meat with bone fragments protruding from it.

They had all lost so much for so little.

Kari took in the ruins. How was she going to get them out of here? The nearest town was Sumar, which was days away. Ronin was in no shape to travel, and Ina's legs were paralyzed. Kari couldn't carry them both.

"Wait here," she said. She needed a horse or a carriage. Surely, someone in the city could assist her. "I'll go find help."

Kari climbed through the rubble, leaving what was once the temple. The city was eerily quiet. There wasn't even the sound of birds chirping or insects buzzing. There was just nothing. Kari's heart broke at the sight. Bodies upon bodies filled the city streets. People and animals alike. Everything was dead.

Vipin had stolen their life energy, then used it to resurrect Ina. He might have thought he was kind to Kari, but he hadn't considered how cruel his actions would be to Ina. Thousands died so Ina could live.

Kari fell to her knees. They were all alone in a dead city. She grabbed at her ring finger. If only she still had her ring, she could use the runestones to call for help. As it was now, they would die, abandoned in Koruzeru.

"Help!" Kari shouting, hoping someone was still alive. "Anybody, please help."

Kari covered her face, sobbing into her hands.

"I don't think that's going to work, little one."

Kari shot upright as Artemis and Chaska approached. Artemis had put her mask back on, hiding the scars given to her by the Immortal Warrior, while Chaska kept her eyes pointed at the ground, afraid to meet Kari's gaze.

"I'm sorry. I'm so sorry," Artemis said. "I believe this is yours."

Artemis held out the interspatial ring. Kari launched forward, snatching it away from her.

"Thank you so much," she exclaimed.

"I collected as many surviving tomes and books as I could find, and I stored them within. The knowledge of our people should survive with you."

Kari didn't care. Right now, the lives of her friends were still in jeopardy. She had to act quickly. Kari summoned the runestones.

"Are those..." Artemis stared at the stones in awe.

"Yes," Kari said. They might not approve, but even they should recognize this as the only way to save her brother. She closed her eyes, trying to recall the order in which they were to be placed. "The Lover's Ballad," she whispered. She might not remember the order, but she remembered what they said. "*Fly on the wings of the wind, united together, outcasts no more.*" She grabbed each stone and laid them out in a circle, according to the poem.

There was only one thing left to do. She stood and gaped at the gate, waiting just as Falcon said.

Nothing happened. There was no purple light, no whirring noise, no help. They were alone.

"He said he would come. He said he would help. He promised." Kari's body quivered, her eyes watered. "Come on, come on, come on."

Please come. Please give me something. Any glimmer of hope would do.

The runestones remained motionless on the ground.

Kari collapsed to her knees, rubbing her face. He wasn't coming. All of his promises were meaningless. She sighed. It might not be by choice. What if he was caught? What if he was found out? Then he could never come or worse, the person who would appear behind the purple wall of light would be Legato.

She jumped as a loud whirring noise emanated from the runestones. A brilliant purple light shot upward. As it faded, it revealed a singular figure standing in the gate. His long blond hair and billowy black cloak were distinctive even before the light entirely dissipated. Falcon had come.

Kari jumped up, throwing her arms around him. "Thank you for coming. We need help."

His eyes scanned the city, his mouth agape. "Looks like I didn't come soon enough. I saw the sky. I take it this was its epicenter. Tell me the truth, how close did we come to an apocalypse?"

Kari stared up into his blue eyes. "Mere moments."

Falcon gulped.

They couldn't dwell on the possibility of endless destruction. Kari grabbed his hand, pulling him toward the remains of Lasan. "My friends are hurt; they need medical attention."

"Show me," Falcon said, matching Kari's pace.

Kari led Falcon back into the ruins of Lasan. Ina sat in the shade of rubble. Ronin lay beside her. Falcon's gaze fixated on Ronin's arm. "I can't even begin to fathom what happened here."

Kari stared at her hands. Words couldn't describe it. "Pain," was all she said.

"Come on," Falcon said. "We need to get them over to the gate, though I'm unsure of how to move your brother with his injuries."

"I can carry him," Kari said. Falcon gave her a sideways look to which Kari responded with a coy smile.

If Vipin hadn't healed her, they would be in even more trouble than they currently were. Should she be thankful or distressed at the thought? Kari strengthened her aura, lifting Ronin the way she had Ina. He was heavier than Ina, but, even so, carrying him was simple with her spirit energy.

Falcon stared, slack jawed.

"Don't let my size fool you. I'm stronger than I look," Kari said, walking toward the Aeolus Gate with Ronin in her arms.

Falcon glanced around the ruins. "Clearly." He helped Ina up, then swept her into his arms and carried her behind Kari and Ronin.

"What will you do now?" he asked, setting Ina down into the center of the runestones.

"I just want to live," Kari whispered as she laid Ronin next to Ina.

"I think that's all any of us want at this point," Ina added, checking on Ronin's tourniquet.

"Legato will search for you. You know that, right?" Falcon asked. Kari nodded. "He's already asked me to gather my team to hunt you down."

"So, what will you do?" Kari asked. "Will you bring me to him? This is but a taste of what my power can do in the wrong hands."

Falcon sighed. "He threatened the children of my close friends if I did not agree to find you."

"You'll do it? Bring me to him? To save the children?"

Falcon shook his head. "I'm calling his bluff. You see, if he makes a move against them, he'll lose our support. The Thunder Five will turn against him. Any power, any control he has over us, will end if he tries to harm them. At the same time, we can only do so much to spite him without risking harm to the kids. It's a stalemate where none of us can fully act or risk fighting the other. He knows it, and we know it.

"It won't stop him from coming for you, however," Falcon continued. "I can hide you beyond his grasp. I know a place in Niwend where you'll be safe. You can make a life there. It won't be glamorous, but I don't think he'll be able to find you."

The Realm of Niwend comprised of a massive ocean, with one lone continent and a multitude of islands. The Niwendian Empire, while it declared control over the innumerable islands that dotted its endless ocean, most weren't even aware they were part of the empire. An island, isolated and remote, would be difficult to find. It was the same principle behind the Shagin island of Mystikos. It would be just like home.

Kari nodded. "That sounds good."

"It'll be a bit of a trip," Falcon said. "The gate can only carry us so far. We'll have to take a ship when we get there."

"That's fine." Kari stared at Ina and Ronin. They would come, too. Everything would change for them. Everything already had.

Artemis and Chaska approached the group. Artemis carried the Golden Rod, while Chaska held tight to Kari's memory stone. Chaska held out the memory stone to Kari, but said nothing. She didn't have to say anything. Kari understood her remorse and guilt. She took the memory stone from her, then tied it around her neck.

"I think going somewhere safe is a wonderful idea for you," Artemis said, planting the staff on the ground. "You deserve to live in peace after everything we put you through."

Kari stared at them. They deserved peace, too. Part of her wanted to offer that they should come with her, yet another part never wanted to see them again. Still, they weren't the monsters they thought they were. They were human, making human mistakes, like everyone else. "What about you two?" Kari asked.

"We've been wrong. Wrong about a great many things," Artemis said, clenching her jaw. "There is no redemption for the things we've done, but maybe we can help others in whatever small way we can. We'll wander and do whatever we can to improve as many lives as possible."

Falcon scoffed. "You're right—that won't bring you redemption."

Kari placed a hand on Falcon's. He understood redemption well. He was the outlaw who chased outlaws. He gazed at her. She was beginning to understand. "It's not your past that defines who you are...only your current actions can do that."

Falcon nodded.

"There's one more thing," Chaska said, finally breaking the silence. She took the Golden Rod from Artemis, holding it out toward Kari. "Ilyia is nowhere to be found. You should have this. It belongs to the Champion of Shagin. It doesn't deserve to be lost here among the ruins. But both of us have lost any right to hold it."

Kari took the staff. "I'm not a champion. But I will keep it safe until it can be returned to our sisters."

The staff glowed at Kari's touch, then was absorbed into the ring.

Falcon looked into Kari's emerald eyes. "Whenever you are ready, I can take you to your new home."

Kari gave one last look at Koruzeru. This was her ancestral home, and it lay in ruin with the dead scattered about yet again. It seemed, once again, Falcon was leading her away to an unknown fate. Only this time, it wouldn't be as a prisoner, but as a friend. He would help her find a new home where she could rebuild and hide the devastating power of the Seed from the clutches of the Guardian. He would be searching for her again. All she had now was to put her trust in Falcon. She hoped he was right that Legato wouldn't be able to find her.

Kari and Falcon stepped into the gate next to Ronin and Ina. On the other side would rest a new home, a new song to sing. Kari closed her eyes. The purple light erupted all around them, then Koruzeru was gone

Also By

About the Author

Joshua Killingsworth is a fantasy lover and author who has spent his life dreaming up worlds to explore. He enjoys stories of heroes set in worlds full of imagination and intrigue. When not writing, he can be found playing video games, spending time with his two kids, or hugging any and every animal he can catch.

Acknowledgements

Thank you to all my family and friends who supported me. A special thank you to Cynthia Shepp for your amazing editing. Thank you to all the readers who have stuck with me over the slowdowns and delays on the road to publication.